David Morrell

DAVID MORRELL

Before I Wake

ALSO BY DAVID MORRELL

NOVELS

First Blood (1972)
Testament (1975)
Last Reveille (1977)
The Totem (1979)
Blood Oath (1982)
The Brotherhood of the Rose (1984)
The Fraternity of the Stone (1985)
Rambo (First Blood Part II) (1985)
The League of Night and Fog (1987)
Rambo III (1988)
The Fifth Profession (1990)
The Covenant of the Flame (1991)
Assumed Identity (1993)
Desperate Measures (1994)
The Totem (Complete and Unaltered) (1994)
Extreme Denial (1996)
Double Image (1998)
Burnt Sienna (2000)
Long Lost (2002)
The Protector (2003)
Creepers (2005)
Scavenger (2007)
The Spy Who Came for Christmas (2008)
The Shimmer (2009)
The Naked Edge (2010)
Murder As a Fine Art (2013)
Inspector of the Dead (2015)
Ruler of the Night (2016)

SHORT FICTION

The Hundred-Year Christmas (1983)
Black Evening (1999)
Nightscape (2004)

GRAPHIC NOVEL

Captain America: The Chosen (2007)

NONFICTION

John Barth: An Introduction (1976)
Fireflies: A Father's Tale of Love and Loss (1988)
The Successful Novelist A Lifetime of Lessons about Writing and Publishing (2008)
Stars in My Eyes: My Love Affair with Books, Movies, and Music (2016)

EDITED BY

American Fiction, American Myth (Essays by Philip Young) edited by David Morrell and Sandra Spanier (2000)
Tesseracts Thirteen (Chilling Tales of the Great White North) edited by Nancy Kilpatrick and David Morrell (2009)
Thrillers: 100 Must Reads edited by David Morrell and Hank Wagner (2010)

Before I Wake

(a story collection)

DAVID MORRELL

Subterranean Press 2019

Signed Limited Edition

ISBN
978-1-59606-912-1

See pages 367-369 for individual story credits.

Subterranean Press
PO Box 190106
Burton, MI 48519

subterraneanpress.com

Manufactured in the United States of America

TABLE OF CONTENTS

9 Introduction

13 Time Was

45 The Architecture of Snow

91 The Companions

113 My Name Is Legion

147 The Interrogator

179 The Granite Kitchen

187 The Spiritualist

209 Vastation

215 Blue Murder

229 The Controller

259 The Attitude Adjuster

295 The Abelard Sanction

313 The Opium-Eater

339 They

365 About the Author

To Charles L. Grant (1942-2006)
Who championed short-story writers and made
a difference as an author, an editor, and a person

INTRODUCTION

BEFORE I WAKE IS MY THIRD story collection, after *Black Evening* (1999) and *Nightscape* (2004). Thinking about all the stories in them, I'm reminded that the first fiction I sold was "The Dripping" to *Ellery Queen's Mystery Magazine* in the long-ago summer of 1971. I'd completed my first novel, *First Blood*, and sent it to my literary agent (in the olden days when typescripts were actually put in a box and mailed as opposed to being sent electronically). I still had a little creative juice after the three years in which I'd worked on *First Blood*. An unusually vivid dream gave me the idea for "The Dripping," and I surprised myself by writing all 3,300 words of it in one day. That typescript too went into the mail.

Imagine my light-headedness when I received an envelope from *Ellery Queen's Mystery Magazine*. Not the stamped, self-addressed manila envelope that I'd sent with the story. *That* would have contained the returned typescript, along with a too-familiar "doesn't suit our needs at the present time" rejection letter. No, this one had a Davis Publications (the owner of *Ellery Queen's Mystery Magazine*) return address and contained a contract, offering $100 for my 3,300 words. (My author friend, Donald E. Westlake, liked to say that this proved inflation didn't exist, because for many years *Ellery Queen's Mystery Magazine* always paid 3 cents a word.)

In 1971 when this miraculous event happened, I was earning $10,500 as an assistant professor in the English department at the University of Iowa. Raising a six-year-old daughter, my wife and I were happy to receive the extra money (I'd have probably settled for one cent per word or even nothing, which is one of the reasons literary agents exist, to protect authors from their insecurities). The validation was more important than the money, as was the discovery that my first sale qualified me for inclusion in Ellery Queen's Department of First Stories. I soon discovered that many authors I revered had also made their first sales to *Ellery Queen's Mystery Magazine*: Jack Finney, Stanley Ellin, and *Columbo* creators William Link and Richard Levinson, to name a few.

A week later, my sense of reality again wavered when my agent phoned with the news that a hardback publisher, M. Evans and Co., had bought *First Blood*. The sequence is important. I finished *First Blood* and then wrote "The Dripping." But I sold "The Dripping" before *First Blood*, thus allowing me the *Ellery Queen's Mystery Magazine* First Story membership, an honor that I treasure as much as any other publishing good fortune that came my way.

"The Dripping" appeared in 1972. For the rest of the decade, I concentrated on novels, with the result that my next story, "The Partnership," wasn't published until 1981 (in another Davis publication, *Alfred Hitchcock's Mystery Magazine*). Thereafter my stories appeared every couple of years. Between novels, they gave me the chance to try new techniques and dramatize situations that fascinated me but couldn't be expanded into a book. Along the way, I was privileged to work with many gifted editors, anthologists, and publishers: T.E.D. Klein at *The Twilight Zone Magazine* and *Night Cry* magazine, Charles L. Grant at the *Shadows* series, Stuart L. Schiff at the *Whispers* series, Paul Mikol at the *Night Visions* series, Douglas L. Winter,

Robert Bloch, Joe and Karen Lansdale, Dennis Etchison, Paul M. Sammon, John Hogan, Otto Penzler, Al Sarrantonio, David Hartwell, Tom Monteleone, Kealan Patrick Burke, James Patterson, Stephen Jones, J. A. Konrath, Del Howison and Jeff Gelb, Richard Chizmar, Bill Schafer, Gardner Dozois and George R.R. Martin, Nelson DeMille, Sam Weller and Mort Castle, Nancy Kilpatrick and Caro Soles, Wes Miller, and Laurie R. King and Leslie S. Klinger. The task of being an editor or an anthologist is mostly unheralded, even with an "edited by" credit on a book's cover. It's my honor to name those people without whom my short stories wouldn't have been written.

Special thanks must go to Charles L. Grant, to whom this collection is dedicated. Charlie didn't only write wonderfully. He also encouraged more short-story authors than anyone I ever knew, especially in the horror genre, pioneering new directions and horizons. He's no longer with us, but he remains in my memory. To be remembered is to be immortal.

The stories in *Black Evening* were arranged chronologically, becoming longer as the collection proceeded (it includes "The Dripping."). Those in *Nightscape* were sequenced for dramatic effect, their chronology jumbled. The latter principle applies here. Genres and topics shift. Some stories are eerie. Others are filled with action. Many are historical. Several have characters I introduced in novels, or else they're about famous authors, such as Henry James, Sir Arthur Conan Doyle, and J.D. Salinger. In one story, Thomas De Quincey performs double duty both as a famous author and a character I featured in three novels. Each story has its own introduction, so I'll leave you for now and rejoin you in a moment.

TIME WAS

Many story ideas came to me during automobile journeys through the vastness of the western United States. This one occurred in 2005 while I was on a promotional tour for Creepers. *Driving from a bookstore in Tucson, Arizona, to one in Scottsdale (The Poisoned Pen, a favorite), I encountered a traffic jam that lasted for hours. I noticed a side road and wondered if it might allow me to bypass the numerous blocked vehicles ahead of me. After all, what could go wrong on a side road in the desert?*

"Time Was" is an example of my eerie Twilight Zone-type stories (Rod Serling was an early influence). You'll encounter a few similarly eerie tales later. This story dramatizes one of my painfully learned themes, that what we think is normal can change quickly and drastically and what we cherish can be taken from us without warning.

"**D**EBBIE, I'M GOING TO BE LATE," Sam Tucker said into his cell phone.

"*Late?*" In the shimmering desert, the weak connection made his wife's voice hard to hear, but the strength of her inflection compensated.

"Maybe not till after dark."

"You promised Lori you'd be at her birthday party."

"I know, but—"

"You missed her birthday *last* year, too."

"Traffic's backed up for miles. The radio says a big motor home flipped over and burst into flames. The reporter says it's going to take hours before the police clear the wreck and get traffic moving again. I'll try to make it up to her. Look, I realize I haven't been home a lot lately, but—"

"*Lately?*"

"You think I enjoy working this hard?" Stuck in an unmoving line of vehicles, Sam watched his Ford Explorer's temperature gauge drift toward the red zone. He turned off the engine and the air conditioning, then opened the window. Despite the desert's dry heat, sweat trickled off his chin.

"I don't mean to complain." Debbie's voice was fainter. "It's just... Never mind. Where *are* you?"

"On I-Ten. The hell of it is, I planned ahead, finished my appointments, and left Tucson an hour ago. If everything had gone smoothly, I'd have been home in time for Lori's party."

Static crackled on the cell phone.

"Debbie?"

"If we hadn't bought the new house, maybe you wouldn't need to work so—"

The static got louder.

"Debbie?"

"Don't rush and maybe get in an accident just because—"

Something ended the transmission. Now Sam didn't even hear static. He almost called back but then thought better. The conversation hadn't turned into an argument. Leave it at that. Besides, the car ahead of him budged forward a little.

Maybe traffic's starting to move sooner than the radio predicted, Sam hoped. Then he realized that the car ahead was only filling a gap created when a vehicle pulled off the highway and followed the shoulder to an exit ahead. A handful of other vehicles did the same. *So what?* he thought. *Maybe those drivers live in whatever town that exit leads to. But I need to get back to Phoenix.*

Traffic inched forward, filling the other gaps. He started his SUV, noted that the heat gauge had fallen to normal, and followed the slow line of vehicles. Now he saw that the exit led to a gas station, a convenience store, and about twenty sun-faded adobe houses whose cracked stucco indicated their losing battle with the desert. Something else caught his attention: A few of the cars that had taken the exit were now throwing up dust as they continued along a sandy road that paralleled the highway.

What do they know that I don't? he wondered. When traffic stopped again, he opened the glove compartment and pulled out a map, spreading it across the steering wheel.

A faint broken line went from a town called Gila Gulch—the name on the exit sign—to a town farther along called Stage Stop. *Must be from when stagecoaches came through here*, Sam thought. The distance looked to be about twenty miles and would bring him back onto I-10 past the mile marker where the radio news had said the motor home was blocking the highway. He looked at the dashboard clock, which showed 5:25. *I've got a chance to get home in time*, he realized.

The next thing, he steered onto the highway's shoulder, reached the exit ramp, drove into Gila Gulch, and stopped at the gas station. His fuel gauge showed between a quarter and a half tank. Enough to get home. But why take chances? As the sun's heat squeezed him, he also bought a jug of radiator fluid and added some to the Explorer's reservoir, which looked slightly low, accounting for the increase he'd noticed on the temperature gauge. He always kept plenty of bottled water in the car. No problem there. Time to hit the road.

"Hit" was almost the word. As Sam headed along the road, which had looked smooth from the highway, he was surprised by its bumps, but if he kept his speed at forty, they were tolerable. Nothing that the Explorer, built for rough terrain, couldn't handle. At this speed, he'd finish the twenty miles in a half hour. A hell of a lot better than sitting in traffic for *three* hours, as the radio had predicted. Pleased that the temperature gauge remained at normal, he closed the window, turned the air conditioner back on, and put a Jimmie Dale Gilmore CD into the car's player. Humming to Jimmie's definitive version of "I'm So Lonesome I Could Cry," he glanced at the traffic jam he passed on his left and smiled. *Imagine the look on Lori's face when I show up*, he thought. *The look on* Debbie's *face will be even better.*

What Sam hadn't told her was that the trip to Tucson had been pointless, that the land his boss thought might be worth developing—Grand Valley Vistas—turned out to have once been a toxic dump site. Lawsuits about it could go on forever. *Another waste of my time*, he thought. If Shepperton—Sam's boss—had done his homework, the site never would have seemed tempting in the first place. It had taken a lot of investigating to discover the liabilities. *But that's why Joe pays me the bucks. To keep him from screwing up. If I had his money, I could make Shepperton Enterprises* (Tucker Enterprises, Sam fantasized) *ten times as successful as it is.*

He glanced to his left and wondered if he was imagining that the traffic jam on the highway seemed a little farther away. There seemed more rocks and saguaro cacti than there'd been before. Probably an optical illusion. But peering ahead, he had to admit that the road did seem to be shifting to the right. No big deal. When they built this road a long time ago, they probably had to adjust for going around obstacles like that hill ahead. Dust clouds beyond it indicated the progress of the handful of cars preceding him. In the rearview mirror, another plume of dust showed a vehicle following. *I'm surprised a lot more drivers haven't realized how to save time*, he thought. *Or maybe they don't have what it takes to try something different. Or they don't have a good enough reason.*

As Jimmie Dale sang another mournful song, Sam's attention drifted to the tall, sentry-like cacti that now stuck up everywhere around him. Many looked sick, with drooping arms and black spots that might have been rot. *That's supposed to be from the thinning ozone layer and unfiltered ultra-violet rays*, he thought. *From air pollution and car exhaust.* He could actually see haze over the blocked traffic on the highway farther to the left.

The hill got bigger. As the road veered to the right around it, noises startled him. *Shots.* He stomped the brakes and gaped at what confronted him. An old-fashioned western town had board sidewalks, mule-drawn wagons, and one of the stagecoaches he'd earlier thought about. Horses were tied to wooden railings. Unlike the adobe buildings in Gila Gulch, these structures were wooden. Most were painted a white that had paled in the sun and the blowing sand, and most had only one level. Men in Stetsons and women in gingham dresses walked the dirt street ahead. The noises he'd heard came from cowboys shooting at each other outside a corral. A man with a rifle fired from a roof. One of the cowboys turned, aimed upward, and shot the man with the rifle, sending him falling onto a second-story porch.

The gunfight might have continued to alarm Sam if anybody else in the town had paid attention. But the men in Stetsons and the women in gingham dresses went on about their business, never once looking toward the shots, making Sam quickly conclude that this was a tourist attraction. He'd heard of a similar Western-town replica called Old Tucson, where tourists paid to see chuck-wagon races and staged gunfights. A lot of Western movies had been made there also, including one of Sam's favorites, *Rio Bravo*, starring John Wayne, directed by Howard Hawks. He'd also heard that Old Tucson had been destroyed in a fire. Perhaps it had never been rebuilt. Perhaps *this* town was its replacement. If so, it was situated awfully far from Tucson to be a success. The lack of cars and tourists made *that* clear. Back at the highway, a couple of signs would have helped.

Maybe they're not open for business yet, Sam thought as the gunfight ended and the survivors carried the bodies away. *Maybe this is a dress rehearsal.* Noticing a sign that read MERIDIAN, he eased his foot onto the accelerator and passed a livery stable, a blacksmith shop, and a general store. They looked as if they'd been recently built and then cleverly made to seem aged. A muscular man came out of the general store, carrying a heavy burlap sack of what might have been flour toward a buckboard wagon.

Impressed by the realism, Sam continued past a restaurant where a sign in the lace-curtained window indicated that a steak dinner could be obtained for fifty cents. A boy rode past on a mule. *I've got to bring Lori and Debbie to see this*, Sam thought. *I won't tell them where we're going. I'll make it a surprise.*

Swinging doors led into a saloon. A large sign boasted about whiskey you could trust, beer that was cold, and (in less bold letters) the best sarsaparilla anybody ever tasted. Sam had heard sarsaparilla referred to in the Westerns he enjoyed watching. A rancher was always buying a bottle for his son, or a gunfighter trying to mend his ways was always being told that he wasn't man enough to drink whiskey anymore, that he had to stick with milk or sarsaparilla. In the movies, they always called it "sasparilla," though. Sam had no idea the word was actually spelled the way the sign indicated.

And what on earth was sarsaparilla anyhow? Sam had always assumed it was a carbonated drink. But what did it taste like? Root beer? He suddenly had an idea. Why not buy a case and take it home for the party? "Have some sarsaparilla," he'd tell Lori and her friends. "What's sarsaparilla?" they'd ask, tripping over the word. "Oh, you've got to try some," he'd say. "It's just out of this world."

And Debbie would give him a smile.

He stopped the car. When he got out, the heat was overwhelming, literally like an oven. *How the hell does anybody think tourists will tolerate coming here?* he thought. There weren't any poles for electricity or phones. The lines must have been underground. Even so, doors and windows were open in every building, indicating that they didn't have air conditioning. A slight breeze did nothing to cool him but did blow dust on his lips.

Well-trained, none of the actors gave him a second look (or a first look for that matter) as he approached the saloon's swinging doors. In Western movies, that type of door—with open space at the top and the bottom—had always seemed fake, as if in the old days people hadn't cared about dirt blowing in. He pushed through, leaving the searing daylight for smoke-filled shadows that felt no cooler than the outside. Then he noticed that, on each side, solid doors had been shoved back. *So the entrance* can *be closed if the weather's bad*, he thought, and was reassured by the realistic detail. He heard a tinny, somewhat out-of-tune piano playing a song that he didn't recognize but that sounded very old. The piano was in the far left corner. No one sat at it as the keys rose and fell and its mechanized music drifted through the saloon. On the far right, stairs led up to rooms off a balcony. *In the old days, that's where the prostitutes would have taken their customers,* Sam thought. On the left, cowboys sat at circular tables, drinking and silently playing cards. Their cigarette smoke thickened, almost making Sam cough. *They'll never get families in here*, he thought.

On the right was a room-length bar, its wood darkened with age and grime. Cowboys leaned against it, silently drinking from beer mugs or shot glasses that probably contained tea or ginger ale. A barkeep wore a white shirt and vest and stood guard, arms crossed, next to the cash register.

Sam went over. "Is that sign outside accurate? Do you sell sarsaparilla?" Realizing that he mispronounced it the way actors in movies did, he hurriedly said, "I mean sarsaparilla." The word felt strange in his mouth.

The barkeep didn't answer. None of the cowboys looked at him. *Part of the show,* Sam thought. *We're supposed to feel like we're back in the 1800s and can't be seen.*

"How much for a case?" Sam asked.

Again no answer.

Sam glanced to the right along the bar and noticed generic-looking soda bottles on a shelf behind it, near the front window. They were made of clear glass that showed dark liquid in them—like root beer. They were labeled sarsaparilla. Corks were held in place with spring devices that he'd occasionally seen on pressurized bottles, indicating that the contents of *these* bottles were probably carbonated. Like root beer.

Sam counted ten bottles. "I'll take them all. How much?"

No answer. The actors maintained the illusion he wasn't there.

Sam went over to the bottles and saw a price tag on each. Five cents.

"This can't be true," he said. "What's the real price?"

The only sound came from the tinny piano.

"Okay then, if that's how you want it. I'll give you a bonus and take the whole lot for a dollar."

Sam put a dollar on the counter and moved to pick up the bottles.

No one bothered to stop him.

"I don't know how you're going to stay in business," he said.

Then he started wondering about what he was buying. Suppose these bottles were merely stage props, or suppose this was the worst-tasting stuff imaginable. Suppose he took it home and gave it to Lori and her friends, only to watch them spit it out.

"Is there anything *wrong* with this stuff?"

No answer.

"Well, if there is, you're about to be involved in a lawsuit." Sam picked up a bottle, freed the spring device, and tugged on the cork, needing a couple of tries to yank it out. Dark fluid fizzed, running over the bottle's mouth.

He sniffed it. *Smells like root beer*, he thought.

"I'm going to drink this now. If it's gone bad and makes me sick or something, you're all lose your jobs."

The piano kept tinkling. No one turned.

Hell, they're not going to let me poison myself, Sam thought.

"You had your chance."

He sipped.

• • •

A TICKLE roused him. On his hand. As the tickle persisted, he forced his heavy eyelids open and found himself lying face down in the sand, his head angled sideways toward his outstretched right arm. The last rays of sunset showed a scorpion on the back of that hand. The creature was about two and a half inches long. Despite the crimson of the dying sun, its yellow was vivid. Its pincers, its eight legs, its curved tail, stinger poised, made him want to scream.

Don't move, he thought. *No matter what, pretend you're paralyzed. If you startle this thing, it'll jab you. You could die out here.*

Here? Sam's mind was so fogged, his head aching so bad, that it took him several moments to remember walking into the saloon and drinking the sarsa...sarsa... His mind couldn't form the word.

But that had been around six o'clock. The sun had still been strong. *So how the hell did it get to be sunset so fast?* he wondered in a panic. *And what am I doing on the ground?*

The scorpion remained poised on his hand. A terrible taste in Sam's mouth made him start to retch. *No! Don't move! Don't scare it!*

The heat of the sunset was against his back. As the blood-tinted light dimmed, he stifled the urge to be sick and stared breathlessly at the scorpion's stinger, which wavered, rose, and seemed about to dart toward his skin. But instead of jabbing him, the scorpion eased forward. One by one, its tickling legs shifted toward the sand.

The instant it was gone, Sam rolled violently in the opposite direction, came to his knees, vomited, and frantically realized that there might be other scorpions around him. Scrambling to his feet, he swatted at his clothes and felt something hard fly off him. *Jesus, did it sting me?* He stared at his hands but saw no swelling and felt no fire. Trembling, he wiped mucus from his lips but couldn't free the terrible taste from his mouth. Like rotten potatoes. He vomited again, rubbed more mucus from his mouth, and stared around in frightened confusion.

The town had vanished. *No, not completely,* he realized. In the swiftly paling sunset, he saw a few charred boards projecting from the sand. Part of a wagon wheel lay among rocks. The ribcage of what might have been a horse was partially exposed next to a mound that could have been collapsed mud-and-straw bricks from a chimney.

What the hell happened? he thought. Continuing to turn, scanning his surroundings, he whimpered with relief when he saw his Explorer. Then the air became gray, and he stumbled toward his car, desperately hurrying despite stiff legs, lest he lose his way if darkness suddenly overcame him.

When he opened the driver's door, the heat in the car shoved him, prompting another attack of dry heaves. He grabbed a bottle of water from next to his briefcase on the passenger seat, rinsed his mouth, spat, couldn't get rid of the taste of rotten potatoes, waited for the spasms to stop, and sipped. Abruptly he was so thirsty that he finished the bottle before he knew what he'd done. Apprehensive, he waited for his stomach to spew it out. Seconds passed. Slowly, he relaxed.

After he managed to buckle his seat belt, he had an irrational fear that the car wouldn't start. But a twist of the ignition key instantly engaged the engine. He turned on the headlights. Ahead, he saw rocks, sand, and diseased cacti, their limbs drooping. But only the tips of charred boards, along with the few other things he'd noticed, gave any indication of where the town had been.

Damn it, what happened? he thought. Immediately, he grasped at a possible answer. *Maybe this isn't the same place. Maybe I collapsed, and somebody moved me.*

But that didn't make sense, either. Why would anybody have moved him? He stared out the windshield toward the shadowy outline of a hill that resembled the hill behind which the town had been situated. On each side of the hill, in the distance, tiny lights drifted through the darkness. In pairs. Headlights. The highway. More evidence that this was the same place where the town had been.

But it couldn't be. His head pounded. Nothing made sense. Having wondered if someone had moved him, he now recalled the solitary dust cloud that had followed him along the road. Surely, whoever was in the car would have found him. After all, the road went directly past where the Explorer was parked. Anyone following couldn't possibly have failed to notice it and the town.

At once, Sam shivered as he realized that, among the rocks, sand, diseased cacti, and occasional tips of charred boards, the one thing his headlights didn't show was the road.

That's impossible, he thought, shivering so hard now that he worried he might have a fever. It hadn't been much of a road. Even so, he couldn't fail to see it. It had been here!

Debbie, he thought. *Lori. They expect me to be home soon.* He picked up his cell phone from the seat, pressed the "start" button, and moaned when it failed to respond. He tried again. Nothing happened. He must have left it on too long. The battery was dead.

He put the car in gear. As his headlights pierced the darkness, he navigated around rocks and cacti. Passing the hill, he lurched over bumps toward the headlights of smoothly moving traffic on I-10. Then he stopped and felt sick again as he came to a dirt road that ran parallel to the highway. It had to be the same road he'd followed. Heading in this direction, he'd seen only one. The map had indicated there was only one. But how in God's name could the road now be in *front* of the hill instead of veering behind it?

• • •

THE HOUSE was dark when he got there. *Good,* Sam thought. *They didn't stay up, waiting for me.* He'd done his best to get home quickly, but several times, he'd felt sick again and had pulled to the side of the highway until he felt better. Now the time was shortly after midnight. His head pounding worse, he reached to press the garage-door opener but quickly changed his mind. The garage was under Lori's bedroom. The rumble might waken her. Then Lori might waken Debbie, and he didn't know how to tell them what had happened. Hell, if *he* didn't understand it, how could *they?* Feeling hungover, straining to think clearly, he parked in the driveway, remembered to take his briefcase, walked past murky bushes, and fumbled to unlock the front door.

Shadows revealed stairs leading up to the bedroom area. On the right was the large living room that they hardly ever used. On the left was the family area with a big-screen TV. In back was the kitchen. Sam made his way in that direction, setting his briefcase on a counter. He turned on the lights, poured a glass of water, finished it in three gulps, and noticed the dried vomit on his shirt. In fact, he smelled it. Jesus, if Debbie saw him like this...

He yanked off his shirt and hurried into the bathroom next to the kitchen. There wasn't a tub or a shower. But at least he could fill the sink and wipe a soapy washcloth over his face, then rinse his mouth and cheeks with warm water. Toweling himself, feeling almost human, he returned to the kitchen and faltered when he saw Lori.

Her hair was in pig tails. She wore her Winnie the Pooh pajamas and her fuzzy, bunny slippers. She rubbed her sleepy eyes.

"Hi, sweetheart," he said. "Sorry if I woke you. Are you thirsty? I'll get you a glass of water while you tell me about the party."

She screamed and raced into the family room.

"Lori?"

Screaming louder, she scrambled up the stairs.

"Lori, it's me." He ran after her. "It's Dad. What's wrong? There's nothing to be afraid of."

A door banged open, followed by loud voices and urgent footsteps.

"Lori?"

Stair lights came on. A muscular man in boxer shorts lunged into view at the top of the stairs.

"Who the hell are *you*?" Sam asked.

"No," the man growled, charging down the stairs. "Who the hell are *you*? What are you doing here? How'd you get in?"

25

Behind the man, Debbie appeared. She wore a hastily put-on housecoat open at the middle, showing the panties and tee-shirt she liked to sleep in. Her red hair was silhouetted by the light up there as she held Lori.

"Debbie?" Sam asked. "Is this some kind of joke?"

"Call the police!" the man yelled.

"Debbie, what's—"

The man reached the bottom of the stairs and punched Sam's stomach, knocking him to the floor.

Landing hard, Sam groaned and fought to catch his breath. He tried to explain, but the man kicked his side, causing him to roll against an end table that crashed in the shadows. At once, the man stumbled back, hopping, holding a bare foot that he'd injured when he'd kicked Sam. The man knocked a lamp over.

"Hurry!" Debbie blurted into a phone. "He's trying to kill my husband!"

Lori screamed again.

Sam struggled to his feet. He saw the man lower his injured foot and pick up the broken lamp to throw at him. He saw Debbie pleading into the phone and Lori screaming. He yanked the front door open and raced into the darkness.

• • •

ALTHOUGH THE confusion of Sam's emotions made him sweat, his shirtless back felt cold against the driver's seat. Speeding from the neighborhood, he heard approaching sirens. He tried to judge the direction from which they came, but no matter the street he took, the sirens wailed nearer, prompting him to steer into a driveway, turn off the engine and the headlights, and slide down out of sight. Fifteen seconds later, flashing lights sped past.

The moment he couldn't see them, he restarted the car and backed onto the street, moving in the opposite direction. He decided he was losing his mind.

• • •

"DEBBIE, IT'S Sam," he said into a cell phone he'd paid a gas-station attendant to let him use.

"*Who?*"

"Quit kidding around. Who *is* that guy? Why did you and Lori pretend you don't know me?"

"We've never seen you before! For God's sake, leave us alone!"

"Are you punishing me for missing Lori's party, for not being home enough, is that it? If you're trying to scare me—"

The phone made bumping noises. A gruff voice came on the line. "This is Sgt. Malone of the Phoenix police department. The penalty for stalking—"

Sam broke the connection.

• • •

"WE DON'T have any non-smoking rooms," the motel clerk said.

Sam's stomach ached where he'd been punched. Too exhausted to try anywhere else, he murmured, "Whatever you've got." His sport coat had been in the Explorer. He wore it buttoned and held the lapels together, concealing his bare chest.

"Fill out this form. All I need is your credit card."

Sam gave it to him, then finished the form. But when he glanced up, the clerk was frowning.

"Something wrong?" Sam asked.

"The credit-card company won't accept this card."

"What?"

"I tried twice."

"Try again. Maybe your scanning machine's broken."

"Worked ten minutes ago." The clerk slid the card through the scanner and studied an indicator on the machine. "Nope. Still won't take it."

"But that's impossible."

"If you say so, but I can't rent you a room without a card."

"Cash. You still take cash, don't you?"

"As long as you don't use the phone or charge incidentals. Eighty-five dollars."

Sam reached into his pocket and came out with two fives.

• • •

SHEPPERTON ENTERPRISES, the sign indicated.

The Explorer's headlights blazed across the large, empty parking lot. At two in the morning, most of the windows in the glass-and-metal building were dark. Exterior lights compensated, so harsh that they aggravated Sam's headache. Barely able to keep his eyes open, he almost parked in the executive area, but then he realized that this was the first place the police would look.

Trembling, he drove from the building and stopped at an apartment complex a block away. Staying in shadows as much as possible, he walked back to Shepperton Enterprises, where he couldn't avoid the lights as he unlocked the side door and entered the building. Before closing the door, he glanced behind him. No flashing lights sped across the parking lot. No one had seen him.

On his left, an intrusion detector gave off a warning beep that stopped as he tapped the security code. He headed up echoing stairs toward the executive offices and their view of a nearby golf course. He unlocked his office, went inside, and kept the lights off as he relocked the door. Huge windows had blinds that he shut. He always kept a shaving kit and a change of clothes here. Tomorrow morning, he could make himself presentable in the washroom down the hall. For now, all he cared about was lying down, trying to understand, trying to make his head stop pounding.

Feeling his way to the couch, he told himself, *Sleep. That's all you need. If you can get some sleep, you'll be able to figure this out.*

• • •

VOICES WOKE him. He struggled to rouse himself from the darkest sleep he'd ever known. As the voices grew louder, he jerked his eyes open, bolted up from the couch, and found two security guards scowling at him while several men and women stood behind them.

"Buddy, how'd you get in here?" a guard asked.

"How'd I…? I work here. This is my office."

"Not likely, friend," the other guard said. "Not when it belongs to Ms. Taylor." He pointed over his shoulder toward a slender, blond woman.

"Who on earth is Ms. Taylor? Look, I'm Sam Tucker and—"

"Never heard of you." The second guard turned toward the people behind him. "Anybody here heard of somebody named Sam Tucker?"

There were puzzled murmurs of "no." Several people shook their heads from side to side.

"*Never heard of me?*"

"Take it easy, buddy."

"What are you talking about? I've worked here nine years! I've been Joe's vice-president since he started the business! Who the hell *are* those people?"

"I said, take it easy, buddy. Don't make this worse. The police'll be here soon. You can sort this out at the station."

"If I didn't work here, how did I get in? How did I get the keys to this building and my office?"

"*You* tell *me*," the first guard said. "Maybe you stole them. Hand them over."

"Where's Joe? Ask Joe! He'll tell you I work for him! He'll tell you I'm his vice-president!"

"We would, except that if you're as close to him as you claim, you'd know he's in Europe."

"On my desk! There's a photo of me and my wife and little girl!" Sam hurried over to show them. But what he saw was a photo of the slender, blond woman behind the guards. She had a geeky-looking man on her right and two children—twin girls—on her left.

He screamed.

• • •

"YOUR NAME'S Sam Tucker?" the detective said.

"Yes."

"Your wife's name is Debbie, and your daughter's name is Lori, both of whom live in the house your broke into last night."

"I didn't break in! I had a key!"

"How did you get the key?"

"I've always had the key!"

"The same as you always had the keys to Shepperton Enterprises."

"Yes! As long as I've worked there! For the past nine years! And the house is new for us! We've only owned it eight months! That's how long I've had the key! Look, I can prove I work for Shepperton Enterprises! Check the documents in the briefcase I left at my house!"

"We'll get to the briefcase in a second. For now, apart from the unlawful entry charges, the ID you gave us is fake."

"*What?*"

"Your social security number belongs to a man named Walter Barry."

"*WHAT?*"

"Who lives in Seattle. The birth place and date you gave us don't pan out, either."

"My briefcase! Look in my briefcase!"

"I already did. It's empty."

• • •

"MY NAME'S Sam Tucker. I..."

• • •

"DEBBIE. I'VE been married to her for eleven years. My daughter's name is…"

• • •

"JOE SHEPPERTON. I've been his vice-president for…"

• • •

MYSTERY MAN STILL NOT IDENTIFIED

PHOENIX, AZ *(May 14)—Authorities continue to be baffled about the identity of a man who broke into a home a year ago and was subsequently discovered sleeping in an office in the real-estate development firm of Shepperton Enterprises.*

"He claims to be my vice-president, but I've never laid eyes on the guy," Joe Shepperton said.

"He says he's my husband," Debbie Bolan told reporters, "but I've been happily married to my husband Ward for the past eleven years. To the best of my knowledge, I've never met this Sam Tucker. I have no idea why he's fixated on me and my daughter. He scares me. I don't know what I'm going to do if they let him go."

"I've never encountered a situation like this," Dr. Philip Kincaid, chief of staff for the Maricopa Mental Health Facility, explained. "After a year, we still haven't been able to identify the man who calls himself Sam Tucker. The FBI has no record of his fingerprints. Neither do any branches of the U.S. military. There haven't been any DNA matches. The social security number he insists on using doesn't belong to him. There's no record that he was born when and where he claims. Nor is there any record of the man and woman he insists are

31

his parents. He claims he has a business degree from UCLA. There's no record of that, either. It's as if he spontaneously appeared with no ties to the past. But of course that's not possible. At first, we classified him as an amnesiac. But he keeps insisting that something happened to him in a town in the desert, a town that doesn't exist, so we're now treating him as delusional, as a schizophrenic with catatonic tendencies. All he does is murmur to himself and read history books."

• • •

...WHICH BRINGS us to one of the least known and most fascinating puzzles of southern Arizona in the nineteenth century: the fate of the town of Meridian. Located along the old stagecoach route between Tucson and Phoenix, Meridian was founded in 1882 by the religious zealot Ebenezer Cartwright, who led a band of pilgrims from Rhode Island in search of what he called the Land of Salvation. After two years of wandering, Cartwright finally settled in the Arizona desert because, as he told a passing stagecoach driver, "its heat will perpetually remind us of the flames of everlasting Hell."

His statement turned out to be prophetic inasmuch as, exactly one year after Meridian came into existence, it was destroyed in a fire. Cartwright chose the town's name, he said, to describe "the highest point of the burning sun, which encourages us to strive for the highest of human endeavor." Whatever his intentions, the reverse turned out to be the case, for during Meridian's brief existence, stagecoach drivers reached Tucson and Phoenix with rumors about a hell town in the desert in which debauchery and drunkenness knew no bounds. Since no one survived the fire, we can only conjecture about Meridian's fate. Perhaps Ebenezer Cartwright's only purpose was to isolate his devoted followers in the middle of nowhere and use them for his own twisted ends. Or perhaps the relentless heat of the desert drove the community insane. After a stagecoach driver reached Phoenix, claiming a false name as well as a home, a wife, and a son that weren't his (delusions that were no doubt the consequence of heat stroke), other drivers avoided the ruins. "Old Cartwright's still out there, trying to suck out our souls," one of them said. Only the desert, which shows a few scorched boards and remnants of wagons and walls of the ghost town, knows the truth.

• • •

"NOW THAT you've met the committee, do you understand the seriousness of this interview?" Dr. Kincaid asked.

"Yes."

"Do you have a wife named Debbie and a daughter named Lori?"

"No."

"Do you own a home at forty-seven Arroyo Road?"

"No."

"Are you a vice-president at Shepperton Enterprises?"

"No."

"What's your name?"

"I don't remember. I know it isn't Sam Tucker, even though that's the name I thought was mine when I came here."

"And which we've decided is convenient for you to use inasmuch as we don't know what your real name is."

"Yes."

"Perhaps one day, you'll remember your actual name or your actual social security number, and we'll be able to connect you with your past. But for now, the best we can do is prepare you to be a productive member of society. We've arranged for you to have a valid social security number. We've tried to get you employment in the area you claim to be

33

expert in—real estate development—but your mental condition and lack of qualifications made our efforts unsuccessful. However, since you enjoy spending most of your time with books, we've obtained employment for you as a custodian at a branch of the Phoenix public library. We've also obtained a room for you at a boarding house near that facility. You'll be obligated, of course, to pay the rent and to keep taking your medication."

"Of course."

"Do you understand that you'll be arrested if you go anywhere near Debbie and Lori Bolan or their home on forty-seven Arroyo Road? Do you also understand that you'll be arrested if you go anywhere near Joe Shepperton or Shepperton Enterprises?"

"I do."

"Have you any questions?"

"One."

"Yes?"

"What happened to my Ford Explorer?"

"Since the license plate and VIN numbers were invalid, the car was impounded and sold at public auction."

"I see."

"How does that make you feel?"

"If the Explorer wasn't mine, I don't have a right to it."

"Exactly. I commend you on your progress."

"Thank you."

• • •

CAREFUL, SAM thought as he stepped from the car. He thanked the driver, a male nurse at the mental-health facility. Squinting from the sun, he watched the vehicle proceed along the shimmering street. Then he turned toward the two-story, Spanish-style boarding house. A stern man stared from the front door. Picking up the cheap suitcase a social worker had given him, Sam approached. For the past two years he had thought only about his lost life, about Debbie and Lori, about the family he'd taken for granted, about hugs and kisses and not being able to see his daughter grow, about family meals and Lori's piano recitals and all the things he'd never made time for. Now they were the most precious things imaginable. With all his heart, he wanted to rush to Debbie and Lori and beg them to help him understand. Free at last, he needed to...

Careful, he warned himself again. *The police and Dr. Kincaid will keep an eye on you. The guy who runs this place will report everything you do. Remember what the police said about the penalties for stalking. You'll never learn the truth if you end up in jail or back at the nut house.*

• • •

THE MOTORCYCLE, which had taken him a month to make a down payment on, transferred every punishing jolt as he followed the primitive road next to I-10. Replicating the route that had destroyed his life, he'd left the highway at Gila Gulch and now headed toward the hill behind which he'd found Meridian. The arms on the human-shaped cacti looked even more limp, black-specked, and diseased than two years earlier. Heat waves radiated off the rocks and the sand. The bleak hill loomed closer. Staring along the road, he noted in distress that it didn't curve to the right of the hill as it had that evening. Instead, it went to the left, remaining parallel with I-10.

Leaving the road, veering to the right, he felt increasingly torturous bumps as he rounded the hill and came to more black-specked cacti. Beneath the goggles that protected his eyes from blowing sand, tears welled. It was a mark of his desperation that he'd managed to convince himself that Meridian would be here when he returned.

Maybe you are in fact insane. Thinking of yourself as "you," as someone apart from you, isn't that one of the signs of schizophrenia? Maybe you're as crazy as everybody thinks you are. Admit it—whatever happened to you out here, it had nothing to do with a place from 1882 that appears and disappears like some kind of evil version of Brigadoon. If you believe that, you are crazy.

He stopped the motorcycle where he estimated he'd parked the Explorer that evening. Amid rocks and sand, he recalled where the livery stable, blacksmith shop, and general store had been. *Where you* imagined *they were*, he thought. *And stop calling yourself "you."*

The restaurant with the fifty-cent steak dinner had been farther along the street, and the saloon with its swinging doors and its sign for whiskey, beer, and sarsaparilla (he still had trouble with the word) had been even farther along. He could see everything in his mind so vividly.

But obviously, they hadn't existed. Heartsick, he got off the motorcycle and propped it on its kickstand. He took off his helmet and felt a dry hot wind on his sweat-matted hair. For a time, after his release from the mental-health facility, he'd followed orders and taken his medication. But it had made him feel so groggy, so out of touch with things, that whatever cure it was supposed to be seemed worse than what Dr. Kincaid had said was wrong with him. Each day, he had taken less and less, his consciousness regaining focus, his senses becoming more alert. And each day, he had felt more certain that he was in fact Sam Tucker, that he did have a wife and daughter, that he worked for Shepperton Enterprises. The only problem was, nobody else in the world agreed with him.

How could it seem so real? he inwardly shouted. *Is that what schizophrenia's like? Do you become convinced that a false world's true?*

Damn it, stop thinking of yourself as "you."

He shuffled along the nonexistent street that he could see so vividly in his memory. Here and there, he noticed charred tips of boards poking from the sand, just as he'd noticed them the evening he'd wakened here. He paused and pulled one of the boards free, studying the scorch marks on it. He stared at the partially exposed bones of a large animal. He had a mental image of the cowboys shooting at each other, of the muscular man carrying the sack of flour. He plodded farther along the nonexistent street.

Here, he thought. The saloon had been just about here. The swinging doors with the gaps at the top and bottom. The tinkly music from the player piano. He stepped through where he imagined the doors had been. He glanced to the left where cowboys had smoked and silently played cards. He looked to the right where other cowboys had leaned against the bar and drank. The sarsa...sarsaparilla bottles had been just about...

Here. This is where you woke up, he thought, staring down at the sand. Something small moved among rocks. A scorpion? So real. So false. *You shouldn't have returned. All you're doing is making yourself worse.* He backed away, as if retreating through the swinging doors, and stopped when a glint in the sand caught his attention: sunlight reflecting off something. *A shiny piece of stone*, he told himself. *Fool's gold or whatever.* The reflection seemed to pierce his eye. He walked toward it and kicked his shoe in the sand. He expected a glinting pebble to roll free. Instead, his shoe dislodged something bigger, something solid enough to resist his shoe.

A circular tip of glass beckoned. He stooped, gripped it, and pulled a bottle from the sand. The bottle was empty. It was the same kind of bottle that had contained the liquid he'd drunk. Despite the sun's heat, he shivered. *How could you have imagined something that you never saw, something that was buried under the sand?* he thought.

That's when he knew he was truly in hell.

• • •

THE NEXT day, he pulled a collapsed tent from the back of the motorcycle and set it up, using a rock to drive the extra-long stakes deep into the sand. The tent had a reflective exterior that made it an excellent shield against the desert sun, he'd been assured. He zipped the entrance shut so scorpions and snakes couldn't get inside. Then he unstrapped a fold-down camp shovel from the motorcycle, opened it, and thrust it into the sand where he'd found the bottle. That was all the equipment he'd been able to fit on the bike. The next time, he'd bring more. If he was going to live out here when he wasn't working at the library, he had to make himself as comfortable as possible. A sleeping bag. A Coleman lantern and stove. A cooler. A portable radio. Maybe a sun umbrella. His janitor's salary didn't allow him to afford all that, and given his lack of history, no bank would give him a loan, but his junk mail (the only mail he received, all of it addressed to "current occupant") brought a never-ending stream of invitations to apply for credit cards, and credit-card companies, he'd discovered, would give a card to everybody, no matter how broke or crazy they were.

Frenzied, he dug the shovel into the sand.

• • •

"SIR, YOU can't stay here," a voice said.

Sam dug harder. After two months, he'd excavated almost the entire length and breadth of where the saloon had been. Mounds of sand marked its perimeter. Stacks of burnt wood rose next to a huge scorched section of the bar. Piles of glasses and bottles lay to one side.

"You can't do this, sir. This is private property. You're trespassing."

A special hoard lay near Sam's tent: the generic-looking soft-drink bottles, from one of which he'd sipped two years ago. He'd been praying that he'd find one that had fluid in it. Maybe, if he drank from it, he could cause Meridian to return. Maybe he could reverse what had happened. Maybe he could get his soul back. But to his dismay, enough to cause him to whimper each time he made a discovery, most of the bottles had been broken, and the few intact ones had been empty. He dug faster.

"*Sir,*" the deep voice insisted.

A hand touched his shoulder.

Trance broken, Sam whirled.

"Don't do anything stupid," a hard-faced man said. He raised his callused hands protectively in case Sam tried to use the shovel as a weapon. The man wore a metal hat, a faded denim shirt, jeans, and construction worker's boots.

To Sam's astonishment, trucks, bulldozers, backhoes, and other earth-moving equipment raised dust, rumbling into view from the side of the hill. He'd been so focused on digging that he hadn't been aware of anything else. Construction workers got out of numerous vans. An SUV jounced across the bumpy terrain and stopped, the words SHEPPERTON ENTERPRISES stenciled on its side. A man in a dress shirt and loosened tie, his sleeves rolled up, got out, put on a metal hat, and barked orders at some of the men. His stomach was more ample than it had used to be, his chin more jowly, his dark hair a little thinner, but there was no mistaking him.

Joe, Sam thought.

After yelling more orders, Joe stared in Sam's direction. "What's going on over there?" he shouted to the worker. "Who the hell's that guy? What's he doing here?"

"Digging," the worker shouted back.

Joe stormed over, yelling, "Don't you think I can see that?"

"Looks like he lives here." The worker pointed at the tent. "Homeless. He's scavenging glass and stuff."

"Jesus."

"Joe," Sam murmured.

"Tear down the tent, and get him out of here," Joe told the worker, then turned to leave.

"Joe," Sam managed to say louder.

"What?" Joe looked back and scowled. "Do I know you?"

"Don't you recognize me?" Immediately, Sam realized how much his sun-leathered skin and two months of beard had changed his appearance. "It's Sam. Sam Tucker."

"Sam?" Joe asked blankly. Apprehension crossed his beefy face. "That nutcase? Sam *Tucker?* The guy who thinks he's my vice-president, for crissake? Call the cops," Joe told the worker. "Tell them he's a stalker. When I come back from Grand Valley, I want this crazy son of a bitch out of here."

"Grand Valley?" Sam asked.

Joe marched through the dust toward a group of workers.

"Did you say *Grand Valley?* Joe! My God, don't tell me you're talking about Grand Valley Vistas outside Tucson?"

Joe scowled back harder. "How come you know about Grand Valley?"

"*You went ahead and bought it?*"

Joe straightened cockily. "In two hours, just about the time the police lock you in a cell, I'll be signing the papers."

"*Carson talked you into it?*"

"Carson? What do you know about Carson? And nobody talks me into *anything!*"

"Yeah, right, like that Hidden Estates deal you so regretted getting tricked into that you hired me to double-check the deals you were tempted to make."

"Hidden Estates?" Joe stormed back to him. "Have you been breaking into my building again? Reading my files?"

"I can save you ten million dollars."

"That's exactly what Carson wants for the land! How did you know? You *have* been reading my files!"

"And I can save you *another* ten million in lawsuits."

"Jesus, you're crazier than I thought."

"It's not going to cost you anything to wait another day, but it'll cost you at least twenty million if you sign those papers."

"Okay, you know so much about my business? Prove it."

"What?"

"Prove I'll be making a mistake."

"And if I can?"

"You poor dumb... The fact is, you *can't* prove it. But maybe that'll make you realize how deluded you are. Maybe you'll finally leave me alone."

"But if I *can?*"

"You mean, will that convince me you used to be my vice-president? No damned way."

"It doesn't matter. That's not what I want. I don't care about that anymore."

"Then what *do* you want?"

"One of the lots here."

"What?"

"*This* lot." Sam pointed toward his excavation. "If I prove buying Grand Valley Vistas would be a disaster, giving me this lot will be the best investment you ever made."

"Fat chance of *that* happening." Joe looked amused. "Fine. Prove I shouldn't buy Grand Valley Vistas, and the lot's yours."

Sam held out his hand. "Shake on it."

"Yeah, sure, right." Joe smirked as he shook Sam's hand.

"You've got your faults, Joe, but breaking your word didn't used to be one of them."

"And it sure as hell isn't now. This man's our witness to the deal. Where's your proof?"

"In the sixties, Grand Valley Vistas used to be a toxic dump site."

"*What?*"

"From a chemical plant that used to be there. It's got enough poisons buried there to cause multiple birth defects and give anybody who lives there cancer."

"And you can *prove* this?" Joe's normally florid face paled.

"I can tell you how to contact a man who was on the crew that dumped the chemicals, and a man who quit working at the plant because of the dumping. They're old now, but their memories are excellent. I can also tell you how to get your hands on the company's records, the ones that authorized the dumping before the plant shut down."

For the first time in Sam's experience, Joe had trouble speaking. "If you're right..."

"You save twenty million, and I get this lot."

• • •

SAM'S SHOVEL clinked against another bottle. In the sweltering sun, he raised the glass container, heartsick that it too was empty. *One day*, he thought. *One day, you'll find a bottle with dark liquid in it, and when you drink from it, you'll have your wife and daughter back. Stop thinking of yourself as "you."*

Around him, saws whined and hammers pounded as homes went up with the speed Joe Shepperton was famous for. Here and there, portable radios played golden oldies or frenzied conversations on political call-in shows. Sam barely noticed them. The saloon was all that mattered. Meridian. Getting his soul back. Impressed with the accuracy of Sam's information, Joe had offered him a position in the company ("Maybe you're a natural."), but Sam had meant what he said. He no longer cared about his former job. *Hell, if it hadn't been for that job,* he thought, *you never would have lost your family.*

What he needed was to retrieve the life he'd taken for granted. *One day, you'll find a bottle filled with liquid in it,* he kept telling himself. *You'll collapse. You'll wake up, and this time you'll be able to return to Debbie and Lori. You'll hug and kiss them. Overjoyed to see you, they'll wonder what kept you all these years.*

They would stare in amazement as he explained. The town would reappear, just as it had reappeared two years earlier. He'd finally be able to get his life back. His *soul* back.

A sudden panic seized him. How could any of that happen if a new town took its place? Time. He didn't have much time.

As the searing sun reached its zenith, he dug and dug with a greater frenzy.

THE ARCHITECTURE
OF SNOW

Few authors had the mystique of J.D. Salinger. In the mid-1960s, having written four much-discussed books, one of which was already being treated as a classic, the revered author of The Catcher in the Rye *stopped publishing and withdrew from public life.*

He never explained why. His final book, a pairing of novellas titled Raise High the Roof Beam, Carpenters *and* Seymour: An Introduction, *received mixed critical reactions. Perhaps Salinger's personality was as fragile as the name of his fictional Glass family implied. Perhaps he decided to stop exposing his work to reviewers and preferred to retreat to a simple life where he listened to "the sound of one hand clapping," a Zen Buddhist phrase that he favored.*

For whatever reason, his walled compound in the town of Cornish, New Hampshire, acquired the reputation of a hermit's lair. Fans who made pilgrimages to the area reported occasional sightings of the lean, aesthetic-looking author, basing their recognition on a solitary, long-ago book photograph that they'd studied. But over the years, the sightings became rarer while the citizens of Cornish closed ranks, refusing to reveal the little information they had about him.

The few reports that surfaced indicate that during the next four decades Salinger wrote obsessively every day and that he had stacks of completed novels in a large safe in his home. In January of 2010, he died at the age of ninety-one. It remains to be seen if those novels will be published. Perhaps they never existed. Perhaps he destroyed them before his death. Perhaps they're unreadable. Or perhaps they're masterpieces, the publication of which will come as unexpectedly as his withdrawal from public life.

These thoughts intrigued me long before Salinger died. In 2004, as I considered the way publishing had changed since my debut novel, First Blood, *appeared in 1972, I wondered what Salinger would make of the international conglomerates that now control the book world. Publicity has become as important as editing. Marketing is often more important than content.*

How would a modern publisher react, I wondered, if—out of nowhere and after so many years—a new Salinger manuscript arrived on an editor's desk? I called the author by another name, and the circumstances of his withdrawal are different, but anyone familiar with Salinger will recognize the inspiration for "The Architecture of Snow." The story was written in 2008. I didn't update the author's age.

O N THE FIRST MONDAY IN OCTOBER, Samuel Carver, who was seventy-two and suddenly unemployed, stepped in front of a fast-moving bus. Carver was an editor for Edwin March & Sons, until recently one of the last privately owned publishing houses in New York City.

"To describe Carver as an editor is an understatement," I said in his eulogy. Having indirectly caused his death, March & Sons, now a division of Gladstone International, sent me to represent the company at his funeral. "He was a legend. To find someone with his reputation, you need to go back to the 1920s, to Maxwell Perkins and his relationships with Ernest Hemingway, F. Scott Fitzgerald, and Thomas Wolfe. It was Perkins who massaged Hemingway's ego, helped Fitzgerald recover from hangovers, and realized that the two feet of manuscript Wolfe lugged into his office could be divided into several novels."

Standing next to Carver's coffin at the front of a Presbyterian church in lower Manhattan, I counted ten mourners. "Carver followed Perkins's example," I went on. "For much of the past five decades, he discovered an amazing number of major authors. He nurtured them through writer's block and discouraging reviews. He lent them money. He promoted them tirelessly. He made them realize the scope of their creative powers. R. J. Wentworth's classic about childhood and stolen innocence, *The Sand Castle*. Carol Fabin's verse novel, *Wagon Mound*. Roger Kilpatrick's Vietnam War novel, *The Disinherited*. Eventual recipients of Pulitzer Prizes, these were buried in piles of unsolicited manuscripts that Carver loved to search through."

Ten mourners. Many of the authors Carver had championed were dead. Others had progressed to huge advances at bigger publishers and ignored their debt to him. A few retired editors paid their respects. *Publishers Weekly* sent someone who took a few notes. Carver's wife had died seven years earlier. The couple hadn't been able to have children. The church echoed coldly. So much for being a legend.

The official explanation was that Carver stumbled in front of the bus, but I had no doubt that he committed suicide. Despite my praise about his past five decades, he hadn't been a creative presence since his wife's death. Age, ill health, and grief wore him down. At the same time, the book business changed so drastically that his instincts didn't fit. He was a lover of long shots, with the patience to give talent a chance to develop. But in the profit-obsessed climate of modern publishing, manuscripts needed to survive the focus groups of the marketing department. If the books weren't easily promotable, they didn't get accepted. For the past seven years, George March, the grandson of the company's founder, loyally postponed forcing Carver into retirement, paying him a small salary to come to the office two days a week. The elderly gentleman had a desk in a corner where he studied unsolicited manuscripts. He also functioned as a corporate memory, although it was hard to imagine how stories about the good old days of publishing could help an editor survive in today's corporate attitude. Not that it mattered—I was one of the few who asked him anything.

Eventually, March & Sons succumbed to a conglomerate. Gladstone International hoped to strengthen its film-and-broadcast division by acquiring a publisher and ordering it to focus on novels suited for movies and television. The trade buzzword for this is "synergy." As usual when a conglomerate takes over a business, the first thing the new owner did was downsize the staff, and Carver was an obvious target for elimination. Maybe he'd felt that his former contributions made him immune. That would account for his stunned reaction when he came to work that Monday morning and received the bad news.

"What am I going to do?" the old man murmured. His liver-spotted hands shook as he studied framed photographs of his wife and authors he'd discovered and put them into a flimsy box. "How will I manage? How will I fill the time?"

Evidently, he'd decided that he wouldn't. The box in one hand, his umbrella in the other, he went outside and let the bus solve his problems.

Because Carver and I seemed to be friends, the new CEO put me in charge of whatever projects Carver was trying to develop. Mostly, that meant sending a few polite rejection letters. Also, I removed some items Carver forgot in his desk drawer: cough drops, chewing gum, and a packet of Kleenex.

• • •

"MR. NEAL?"

"Mmmm?" I glanced up from one of the hundreds of emails I received each day.

My assistant stood in my office doorway. His black turtleneck, black trousers, and black sports coat gave him the appearance of authority. Young, tall, thin, and ambitious, he held a book mailer. "This arrived for Mr. Carver. No return address. Should I handle it for you?"

In theory, it was an innocent suggestion. But in the new corporate climate, I doubted there was any such thing as an innocent suggestion. When my assistant offered to take one of my duties, I wondered if it was the first step in assuming *all* of my duties. After Carver was fired, three other editors, each over fifty, received termination notices. I'm forty-six. My assistant keeps calling me Mr. Neal, even though I've asked him to call me Tom. "Mister" isn't only a term of respect—it's also a way of depersonalizing the competition.

"Thanks, but I'll take care of it."

Determined to stake out my territory, I carried the package home. These days, manuscripts are nearly always submitted electronically, so one that arrived via snail mail was almost certainly from someone who didn't understand the business. I forgot about it until Sunday afternoon after I'd worked through several chunky submissions that included two serial-killer novels and a romantic saga about California's wine country. The time-demanding tyranny of those manuscripts is one reason my wife moved out years earlier. She said she lived as if she were single, so she might as well *be* single. Most days, I don't blame her.

A Yankees game was on television. I opened a beer, noticed the package on a side table, and decided to flip though its contents during commercials. When I tore it open, I found a typed manuscript, double-spaced in professional format. With unsolicited submissions, you can't count on any of that. It didn't reek of cigarette smoke or food odors, and that too was encouraging. Still, I was troubled not to find an introductory letter and return postage.

The manuscript didn't have the uniform typeface that word processors and printers create. Some letters were faint, others dark. Some were slightly above or below others. The author had put this through an actual typewriter. It was a novel called *The Architecture of Snow.* An evocative title, I decided, although the marketing department would claim that bookstore clerks would mistakenly put it in the arts-and-architecture section. The writer's name was Peter Thomas. Bland. The marketing department preferred last names that had easily remembered concrete nouns like "King" or "Steel."

With zero expectation, I started to read. Hardly any time seemed to pass before the baseball game ended. My beer glass was empty, but I didn't remember drinking its contents. Surprised, I noticed the darkness outside my apartment's windows. I glanced at my watch. Ten o'clock? Another fifty pages to go. Eager to proceed, I made a sandwich, opened another beer, shut off the TV, and finished one of the best novels I'd read in years.

You dream about something like that. An absolutely perfect manuscript. Nothing to correct. Just a wonderful combination of hypnotic tone, powerful emotion, palpable vividness, beautiful sentences, and characters you never want to leave. The story was about a ten-year-old boy living alone with his divorced father on a farm in Vermont. In the middle of January, a blizzard hits the area. It knocks down electricity and telephone lines. It disables cell-phone relays. It blocks roads and imprisons the boy and his father.

• • •

"THE FATHER starts throwing up," I told the marketing/ editorial committee. "He gets a high fever. His lower right abdomen's in terrific pain. There's a medical book in the house, and it doesn't take them long to realize the father has appendicitis. But they can't telephone for help, and the father's too sick to drive. Even if he could, his truck would never get through the massive drifts. Meanwhile, with the power off, their furnace doesn't work. The temperature in the house drops to zero. When the boy isn't trying to do something for his father, he works to keep a fire going in the living room, where they retreat. Plus, the animals in the barn need food. The cows need milking. The boy struggles through the storm to reach the barn and keep them alive. With the pipes frozen, he can't get water from the well. He melts snow in pots near the fire. He heats canned soup for his dad, but the man's too sick to keep it down. Finally, the boy hears a snowplow on a nearby road. In desperation, he dresses as warmly as he can. He fights through drifts to try to reach the road."

"So basically it's a Young Adult book," the head of marketing interrupted without enthusiasm. Young Adult is trade jargon for Juvenile.

"A teenager might read it as an adventure, but an adult will see far more than that," I explained. "The emotions carry a world of meaning."

"Does the boy save the father?" the new CEO asked. He came from Gladstone's broadcast division.

"Yes, although the boy nearly dies in the process."

"Well, at least it isn't a downer." The head of marketing shook his head skeptically. "A couple of days on a farm in a blizzard. Feels small. Bestselling novels need global threats and international conspiracies."

"I promise—on the page, those few days feel huge. The ten-year-old becomes the father. The sick father becomes the son. At first, the boy's overwhelmed. Then he manages almost superhuman efforts."

"Child in jeopardy. The book won't appeal to women. What's the title mean?"

"The epigraph indicates that *The Architecture of Snow* is a quote from an Emerson poem about how everything in life is connected as if covered by snow."

The CEO looked bored. "Has anybody heard of the author?"

"No."

"A first novel. A small subject. It'll be hard to persuade the talk shows to promote the book. I don't see movie potential. Send the usual rejection letter."

"Can't." I felt on the verge of risking my job. "The author didn't give a return address."

"A typical amateur."

"I don't think so." I paused, about to take the biggest gamble of my career. But if my suspicion was correct, I no longer needed to worry about my job. "The book's beautifully, powerfully written. It has a distinctive, hypnotic rhythm. The punctuation's distinctive also: an unusual use of dashes and italics. A father and a son. Lost innocence. The book's style and theme are synonymous with..." I took the chance. "They remind me of R. J. Wentworth."

The CEO thought a moment. "*The Sand Castle?*"

"We sold eight million copies so far, a hundred thousand paperbacks to colleges this year alone," I said.

"You're suggesting someone imitated his style?"

"Not at all."

"Then...?"

"I don't believe it's an imitation. I think Peter Thomas *is* R. J. Wentworth."

The room became so quiet, I heard traffic outside twenty stories below us.

"But isn't Wentworth *dead?*" a marketer asked. "Wasn't he killed in a car accident in the sixties?"

"Not exactly."

• • •

OCTOBER 15, 1966. Three disasters happened simultaneously. A movie based on one of Wentworth's short stories premiered that month. The story was called "The Fortune Teller," but the studio changed the title to "A Valentine for Two." It also added a couple of songs. Those changes confirmed Wentworth's suspicions about Hollywood. The only reason he sold the rights to the short story was that every producer was begging for *The Sand Castle* and he decided to use "The Fortune Teller" as a test case. He lived with his wife and two sons in Connecticut. The family begged him to drive them into Manhattan for the premiere, to see how truly bad the film was and laugh it off. En route, rain turned to sleet. The car flipped off the road. Wentworth's wife and two sons were killed.

The film turned out to be dreadful. The story's New England setting became a cruise ship. A teenage idol played the main character—originally a college professor but now a dance instructor. Every review was scathing. Nearly all of them blamed Wentworth for giving Hollywood the chance to pervert a beloved story. Most critics wrote their attacks in mock Wentworth prose, with his distinctive rhythms and his odd use of dashes and italics.

Meanwhile, his new book, a collection of two novellas, *Opposites Attract*, was published the same day. March & Sons wanted to take advantage of the movie publicity. Of course, when the date was originally chosen, no one could have known how rotten the movie would be. By the time rumors spread, it was too late to change the schedule. Reviewers already had the book in their hands. It was charming. It was entertaining. In many places, it was even meaningful. But it wasn't as magnificent as *The Sand Castle*. Anticipation led to disappointment, which turned to nastiness. Many reviewers crowed that Wentworth wasn't the genius some had reputed him to be. They took another look at *The Sand Castle* and now faulted passages in it.

• • •

"ALL ON the same day," I told the marketing/editorial committee. "October 15, 1966. Wentworth blamed everything on himself. His fiction is influenced by transcendental writers like Emerson and Thoreau, so it isn't surprising that he followed Thoreau's example and retreated to the New England countryside, where he bought a house on two acres outside a small town called Tipton in Vermont. He enclosed the property with a high fence, and that was the end of his public life. College students began romanticizing his retreat to the countryside—the grieving, guilt-ridden author, father, and husband living in isolation. When the paperback of *Opposites Attract* was published, it became a two-year bestseller. More than that, it was suddenly perceived as a minor masterpiece. Not *The Sand Castle*, of course. But far superior to what critics had first maintained. With each year of his seclusion, his reputation increased."

"How do you know so much about him?" the head of marketing asked.

"I wrote several essays about him when I was an undergrad at Penn State."

"And you're convinced this is a genuine Wentworth manuscript?"

"One of the tantalizing rumors about him is that, although he never published anything after 1966, he kept writing every day. He implied as much to a high school student who knocked on his gate and actually got an interview with him."

"Those essays you wrote made you an expert? You're confident you can tell the real thing from an imitation?"

"The book's set in Vermont, where Wentworth retreated. The boy limps from frostbite on his right foot, the same foot Wentworth injured in the accident. But I have another reason to believe it's genuine. Wentworth's editor, the man who discovered him, was Samuel Carver."

"*Carver?*" The CEO leaned forward in surprise. "After more than forty years, Wentworth finally sent his editor a manuscript? Why the pseudonym? That doesn't make sense."

"I don't have an answer. But the absence of a letter and a return address tells me that the author expected Carver to know how to get in touch with him. I can think of only one author who could take that for granted."

"Jesus," the CEO said, "if we can prove this was written by Wentworth—"

"Every talk show would want him," the head of marketing enthused. "A legendary hermit coming out of seclusion. A solitary genius ready to tell his story. CNN would jump at the chance. The *Today* show. *Sixty Minutes.* He'd easily make the cover of the major magazines. We'd have a guaranteed number-one bestseller."

"Wait a second," a marketer asked. "How *old* is he?"

"In his early eighties," I answered.

"Maybe he can barely talk. Maybe he'd be useless on the *Today* show."

"That's one of a lot of things you need to find out," the CEO told me. "Track him down. Find out if he wrote this manuscript. Our parent company wants a twenty-percent increase in profits. We won't do that by promoting authors who sell only fifty thousand hardbacks. We need a million seller. I'm meeting the Gladstone executives on Monday. They want to know what progress we're making. It would be fabulous if I could tell them we have Wentworth."

• • •

I TRIED to telephone Wentworth's agent to see if she had contact information. But it turned out that his agent had died twelve years earlier and that no arrangements were made for anyone else to represent Wentworth, who wasn't expected to publish again. I called Vermont's telephone directory assistance and learned that Wentworth didn't have a listed phone number. The Author's Guild couldn't help, either. There was no personal information about him on the Internet.

My CEO walked in. "What did he tell you? Does he admit he's the author?"

"I haven't been able to ask him. I can't find a way to contact him."

"This is too important. Go up to Vermont. Knock on his door. Keep knocking until he answers."

I checked Google Maps and located Tipton in the southern part of Vermont. A Google search revealed that few people lived there. It was difficult to reach by plane or train, so the next morning, I rented a car and drove six hours north through Connecticut and Massachusetts.

In mid-October, Vermont's maple-tree-covered hills had glorious colors, although I was too preoccupied to give them full attention. With difficulty—because a crossroads wasn't clearly marked—I reached Tipton (population 5,073) only after dark and checked into one of its few motels without getting a look at the town.

At eight the next morning, I stepped from my room and breathed cool, clean air. Rustic buildings lined the main street, mostly white clapboards with high-pitched roofs. A church steeple towered above a square. Calm. Clean. Quiet. Ordered. The contrast with Manhattan was dramatic.

Down the street, a sign read MEG'S PANTRY. As I passed an antique store, I had the palpable sense of former years. I imagined that, except for satellite dishes and SUVs, Tipton looked the same now as it had a hundred years earlier, perhaps even *two* hundred years earlier. A plaque confirmed my suspicion: JEREMIAH TIPTON CONSTRUCTED THIS BUILDING IN 1792.

When I opened the door, the smell of coffee, pancakes, eggs, bacon, and hash browns overwhelmed me. A dozen ruddy-faced patrons looked up from their breakfasts. My pale cheeks made me self-conscious, as did my slacks and sports coat. Amid jeans and checkered wool shirts, I obviously wasn't a local. Not that I sensed hostility. A town that earned its income from tourists tolerated strangers.

As they resumed their murmured conversations, I sat at the counter. A gray-haired woman with spectacles came over, gave me a menu, and pulled a notepad from an apron.

"What's the special?" I asked.

"Corned beef and poached eggs."

I didn't have an appetite, but I knew I couldn't establish rapport if my bill wasn't high enough for the waitress to expect a good tip. "I'll take it."

"Coffee?"

"You bet. Regular. And orange juice."

When she brought the food, I said, "Town's kind of quiet."

"Gets busy on the weekends. Especially now that the leaves are in color."

When she brought the check, I said, "I'm told there's a writer who lives in the neighborhood. R. J. Wentworth."

Everyone looked at me.

"Wentworth? I don't think I ever heard of him," the waitress said. "Mind you, I'm not a reader."

"You'd love his books." The obvious response to a statement like that is, "Really? What are they about?" But all I received was a guarded look. "Keep the change," I said.

Subtlety not having worked, I went outside and noticed a little more activity on the street. Some of it wasn't reassuring. A rumpled guy in ragged clothes came out of an alley. He had the vacant look of a drunk or a drug addict.

Other movement caught my attention. A slender man wearing a cap and a windbreaker reached a bookstore across the street, unlocked its door, and went in. When I crossed to it, I saw that most of the volumes in the window had lush covers depicting covered bridges, autumn foliage, or snow-covered slopes, with titles related to Vermont's history and beauty. But one volume, small and plain, was a history of Tipton. I tried the door and found it was locked.

Through the window, I saw the slender man take off his windbreaker. His cap was already off, revealing thin, gray hair. He turned toward the rattling doorknob and shook his head, motioning courteously for me to leave. When I pretended to be confused, he walked over and unlocked the door.

"I'm not open yet. Can you come back in an hour?"

"Sure. I want to buy that book in the window—the history of Tipton."

That caught his attention. "You've got excellent taste. Come in."

An overhead bell rang when he opened the door wider. The store was filled with pleasant mustiness. He tugged a pen from his shirt pocket.

"I'll autograph the book for you," he said.

"You're the author?"

"Guilty."

I looked at the cover. *Tales of Historic Tipton* by Jonathan Wade. "I'm from New York. An editor for March & Sons. It's always a pleasure to meet an author."

"You're here to see the colors?"

"A little pleasure with business." I paid for the book.

"Business?"

"An author lives around here."

"Oh?"

"R. J. Wentworth."

"Oh?"

"I need to speak to him."

"Couldn't you just write him a letter?"

"I don't have his address."

"I see." Wade pointed at the book in my hands. "And you thought perhaps the address is in *there?*"

"The thought crossed my mind."

"You won't find it. Still want to buy the book?"

"Absolutely. I love history, and when I meet an author, I'm always curious to see how he writes."

"Not with the brilliance of R. J. Wentworth, I regret to say. We used to get people asking about him all the time. Thirty years ago, my father had a thriving business, selling Wentworth's books to people who asked about him. In fact, without Wentworth, my father wouldn't have made a living. Nor would anybody else in town, for that matter. Tipton would have dried up if not for the tourists Wentworth attracted."

"But not anymore?"

"His fans got old, and people don't read much these days."

"So a waitress across the street told me."

"This town owes him a lot, even if he didn't intend to do us a favor. In these parts, if you're not born here, you're always an outsider. But after more than forty years of living here, he's definitely one of us. You won't find anybody who'll tell you where he is. I wouldn't be able to look him in the eyes if I violated his privacy."

"In the eyes?" I asked, feeling a chill. "You mean you've spoken with him?"

"Despite Bob's reputation for being a hermit, he isn't anti-social."

"'Bob'?" I asked in greater amazement. The familiarity sounded almost profane.

"His first name is Robert, after all. He insists on being called Bob. He comes into town on occasion. Buys books. Eats at the Pantry. Gets a haircut. Watches a baseball game at the tavern down the street."

I continued to be astounded.

"Not often and certainly never on a weekend during peak tourist season," Wade continued. "He picks times when he knows he can move around without being bothered."

"Even at his age?"

"You'd be surprised."

"But what's he like?"

"Polite. Considerate. He doesn't make assumptions about himself. What I mostly notice is how clear his eyes are. You've read his work?"

"Many times."

"Then you know how much he's influenced by Transcendental writers like Emerson and Thoreau. Calm. Still. Reflective. It's soothing to be around him."

"But you won't help me meet him?"

"Definitely not."

"Could you at least phone him and try to arrange a meeting?"

"Can't."

"Okay, I understand."

"I'm not sure you do. I literally can't. Bob doesn't have a telephone. And I'm not about to knock on his door. Why do you need to talk to him?"

I told Wade about the manuscript. "I think it's his work, but it doesn't have his name on it." I added the detail that I hoped would made Wade cooperate. "It was addressed to his editor. But unfortunately, his editor died recently. They were friends. I wonder if he's been told."

"I only have your word that you're an editor."

"Here's my business card."

"Twenty years ago, a man showed me a business card, claiming he worked in the White House. He said the President wanted to give Bob an award, but he turned out to be an assistant to a Hollywood producer who wanted the movie rights for *The Sand Castle*."

"What harm would it do to put a note in his mailbox?"

"I've never intruded on him. I'm not about to start now."

• • •

OUTSIDE, A pickup truck rattled past. A few more locals appeared on the sidewalk. Another rumpled guy came out of an alley. A half-block to my right, a Jeep was parked outside an office marked TIPTON REALTY. I walked over and pretended to admire a display of properties for sale: farms, cabins, and historic-looking homes.

When I stepped inside, the hardwood floor creaked. The smell of furniture polish reminded me of my grandmother's house.

At an antique desk, an attractive red-haired woman looked up from a computer screen. "May I help you?" Her voice was pleasant.

"I was wondering if you had a map of the roads around here. My Vermont map doesn't provide much detail."

"Looking for property?"

"Don't know yet. As you can probably tell, I'm not from around here. But the scenery's so magnificent, I thought I might drive around and see if anything appeals to me."

"A weekend place to live?"

"Something like that."

"You're from New York, right?"

"It's that obvious?"

"I meet a lot of people passing through. I'm a good judge of accents. New York's a little far to have a weekend place here."

"I'm not sure it would be just for weekends. I'm a book editor. But I've given some thought to writing a novel."

This attracted her interest.

"I hear the location has inspired other writers," I said. "Doesn't John Irving live in Vermont?"

"And David Mamet and Grace Paley."

"And R. J. Wentworth," I said. "Doesn't he live around here?"

Her expression became guarded.

"Great writer," I said.

Her tone was now curt. "You'll find maps on that table."

• • •

As I walked to my car, I thought that the CIA or the mafia ought to send their recruits for training in Tipton. The townspeople knew how to keep secrets. I chose north, driving along brilliantly wooded back roads. The fragrance of the falling leaves was powerful, reminding me of my boyhood in a pleasant old house on Long Island, of helping my father rake the yard. He burned the leaves in a pit behind the house. He always let me strike the match. He died from a heart attack when I was twelve.

I turned up a dirt road, passed a cabin, reached a wall of

trees, and went back to the main road. Farther along, I turned up another dirt road, passed *two* cabins, reached a stream that blocked the road, and again went back.

My search wasn't as aimless as it seemed. After all, I knew what I was looking for: a high fence that enclosed a couple of acres. The female high school student who'd been fortunate enough to get an interview with Wentworth years earlier described the property. The high wooden gate was almost indistinguishable from the fence, she wrote. The mailbox was embedded in the fence and had a hatch on the opposite side so that Wentworth didn't need to leave the compound to get his mail. A sign warned NO SOLICITORS. NO TRESPASSING.

But nothing in the north sector matched that description. Of course, the student's interview was two decades old. Wentworth might have changed things since then, in which case I was wasting my time. How far away from town would he have wanted to live? I arbitrarily decided that fifteen miles was too far and switched my search to the side roads in the west. More farms and cabins, more falling leaves and wood smoke. By the time I finished the western sector and headed south, the afternoon light was fading.

My cell phone rang.

"Have you found him yet?" my boss demanded.

The reception was so poor, I could barely hear him. When I explained the problems I was having, he interrupted. "Just get it done. If Wentworth wrote this book, remind him his last contract with March & Sons gives us the option on it. There's no way I'm going to let anybody else publish it. Do you have the agreement with you?"

"In my jacket."

"Make sure you get him to sign it."

"He'll want to talk to an agent."

"You told me his agent's dead. Anyway, why does he need an agent? Within reason, we'll give him whatever he wants." The transmission crackled. "This'll go a long way toward proving you're a necessary part of the team." The crackle worsened. "Don't disappoint... Call...soon...find..."

With renewed motivation, I searched the southern sector, not giving up until dark. In town, I refilled the gas tank, ready for an early start the next morning. Then I walked along the shadowy main street, noticing FOR SALE signs on a lot of doors. The town's financial troubles gave me an idea.

• • •

TIPTON REALTY had its lights on. I knocked.

"Come in," a woman's voice said.

As I entered, I couldn't help noticing my haggard reflection on the door's window.

Again the hardwood floor creaked.

"Busy day?" The same woman sat at the desk. She was about thirty-five. Her lush red hair hung past her shoulders. Her bright green eyes were hard to look away from.

"I saw a lot of beautiful country."

"Did you find him?"

"Find...?"

"Bob Wentworth. Everybody in town knows you're looking for him."

I glanced down. "I guess I'd make a poor spy. No, I didn't find him." I held out my hand. "Tom Neal."

She gripped it. "Becky Shafer."

"I can't get used to people calling him 'Bob.' I gather you've met him."

"Not as much as other people in Tipton. I'm new."

"Oh?"

"Yeah, I came here only twelve years ago."

I chuckled.

"I drove into town with my artist boyfriend," she explained. "We loved the quiet and the scenery. We decided to stay. The boyfriend's long gone. But I'm still a newcomer."

"Sorry about the boyfriend." I noticed she didn't wear a wedding ring.

"No need to be sorry. He turned out to be a creep."

"A lot of that going around." I thought of my CEO.

She gave me a look that made me think she applied the word to me.

"I do have an important reason to see him," I said.

After I told her about the manuscript, she thought a moment. "But why would he use a pseudonym?"

"That's one of many things I'd like to ask him." Thinking of the FOR SALE signs, I took my chance to propose my idea. "To hear the old timers tell it, things got crazy here with so many fans wanting to talk to him. You can imagine the effect a new book would create. The publicity. The pent-up demand. This town would attract a lot of fans again. It would be like the excitement of thirty years ago."

I let the temptation sink in.

Becky didn't respond for several moments. Her gaze hardened. "So all I need to do is show you where Bob lives, and in exchange, next year I'll have more business than I can handle?"

"When you put it that way, I guess that's right."

"Gosh, I didn't realize it was so late." She pulled her car keys from her purse. "You'll have to excuse me. I need to go home."

• • •

THE WEATHERED old Tipton Tavern was presumably the place Wade told me about, where Wentworth sometimes watched a baseball game. There was indeed a baseball game on the televison, but I was the main interest, patrons setting down their drinks and looking at me. As much as I could tell from recalling the photograph on Wentworth's books (a lean-faced, dark-haired man with soulful eyes), he wasn't in the room.

Heading back to the motel, I didn't go far before I heard wary footsteps behind me. A cold breeze made me shiver as I glanced back toward the shadowy street. The footsteps ended. I resumed walking and again heard the footsteps. My Manhattan instincts took charge. Not quite running, I passed my car and reached the motel. My cold hands fumbled with the room key, finally managing to hurry inside.

In the middle of the night, glass broke outside my room and woke me. I phoned the front desk, but no one answered. In the morning, not having slept well, I went out to my car and found the driver's window shattered. A rock lay on the seat. Nothing seemed missing until I checked the glove compartment. A zippered pouch of coins and dollar bills that I keep there was gone.

The surprised desk clerk told me, "The town constable runs the barbershop."

• • •

"YES, WE'VE been having incidents lately." The heavyset barber/constable trimmed an elderly man's spindly hair. "A bicycle was stolen. A cabin was broken into."

I took a close look at the man in the chair and decided he wasn't Wentworth.

"Town's changing. Outsiders are hanging around," the barber continued.

I recalled the two druggies I'd seen emerge from an alley the previous day. "What are you going to do about it?"

"Contact the state police. I hoped the problem would go away as the weather got colder."

"Please remember I reported the break-in. The rental car agency will contact you." Trying to catch him off guard, I added, "Where does Bob Wentworth live?"

The barber almost responded, then caught himself. "Can't say."

But like a bad poker player, he hadn't been able to repress a glance past me toward the right side of the street.

• • •

I WENT to the left to avoid suspicion. Then I walked around the block and returned to the main street, out of sight of the barbershop. As I stepped from an alley, I again had the sense that someone followed, but when I looked behind me, I seemed alone.

More people were on the sidewalk, many dressed like outsiders, the town finally attracting business as the weekend approached. But the locals paid attention only to me. Trying to look casual, I went into a quilt shop, then continued along the street. Wentworth didn't live on a country road, I now realized with growing excitement. He lived in town. But I'd checked all the side streets. In fact, I'd used some of those streets to drive north, west, south, and east. Where was he hiding?

I walked to the end of the street. In a park of brilliant maples, dead leaves crunched under my shoes as I followed a stream along the edge of town. I soon reached a tall fence.

My cell phone rang.

"I hope you've found him," a stern voice warned.

"I'm making progress."

"I want more than progress. The Gladstone executives phoned to remind me they expect a better profit picture when I report on Monday. I hinted I'd have major news. Get Wentworth."

A locked gate sealed off a lane. I managed to climb over, tearing a button off my sports jacket.

Sunlight cast the shadows of branches. To my left were the backyards of houses. But on my right, the fence stretched on. A crow cawed. A breeze rattled leaves as I came to a door that blended with the fence. Signs warned NO SOLICITORS and NO TRESPASSING. A mailbox was recessed into the fence.

When I knocked on the door, the crow stopped cawing. The door shook. I waited, then knocked again, this time harder. The noise echoed. I knocked a third time.

"Mr. Wentworth?"

Leaves fell.

"Mr. Wentworth? My name's Tom Neal. I work for March & Sons. I need to talk to you about a manuscript we think you sent."

The breeze chilled my face.

I knocked a fourth time. *"Mr. Wentworth?"*

Finally, I took out a pen and a notepad. I thought about writing that Carver was dead, but that seemed a harsh way for Wentworth to get the news. So I gave him the name of the motel where I was staying and left my cell-phone number. Then I remembered that Wentworth didn't have a phone. But if he sometimes left his compound, he could use a phone in town, I concluded. Or he could walk to the motel.

"I'm shoving a note under the gate!"

Back in the park, I sat on a bench and tried to enjoy the view, but the breeze got cooler. After an hour, I returned to Wentworth's gate. A corner of my note remained visible under it.

"Mr. Wentworth, *please*, I need to talk to you! It's important!"

Maybe he's gone for a walk in the woods, I thought. *Or maybe he isn't even in town.*

Hell, he might be in a hospital somewhere.

• • •

"Did you find him?"

In the tavern, I looked up from a glass of beer. "No." Strictly speaking, it wasn't a lie.

Becky Shafer stood next to me at the bar. Her green eyes were as hypnotic as on the previous evening. "I thought about our conversation last night. I came to apologize for being abrupt."

"Hey, I'm from New York, remember? It's impossible to be abrupt to me. Anyway, I can't blame you for trying to protect someone who lives here."

"May I sit down?"

"I welcome the company. Can I buy you a beer?"

"Rye and diet Coke."

"Rye? I admire an honest drinker."

She laughed as the bartender took my order. "Maybe it *would* be good for the town if Bob published another book. Who knows? It's just that I don't like to feel manipulated."

"I'm so used to being manipulated, it feels normal."

She gave me a questioning look.

"When I first became an editor, all I needed to worry about was helping an author write a good book. But now conglomerates own just about every publisher. They think of books as commodities. If authors don't sell a hundred thousand copies, the head office doesn't care about them, and editors who don't find the next blockbuster are taking up space. Every morning, I go to March & Sons, wondering if I still work there."

"I know what you mean." Becky sipped her drink. "I'm also an attorney." My surprised look made her nod. "Yep. Harvard Law School."

"I'm impressed."

"So was the Boston law firm that hired me. But I couldn't bear how the senior partners pitted us against each other to see who generated the most fees. Finally I quit. I don't earn much money here, but I sure enjoy waking up each morning."

"In my office, I don't hear many people say *that*."

"Stay here longer. Maybe *you'll* be able to say it."

• • •

WALKING BACK to the motel, I again heard footsteps.

As on the previous night, they stopped when I turned toward the shadows. Their echo resumed when I moved on. Thinking of my broken car window, I increased speed. My cell phone rang, but I didn't have time to answer it. Only after I hurried into my room and locked the door did I listen to the message, hoping it was from Wentworth.

But the voice belonged to my CEO. "You're taking too long," he told me.

• • •

"MR. WENTWORTH?" At nine the next morning, amid a stronger breeze, I pounded on his gate. "It's really important that I talk to you about your manuscript! And Sam Carver! I need to talk to you about *him!*"

I stared at the bottom of the gate. Part of my note still remained visible. A thought from yesterday struck me. *Maybe he isn't home. Maybe he's in a hospital somewhere. Or maybe*—a new thought struck harder—*maybe he is home. But maybe he's sick. Too sick to go outside.*

"Mr. Wentworth?" I hammered the gate. "Are you all right?" I tried the knob, but it didn't turn. "Mr. Wentworth, can you hear me? Is anything wrong? *Do you need help?*"

Perhaps there was another way in. Chilled by the worsening breeze, I returned the way I had come and climbed back into the park. I followed the fence to a corner, then continued along the back, struggling through dense trees and undergrowth.

Indeed, there *was* another way in. Hidden among bushes, a gate shuddered as I pounded. "Mr. Wentworth?" I shoved a branch away and tried the knob, but it too wouldn't turn. I rammed my shoulder against the gate, but it held firm. A tree grew next to the fence. I grabbed a branch and pulled myself up. Higher branches acted as steps. Buffeted by the wind, I straddled the fence, squirmed over, dangled, and dropped to a pile of soft leaves.

• • •

IMMEDIATELY, I felt a difference. The wind stopped. Sounds were muted. The air became cushioned, as if a bubble enclosed the property. A buffer of some kind. No doubt, the tall fence caused the muffling effect. Or maybe it was because I'd entered sacred territory. As far as I knew, I was one of the few ever to set foot there. Although I breathed rapidly from struggling over the fence, I felt a hush.

Apples hung on trees or lay on the ground amid leaves. A few wrinkled raspberries remained on bushes. A vegetable garden contained the frost-browned remnants of tomato plants. Pumpkins and acorn squash bulged from vines. Continuing to be enveloped in a hush, I walked along a stone path. Ahead were a gazebo, a clapboard cottage, and a smaller building.

"Mr. Wentworth?"

When I rounded the gazebo and headed toward the cottage, I heard a door creak open. A man stepped out. He wore sneakers, jeans, and a sweater. He was slender, with graying hair. His thin, soulful features emphasized his dark, intense eyes.

He had a pistol in his hand.

"Wait." I jerked up my hands.

"Walk to the front gate."

Wentworth would have been in his early eighties, but this man looked twenty years younger, his cheeks aglow, only slightly wrinkled.

"Walk to the front gate."

"This isn't what it looks like." As he kept pointing the gun, my chest cramped. "I'm looking for Mr. Wentworth. I thought he might be ill. I came to see if I could help."

"Stay ahead of me."

"My name's Tom Neal. I knocked on the gate."

"*Move.*"

"I left a note. I'm an editor for March & Sons. Please. I need to talk to Mr. Wentworth about a manuscript I think he sent us. It was addressed to Sam Carver. He's dead. I took over his duties. That's why—"

"Stop," the man said.

His command made the air feel stiller. Crows cawing, squirrels scampering along branches, leaves rustling—everything seemed to halt.

"Sam's dead?" The man frowned, as if the notion was unthinkable.

"A week ago Monday."

Slowly, he lowered the gun.

"Who *are* you?" I asked.

The man rubbed his forehead in shock. "What? Who...? Nobody. Bob's son. He's out of town. I'm watching the house for him."

Bob's son? But that didn't make sense. Because Wentworth's family was killed in a car accident, another child would need to have been born when Wentworth was around twenty, before he got married, before *The Sand Castle* was published. Later, the furor of interest in Wentworth was so great that it would have been impossible to keep an illegitimate child a secret.

The man continued to look shocked. "What happened to Sam?"

I explained about the firm's new owner and how Carver was fired.

"The way you talk about the bus, are you suggesting..."

"I don't think Sam had much to live for. The look on his face when he carried his belongings from the office..."

The man seemed to peer at something far away. "Too late."

"What?"

Despondent, he shook his head from side to side. "The gate self-locks. Let yourself out."

As he turned toward the cottage, he limped.

"You're not Wentworth's son."

He paused.

"The limp's from your accident. You're R. J. Wentworth. You look twenty years younger. I don't know how that's possible, but that's who you are."

No one has ever looked at me so deeply. "Sam was your friend?"

"I admired him."

His dark eyes assessed me. "Wait here."

• • •

WHEN HE returned from the house, continuing to limp, he held a teapot and two cups. He looked so awkward that I reached to help.

We sat in the gazebo. The air felt more cushioned and soothing. My sense of reality was tested. R. J. Wentworth. Could I actually be talking to him?

"How can you look twenty years younger than you are?"

Wentworth ignored the question and poured the tea.

He stared at the steaming fluid. His voice was tight. "I met Sam Carver in 1958 after he found *The Sand Castle* in a stack of unsolicited manuscripts. At the time, I was a teacher in a grade school in Connecticut. My wife taught there, also. I didn't know about agents and how publishing worked. All I knew about was children and the sadness of watching them grow up. *The Sand Castle* was rejected by twenty publishers. If Sam hadn't found it, I'd probably have remained a teacher, which in the long run would have been better for me and certainly for my family. Sam understood that. After the accident, he was as regretful as I that *The Sand Castle* gained the attention it did." Wentworth raised his cup. "To Sam."

"To Sam." I sipped, tasting a hint of cinnamon and cloves.

"He and his wife visited me here each summer. He was a true friend. Perhaps my only one. After his wife died, he didn't come here again, however."

"You sent him *The Architecture of Snow?*"

Wentworth nodded. "Sam wrote me a letter that explained what was happening at March & Sons. You described his stunned look when he was fired. Well, he may have been stunned, but he wasn't surprised. He saw it coming. I sent the manuscript so he could pretend to make one last discovery and buy himself more time at the company."

"But why didn't you use your real name?"

"Because I wanted the manuscript to stand on its own. I didn't want the novel to be published because of the mystique that developed after I disappeared. The deaths of my wife and two sons caused that mystique. I couldn't bear using their deaths to get the book published."

"The manuscript's brilliant."

He hesitated. "Thank you." I've never heard anyone speak more humbly.

"You've been writing all these years?"

"All these years."

He sipped his tea. After a thoughtful silence, he stood and motioned for me to follow. We left the gazebo. Limping, he took me to the small building next to the cottage. He unlocked its door and led me inside.

• • •

HIS WRITING studio. For a moment, my heart beat faster. Then the hush of the room spread through me. The place had the calm of a sanctuary. I noticed a fireplace, a desk, a chair, and a typewriter instead of a computer.

"I have five more machines just like it—in case I need parts," Wentworth said.

I imagined the typewriter's bell sounding when Wentworth reached the end of each line. A ream of paper lay next to the typewriter, along with a package of carbon paper. A window directed light from behind the desk.

And to the side of the desk? I approached shelves upon which were arranged twenty-one manuscripts. I counted them. *Twenty-one*. They sent a shiver through me. "All these years," I repeated.

"Writing can be a form of meditation."

"And you never felt the urge to have them published?"

"To satisfy an ego I worked hard to eliminate? No."

"But isn't an unread book the equivalent of one hand clapping?"

He shrugged. "It would mean returning to the world."

"But you did send a manuscript to Sam."

"As Peter Thomas. As a favor to my friend. But I had doubts that the ploy would work. In his final letter, Sam said the changes in publishing were too grim to be described."

"True. In the old days, an editor read a manuscript, liked it, and bought it. But now the manuscript goes to the marketing department first. If the marketers don't estimate high sales, the book usually isn't accepted."

Wentworth was appalled. "How can a book with an original vision get published? After a while, everything will be the same. The strain on your face. Now I understand. You hate the business."

"The way it's become."

"Then why do you stay?"

"Because, God help me, I remember how excited I felt when I discovered a wonderful new book and found readers for it. I keep hoping corporations will realize books aren't potato chips."

Wentworth's searching eyes were amazingly clear. I felt self-conscious, as if he saw directly into me, sensing my frustration.

"It's a pleasant day. Why don't we go back to the gazebo?" he suggested. "I have some things I need to do. Perhaps you could pass the time by reading one of these manuscripts. I'd like your opinion."

For a moment, I was too surprised to respond. "You're serious?"

"An editor's perspective would be helpful."

"The last thing you need is my help." I couldn't believe my good fortune. "But I'd love to read something else you've written."

• • •

WENTWORTH'S CHORES turned out to be raking leaves, putting them in a compost bin, and cleaning his gardens for winter. Surrounded by the calming air, I sat in the gazebo and watched him, reminded of my father. Amid the muted sounds of crows, squirrels, and leaves, I finished my cup of tea, poured another, and started the manuscript, *A Cloud of Witnesses*.

I read about a slum in Boston, where a five-year-old boy named Eddie lived with his mother, who was seldom at home. The implication was that she haunted bars, prostituting herself in exchange for alcohol. Because Eddie was forbidden to leave the crummy apartment (the even worse hallways were filled with drug dealers and perverts), he didn't have any friends. The television was broken. He resorted to the radio and, by trial and error, found a station with an afternoon call-in program, "You Get It Straight from Jake," hosted by a comedian named

Jake Barton. Jake had an irreverent way of relating the day's events, and even though Eddie didn't understand most of the events referred to, he loved the way Jake talked. In fact, Jake accomplished a rare thing—he made Eddie laugh.

As I turned the pages, I heard Wentworth raking but as if from a great distance, farther and fainter. My vision narrowed until I was conscious only of each page in front of me and then only of Eddie looking forward to each day's broadcast of "You Get It Straight from Jake," Eddie laughing at Jake's jokes, Eddie wishing he had a father like Jake, Eddie...

A hand nudged my shoulder, the touch so gentle I barely felt it.

"Tom," a voice whispered.

"Uh."

"Tom, wake up."

My eyelids flickered. Wentworth stood before me. It was difficult to see him; everything was so shadowy. I was flat on my back on the bench. I jerked upright.

"My God, I fell asleep," I said.

"You certainly did." Wentworth looked amused.

I glanced around. It was dusk. "All day? I slept all day? I'm so sorry."

"Why?"

"Well, I barge in on you, but you're generous enough to let me read a manuscript, and then I fall asleep reading it, and—"

"You needed the rest. Otherwise, you wouldn't have dozed."

"Dozed? I haven't slept that soundly in years. It had nothing to do with... Your book's wonderful. It's moving and painful and yet funny and...I just got to the part where Jake announces he's been fired from the radio station and Eddie can't bear losing the only thing in his life he enjoys."

"There's plenty of time. Read more after we eat."

"Eat?"

"I made soup and a salad."

"But I can't impose."

"I insist."

• • •

EXCEPT FOR a stove and refrigerator, the kitchen might have looked the same two hundred years earlier. The floor, the cabinets, and the walls were polished wood, with a golden hue that made me think they were maple. The table and chairs were dark, perhaps oak, with dents here and there. Flaming logs crackled in a fireplace.

I smelled freshly baked bread and, for the first time in a long while, felt hungry. I ate three bowls of soup and two helpings of salad, not to mention a half loaf of bread.

"The potatoes, tomatoes, onions, and carrots, everything in the soup comes from my garden," Wentworth explained. "The growing season is brief here. I need to be resourceful. For example, the lettuce comes from a late summer planting that I keep in a glass frame so I can harvest it in the winter."

The fresh taste was powerful, warming my stomach. Somehow, I had room for two slices of apple pie, which was also homemade, from Wentworth's trees. And tea. Two cups of tea.

Helping to clean the dishes, I yawned. Embarrassed, I covered my mouth. "Sorry."

"Don't be. It's natural to feel sleepy after we eat. That's what mammals do. They eat. Then they sleep."

"But I slept all day."

"A sign of how much rest you need. Lie down on the sofa in the living room. Read more of my book."

"But I ought to go back to my motel room."

"Nonsense." Limping, Wentworth guided me into the living room. The old furnishings reminded me of those I saw long ago in my grandmother's house. The sofa was covered with a blanket.

"I won't be an imposition?"

"I welcome your reaction to my manuscript. I won't let you take it with you to the motel, so if you want to read it, you need to do it here."

I suppressed another yawn, so tired that I knew I wouldn't be alert enough to deal with anyone following me to the motel. "Thank you."

"You're more than welcome." Wentworth brought me the rest of the manuscript, and again I felt amazed that I was in his company.

The fireplace warmed me. On the sofa, I sat against a cushion and turned the pages, once more absorbed in the story. Jake announced that his sense of humor had gotten him fired from the radio station. He told his listeners that he had only two more broadcasts and then would leave Boston for a talk show in Cincinnati. Eddie was devastated. He hadn't seen his mother in two days. All he had to eat was peanut butter and crackers. He put them in a pillowcase. He added his only change of clothes, then went to the door and listened. He heard footsteps. Somebody cursed. When the sounds became distant, Eddie did the forbidden—he unlocked and opened the door. The lights were broken in most of the hallway. Trash was stacked in corners. The smell of urine and cooked cabbage made Eddie sick. Shadows threatened, but the curses and footsteps were more distant, and Eddie stepped through the doorway.

The crackling in Wentworth's fireplace seemed to come from far away, reminding me of the faint tap of a typewriter.

• • •

THE HAND on my shoulder was again so gentle I barely felt it. When I opened my eyes, Wentworth stood over me, but this time he was silhouetted by light.

"Good morning." He smiled.

"Morning?"

"It's eleven o'clock."

"I slept thirteen hours?" I asked in shock.

"You're more tired than I imagined. Would you like some breakfast?"

My stomach rumbled. I couldn't recall waking up with so strong an appetite. "Starved. Just give me a moment to..."

"There's an extra toothbrush and razor in the bathroom."

As I washed my face, I was puzzled by my reflection in the mirror. My cheeks were no longer drawn. Wrinkles on my brow and around my eyes were less distinct. My eyes looked bright, my skin healthy.

At the kitchen table, I ate a fruit salad Wentworth prepared— oranges, bananas, pears, and apples (the latter two from his trees, he reminded me). I refilled my bowl three times. As always, there was tea.

"Is it drugged? Is that why I'm sleeping so much?"

Wentworth almost smiled. "We both drank from the same pot. Wouldn't I have been sleepy, also?"

I studied him as hard as he had studied me. Despite his age, his cheeks glowed. His eyes were clear. His hair was gray instead of white. "You're in your early eighties, correct?"

"Correct."

"But you look at least twenty years younger. I don't understand."

"Perhaps you do."

I glanced around the old kitchen. I peered toward the trees and bushes outside. The sun cast a glow on falling leaves. "This place?"

"A similar compound in another area would have produced the same effect. But yes, this place. Over the years, I acquired a natural rhythm. I lived with the land. I blended with the passage of the sun and moon and seasons. After a while, I noticed a change in my appearance, or rather the *lack* of change in my appearance. I wasn't aging at the rate that I should have. I came to savor the delight of waking each day and enjoying what my small version of the universe had in store for me."

"That doesn't seem compatible with the gun you aimed at me."

"I brought that with me when I first retreated here. The loss of my family... Each morning was a struggle not to shoot myself."

I looked away, self-conscious.

"But one day crept into another. Somehow, I persisted. I read Emerson and Thoreau again and again, trying to empty myself of my not-so-quiet desperation. Along with these infinite two acres, Emerson and Thoreau saved my life. I came to feel my family through the flowers and trees and... Nothing dies. It's only transformed. I know what you're thinking—that I found a sentimental way to compensate. Perhaps I did. But compare your life to mine. When you came here, when you snuck onto my property, you looked so desperate that for the first time in many years I was frightened. I knew that several homes had been broken into recently. I got the gun from a drawer. I hoped I wouldn't need to defend myself."

Shame burned my cheeks. "Perhaps I'd better go."

"Then I realized you were truly desperate, not because of drugs or greed, but because of a profound unhappiness. I invited you to stay because I hoped this place would save you."

As so often with Wentworth, I couldn't speak. Finally, I managed to say "Thank you," and was reminded of how humbly he used those words when I told him how brilliant *The Architecture of Snow* was.

"I have some coveralls that might fit you," he said. "Would you like to help me clean my gardens?"

• • •

IT WAS one of the finest afternoons of my life, raking leaves, trimming frost-killed flowers, putting them in the compost bin. We harvested squash and apples. The only day I can compare it to was my final afternoon with my father so long ago, a comparably lovely autumn day when we raked leaves, before my father bent over and died.

A sound jolted me: my cell phone. I looked at the caller ID display. Finally, the ringing stopped.

Wentworth gave me a questioning look.

"My boss," I explained.

"You don't want to talk to him?"

"He's meeting the company's directors on Monday. He's under orders to squeeze out more profits. He wants to announce that *The Architecture of Snow* is on our list."

Wentworth glanced at the falling leaves. "Would the announcement help you?"

"My instructions are not to come back if I don't return with a signed contract."

Wentworth looked as if I'd told a slight joke. "That explains what drove you to climb over my fence."

"I really did worry that you were ill."

"Of course." Wentworth studied more falling leaves. "Monday?"

"Yes."

"If you go back, you'll lose sleep again."

"Somebody's got to fight them."

"Maybe we need to save ourselves before we save anything else. How would you like to help me split firewood?"

• • •

FOR SUPPER, we ate the rest of the soup, the bread, and the apple pie. They tasted as fresh as on the previous night. Again, I felt sleepy, but this time from unaccustomed physical exertion. My skin glowed from the sun and the breeze.

I finished my tea and yawned. "I'd better get back to the motel."

"No. Lie on the sofa. Finish my manuscript."

The logs crackled. I might have heard the distant clatter of a typewriter as I turned the pages.

In the story, Eddie braved the dangers of the rat-infested apartment building, needing all his cleverness to escape perverts and drug dealers. Outside, on a dark rainy street, he faced greater dangers. Every shadow was a threat. Meanwhile, a chapter about Jake revealed that he was a nasty drunk when he wasn't on the air. The station's owner was glad for the chance to fire him when Jake insulted one of the sponsors during the program. But Eddie idealized him and was ready to brave anything to find him. As the rain fell harder, he wondered how to find the radio station. He couldn't just ask a stranger on the street. He saw a store that sold newspapers and magazines and hurried toward it.

• • •

THIS TIME, Wentworth didn't need to touch me. I sensed his presence and opened my eyes to the glorious morning.

"Did you sleep well?"

"Very. But I'm afraid I didn't finish it. I'm where Eddie found the radio station's address in—"

"Next time," Wentworth said.

"Next time?"

"When you come back, you can finish it."

"You'd like me to come back?"

Instead of answering, Wentworth said, "I've given your problem a lot of consideration. Before I tell you my decision, I want you to tell me what you think of my manuscript so far."

"I love it."

"And? If I were your author, is that all you'd say to me as an editor? Is there nothing you want changed?"

"The sentences are wonderful. Your style's so consistent, it would be difficult to change anything without causing problems in other places."

"Does that imply a few sections would benefit from changes?"

"Just a few cuts."

"A few? Why so hesitant? Are you overwhelmed by the great man's talent? Do you know how Sam and I worked as editor and author? We fought over every page. He wasn't satisfied until he made me justify every word in every sentence. Some authors wouldn't have put up with it. But I loved the experience. He challenged me. He made me try harder and reach deeper. If *you* were my editor, what would you say to challenge me?"

"You really want an answer?" I took a breath. "I meant what I said. This is a terrific book. It's moving and dramatic and funny when it needs to be and...I love it."

"But..."

"In *The Architecture of Snow*, the boy struggles through a blizzard to save his father. In *this* novel, Eddie struggles to get out of a slum and find a father. You're running variations on a theme. An important theme, granted. But the same one as in *The Sand Castle*."

"Continue."

"That may be why the critics turned against your last book. Because *it* was a variation on *The Sand Castle*, also."

"Maybe some writers only have one theme."

"Perhaps that's true. But if I were your editor, I'd push you to learn if that were the case."

Wentworth considered me with those clear probing eyes. "My father molested me when I was eight."

I felt as if I'd been hit.

"My mother found out and divorced him. We moved to another city. I never saw my father again. She never remarried.

Fathers and sons. A powerful need when a boy's growing up. That's why I became a grade-school teacher: to be a surrogate father for the children who needed one. It's the reason I became a writer: to understand the hollowness in me. I lied to you. I told you that when I heard you coming across the yard, when I saw your desperate features, I pulled my gun from a drawer to protect myself. In fact, the gun was already in my hand. Friday. The day you crawled over the fence. Do you know what date it was?"

"No."

"October 15."

"October 15?" The date sounded vaguely familiar. Then it hit me. "Oh... The day your family died in the accident."

For the first time, Wentworth started to look his true age, his cheeks shrinking, his eyes clouding. "I deceive myself by blaming my work. I trick myself into thinking that, if I hadn't sold 'The Fortune Teller' to Hollywood, we wouldn't have driven to Manhattan to see the damned movie. But the movie didn't kill my family. The movie wasn't driving the car when it flipped."

"The weather turned bad. It was an accident."

"So I tell myself. But every time I write another novel about a father and a son, I think about my two boys crushed in a heap of steel. Each year, it seems easier to handle. But some anniversaries... Even after all these years..."

"The gun was in your hand?"

"In my mouth. I want to save *you* because you saved *me*. I'll sign a contract for *The Architecture of Snow*."

• • •

THROUGHOUT THE long drive back to Manhattan, I felt a familiar heaviness creep over me. I reached my apartment around midnight, but as Wentworth predicted, I slept poorly.

"Terrific!" My boss slapped my back when I gave him the news Monday morning. "Outstanding! I won't forget this!"

After the magic of the compound, the office was depressing. "But Wentworth has three conditions," I said.

"Fine, fine. Just give me the contract you took up there to get signed."

"He didn't sign it."

"*What?* But you said—"

"That contract's made out to R. J. Wentworth. He wants *another* contract, one made out to Peter Thomas."

"The pseudonym on the manuscript?"

"That's the first condition. The second is that the book needs to be published with the name Peter Thomas on the cover."

The head of marketing gasped.

"The third condition is that Wentworth won't do interviews."

Now the head of marketing turned red, as if choking on something. "We'll lose CNN and the *Today* show and the magazine covers and—"

"No interviews? That makes it worthless," my CEO complained. "Who the hell's going to buy a book about a kid in a snowstorm when its author's a nobody?"

"Those are his conditions."

"*Couldn't you talk him out of that?*"

"He wants the book to speak for itself. He says part of the reason he's famous is that his family died. He won't capitalize on that, and he won't allow himself to be asked about it."

"Worthless," my boss moaned. "How can I tell the Gladstone executives we won't have a million seller? I'll lose my job. You've already lost *yours*."

"There's a way to get around Wentworth's conditions," a voice said.

Everyone looked in that direction, toward the person next to me: my assistant, who wore his usual black turtleneck and black sports jacket.

"Make out the contract to Peter Thomas," my assistant continued. "Put in clauses guaranteeing that the book will be published under that name and that there won't be any interviews."

"Weren't you listening? An unknown author. No interviews. No serial killer or global conspiracy in the plot. We'll be lucky to sell ten copies."

"A million. You'll get the million," my assistant promised.

"Will you *please* start making sense?"

"The Internet will take care of everything. A month from pub date, I'll leak rumors to hundreds of chat groups. I'll put up a fan website. On the social networks, I'll spread the word that Wentworth's the actual author. I'll point out parallels between his early work and this one. I'll talk about the mysterious arrival of the manuscript just as his editor died. I'll mention that a March & Sons editor, Robert Neal, had a weekend conference at Wentworth's home in October, something that can be verified by checking with the motel where Mr. Neal stayed. I'll juice it up until everyone buys the rumor. Believe me, the Internet thrives on gossip. It'll get out of control fast. Since what passes for news these days is half speculation, reporters and TV commentators will do pieces about the rumors. After a week, it'll be taken for granted that Peter Thomas is R. J. Wentworth. People will want to be the first to buy the book to see what all the fuss is about. Believe me, you'll sell a million copies."

I was too stunned to say anything.

So were the others.

Finally my boss opened his mouth. "I love the way this guy thinks." He gave me a dismissive glance. "Take the new contract back to Wentworth. Tell him he'll get everything he wants."

• • •

SO, ON Tuesday, I drove back to Tipton. Because I was now familiar with the route, I made excellent time and arrived at four in the afternoon. Indeed, I often broke the speed limit, eager to see Wentworth again and warn him how March & Sons intended to betray him.

I saw the smoke before I got to town. As I approached the main street, I found it deserted. With a terrible premonition, I stopped at the park. The smoke shrouded Wentworth's compound. His fence was down. A fire engine rumbled beyond it. Running through the leaves, I saw townspeople gathered in shock. I saw the waitress from Meg's Pantry, the waiter from the Tipton Tavern, Jonathan Wade from the bookstore, the barber who was the town constable, and Becky. I raced toward her.

"What happened?"

The constable turned from speaking to three state policemen. "The two outsiders who've been hanging around town broke into Bob's place. The state police found fresh cigarette butts at the back fence. Next to a locked gate, there's a tree so close to the fence it's almost a ladder."

My knees weakened when I realized he was talking about the tree I'd climbed to get over the fence. *I showed them the way,* I thought. *I taught them how to get into the compound.*

"Some of the neighbors thought they heard a shot," the constable said, "but since this is hunting season, the shot didn't seem unusual, except that it was close to town. Then the neighbors noticed smoke rising from the compound. Seems that after the outsiders stole what they could, they set fire to the place—to make Bob's death look like an accident."

"Death?" I could barely say the word.

"The county fire department found his body in the embers."

My legs were so unsteady that I feared I'd collapse. I reached for something to support me. Becky's shoulder. She held me up.

"The police caught the two guys who did it," the constable said

I wanted to get my hands on them and—

"Bob came to see me after you drove back to New York," Becky said. "As you know, he needed an attorney."

"What are you talking about?"

Becky looked puzzled. "You aren't aware he changed his will?"

"*His will?*"

"He said you were the kind of man he hoped that his sons would have grown up to be. He made you his heir, his literary executor, everything. This place is yours now."

Tears rolled down my cheeks. They rolled even harder an hour later when the firemen let Becky and me onto the property and showed us where they'd found Wentworth's body in the charred kitchen. The corpse was gone now, but the outline in the ashes was vivid. I stared at the blackened timbers of the gazebo. I walked toward Wentworth's gutted writing studio. A fireman stopped me from getting too close. But even from twenty feet away, I saw the clump of twisted metal that was once a typewriter. And the piles of ashes that had once been twenty-one manuscripts.

• • •

I SPEND a lot of time trying to rebuild the compound, although I doubt I'll ever regain its magic. Becky often comes to help me. I couldn't do it without her.

But *The Architecture of Snow* is what I mostly think about. I told March & Sons to go to hell, with a special invitation to my assistant, my boss, and the head of marketing. I arranged for the novel to be privately printed under the name Peter Thomas. A Tipton artist designed a cover that shows the hint of a farmhouse within gusting snow, almost as if the snow is constructing the house. There's no author's biography. Exactly as Wentworth intended.

I keep boxes of the novel in my car. I drive from bookstore to bookstore throughout New England, but only a few will take the chance on an unknown author. I tell them it's an absolutely wonderful book, and they look blank as if "wonderful" isn't what customers want these days. Is there a serial killer or a global conspiracy?

Wade has dozens of copies in his store. His front window's filled with it. He tries to convince visitors to buy it, but his tourist customers want books that have photographs of ski slopes and covered bridges. He hasn't sold even one. The townspeople? The waitress at Meg's Pantry spoke the truth. She isn't much of a reader. Nor is anybody else. I tried until I don't know what else to do. I'm so desperate I finally betrayed Wentworth's trust and told you who wrote it. Take my word—it's wonderful. Buy it, will you? Please? For God's sake, buy this book.

THE COMPANIONS

In my introduction to "Time Was," I mentioned that Rod Serling influenced my early stories. (See my essay about him in Stars in My Eyes: My Love Affair with Books, Movies, and Music.*) Ray Bradbury also influenced me. "The Companions" is an opposite version of his "The Crowd." Parts of it are unusually autobiographical. Everything in the first section—all the events at the Santa Fe opera—actually happened to my wife and me. It was one of the strangest nights of our lives, making us wonder if we had entered Bradbury's October country.*

FRANK SHOULDN'T HAVE BEEN THERE. ON Thursday, unexpected script meetings required him to fly from Santa Fe to Los Angeles. His discussions with the film's director and its star ended on Friday evening. Usually, he would have spent the weekend with friends in Los Angeles, but he loved opera, and he had tickets for the next night when Santa Fe's opera company was premiering Poulenc's *The Dialogues of the Carmelites*, a work Frank had never seen. The tickets included a pre-performance dinner, along with a lecture about the composer.

"You just arrived in L.A. and now you want to fly back?" his wife, Ellen, asked when he phoned. "If there's an 'ultimate commuter' award, I'll nominate you for it."

"I've really been looking forward to this," Frank answered. Using his cell phone, he sat in his rented car outside the newest, trendiest Beverly Hills restaurant where the final meeting had ended. "Do you remember how many times I called the box office and kept getting a busy signal? The person I spoke to said I got the last two tickets."

"The dinner's supposed to be in a tent behind the opera house, right?"

"Right."

"Well, the tent might not be standing. Yesterday, the monsoons started."

Ellen referred to a July weather pattern in which moist air from the Pacific streamed into New Mexico, creating rains that were often violent.

"The storm was really bad," Ellen continued. "In fact, there's another one coming. I shouldn't be on the phone. It isn't safe with the lightning this close."

"I bet tomorrow will be bright and sunny."

"It's not supposed to be, according to the weather guy on channel seven. How were your meetings?"

"The director wants me to change the villains from presidential advisors to advertising executives. The star wants me to include a part for his new girlfriend. This opera will be my reward for listening to them."

"You're that determined? Be prepared to get wet." The prolonged boom of thunder echoed behind Ellen's voice. "I'd better hang up. Love you."

"Love you," Frank said.

• • •

FRANK'S PLANE was scheduled to leave Los Angeles at ten in the morning, but it didn't take off until two.

"Bad weather in New Mexico," the American Airlines attendant explained.

The jet descended through dark, churning clouds for a bumpy landing in Santa Fe shortly after five.

"It's been raining all day," an airline employee told Frank. "This is the first break we've had."

But a new storm beaded Frank's windshield as soon as he got in his car. Poor visibility slowed traffic so that the usual fifteen-minute drive home took three times that long. Frank pulled into his garage at six. The dinner at the opera was supposed to start at seven.

He'd made various cell-phone reports to his wife. Even so, Ellen looked relieved, as if she hadn't seen him for weeks, when he walked in. To her credit, she was dressed, ready for the evening. "If you're game, *I* am. But I think we're both nuts."

"I'm afraid I'm more nuts than you."

"The umbrella's in here." Ellen pointed to a knapsack that they always took to the opera. The theater's sides were open—people who dressed for daytime summer temperatures could feel frozen as the mountain air dropped from ninety to fifty degrees at night. "I've also got a blanket, a thermos of hot chocolate, and our rain coats. This had better be a good opera."

"Look." Frank smiled out the kitchen window, pointing toward sunlight peeking through the clouds. "The rain stopped. Everything's going to work out."

• • •

THE THEATER was eight miles north of town. As Frank headed up Route 285, traffic was fast and crazy as usual, drivers changing lanes regardless of how slick the pavement was.

Ellen pointed toward a police car, an ambulance, and two wrecked cars at the side of the road. "They're putting somebody into the ambulance. My God, somebody must have died. They covered the body."

Traffic threw a gritty spray that speckled Frank's windshield. Troubled by the accident, he turned on the windshield wipers and reduced his speed. Horns blared behind him, vehicles racing past. Straining to see beyond the streaks on his window, he steered toward an exit ramp and headed up a hill toward the opera house.

There, he walked with Ellen to a tent behind the theater. A bottle of wine stood on each table.

Half the seats were empty.

"See, not everybody's crazy like us," Ellen said.

"Like *me*."

After choosing salad and chicken from a buffet, they sat at a table.

Frank glanced toward the entrance. Two men entered, surveyed the empty seats, saw Frank and Ellen alone, and came over.

One of the men was short, slight, and elderly, with white hair and a matching goatee that made him look rabbinical. The other man was tall, well built, and young, with short, dark hair and a clean-shaven, square-jawed face. They both wore dark suits and white shirts. Their eyes were very clear.

"Hello," the elderly man said. "My name's Alexander."

"And I'm Richard," the other man said.

"Pleased to meet you." Frank introduced Ellen and himself.

"Terrible weather," the elderly man, Alexander, said.

"Sure is," Ellen agreed.

"We drove all the way from Albuquerque," the younger man, Richard, said.

"I can beat that," Frank told them. "I came all the way from Los Angeles."

The two men went to get their food. Frank poured wine for Ellen and himself, then offered to pour for Alexander and Richard when they came back.

"No, thanks," Alexander said.

"It makes me sleepy," Richard said.

The pair bowed their heads in a silent prayer. Self-conscious, Frank and Ellen did the same. Then the four of them ate and discussed opera, how they preferred the Italian ones, could tolerate the German ones, and felt that French operas were an ordeal.

"The rhythm's so ponderous in some of them," Frank said. "It's like being on a Roman slave ship, rowing to a drumbeat, like that scene in *Ben Hur*."

"But *Carmen*'s good. A French opera set in Spain." Richard laughed at the idea. "And tonight's opera is French. I've never heard it, so I have no idea whether it's worth our time."

Frank enjoyed how easy they were to talk to. They had an inner stillness that soothed him after his frustrating Hollywood meetings and his difficult journey home.

"So you live in Albuquerque?" Ellen asked the young man.

"No, *he* doesn't live there. *I* do," the elderly man said. "I'm a retired computer programmer."

"And I'm a monk," Richard said. "I live at Christ in the Desert." He referred to a monastery about thirty miles north of Santa Fe.

Frank hid his surprise. "I assumed the two of you were together."

"We are," Alexander said. "I often go on weekend retreats to the monastery. That's where Brother Richard and I became friends." Alexander referred to the practice of leaving the clamor of everyday life and spending time in the quiet of a monastery, meditating to achieve spiritual focus.

"Alexander doesn't drive well at night anymore," Brother Richard said. "So I went down to Albuquerque to get him. This opera has a subject of obvious interest to us."

What he meant was soon explained as the after-dinner lecture began. An elegant woman stood at a podium and explained that *The Dialogues of the Carmelites* was based on a real event during the French Revolution when a convent of Carmelite nuns was executed during the anti-Catholic frenzy of the Reign of Terror. The composer, the speaker explained, used the incident as a way of exploring the relationship between religion and politics.

As the lecture concluded, Frank wished that he'd followed Alexander and Brother Richard's example, abstaining from the wine, which had made him sleepy.

The group got up to walk from the tent to the opera house.

"It was good to chat with you," Frank said.

"Same here," Brother Richard said.

By then, it was half past eight. Santa Fe's operas usually started at nine. Darkness was gathering. Alexander and Brother Richard proceeded into the gloom while Frank and Ellen went to restrooms near the tent.

Minutes later, after a chilly walk, Frank and Ellen entered the opera house, made their way through the crowd, found the row they were in, and stopped in surprise.

Alexander and Brother Richard were in the same row, five seats from Frank and Ellen.

Smiling, the two men looked up from their programs.

"Small world," Ellen said, smiling in return.

"Isn't it," Alexander agreed. Frail, he shivered as the wind increased outside, gusting through the open spaces on each side of the opera house.

"Could be a better night," Brother Richard said. "Let's hope the opera's worth it."

Frank and Ellen took their seats. A row ahead, a well-coiffed woman in a flimsy evening gown hugged herself, typical of many in the audience, presumably visitors who hadn't been warned about Santa Fe's sudden temperature drops.

As the wind keened, Ellen looked over at Alexander, noticing that he shivered more violently.

"I'll lend him our blanket," she told Frank.

"Good idea."

The five intervening seats remained empty. Ellen went over, offered the blanket, which Alexander gladly took, and held out the thermos of hot chocolate, which he also took.

"Bless you, how thoughtful."

"My good deed for the day," Ellen said.

• • •

TEN MINUTES into the opera, Frank wished that he'd stayed with his friends in Los Angeles. *The Dialogues of the Carmelites* turned out to be aptly named, for the cast droned its musical lines in a dreary operatic approximation of dialogue. Although the female singers needed to lower their pitch to accommodate the atonal effects, they nonetheless gave the effect of screeching.

Worse was the libretto, which had been translated into English and took one of the most *un*spiritual approaches to religion that Frank had encountered, claiming that the Carmelite nuns were emotional invalids dominated by a masochistic abbess who convinced her charges to linger and wait to be executed so that she could prove how powerfully she controlled them.

Halfway through the first act, lightning flashed. The storm clouds unloaded, sending a torrent past the open sides of the opera house, prompting the audience in those sections to retreat up the aisles.

Nature as critic, Frank thought.

• • •

He had a headache by the time the seemingly interminable first act ended. Ushers hurried to the wet seats near the open sides, toweling them. As Frank and Ellen stood, they found Alexander and Brother Richard coming over.

"I don't know how I'd have gotten through that act without your charity," the elderly man said, looking even colder.

"A terrible opera," Brother Richard added. "You should have stayed in Los Angeles."

"Don't I wish."

"Thanks for the blanket and the thermos." Alexander returned them. "We're going home."

"That bad?"

"Worse."

"Well, we enjoyed meeting you."

"Same here," Brother Richard said. "God bless."

They disappeared among the crowd.

"Well, if I'm going to be able to sit through the second act, I'd better stretch my legs," Frank said.

"You're determined to stay?" Ellen asked.

"After all the trouble I went through to get here? This damned opera isn't going to beat me."

• • •

They followed the crowd to an outside balcony. The rain had again stopped. There were puddles in the courtyard below them, where well-dressed men and women drank cocktails, coffee, or hot chocolate. In the distance, lightning lit the mountains. Everybody oohed and awed.

Frank shivered, then pointed at something in the courtyard. "Look."

About a third of the audience was leaving through the front gate. But coming from the opposite direction, from the parking lot, Alexander and Brother Richard emerged from the darkness, making their way through the courtyard. What puzzled Frank wasn't that they had left and were coming back. Rather, what caught his attention was that a spotlight seemed to be following them, outlining them, drawing Frank's attention to their progress through the crowd. They almost glowed.

The two men went into the gift shop across from the balcony. Almost immediately, they returned without having bought anything and again made their way through the crowd. They disappeared into the darkness past the gate.

"What was *that* all about?" Ellen asked.

"I have no idea." Frank couldn't help yawning.

"Tired?"

"Very."

"Me too."

Frank yawned again. "Know what? If this opera's bad enough for Alexander and Brother Richard to leave, I'm going to bow to their superior taste."

"After all the trouble you took?"

"It takes a real man to admit a mistake."

"That 'real man' stuff turns me on. Yeah, let's go home."

· · ·

THE PARKING lot was well lit. Even so, the low clouds made everything gloomy as Frank and Ellen stepped over puddles, trying to find their car.

"Has to be around here some place." Frank sensed that the angry sky was going to unload again. "Keep that umbrella handy."

Behind him, from the theater, he heard faint music as the orchestra started the second act. The only two people in the parking lot, he and Ellen walked along another row of cars when movement to the left attracted his attention. He turned toward the edge of the parking lot, seeing two men emerge from the darkness and approach them.

Alexander and Brother Richard.

"What are *you* doing here?" Frank asked in surprise. "You left ahead of us."

"We're looking for our car," Alexander told him.

"There." Brother Richard pointed. "Over there."

With a tingle of amazement, Frank saw that his SUV was next to the sedan that Brother Richard indicated.

"Good heavens," Ellen murmured.

Thunder rumbled.

"Drive safely." Alexander eased his frail body into the passenger seat.

"You, too," Frank said.

Brother Richard got behind the steering wheel.

Watching them drive away, Frank said, "Can you believe that? All those coincidences?"

"Weird," Ellen said.

Following them down the winding road that led to Route 285, they watched Alexander's headlights find an opening in the speedy traffic. The sedan headed north.

"And weird again," Frank said.

"What do you mean?" Ellen asked.

"They told us Alexander lived in Albuquerque and that Brother Richard had driven down there to get him."

"So?"

"Why are they going in the opposite direction, north instead of south?"

"Maybe Alexander's too tired for a long drive and they're taking a shorter trip up to the monastery."

"Sure."

Another thunderstorm hit just as they arrived home.

• • •

THE NEXT morning, Frank opened *The Santa Fe New Mexican* and found an article about the return of the monsoons. A weather expert commented that the storms were expected to linger for several weeks and would help to replenish the city's reservoirs, which were low because of a dry spring. A forest-service official hoped that the rains would reduce the risk of fires in the mountains. Along with the good news, however, there had been numerous traffic accidents, including one that had killed two men the previous evening.

One of the victims had been a monk, Brother Richard Braddock, who lived at Christ in the Desert monastery, while the other victim had been a companion, Alexander Lane, from Albuquerque.

"No," Frank said.

Ellen peered up. "What's the matter?"

"Those two men we met last night. It looks like they got killed."

"*What?*"

"In a traffic accident. After they left the opera." Frank quoted from the story. "'Saturday evening, wet pavement is blamed for causing a pickup truck to lose control and slam into a vehicle driven by Brother Richard Braddock on Route Two Eighty-Five one mile south of the Santa Fe opera exit.'"

"South of the opera exit? But we saw them go north."

Frank stared. "You're right. They *couldn't* have been in an accident south of the exit." He re-read the story to make sure he'd gotten the details right. "'Last evening'?"

"What's wrong?"

"'*Last evening*'? That doesn't make sense." Frank went into the kitchen, looked for a number in the phone book, and pressed buttons on his cell phone.

"State police," a man's Hispanic-accented voice answered.

Frank explained what he needed to know.

"Are you a relative of the victims?"

"No," Frank said. "But I think I met them at the opera last night."

The voice paused. Frank heard a page being turned, as if the officer were reading the report.

"Not likely," the voice said.

"Why not?"

"The operas usually start at nine, I hear."

"Yes."

"This accident happened almost two and a half hours before that. At six-forty."

"No," Frank said. "At the opera, I talked to a man named Richard who said he was a monk at Christ in the Desert. He had a friend named Alexander, who lived in Albuquerque. That matches the details in the newspaper."

"Sure does, but it couldn't have been them, because there's no mistake—the accident happened at six-forty. Must have been two other guys named Richard and Alexander."

Frank swallowed. "Yes, it must have been two others." He set down the phone.

"Are you okay?" Ellen asked. "You just turned pale."

"Do you remember when we were driving to the opera last night, we passed an accident?"

Ellen nodded, puzzled.

"You saw a body with a sheet over it being loaded into an ambulance. There were actually *two* bodies."

"Two?"

"I'd think we'd better take a drive to Christ in the Desert."

• • •

A MAP led them through a red canyon studded with juniper trees. With a wary eye toward new storm clouds, Frank rounded a curve and navigated the narrow, muddy road down to a small pueblo-style monastery on the edge of the Chama River.

When he and Ellen got out of their SUV, no one was in sight.

A breeze gathered strength, scraping branches together. Otherwise...

"Sure is quiet," Ellen said.

"Looks deserted. You'd think somebody would have been curious about an approaching car."

"I think I hear something." Ellen turned toward the church.

"We pray to the Lord," a distant voice echoed from inside.

"Lord hear our prayers," other distant voices replied.

"We'd better not intrude. Let's wait until they're finished," Frank said.

Quiet, they leaned against the Jeep, surveying the red cliffs on one side and the muddy, swollen river on the other.

Storm clouds thickened.

"Looks like we'll soon have to go inside whether we want to or not," Ellen said.

The church's front door opened. A bearded man in monk's robes stepped out, noticed Frank and Ellen, and approached them. Although his expression was somber, his eyes communicated the same inner stillness that Richard's had the night before.

"I'm Brother Sebastian," the man said. "May I help you?"

Frank and Ellen introduced themselves.

"We're from Santa Fe," Frank said. "Last night, something odd happened, and we're hoping you might help explain it."

Puzzled, Brother Sebastian waited for them to continue.

"Yesterday..." Ellen looked down at her hands. "Was a monk from here killed in a car accident?"

Brother Sebastian's eyes lost their luster. "I just came back from identifying his body. We've been saying prayers for him. I wish he'd never been given permission."

"Permission?"

"We're Benedictines. We're committed to prayer and work. We vowed to live the rest of our lives here. But that doesn't mean we're cloistered. Some of us even have driver's licenses. With special permission, we're sometimes allowed to leave the monastery—to see a doctor, for example. Or, in yesterday's case, Brother Richard was given permission to drive down to Albuquerque, get a friend who often comes for retreats here, and attend the opera, which has a religious theme and which we thought might have a spiritual benefit."

"It wasn't very spiritual," Ellen said. She explained about the bleak nature of the opera and then said, "Last night at the theater, we met a man named Richard who said he was a monk here. He had an elderly friend named Alexander who said Richard had driven him up from Albuquerque."

"Yes, Brother Richard's friend was named Alexander."

"They sat next to us at a pre-opera dinner," Ellen said. "Then it turned out they were just a few seats away from us in the same row at the opera. When we left early, we crossed paths with them in the parking lot. Their car was next to ours. The whole thing felt strange."

"And strangest of all..." Frank spoke quickly. "The state police say Brother Richard and his friend Alexander died at six-forty south of the opera, so how could we have met them at the opera and watched them drive north afterwards?"

Brother Sebastian's inner stillness changed to unease. "Perhaps you're misremembering the names."

"I'm sure I wouldn't misremember one of them said he was a monk here," Frank said.

"Perhaps the newspaper got the time and place of the accident wrong. Perhaps it happened *after* the opera."

"No," Frank said. "I phoned the state police. They agree with the newspaper. The accident happened at six-forty."

"Then you couldn't have met Brother Richard and his friend at the opera."

"It certainly seems that way," Ellen said. "But this is making us crazy. To help us stop thinking about this, if you have a photograph of Brother Richard, would you mind showing it to us?"

Brother Sebastian studied them. "Superstition isn't the same as spirituality."

"Believe me, we're not superstitious," Frank said.

Brother Sebastian studied them another long moment. "Wait here, please."

Five minutes later, the monk returned. The wind was stronger, tugging at his brown robe and kicking up red dust. He held a folded newspaper.

"A journalist from Santa Fe came here last summer to write a story about us. We saw no harm in it, especially if it encouraged troubled people to attend retreats here."

Brother Sebastian opened the newspaper and showed Frank and Ellen a color picture of a man in robes standing outside the church.

Frank and Ellen stepped closer. The photograph was faded, but there was no mistaking what they saw.

"Yes," Frank said. "That's the man we met at the opera last night." The wind brought a chill.

"No," Brother Sebastian said. "Unless the state police are wrong about the time and place of the accident, what you're telling me isn't possible. As I said, superstition isn't the same as spirituality."

• • •

"I DON'T care how logical he insists on being," Frank said. "Something happened to us." Guiding the SUV along the muddy road, he added, "Last night, do you remember how bad the storm was when we arrived home?"

"Yes. I was glad we weren't on the road."

"Right. The storm didn't quit until after midnight. It shook the house. If we hadn't left the opera early, we'd have been caught in it. The newspaper said there were several accidents."

"What are you getting at?" Ellen asked.

"If Brother Sebastian heard me now, he'd say I was definitely superstitious. Do you suppose…"

"Just tell me what you're thinking."

Frank forced himself to continue. "Alexander and Brother Richard gave us the idea of leaving early. We followed them. As crazy as it sounds, if we'd stayed for the entire opera and driven home in the storm, do you suppose we might have been killed?"

"Are you actually suggesting they saved our lives? Two ghosts?"

"Not when you put it that way."

"It's impossible to know what might have happened if we'd driven home later," Ellen emphasized.

"Right. And as for ghosts…"

Frank's voice drifted off. He reached the solid footing of the highway and headed back to Santa Fe.

• • •

ONE YEAR later, Frank again saw Alexander and Brother Richard.

It was a Saturday morning in late August. He and Ellen were in downtown Santa Fe, buying vegetables at the farmer's market. As they carried their sacks toward where they'd parked on a side street, Frank saw a short, slight, elderly man with white hair and a matching goatee. Next to him was a tall, well-built, young man, with short, dark hair and a square-jawed face. Unusual in the farmer's market atmosphere at nine in the morning, they both wore dark suits and white shirts. Their eyes were very clear.

"Those two men over there," Frank said, pausing.

"Who?" Ellen asked. "Where?"

"Next to the bakery stand over there. An old guy and a young guy. You can't miss them. They're wearing black suits."

"I don't notice any..."

"They're staring straight at us. I feel like I've seen them before. They have a..."

"Have a what?"

"Glow. My God, do you remember the two guys from...?"

As Frank moved toward them, they turned and walked into the crowd.

He increased speed.

"What are you doing?" Ellen called.

Frank caught a glimpse of the black suits within the crowd, but no matter how urgently he tried to shift past people buying from various stands, he couldn't get closer.

"Wait!" he shouted.

Vaguely aware of people staring at him, he saw the black suits disappear in the crowd. After another minute of searching, he had no idea which direction to take.

Baffled, Ellen reached him.

"The two guys from the opera," Frank explained. "It was them."

"The opera?"

"Don't you remember?"

People bumped past him, carrying sacks. Frank stepped up onto a crate and scanned the crowd, looking for two men in black suits, but all he saw were people in shorts and T-shirts.

"Damn it, I had so many questions."

Ellen looked at him strangely.

Tires squealed. Metal and glass shattered. A woman screamed.

Frank ran toward a side street. Peering through the crowd, he and Ellen saw what used to be their Jeep. A pickup truck had slammed into it. A woman lay on the pavement, next to a bicycle, its wheels spinning.

"I saw the whole thing," a man said. "The truck was weaving. Driver must be drunk. He swerved to avoid the girl on the bicycle and hit that car parked over there. It's a lucky thing no one was killed."

• • •

"IF I hadn't noticed them," Frank said, watching a tow truck haul their SUV away, "if they hadn't distracted me, we'd have been at our car when the accident happened. They saved us. Saved us for a second time."

"I didn't see them," Ellen said. "The opera? How could it be the same two men?"

• • •

THE THIRD time Frank noticed them was five years later. Thursday. December 10. Seven p.m. Ellen had been recovering from a miscarriage, her fourth in their fifteen-year marriage. Finally accepting that they would never have children of their own, they discussed the possibility of adopting. Now that Ellen felt well enough to leave the house, Frank tried to raise her spirits by taking her to a restaurant that had recently opened and was receiving fabulous reviews.

The restaurant was near Santa Fe's historic plaza, so after they parked, they walked slightly out of their way to appreciate the Christmas lights on the trees and the pueblo-style buildings.

"God, I love this town," Frank said. Snow started to fall, making him ask, "Are you warm enough?"

"Yes." Ellen put her hood up.

"Those two guys... No, it can't be," Frank said, noticing the only two other people in the area.

"Where?"

"There. Over by the museum. In this weather, all they're wearing are black suits."

Frank realized that one of them was short, slight, and elderly, with white hair and a matching goatee. Next to him was a tall, well-built, young man, with short, dark hair and a square-jawed face.

"My God, it's them," he said.

"Who?"

Even at a distance, their eyes were intense.

"Hey," he called, "wait. I want to talk to you."

They turned and walked away.

"Stop!"

They receded into the falling snow.

Frank hurried toward them, leaving the plaza, heading along a quiet street. The snow fell harder.

"Frank!" Ellen called.

He looked back. "They went toward the restaurant!"

"Frank!" This time the word came from Alexander where he waited with Brother Richard in front of the restaurant.

Frank stepped toward them and felt his shoes slip on ice under the snow. He arched backward. His skull shattered against a lamppost.

• • •

STANDING NEXT to Alexander and Brother Richard, Frank watched Ellen slump beside his body, sobbing. A siren wailed in the distance. People emerged from the restaurant and approached in shock.

Oddly numb, Frank couldn't feel the cold or the snow falling on him. "What's happening?"

They didn't reply.

"How can I be looking down past Ellen toward me on the ice?"

Again, they didn't reply.

"How...? Am I...?"

"Yes," the elderly man said.

"No."

"Yes," the young man said.

"Ellen...I don't..."

"We understand," Alexander said. "There were people *we* didn't want to leave either."

He continued to looked down as snow fell on Ellen, covering her coat while she sobbed next to his body. Bystanders gathered around her.

"Ice under the snow?" Frank asked. "I died because of a crazy accident?"

"Everything in life is an accident."

"But you lured me toward it. You distracted me so I'd walk faster than I should have. I told Ellen you were guarding us, but she didn't believe me."

"She was right. We're not your guardians."

"Then what *are* you?"

"Your companions."

"What?"

"We stopped you from dying when you weren't supposed to, and we helped you to die when it was your time," Alexander said.

"We died as you drove past our wrecked car on the highway, going to the opera," Brother Richard continued. "The rule is you bond to someone near where you die. Then you help that person die when he or she is supposed to, and you stop it from happening sooner than it's supposed to. Everything in its time."

"The opera?"

"You weren't supposed to be there. The storms, the difficulty of flying home from Los Angeles, they were supposed to make you stay away. When you went to extreme efforts to come back to Santa Fe and go to the opera, we had to convince you to leave early."

"You're saying Ellen and I would have been killed in a car accident if we'd stayed until the opera was finished?"

"In a crash in the storm. But only you. Your wife would have survived."

"And at the farmer's market?"

"You'd have been killed when the truck swerved to avoid the bicyclist."

"Only me?"

"Yes. Again your wife would have survived."

"I don't want to..."

"Everybody dies. But you won't be leaving her. She was so near you when you died that you're now her companion."

Frank slowly absorbed this information. "I can be with her until...?"

"Until you make sure that she dies when she's supposed to," Brother Richard said. "Eight months from now, she will die falling from a step ladder. Unless you stop her. Because that's not her time. Six years from now, she will die in a fire. Unless you stop her from going to a particular hotel. Because, again, that's not her time."

"When *will* she die?"

"Twelve years from now. From kidney cancer. That will take its natural course. You won't need to assist her."

Frank's heart ached.

"She'll have remarried by then," Alexander said. "She and her new husband will adopt a little boy. Because you love her, you'll share her happiness. Afterward, she, too, will become someone's companion."

"And after that?" Frank asked.

"We're allowed to find peace."

Frank gazed down at his sobbing wife as she kneeled beside his body. Blood flowed from his skull, congealing in the cold.

"One day I'll be allowed to talk to her as you and I are talking?" he asked.

"Yes."

"But in the meantime, she'll eventually love someone else and adopt a child?"

"Yes."

"For fifteen years, I was her companion. All I want is for her to be happy. Even if it means not sharing her happiness..."

Frank at last felt something: the sting of tears on his cheeks.

"...I'll be glad to be a different sort of companion to her for the rest of her life."

MY NAME IS LEGION

While researching one of my novels, The Protector, *I came across a troubling account of a World War II battle in which separate units of the French Foreign Legion fought each other to the death. The Allies commanded one unit. German-controlled France commanded the other. Although the men in these units had trained together, eaten together, and slept in the same barracks together for many years, these brothers-in-arms were now obligated to kill one another.*

The complexity of the situation—professional duty versus personal loyalty—haunted me until I felt compelled to explore it. Kline, Rourke, and Durado are invented characters. Otherwise the details are based on historical sources, including dialogue taken from eyewitness accounts of the 1863 Battle of Camerone in Mexico, the Legion's most important event.

The mission is sacred. You will see it through to the end, at any price.

— From the French Foreign Legion's Code of Honor

Syria. June 20, 1941.

"THE COLONEL FOUND SOMEONE TO CARVE a wooden hand."

Hearing Durado's voice behind him, Kline didn't turn. He kept his gaze focused between the two boulders that protected him from sniper fire. Propped against a rocky slope, he stared toward the yellow, sandstone buildings in the distance.

"Wooden hand?" The reference didn't puzzle Kline, but the timing did. "This isn't April."

"I guess the colonel figures we need a reminder," Durado answered.

"Considering what'll happen tomorrow, he's probably right."

"The ceremony's at fifteen hundred hours."

"Can't go," Kline said. "I'm on duty here till dark."

"There'll be a second ceremony. The sergeant told me to come back later and take your place so you can attend."

Kline nodded his thanks. "Reminds me of when I was a kid and my family went to church. The colonel's become our preacher."

"See anything out there?" Durado asked.

"Nothing that moves—except the heat haze."

"Tomorrow will be different."

Kline heard the scrape of rocks under combat boots as Durado walked away. A torn blanket was over him. His uniform was minimal—tan shorts and a matching short-sleeved shirt, faded by the desert sun. His headgear was the Legion's famed *kepi blanc*, a white cap with a flat, round top and black visor. It too was badly faded. A flap at the back covered his neck and ears, but for further protection, Kline relied on the blanket to shield his bare legs and arms and keep the rocks on each side from absorbing so much heat that they burned him.

His bolt-action MAS 36 rifle was next to him, ready to be used if he saw a sniper moving. Of course, that would reveal Kline's position, attracting enemy bullets, forcing him to find a new vantage point. Given that he'd smoothed the ground and made this emplacement as comfortable as possible, he preferred to hold his fire until tomorrow.

Enemy bullets? Those words had automatically come to mind, but under the circumstances, they troubled him. Some of the men over there weren't his enemy.

Yes, pulling the trigger could wait until tomorrow.

• • •

KLINE WASN'T his real name. Seven years earlier, in 1934, he'd arrived at the Old Fort in the Vincennes area of Paris, where he'd volunteered to join the French Foreign Legion, so-called because the unit was the only way foreigners could enlist in the French army.

"American," a sergeant had sniffed.

Kline had received a meal of coffee, bread, and watery bean soup. In a crowded barracks, he slept on a straw-filled mattress at the top of a three-tiered metal bunk. Two days later, he and twenty other newcomers, mostly Spaniards, Italians, and Greeks, with a solitary Irishman, were transported via train south to Marseilles. They were herded into the foul-smelling, lower hold of a ship, where they vomited for two days during a rough voyage across the Mediterranean to Algeria. At last, trucks took them along a dusty, jolting road to the Legion's headquarters at the remote desert town of Sidi-bel-Abbes. The heat was overwhelming.

There, Kline's interrogation had started. Although the Legion had a reputation for attracting criminals on the run from the law, in reality it understood the difficulty of making disciplined soldiers out of them and didn't knowingly accept the worst offenders. As a consequence, each candidate was questioned in detail, his background investigated as thoroughly as possible. Many volunteers, while not criminals, had reached a dead end in their lives and wanted a new start, along with the chance to become French citizens. If the Legion accepted them, they were allowed to choose a new name and received new identities.

Certainly, Kline had reached a dead end. Before arriving in France and volunteering for the Legion, he'd lived in the United States, in Springfield, Illinois, where the Great Depression had taken away his factory job and prevented him from supporting his wife and infant daughter. He'd made bad friends and acted as the lookout for a bank robbery in which a guard was killed and the only cash was $24.95. During the month he'd spent eluding the police, his daughter had died from whooping cough. His grief-crazed wife had slit her wrists, bleeding to death. The single thing that had kept Kline from doing the same thing was his determination to punish himself, and that goal had finally prompted him to do the most extreme thing he could imagine. Responding to an article in a newspaper that he happened to find in a trash barrel, he ended his anguished wandering by working as a coal shoveler on a ship that took him to Le Havre in France, from where he walked all the way to Paris and enlisted in the Legion.

According to the newspaper article, no way of life could be more arduous, and Kline was pleased to discover that the article understated the hardship. Managing to hide his criminal past, he endured a seemingly endless indoctrination of weapons exercises, hand-to-hand combat drills, forced marches, and other tests of endurance that gave him satisfaction because of the pain they inflicted on him. In the end, when he received the certificate that formally admitted him to the Legion, he felt that he had indeed made a new start. Never forgiving himself or the world or God for the loss of his family, he felt an unexpected deep kinship with a group that had "Living by Chance" as part of its credo.

• • •

THE IRISHMAN called himself Rourke. Because he and Kline were the only men who spoke English in their section of volunteers, they became friends during their long months of training. Like everyone else in the Legion, Rourke referred only vaguely to his past, but his skill with rifles and explosives made Kline suspect that he'd belonged to the Irish Republican Army, that he'd killed British soldiers in an effort to make the British leave his country, and that he'd sought refuge in the Legion after the British Army had vowed to use all their resources to hunt him.

"I don't suppose you're a Roman Catholic," Rourke said one night after they completed a fifty-mile march in punishing heat. His accent sounded melodic, despite his pain as they bandaged the blisters on their feet.

"No, I'm a Baptist," Kline answered. "At least, that's how I was raised. I don't go to church anymore."

"I didn't see many Baptists in Ireland," Rourke joked. "Do you know your Bible?"

"My father read from it aloud every night."

"'My name is legion'," Rourke quoted.

"'For we are many'," Kline responded. "The gospel according to Mark. A possessed man says that to Jesus, trying to explain how many demons are in him... Legion." The word made Kline finally understand where Rourke was taking the conversation. "You're comparing us to devils?"

"After putting us through that march, the sergeant qualifies as one."

Kline chuckled.

"For certain, the sergeant wants the *enemy* to think we're devils," Rourke continued. "That's what the Mexican soldiers called the legionnaires after the battle at Camerone, isn't it?"

"Yes. 'These are not men. They're demons.'"

"You have a good memory."

"I wish I didn't."

"No more than I." Rourke's normally mischievous eyes looked dull. His freckled face was covered with dust. "Anyway, after a march like that, we might as well *be* devils."

"How do you figure?"

Wiping blood from his feet, Rourke somehow made what he said next sound like another joke. "We understand what it feels like to be in hell."

• • •

ROURKE WAS gone now.

Kline's years in the Legion had taught him to banish weak emotions. Nonetheless, the loss of his friend made him grieve. As he stared between the boulders toward the seemingly abandoned, sandstone buildings, he thought about the many conversations he and Rourke had shared. In 1940, as Germany increasingly threatened Europe, they'd fought side-by-side in the concrete fortifications of the Maginot Line that France had built along its border with Germany. Their unit endured relentless assaults from machine guns, tanks, and bombers, counterattacking whenever the Germans showed the slightest sign of weakness.

The casualties were massive. Nonetheless Kline, Rourke, and their fellow legionnaires continued fighting. When the officer in charge of a regular French unit insisted that no one had a chance and that surrender to the Germans was the only reasonable choice, the Legion commander had shot him to death. A second French officer tried to retaliate, and this time, it was

Kline who pulled the trigger, defending his commander whose back was turned. Every legionnaire understood. From their first day of training, absolutes were drilled into them, and one of them was, *Never surrender your arms.*

"What do Baptists believe?" Rourke asked the night after another battle. They were cleaning their rifles.

"God punishes us for our sins," Kline answered.

"What can you do to be saved?"

"Nothing. It all depends on Christ's mercy."

"Mercy?" Rourke's thin face tightened as he considered the word. "Seen much of that?"

"No."

"Me, neither," Rourke said.

"What do *Catholics* believe about being saved?" Kline asked.

"We say we're sorry for our sins and do penance to prove we mean it."

Thinking of his wife and daughter, of how he'd left them alone while he'd helped in the bank robbery, of how his wife had committed suicide after his daughter had died, Kline asked, "But what if your sin's so bad that you can't possibly make up for it?"

"I ask myself that a lot," Rourke answered. "I was an altar boy. I almost went into the seminary. But maybe I'm in the wrong religion. You say God punishes us for our sins and our only hope is to depend on His mercy? Makes sense to me."

That was when Kline decided that Rourke hadn't joined the Legion to avoid being hunted by the British army. No, he was in the Legion because, like Kline, he'd done something horrible and was punishing himself.

• • •

KLINE MISSED his friend. Staring between the boulders, he sought distraction from his regrets by reaching for his canteen under the blanket that protected him from the sun. He unscrewed it and withdrew his gaze from the ancient buildings only long enough to drink the warm, metallic-tasting water.

He focused again on the target. Men with rifles were over there, watching this ridge. Of that, he had no doubt. There would be a battle tomorrow. Of that, he had no doubt, either.

Behind him, footsteps approached, dislodging rocks.

Durado's voice said, "The first ceremony's over. I'll take your place."

"Everything's quiet," Kline reported.

"It won't be quiet tomorrow. The captain says we're definitely going in."

Kline pulled the blanket off himself, feeling the harsh rays of the sun on his now-exposed arms and legs. Careful to stay low, he made his way along the bottom of the rocky slope. After passing other sentry emplacements, he reached the main part of camp, where half the Thirteenth Demi-Brigade was in formation next to its tents.

The air was blindingly bright as the colonel stepped onto a boulder, facing them. His name was Amilakvari. He was a Russian who'd escaped the Communist revolution when he was eleven and joined the Legion when he was twenty. Now in his mid-thirties, he looked gaunt and sinewy after months of desert combat. Nonetheless, he wore a full dress uniform.

Despite his Russian background, the colonel addressed the legionnaires in French, their common language, even though privately most still spoke their native language and formed friendships on the basis of it, as Kline had done with Rourke. Solemn, the colonel raised a hand, but the hand didn't belong to him. It had been carved from a block of wood, the palm and the fingers amazingly lifelike.

Neither Kline nor anyone else needed to be told that it was supposed to be a replica of the wooden hand of the Legion's greatest hero, Captain Jean Danjou. All of them knew by heart the events that the captain was about to describe, and every battle-hardened one of them also knew that, before the ceremony was completed, tears would stream down his face.

• • •

CAMARÓN, MEXICO. The Legion spelled it Camerone.

As often as Kline had heard the story, with each telling it became more powerful. Listening to the colonel recite it, Kline sensed he was there, feeling the cool night air as the patrol set out at one a.m. on April 30, 1863.

They were on foot: sixty-two soldiers, three officers, and Captain Danjou, a decorated combat veteran with a gallant-looking goatee and mustache. Few understood why they were in Mexico, something to do with a pact between Napoleon III of France and Emperor Maximilian of Austria. The two rulers schemed to invade Mexico while the United States was distracted by its Civil War. But legionnaires were indifferent to politics. All they cared about was completing any mission they were assigned.

The French force had arrived at the port of Veracruz in the Gulf of Mexico, where they immediately discovered an enemy as lethal as the Mexican soldiers and furious civilians who resisted them. The ravages of Yellow Fever killed a third of them and forced them to move their headquarters sixty miles inland to the elevated town of Cordoba, where they hoped the air would be less contaminated. The shift in location meant that the supply route between Veracruz and Cordoba needed to be kept open, and the responsibility for doing that fell to patrols like the one Captain Danjou commanded.

Kline imagined the long night of walking along the remote, barren road. At dawn, the legionnaires were allowed to stop for breakfast, but as they searched for wood to build cook fires, a sentry pointed to the west.

"Mexican cavalry!"

The dust raised by the approaching horses made it difficult to count the number of riders, but this much was clear—there were hundreds and hundreds of them.

"Form a square!" Danjou ordered.

The men assembled in rows that faced each direction. The first row knelt while the second stood, their rifles aimed over the heads of the men kneeling in front.

The Mexican cavalry charged. As one, the legionnaires in the first row fired, breaking the attack. While they reloaded, the men behind them aimed, ready to fire if ordered.

Knowing that he'd gained only a little time, Danjou studied the open area around him, in search of cover. To the east, a ruined hacienda attracted his attention. He urged his men toward it, but again the Mexicans charged, and again the legionnaires fired, their fusillade dispersing the attack.

"Keep moving!" Danjou yelled.

Nearing the ruins, he peered over his shoulder and saw foot soldiers joining the Mexican cavalry. Out of breath, he and his patrol raced into a rubble-littered courtyard.

"Close the gates! Barricade them!"

Danjou assessed where they were. Dilapidated farm buildings formed a fifty-yard square. A stone wall enclosed it. In places, the barrier was ten feet high, but at other spots, the wall had collapsed, forming a chest-high heap of stones.

"Spread out! Take cover!"

A sentry scurried up a ladder to the top of a stable and reported the dust of more horsemen and infantry arriving. "I see sombreros in every direction!"

"How many?"

"At least two thousand."

Danjou quickly calculated the ratio: thirty to one.

"There'll soon be a lot less of them," he shouted to his men.

He got the laugh that he'd hoped for. But his billowy red pants and dark blue jacket were soaked with sweat from the urgent retreat toward the hacienda. In contrast, his mouth was dry, and he knew that, as the day grew hotter, his men would be desperate for water.

A quick search of the ruins revealed that there wasn't any. But that wasn't the case with the Mexicans. A nearby stream provided all the water the enemy could want. Danjou's lips felt drier at the thought of it.

"A rider's coming!" the sentry announced. "He's got a white flag!"

Danjou climbed the ladder to the top of the stable. The movement was awkward for him. He had only one hand. Years earlier, his left one had been blown off by a musket. Undaunted, he'd commissioned a carver to create an ornate wooden replacement. Its lacquer was flesh-colored. Its fingers had hinges that made them flexible. It had a black cuff into which he inserted the stump of his wrist. By moving the stump against leather strips inside the cuff, he had taught himself to make the wooden fingers move.

Keeping that artificial hand out of sight behind his back, lest it be interpreted as a weakness, Danjou peered down at a Mexican officer who rode to him. The many languages of Danjou's legionnaires had taught him to become multilingual.

"You're outnumbered," the Mexican officer said in Spanish. "You don't have water. You'll soon run out of food. Surrender. You'll be treated fairly."

"No," Danjou responded.

"But to stay is to die."

"We won't lay down our arms," Danjou emphasized.

"This is foolish."

"Try to attack us, and you'll learn how foolish *that* is."

Enraged, the Mexican officer galloped away.

Danjou descended the ladder as quickly as he could. Even though he shouted encouragement to his men, he was troubled that the hacienda was situated in low terrain. The elevated ground beyond it allowed enemy riflemen to shoot down past the walls and into the compound.

Mexican snipers opened fire, providing cover for another cavalry charge. The dust the horses raised concealed advancing infantry. Bullets walloped through the wooden buildings and shattered chunks of stone off the walls. But despite the unrelenting barrage, the disciplined volleys from the legionnaires repelled attack after attack.

By eleven a.m., the heat of the sun was crushing. The barrels of their rifles became too hot to touch. Twelve legionnaires were dead.

Danjou urged the remainder to keep fighting. Gesturing with his wooden hand, he rushed from group to group and made each man know that he counted on him. But as he crossed the courtyard to help defend a wall, he staggered and fell. Blood erupted from a bullet to his chest.

A legionnaire who ran to help him heard him murmur, "Never give up."

Danjou's second-in-command took charge, making the men swear to fight harder in Danjou's honor. "We may die, but by God, we'll never surrender!"

With two thousand Mexicans shooting, the enormous number of bullets hitting the compound—perhaps as many as 8,000 per minute—would have felt overwhelming, Kline knew, the equivalent of being strafed by numerous machine guns in the current war. The noise alone would have been agonizing. He imagined buildings crumbling and gun smoke making it almost impossible to see.

The farmhouse caught fire, ignited by muzzle flashes. Smoke from it further hampered vision and made the legionnaires strain to breathe. But they kept shooting, repelling more attacks, ignoring more pleas to surrender.

By four in the afternoon, only twelve legionnaires remained alive. By six p.m., the number of men able to fight had been reduced to five. As the Mexicans burst into the compound, the handful of survivors fired their last remaining ammunition, then attacked with fixed bayonets, rushing through the smoke, stabbing and clubbing.

A private was shot nineteen times while he tried to shield his lieutenant. Two others were hit and fell, but one struggled to his feet and joined his last two comrades. They stood back to back, thrusting with their bayonets.

The Mexican commander had never seen fighting like it.

"Stop!" he ordered his men.

He spun toward the survivors. "For God's sake, this is pointless! Surrender!"

"We won't give up our weapons," a wounded legionnaire insisted.

"Your weapons? Are you trying to negotiate with me?" the Mexican officer asked in amazement.

The bleeding legionnaire wavered, trying not to fall. "We might be your prisoners, but we won't give up our weapons."

The Mexican gaped. "You don't have any ammunition. Your rifles are almost useless anyhow. Keep the damned things."

"And you need to allow us to take care of our wounded."

Astonished by their audacity, the Mexican officer grabbed the sinking legionnaire and said, "To men like you, I can't refuse anything."

• • •

KLINE STOOD under the stark Syrian sun, listening to his commander describe the battle at Camerone.

Kline had heard the details many times, but with each telling, they gained more power. In his imagination, he smelled the blood, heard the buzzing of the flies on the corpses, and tasted the bitter smoke from the burning buildings. The screams of the dying seemed to echo around him. He felt his eyes mist with emotion and took for granted that the men around him felt the same.

All the while, the colonel held up the wooden hand, a replica of Danjou's wooden hand, which had been recovered after the long-ago battle. The original hand was now protected in a glass case at Legion headquarters in Aubagne, France. Each year on April 30, the anniversary of the battle, the hand was carried around a crowded assembly room, allowing everyone to gaze at the Legion's most precious relic. On that same day, a similar memorial—minus the hand—occurred at every Legion base around the world. It was the most important ritual in the Legion's year.

But no one had ever arranged for a replica of Danjou's hand to be carved. No one had ever gone this far to imitate the ceremony as it took place each year at Legion headquarters. Moreover, this wasn't April 30. Given what was scheduled to happen the next morning, Kline understood how determined the colonel was to remind him and his fellow legionnaires of their heritage.

Standing on the boulder, holding the wooden hand above his head, the colonel spoke so forcefully that no one could fail to hear.

"Each of the sixty-six legionnaires at that battle carried sixty rounds of ammunition. Every round was used. That means they fired thirty-eight hundred rounds. Despite the heat and thirst and dust and smoke, they killed almost four hundred of the enemy. Think of it—one out of every ten bullets found its mark. Astonishing, given the circumstances. Those legionnaires were offered repeated opportunities to surrender. At any time, they could have abandoned their mission, but they refused to dishonor the Legion or themselves.

"Tomorrow, remember those heroes. Tomorrow, *you* will be heroes. No legionnaire has ever encountered what all of you will face in the morning. We never walk away from a mission. We never fail to honor our obligations. What is our motto?"

"The Legion Is Our Country!" Kline and everybody else automatically shouted.

"I can't hear you!"

"The Legion Is Our Country!"

"*What is our second motto?*"

"Honor and Nobility!"

"Yes! Never forget that! Never forget Camerone! Never disgrace the Legion! Never fail to do your duty!"

• • •

BROODING ABOUT the bleak choice he would face the next morning, Kline returned along the bottom of the rocky slope. Barely noticing the numerous sentries along the way, he came to where Durado lay under a blanket and peered between the two boulders toward the outskirts of Damascus.

"You're back already? Just when I was getting comfortable," Durado joked.

Kline half-smiled. The humor reminded him of the jokes that Rourke had used to make.

Heat radiated off the rocks.

"Do you think the colonel's speech made a difference?" Durado squirmed to the bottom of the slope, staying hidden from the snipers over there.

"We won't know until tomorrow," Kline answered, taking his place between the boulders. "No legionnaire's ever been forced into this situation before."

"Well, we do what we need to," Durado said, starting to walk away.

"Yes, God punishes us for our sins," Kline murmured.

Durado stopped and turned. "What? I didn't hear what you said."

"Just talking to myself."

"I thought you said something about God."

"Did you ever realize that it didn't need to happen?" Kline asked.

"Realize that *what* didn't need to happen?"

"Camerone. The legionnaires were out of water. They had almost no food. Their ammunition was limited. In that heat, after three days without anything to drink, they'd have been unconscious or worse. All the Mexicans needed to do was wait."

"Maybe they were afraid reinforcements would arrive before then," Durado suggested.

"But why would the Mexicans have been afraid?" Kline asked. "There were so many of them that a rescue column wouldn't have had a chance. If they'd set it up properly and made it seem that only a couple of hundred Mexicans surrounded the hacienda, they could have lured the reinforcements into an ambush."

"So what's your point?"

"Just what I said—sometimes, battles don't need to happen."

"Like tomorrow's?" Durado asked.

Kline pointed toward the buildings. "Maybe they'll surrender."

"Or maybe they hope *we'll* surrender. Is that going to happen?"

"Of course not." Kline quoted from the Legion's Code of Honor, which all recruits were required to memorize at the start of their training. "'Never surrender your arms.'"

"And *they* won't do it, either," Durado said.

"But in the end, France was forced to leave Mexico. Camerone made no difference."

"Be careful. You'd better not let the colonel hear you talking this way."

"Maybe tomorrow's battle won't make a difference, either."

"Thinking isn't our business." Now it was Durado's turn to quote from the Legion's Code of Honor. "'The mission is sacred. You will see it through to the end, at any price.'"

"'At any price'." Kline exhaled. "You're absolutely right. I'm not paid to think. Tomorrow, I'll fight as hard as you."

"God punishes us for our sins? Is that what you said earlier?" Durado asked. "The things I've seen in this war prove God doesn't exist. Otherwise, they never would have been allowed to happen."

"Unless this battle tomorrow is God's way of paying us back."

"For our sins?"

"For the things we'd give anything to forget."

"In that case, God help us." Again, the irony in Durado's voice reminded Kline of Rourke.

● ● ●

KLINE LAY under the blanket, staring across the rocky hill toward the buildings that seemed to waver in the heat. He knew that soldiers just like him watched from their own hiding places over there. With their weapons beside them, they brooded behind the city's walls, parapets, turrets, and gates, knowing that soon, probably the next morning, the battle would begin.

Kline was struck by how much different things had been a year earlier. When the Germans had broken through the concrete battlements of the Maginot Line and invaded France, the only tactic that had made sense was for him and Rourke and the rest of the legionnaires in their unit to fight a retreating action, trying to slow the German advance as much as possible.

And we still might have beaten them, Kline thought, *if the Germans hadn't realized the mistake they were about to make.*

The risk to the invading army had been that a rush to occupy all of France would overextend their supply lines, leaving them vulnerable to devastating hit-and-run attacks by French civilians and the remainder of the French military. Without supplies, the Germans would have been helpless. To prevent that from happening, they'd developed the brilliant strategy of consolidating their forces in the northern and western parts of France, an area that included Paris. Meanwhile, their massive threatening presence had convinced the rest of France that total occupation was only a matter of time, that it was better to capitulate and negotiate for favorable terms.

So the bastards in the south became collaborators, Kline thought.

The deal was that the southern two-fifths of France would remain free of German soldiers. Meanwhile, France would form a new government based in the community of Vichy in the central part of the country. In theory, this government was neutral to Germany, but in reality, the Vichy regime was so eager to placate the Germans that they were more than happy to hand over Jews or any other "undesirables" that the Germans wanted.

The rest of France might as well have been invaded. The result was the same, Kline thought. *Maybe they could justify collaborating if they'd made an effort to resist. But as it was, they just surrendered and acted like the enemy.*

He painfully remembered the last time he'd seen Rourke. Along with a remnant of their legionnaire unit, they'd been hiding in a French barn, waiting for nightfall when they could slip out and elude patrols by the Vichy militia.

Their radioman picked up a wireless signal that he quickly reported. "The Thirteen Demi-Brigade shipped back from fighting in Norway."

All the men hiding in the barn sat up from the straw they lay on. The context didn't need to be explained—the Legion had been fighting on two fronts, and the Thirteenth's objective had been the defense of Norway. But like the Legion's unit on the Maginot Line, the Thirteenth had been forced to withdraw.

"They landed at Brest," the radioman continued.

The men nodded, well aware that Brest was the westernmost port in France.

"When they realized France had capitulated and that the Germans were about to occupy the port, they hurried back on the ships and headed toward England."

"So they're going to help the Allies try to retake France?" Kline asked.

"Yes," the radioman answered. "But not all of them went to England."

Rourke straightened. "What do you mean?"

"Some decided to go back to headquarters in Algeria."

The legionnaires remained silent for a moment, analyzing the significance of this information. Another reason Germany had resisted invading all of France was that the move would have made enemies of Algeria and Morocco: French territories in North Africa. But by persuading France to form the Vichy government, a supposedly neutral regime that was in effect a puppet government, Germany gained indirect control of those French territories and prevented the legionnaires stationed there from helping England.

"They're going to fight *against* the Brits?" Kline asked in shock.

"It's more like they're hoping Algeria will remain neutral. That way, they'll be able to sit out the rest of the war without fighting *anybody*," the radioman explained.

"Lots of damned luck to them," someone said.

"The message came from England," the radioman continued. "From Brigadier General de Gaulle."

"Who's he?"

"I never heard of him, either," the radioman continued.
"But apparently he's in charge of something called the Free
French Forces, and that includes the legionnaires who went to
England. He wants every French soldier to get there somehow
and regroup. The fight's not over."

"Thank God, somebody's got some balls," another
legionnaire said. "I guess we know which way we're going
tonight. To the coast. We'll get our hands on a boat and head
toward England."

Most of the men readily agreed. They'd been born and
raised in Spain, Portugal, Greece or any number of other countries, but all were now French citizens and felt loyal to the
nation they'd been fighting to protect.

But Kline couldn't help noticing that some were pensively
quiet. Evidently, the previous year of fighting made the idea of
sitting out the war in Algeria appealing.

Kline also couldn't help noticing that Rourke was one of
the men who remained quiet.

• • •

AT DARK, as the group snuck from the barn, Kline motioned
for Rourke to wait.

"I get the feeling you're not going to England with us," he
said when the two were alone.

In the shadows, Rourke took a moment to answer. "Yes.
When we reach the coast, I'll find a way to Algeria."

"You've had enough fighting?"

"It's got nothing to do with sitting out the war. Believe me,
I'm happy to fight the Germans." Rourke paused. "But I can't
go to England."

"I don't understand."

"You and I never talked about our pasts, my friend." Rourke put a hand on Kline's shoulder. "But I think you guessed a lot about mine. If I go back to England, I might end up serving next to the same British soldiers who hunted me in Ireland before I joined the Legion. Don't get me wrong. I didn't join the Legion to escape them."

"I know. You joined to do penance."

"See, we understand each other," Rourke said. "I once told you that Catholics need to tell God they're sorry for their sins and then do whatever's necessary to prove they mean it."

"I remember."

"Well, how can I keep doing penance if some bastard British Tommy recognizes me and shoots me?"

From the darkness outside the barn, a legionnaire whispered, "Kline, we need to get moving."

"In a moment." Kline turned to Rourke. "Take care of yourself."

"Don't worry," Rourke said, shaking hands with him. "We'll cross paths again after the war."

• • •

BUT ROURKE had been wrong. It wasn't after the war that they would cross paths. Soon after the split in the Legion, some men going to England, others going to Algeria, the Vichy government ordered the legionnaires in Algeria to assist the German army.

By June of 1941, when the Allies fought to liberate Syria from the invaders, Kline's Legion unit was helping the British. Meanwhile, a different Legion unit, the Vichy brigade, was helping the Germans.

In the morning, the unthinkable would occur. Battling for Damascus, legionnaires who had trained together, bivouacked together, eaten together, gotten drunk together, and fought together, would now fight each other, and unless Rourke had already died in combat, he would be one of those whom Kline would attack.

• • •

As the sun began to set, Durado returned one last time, assigned to sentry duty for the night. The intense heat continued to weigh on them.

"Still quiet over there?" Durado asked.

"No sign of anyone. Maybe they pulled back," Kline hoped.

"I doubt it."

"Me, too. They know *we* won't pull back."

"But surely they realize they're on the wrong side," Durado said.

"Probably they're saying the same thing about us."

"What do you mean?"

"*They're* the ones fighting for France."

"For a government doing everything it can to please the damned Germans," Durado insisted.

"Even so, it's the only French government there is. Do you remember what Commander Vernerey said when the Allies told him to fight the Germans in Norway?"

"If I heard, I've forgotten."

"Legionnaires fighting in snow instead of sand. He knew how crazy that was. But he didn't argue with his orders. He said, 'What is my aim? To take the port of Narvik. For the Norwegians? The phosphates? The anchovies? I haven't the slightest idea. But I have my mission, and I shall take Narvik.'"

"Yes," Durado said. "We have our mission."

"Something's moving over there." Kline pointed.

Durado squirmed next to him and peered between the boulders.

At a gate in the Damascus wall, a white flag appeared. Several legionnaires emerged, recognizable because each man's cap was the Legion's traditional white *kepi*. Unlike the shorts and short-sleeved shirts that Kline's unit wore, the uniform of the opposing legionnaires consisted of full-length sleeves and pants.

In the last of the setting sun, they formed a line against the wall, stood at attention, and formally presented arms to Kline's unit.

Kline strained to distinguish their faces, unable to tell if Rourke was among them. Even so, he had no doubt that, if he got closer, he'd be able to call each of them by his first name.

At once, he gripped the boulder on his right. Using it for leverage, he stood.

"What are you doing?" Durado asked in alarm.

But Kline wasn't the only man who stood. All along the ridge, sentry after sentry rose to his feet.

Soon Durado did, also.

Someone yelled, "Present...arms!"

The line of sentries imitated their brethren across the way. Kline's chest felt squeezed as he went through the ritual that ended with him holding his rifle close to him, the butt toward the ground, the barrel toward the sky.

From somewhere in Damascus, a bugle played, echoing across the valley. The song, *"Le Boudin,"* was familiar to every legionnaire, who learned it by heart at the start of his training. It dated back to the nineteenth century when Belgium had refused to allow its citizens to join the Legion. As the pulsing melody faded to a close, a bugler on the Demi-Brigade's side took it up. Soon voices joined in, filling the valley with the normally comical lyric about blood sausage and how the Legion wouldn't share any with the Belgians because they were shitty marksmen.

"*Le Boudin*" was followed by another favorite from the first day of training, "*La Legion Marche.*" Its energy expanded Kline's chest and made him sing so hard that he risked becoming hoarse. Even though his voice was only one of thousands on both sides of the valley, he tried his best to make Rourke hear him.

The Legion marches toward the front.
Singing, we are heirs to our traditions,
One with the Legion.

The song praised Honor and Loyalty, virtues that gave the Legion strength. But Kline's voice faltered as he realized that absolute loyalty to a mission was what had brought the Legion to this moment.

When the lyrics reached their refrain, a section of it made Kline stop singing.

We don't only have weapons.
The devil marches with us.

He remembered the conversation he'd had with Rourke when they'd enlisted long ago.

"'My name is Legion'," Rourke had said.

"'For we are many'," Kline had responded. "A possessed man says that to Jesus, trying to explain how many demons are in him."

From Damascus and from this ridge, each side now repeated the song's refrain, their voices rising.

The devil marches with us.

As the sun dipped completely behind the horizon, the music sank as well, echoing faintly, descending into silence.

Enveloped by darkness, Kline went to the bottom of the ridge and stared up at the cold glint of the emerging stars.

He left Durado and made his way to the mess tent. Although he had no appetite, he knew that he would need all his strength in the morning, so he ate the bread and bacon that were served, and drank bitter coffee. Many other men sat around him. None said a word.

Later, in the shadows of his tent, he wondered what Rourke had done that was so horrible it had made him join the Legion as his punishment. Had he set a road-side bomb intended for a British army convoy, only to see it blow apart a school bus full of children? Or had he set fire to a house occupied by an Irish family who supposedly had revealed the IRA's battle plans to the British, only to discover that he'd set the wrong house ablaze, that the family he'd burned to death was innocent? Would those things be terrible enough to make someone like Rourke hate himself? In his nightmares, did he hear the screams of the dying children, just as Kline imagined his wife sobbing over the corpse of their daughter, reaching for a knife to slit her wrists while Kline hid from the police because of a bank robbery in which a guard had been killed for $24.95?

Everybody ran in different directions, Kline remembered. *One of them had the money. I never got even a dollar.*

Imagining the relentless coughing that had racked and smothered his daughter, he thought, *I should have been with my family.*

He remained awake for a long time, staring at the top of his tent.

• • •

EXPLOSIONS SHOOK him from a troubled sleep, so many roaring blasts that he couldn't distinguish them. The ground, the tent, the air—everything trembled. The first shockwaves slapped his ears, making them ring. But amid the persistent heavy rumbles, his ears became numb, as if muffled by cotton batting. He grabbed his rifle and charged from the tent, seeing the chaos of a camp being struck by artillery shells. Powerful flashes illuminated the darkness as rocks, tents, and men disintegrated in the blasts.

Murky silhouettes of legionnaires ran desperately toward the cover of boulders, toward pits they'd dug, toward anything that would shield them from flying debris. The camp's own artillery returned fire, howitzers and tanks shuddering as they blasted shells toward Damascus.

Burning explosions erupted from the sandstone buildings over there. They and the muzzle flashes of the cannons turned the darkness into a pulsing twilight that allowed Kline to see his way toward a rock wall behind which he dove before a nearby blast sent shrapnel streaking over it.

The bombardment persisted for hours. When it finally ended, the air was thick with dust and smoke. Despite the continued ringing in Kline's ears, he heard officers yelling, "*Allez! Allez!* Get on your feet, you lazy bastards! Attack!"

Kline came to his feet, the dust so thick that he sensed more than saw the men around him doing the same.

He and the others scurried up the ridge. Sometimes they slipped on loose stones, but that was the only thing that held them back. Kline sensed their determination as they reached the top and increased speed, charging past boulders toward the wall.

The dust still hovered, giving them shelter, but soon it thinned, and the moment they emerged from it, visible now, running toward the wall, the legionnaires opposing them opened fire. Kline felt a man beside him stagger. A man ahead of him dropped.

But Kline kept charging, shooting toward movement on the parapets. At once, a portion of the wall blew apart from a cannon shell. A second explosion widened the opening.

Kline paused only long enough to yank the pin from a grenade and hurl the grenade as far as he could through the gap in the wall. Other legionnaires did the same, diving to the ground the same as Kline did, waiting for the multiple blasts to clear their way.

He scrambled over the rubble and entered a courtyard. Among stone buildings, narrow alleys led in various directions. A bullet struck near him, throwing up chunks of sandstone. He whirled toward a window and fired, not knowing if he hit anyone before he charged on. Then he reached one of the alleys and aimed along it. Joined by other legionnaires, he moved slowly now, prepared to fire at any target.

Shots seemed everywhere. Explosions rumbled as Kline pressed forward, smelling gunpowder and hearing screams. The buildings were no taller than three stories. Smoke drifted over them, some of it settling into the alley, but he didn't allow it to distract him. The doors and windows ahead were all he cared about.

A man next to him screamed and fell. Kline fired toward the ground-floor window from which the shot had come, and this time, he saw blood fly. A legionnaire near him hurled a grenade through the same window, and the moment it exploded, they crashed through a doorway, firing.

Two soldiers lay dead on the floor. Their white legionnaire's caps were spattered with blood. Their uniforms had the long sleeves and full-length pants of the opposing side. Kline recognized both of them. Rinaldo and Stavros. He'd trained with them, marched with them, shared tents with them, and sung with them at breakfast in the mess hall at Sidi-bel-Abbes.

Stairs led upward. From above, Kline heard shots. Aiming, he and the other legionnaire checked a neighboring room, then approached the steps. As they climbed, a quick glance toward his companion showed Kline that he was again paired with Durado. The Spaniard's normally tan complexion was now sallow.

Neither spoke as they stalked higher.

Above, the shots persisted, presumably directed toward the alley they'd left or else toward the alley on the opposite side of the building. Perhaps the numerous explosions in the area had prevented the shooter from realizing that this building had been hit by a grenade. Or perhaps the shooter wasn't alone. Perhaps he continued firing while another soldier watched the stairs, hoping to draw Kline and Durado into a trap.

Sweat trickled down Kline's face. Nearing the top, he armed another grenade and threw it into a room. Immediately, he and Durado ducked down the stairs, protecting themselves from the force of the blast. They straightened and charged the rest of the way up, shooting as they entered the room.

No one was there. A neighboring room was deserted, also. At the last moment, the shooter must have hurried the rest of the way up the stairs, taking refuge on the third and final floor.

Kline and Durado took turns replacing the magazines on their rifles. Again they crept up, and this time, it was Durado who threw the grenade. An instant after the explosion, they ran to the top, but amid the smoke of the explosion, they still didn't find anyone.

In the far corner, a ladder led to an open hatch in the roof.

Durado's voice was stark. "I'm not going up there."

Kline understood. Their quarry was probably lying on the roof, aiming toward the hatch, ready to shoot the head of anyone who showed himself through the small opening. There was no way to know which way to throw a grenade to try to clear the roof.

"Maybe he ran across to another building," Kline said.

"And maybe not. I won't climb up there to find out."

"Right. To hell with him," Kline decided. He peered through an open window and saw a sniper in a window across from him. The sniper wore a white legionnaire's cap. His sleeves were long. As the man aimed down toward an alley, Kline shot him before he had the chance to pull the trigger.

Durado pointed. "Snipers all along the roofs!"

Kline worked the bolt on his rifle and fired through the window. Worked the bolt and fired. The movement became automatic. Hearing Durado do the same through an opposite window, he loaded a fresh magazine and continued shooting in a frenzy. His uniform was drenched with sweat. Struck by his bullets, white-capped men with long-sleeved shirts slumped on the roofs or else toppled into the alleys.

An explosion shoved Kline forward, almost propelling him through the window. He managed to twist sideways and slam against the window's frame before he would have gone through. His back stung, and his shirt felt more soaked, but this time, he knew it was from blood.

Trying to recover from the shockwave, he spun toward the room and realized that the explosion had come from the far corner. The ladder was in pieces. The man on the roof had dropped a grenade through the hatch.

"Durado!"

There wasn't any point in running to try to help him. Durado had been shooting through a window near the ladder. The grenade had exploded next to him, tearing him open. His blood was everywhere. His gaping intestines lay around him. Already, the flies settled on him.

Kline aimed toward the ceiling's open hatch. Abruptly, numerous bullets sprayed through the window next to him. The snipers across from him had realized the direction from which his shots had come. If the wall hadn't been made of thick sandstone, their bullets would have come through and killed him. Even so, the wall would eventually disintegrate from the unrelenting barrage. He couldn't stay in the room much longer.

When another grenade dropped through the hatch, Kline dove toward the stairs. The impact made him wince as he rolled down, feeling the edges of the steps against his bleeding back. The explosion roared behind him. He groaned when he hit the bottom, but he kept rolling.

He deliberately made loud noises, striking his boots hard as he clattered down the final section of the stairs. At the bottom, he fired once, hoping to give the impression that he shot at someone before he left the building. Then he silently crept up to the middle floor and hid in the adjacent room.

The most difficult part about standing still and waiting was trying to control the sound of his breathing. His chest heaved. He was sure that the strident sound of air going through his nostrils would give him away. He worked desperately to breathe less fast, but that only increased the urgency in his lungs. His heart seemed about to explode.

A minute passed.

Two.

Blood trickled down Kline's injured back. Outside, the explosions and shots continued.

I'm wasting my time, Kline thought. *I ought to be outside, helping.*

The moment he started to leave, he smiled when he heard a shot from the floor above him. The man on the roof had finally decided that the building was clear. He'd dropped down to continue shooting from the cover of a window.

Kline emerged from the room. Hearing another shot above him, he eased up the stairs. He paused, waiting for another shot and the sound of the rifle's bolt being pulled back. Those noises concealed his own sounds as he came to the top of the stairs and fired, hitting the man in the back.

The legionnaire, who wore long pants, slumped forward, his head on the window sill. Kline recognized the back of his brawny neck. His name was Arick. He was a German, who'd been part of Kline's group of volunteers back in 1934. Outside, other Germans fought each other, some for the Vichy Legion, some for the Free French Legion. But where a legionnaire had been born and raised made no difference.

The Legion Is Our Only Country, Kline thought.

God help us.

He turned to race down the stairs and re-enter the battle. He reached the second floor. He hurried to the first at the same moment a man left the chaos outside, rushing into the demolished room. He wore the Legion's white *kepi*. Long pants.

He gaped at Kline.

Kline gaped, as well.

The man was even thinner than when Kline had last seen him, his freckles almost hidden by the dust of battle.

"Rourke."

The name barely escaped Kline's mouth before he shot Rourke in the chest. The pressure of his finger on the trigger was automatic, the result of countless drills in which self-preservation preceded thought.

Rourke staggered back, hit a wall, and slid down, leaving a streak of blood. He squinted at Kline, as if trying to focus his dimming eyes.

He trembled and lay still.

"Rourke," Kline said again.

He went to the open doorway, fired at an opposing legionnaire, and hurried into the tumult of the alley, hoping to die.

• • •

THE BATTLE persisted into the next day. By sunset, the Vichy Legion had been routed. Damascus had fallen to the Allies.

Exhausted, his back crusted with scabs, Kline lay with other legionnaires in the rubble of a building. It was difficult to find a comfortable position among the debris. They licked the last drops of water from the brims of their canteens. They chewed the last of the stale biscuits in their rations.

As the sun set and the cold stars appeared, Kline peered up at the vastness. He was puzzled by the casualty figures that had been reported to his group of men. On his side, only 21 legionnaires had been killed and 47 wounded. But of the opposing legionnaires, 128 had been killed while 728 had been wounded.

The contrast was so great that Kline had difficulty making sense of it.

They had plenty of time to secure their defenses within the city, he thought. *They had buildings to shield them from our bullets while we attacked across open ground. We were easy targets. They should have been able to stop us from reaching the walls.*

An unnerving thought squirmed through his mind. *Did they hold back? Did they shoot to miss? Did they hope to appear to fight when all they wanted was for the battle to end as soon as their pride would allow?*

Kline recalled speaking with Durado about whether the men in the Vichy Legion knew they were on the wrong side, the aggressor's side, the invader's side.

The snipers whom Kline had seen in windows and on rooftops—had they been merely firing but not aiming? Had they been looking for an honorable way to lose the fight?

Kline remembered turning in surprise as Rourke had hurried through the doorway into the wreckage of the room. Kline had shot him reflexively. Searching his memory, Kline struggled to focus on Rourke's rifle. Had Rourke been raising it, about to shoot? Or had Rourke been about to lower it and greet his friend?

There was no way to tell. Everything had happened too quickly.

I did what I was trained to do, Kline thought. *The next instant, Rourke might have shot me.*

But then again, he might not have.

Would our friendship have meant more to him than his duty as a legionnaire? Kline wondered. *Or would Rourke's training have made him pull the trigger?*

Peering up toward the sky, Kline noticed that there were even more stars. Their glint was colder—bitterly so—as a new, more unnerving thought took possession of him. He remembered the many times that he and Rourke had talked about salvation.

"What do Baptists believe?" Rourke had asked.

"God punishes us for our sins," Kline had answered.

Kline now suspected that manipulating him into killing his friend was another way for God to punish him.

"What do *Catholics* believe about being saved?" Kline had asked.

The former altar boy had replied, "We tell God we're sorry for our sins and do penance to prove we mean it."

Penance.

Thinking of his dead wife and daughter, thinking of the dead bank guard, thinking of Rourke, he murmured, his voice breaking, "I'm sorry."

THE INTERROGATOR

There's a joke about two psychoanalysts walking past each other on a street.

One says, "Hello," and keeps going.

The other murmurs, "I wonder what he meant by that."

The joke can also apply to the way espionage experts look for significance in the slightest things their opponents say or do.

"Hello."

"I wonder what he meant by that."

Intelligence data comes from various sources: human and electronic, civilian and military. Each has strengths and weaknesses. Humans observe subjectively but are capable of informed judgments. Satellites see objectively but can't supply memory and context. A civilian observer might not recognize a threat while a military observer might be conditioned to see a threat that is not in fact there.

Thus intelligence data needs to be verified, interpreted, and shaped. It is then passed on to policy makers who interpret it further for their own purposes, sometimes seeing only what they want to see. There are many flaws in this sequence, with the result that the spy world can be a "wilderness of mirrors," as legendary counter-espionage master James Jesus Angleton described it. Often it becomes a contest of out-guessing, second-guessing, and triple-guessing.

In World War II, for example, Allied military intelligence was able to use disinformation (corpses with fake battle plans; wooden outlines of tanks in mock invasion-staging areas) to trick German military intelligence into believing that the D-Day invasion would be somewhere other than Normandy.

Similarly, prior to the Iraq War, Middle Eastern informants knew that American policy makers were eager to find proof that Iraq had weapons of mass destruction. To ingratiate themselves with their espionage employers, some of these well-paid informants exaggerated what could possibly be interpreted as the evidence the U.S. was looking for. Beginning intelligence reports moderated what the informants said, but as the reports were passed higher and as political demands increased, the qualifiers became harder to find until "maybe" became "almost certainly."

These examples show that, despite an intelligence agency's best efforts, it's possible to make errors. The problem becomes more critical when the stakes are high and the time in which a decision needs to be made is extremely short. That is the situation I describe in the following story, which is based on unofficial espionage training that I received over three decades.

This is how my training happened. In 1984, I published a spy novel, The Brotherhood of the Rose, *in which I tried something new in the genre. Until that time, espionage novels tended to fit into one of two categories. The British tradition, as represented by John le Carré, had authentic tradecraft but almost no action. Glum English spymasters sat in gloomy offices, trying to outwit their counterparts behind the Iron Curtain. In contrast, the American tradition, as exemplified by Robert Ludlum, had imaginary, sometimes preposterous spy tradecraft but plenty of entertaining chases and gunfights.*

My goal in The Brotherhood of the Rose *was to combine the strengths of both. This had seldom been tried before. The problem was that John le Carré, whose real name is David Cornwall, had actually been an operative in England's MI6, the equivalent of America's CIA. When he described the way spies handled themselves, he based those scenes on tactics he had actually been trained to employ. But how could I, an outsider, learn the tradecraft? I didn't want state secrets. I just wanted to know how spies thought and went about their business.*

These days, it's possible to learn almost anything instantly on the Internet. In the 1980s, however, research was done the old-fashioned way, beginning with the card catalogue in a library. But as The Brotherhood of the Rose *evolved into a trilogy that included* The Fraternity of the Stone *and* The League of Night and Fog, *I exhausted the information I found in books. That's when I noticed a newspaper item about something called The G. Gordon Liddy Academy of Corporate Security and Private Investigation.*

For some, the political crisis involving Liddy might not be familiar, but there was a time when it seemed that America talked about nothing else. On June 19th, 1972, a security guard at the Watergate office complex in Washington, D.C., became suspicious about an office lock that had been tampered with. He contacted the police, who found five burglars in the Democratic National Committee's headquarters. The goal of the burglars was to discover tactics that the Democratic Party planned to use against then-President Nixon in the upcoming national election and also to determine who in the government was leaking sensitive information that damaged the Republican side.

The burglars were soon linked to a higher-up, G. Gordon Liddy, who hardly seemed your typical criminal. A lawyer, a former assistant district attorney, and a former FBI agent, Liddy had worked for the Treasury Department, had been attached to the White House for special duties, and had then become legal counsel for the Committee to Re-elect the President.

In the ensuing investigation, the trail to the people who sanctioned the burglary led higher and higher in the White House until President Nixon was forced to resign. Many government officials readily implicated others in exchange for immunity or a reduced sentence. But Liddy kept his mouth shut, mentioned no one else, and was sentenced to twenty years in prison, a duration that President Jimmy Carter reduced in what he called "the interest of fairness based on a comparison of Liddy's sentence with the much lighter sentences of others convicted of Watergate-related prosecutions."

In 1977, Liddy was released after fifty-two and a half months. He was an unemployed felon with a huge government fine and a mountain of attorneys' fees. But he now had an asset: a reputation for being strong, true, and unwaveringly loyal. His word was his bond, a rare commodity in politics or anywhere else.

After prison, Liddy earned income by giving lectures and writing an autobiography, Will. *The title referred to his will power. He described overcoming his fear of fire by holding a hand over a flame and ignoring the damage to his flesh. To subdue his fear of rats, he claimed that he killed one, roasted it, and ate it.*

Liddy also earned money by helping to form what People *magazine called "a commando-for-hire" organization in which former special-operations personnel were available for missions that couldn't be conducted through normal channels. The unit was called Hurricane Force, and a typical scenario ran like this. A Middle-Eastern businessman comes to the United States. He meets an American woman. They marry. A son results. But marital bliss turns to strife. A divorce court grants custody of the boy to his mother. Fuming, the Middle Eastern businessman waits for his chance, picks up his son on visitation day, goes to the airport, and flies to his country of origin, where U.S. laws don't apply and a mother doesn't have rights. If the woman had enough money, she could hire Hurricane Force, whose members would go to the Middle Eastern country, establish surveillance, and separate the son from his father, extracting him back to the United States. Whether this operation was ever put into motion, I don't know, but it's the sort of thing that Hurricane Force was designed for, along with ransom payments and hostage negotiation. (If you want an idea of what that world is like, take a look at the film,* Proof of Life. *The tradecraft details are accurate. Or else look at the kidnap/ransom/retrieval novels by my author friend, K. J. Howe.)*

A third way Liddy earned income was The G. Gordon Liddy Academy of Corporate Security and Private Investigation. An extension of Hurricane Force, this three-week course had a faculty that included former members of the CIA, FBI, DEA, and Mossad. The executive-protection instructor was a former U.S. marshal who served on the team that protected John Hinckley, Jr. after he shot President Reagan. The intrusion-detector specialist, John Strauchs, discussed the principles of what civilians might call sophisticated burglar alarms. A medical examiner from Florida's Dade County analyzed the complexities of crime-scene investigation. A polygraph expert explained the principles of the so-called lie detector and ways in which it might be fooled. A lock expert demonstrated ways in which locks could be defeated. An explosives expert illustrated ways in which homemade bombs could be assembled.

When the Liddy Academy's directors received my application, they investigated me to make sure I could be trusted with the powerful information that the instructors provided. Evidently my status as a professor of American literature at the University of Iowa convinced them that, as Rambo's creator, I wouldn't show up wearing a bandana and a bandoleer. For a fee of $2,700 (in 1986 dollars), I was allowed to attend.

The Academy happened only three times, once in Miami, once outside New York City, and once near Los Angeles. I chose the New York area. After arranging for some time away from my university teaching duties, I said goodbye to my wife and two children and disappeared for three weeks to Nanuet, NY. Those three weeks—from early morning until midnight, weekends included—turned out to be a condensed version of what CIA field operatives experience at Camp Peary, the Agency's training facility in Virginia, often referred to as The Farm. (For a sense of what that training is like, take a look at the films Spy Games *and* The Recruit.*)*

My fellow students were professionals in law enforcement and corporate security. The most distinctive of them was an extremely short investigator. In pre-politically-correct times, he would have been called a midget. He worked undercover, going into mob-owned bars, where no one paid attention to him as he overheard incriminating conversations. Another student was President Reagan's son, Ron Reagan, Jr., who was researching an article about the Academy for Playboy *magazine. It was an eerie experience to sit next to Ron while we discussed his father as we watched the president conduct a press conference on television.*

Based on lectures that various instructors delivered, these were some of the training exercises:

At 9 P.M. in the middle of a week, I was told to go to the cocktail lounge of a hotel that catered to traveling businessmen. My assignment was to sit next to a stranger at the bar and throughout the evening to learn as much as I could about him: his name, where he lived, whether he was married and had children, whom he worked for, and if possible, his social security number.

The way I obtained the latter probably wouldn't work these days because many people are paranoid about identity theft. But this is how I did it.

After each of us consumed a couple of beers, I told my new companion, "You know, today I learned something interesting about social security numbers."

"Yeah?"

"Yeah. There are three sections of digits, right?"

My companion thought a moment. "Right."

"I'll show you what I mean. Here's mine," I said.

I wrote a bogus social security number on a cocktail napkin. "The first three digits refer to a state," I continued.

My companion sipped his beer and nodded, studying my supposed social security number, trying to concentrate on what I was telling him.

"Those first three digits indicate where my family lived when my parents applied to get me a social security number. Four seven eight. If somebody had this list..." I pulled out a piece of paper that had digits next to the names of states, a document readily available from the Social Security Administration. "...they'd know I was from Iowa."

"Yeah?" My companion thought a moment longer, looking toward the list in my hand. "I wonder if that works for mine."

He wrote his social security number on the cocktail napkin.

I read the first three digits. "Two one two." Then I looked at the sheet in my hand. "New Hampshire," I announced.

"By God, that's right," my companion said, unaware that I'd tricked him into providing his number. "That's where I lived when I was a kid."

A few days later, in an unrelated assignment, I was in a parking lot of a Nanuet shopping mall, part of a team scattered throughout the lot and in the mall. We were waiting for a man to arrive. He was someone hired by the Academy. We had photographs of him and the car he would use. He had an envelope that he intended to pass to someone in the mall (another person hired by the Academy). Our mission was to notice when the envelope was exchanged and to follow the other man. But we didn't know what the other man looked like, and we didn't know if the envelope would be passed directly or if the courier might select a pair of trousers in a department store, go into a changing room, and tape the envelope under a seat there. Or he might tape it under a restaurant table while eating a hamburger. Meanwhile, both men would be watching for surveillance, and if they noticed us, they wouldn't complete the transfer. To complicate matters, security guards in the mall were nervous after a recent armed bank robbery in the area. If we weren't careful, they would become suspicious about the covert drama that was supposed to be invisible to them. In fact, the security guards did step in and question two members of our team, who followed their quarry too zealously. The exercise was aborted. The debriefing was uncomfortable but informative.

Thus we practiced the various tools of the spy profession: elicitation, target assessment, surveillance, information transfer, and so on, the sort of techniques that I mention in the first paragraph of "The Interrogator." Elicitation (the ability to learn information from someone without that person being aware of what's really happening in a conversation) is a fundamental of the spy world. Give people the opportunity, and they will reveal the most amazing things about themselves, as my anecdote about the social security number demonstrates.

Neuro-linguistic programming was the key to it, our elicitation instructor emphasized. At that time (and perhaps now), almost all CIA field operatives received extensive training in NLP for purposes of recruiting and debriefing. NLP divides people into three types. An operative can identify a person's type and mirror the language patterns and body movements of that type, making a stranger feel as if she or he has been friends with the operative for a very long time. I'll forego a detailed explanation of NLP here because I devote a couple of pages to it in "The Interrogator," but I can't resist adding that its principles allowed me to know that when President Clinton appeared at a press conference to deny having had sex with Monica Lewinsky, the direction of his eyes made clear that he was lying.

Liddy delivered several lectures at the Academy. I got to know him well enough that I'll call him Gordon from now on. We had numerous dinner conversations in which (I do not exaggerate) the topic was often opera. I continued to cross paths with him over the years and was interviewed on his radio talk show when I had new novels to discuss. Controversial, strong willed, and devoted to his wife of many years, Gordon was always fascinating and, in private, a gentleman quite different from his gruff public persona. I often repeat something that he told me and that strikes me as being truer now than ever: "The world is a bad neighborhood."

For me, the gates were now open. I had a personal relationship with professionals in the worlds I wanted to write about. They provided technical advice for numerous novels, such as The Fifth Profession, The Protector, *and* Assumed Identity. *In fact, the latter is dedicated to Martin E. Wingate, one of the many identities that one of my Academy instructors assumed during his career in Army military intelligence.*

These professionals introduced me to other espionage experts, who generously increased my knowledge even further (I provide a list of many at the start of The Protector *and* The Naked Edge). *I became an honorary lifetime member of the Association for Intelligence Officers. I also became an honorary lifetime member of the Special Operations Association, which is connected to espionage because many former special-operations personnel work as contract operatives for civilian security and information-gathering companies that are sometimes covertly used by intelligence agencies. If these contract operatives are caught practicing espionage against a foreign* power, so many barriers exist between the companies the operatives work for and whatever government agency hired them that there's no way to link the two.

I once spent a weekend training with one of these operatives. He liked to play blackjack, so I met him in Las Vegas. When he wasn't at the tables, he led me through exercises comparable to what the CIA teaches at The Farm. One exercise involved finding a place to leave information that an associate could easily retrieve without being noticed. We pretended that an empty aspirin bottle contained secrets and we walked outside a casino, looking for a suitable hiding place.

The way this usually works is, you put a small chalk mark on a lamppost or some such, where an associate knows to look each day. If she or he sees the mark, it's a signal to go to a prearranged spot where the material has been hidden. The trick is that nobody else should be able to see the material being deposited and picked up, even when both people involved in the exchange are being followed.

Las Vegas has a lot of surveillance cameras, which made the assignment difficult. Outside the casino, we studied the parking garage. Cameras were aimed toward the garage's entrance. Cameras were also on the inside of the garage. But there was a five-foot tunnel from the outside to the inside that, for a few seconds, couldn't be observed.

In the tunnel, my instructor looked up and saw a small ledge. "This is perfect." He reached up to show me how to position the aspirin bottle so that it would be out of sight but easy to retrieve by someone who passed through quickly.

His face changed expression as he pulled down a small package. "Looks like somebody already figured this is a perfect place for a drop."

He hastily returned the package to where it had been. We got the hell out of there.

After I resigned my professorship at the University of Iowa and moved from Iowa City to Santa Fe, New Mexico, I discovered that Santa Fe had an NLP Institute. I received ten weekends of training and earned my certification. In one of those coincidences that you wouldn't believe in fiction, I discovered that the house I bought in Santa Fe had been owned by social anthropologist Edward T. Hall, who's a grandfather of NLP because of his pioneering work in the concepts of body language and personal space. He's one of the few authentic geniuses I ever met. His The Hidden Dimension *and* The Silent Language *offer profound insights into the way human beings relate to one another, which is what the spy business is about. Hall taught State Department diplomats and CIA operatives back in the days when the Dulles brothers ran those places. When I moved into Hall's house, the neighbors told me that there used to be abundant radio antennae on the roof and that robust young men used to park their cars in front of his house at nine each morning in the summer and then drive away at five. My house has a swimming pool behind a high wall. Visiting me one day, Hall explained that the "government" had built the swimming pool for him. I can only imagine what Hall taught those young men on hot summer days as they gathered around that pool.*

The anecdote with which "The Interrogator" begins is one that an operative told me about part of his training. The concluding reference to the two double agents who paralyzed the CIA is factual. While the story's central event is invented, it's based on any number of real ones. In many ways, what you're about to read is fact more than fiction.

WHEN ANDREW DURAND WAS GROWING UP, his father never missed an opportunity to teach him espionage tradecraft. Anything they did was a chance for the boy to learn about dead drops, brush contacts, cut outs, elicitation, and other arts of the profession.

Not that Andrew's father spent a great deal of time with him. As a senior member of the CIA's Directorate of Operations, his father had global responsibilities that constantly called him away. But when circumstances permitted, the father's attention to Andrew was absolute, and Andrew never forgot their conspiratorial expeditions.

In particular, Andrew recalled the July afternoon his father took him sailing on the Chesapeake to celebrate his sixteenth birthday. During a lull in the wind, his father told him about his graduate-student days at George Washington University and how his political-science professor introduced him to a man who turned out to be a CIA recruiter.

"It was the Cold War years of the nineteen fifties," his father said with a nostalgic smile as waves lapped the hull. "The nuclear arms race. Mushroom clouds. Bomb shelters. In fact, my parents installed a bomb shelter where we now have the swimming pool. The shelter was deep enough that when we tore it out later, we didn't need to do much excavating for the pool. I figured handling the Soviets was just about the most important job anybody could want, so when the recruiter finally ended the courtship and popped the question, I didn't need long to decide. The Agency had already done its background check. A few formalities still remained, like the polygraph, but before they got to that, they decided to test my qualifications for the job they had in mind."

The test, Andrew's father explained, was to make him sit in a windowless room and read a novel. Written by Henry James, published in 1903, the book was called *The Ambassadors*. In long, complicated sentences, the first section introduced a middle-aged American with the odd name of Lambert Strether, who traveled to Paris on a mission.

"James has a reputation for being difficult to read," Andrew's father said. "At first, I thought I was being subjected to a practical joke. After all, what was the point of just sitting in a room and reading? After about a half hour, music started playing through a speaker hidden in the ceiling, something brassy by Frank Sinatra, 'I've Got You under My Skin.' I remember the title because I later understood how ironic it was. Another brassy Sinatra tune followed. Then another. Abruptly, the music stopped, and a male voice I'd never heard before instructed me to put the book in my lap and describe what was happening in the plot. I replied that Strether worked for a rich woman in a town in New England. She'd sent him to Paris to learn why her son hadn't returned home after a long trip abroad. 'Continue reading,' the voice said. The moment I picked up the novel, another brassy Sinatra tune began playing.

"As I turned the pages, I was suddenly aware of faint voices behind the music, a man and a woman. Their tone was subdued, but I could tell they were angry. At once, the music and the voices stopped.

"'What's happening in the book?' the voice asked from the ceiling.

"I answered, 'Strether's worried that he'll lose his job if he doesn't persuade the son to go home to his mother.'

"'Lose only his job?' the voice asked.

"'Well, the rich woman's a widow, and there's a hint that she and Strether might get married. But that won't happen if Strether doesn't bring her son home.'

"'There were people talking behind the music.'

"'Yes. A man and a woman.'

"'What were they discussing?'

"'They were supposed to meet at a restaurant for dinner. But the man arrived late, claiming last-minute responsibilities at his office. His wife believes he went to see another woman.'

"'Continue reading,' the voice said."

Andrew remembered listening to his father explain how the test persisted for hours. In addition to the music, two and then three conversations took place simultaneously behind the songs. Periodically, the voice asked about each of them (a woman was fearful about an impending gall-bladder surgery; a man was angry about the cost of his daughter's wedding; a child was worried about a sick dog). The voice also wanted to know what was happening in the densely textured novel.

"Obviously, it was an exercise to determine how much I could be aware of at the same time, or whether the examiner could distract me and get under my skin," Andrew's father said. "It turned out that my political-science teacher recommended me to the Agency because of my ability to hold various thoughts at once without being distracted. I passed the test and was initially assigned to hot-bed cities like Bonn, which in those days was the capital of West Germany. Pretending to be an attaché, I made chit-chat at crowded embassy cocktail parties while monitoring the voices of foreign diplomats around me. No one expected state secrets to be revealed. Nonetheless, my superiors were surprised by the useful personal details I was able to gather at those diplomatic receptions: who was trying to seduce whom, for example, or who had money problems. Alcohol and the supposed safety of the chaos of voices in a crowded room made people careless. After that, I was promoted to junior analyst, where I rose through the ranks because I could balance the relative significance of various crises that erupted simultaneously around the globe."

The waves lapped stronger against the hull. The boat shifted. The memories made Andrew's father hesitate. Drawn into the past, he took a moment before glancing toward clouds moving across the sky.

"Finally, the wind's picking up. Grab the wheel, son. Check the compass. Take us southwest toward home. By the way, that James book, *The Ambassadors?* After all my effort, I was determined to finish it. In the end, it turned out that Strether's experience in Paris was so broadening that he felt he'd become smarter, aware of everything around him. But he was wrong. The rich woman's son gained his trust, only to make a fool of him. Despite all his awareness, Strether returned to America, where he assumed he'd lose everything."

• • •

"FOUR DAYS," Andrew promised the somber group in the high-security conference room. He was thirty-nine and spoke with the authoritative tone of his father.

"Is that a guarantee?"

"I can possibly get results sooner, but definitely no later than four days."

"There's a time element," a grim official warned, "the probability of smallpox dispersal in a subway system during peak hours. Ten days from now. But we don't know the exact time or which country, let alone which city. Our people apprehended the subject in Paris. His fellow conspirators were with him. One escaped, but the rest died in a gun battle. We have documents that indicate what they set in motion—but not the particulars. Just because they were in Paris, that doesn't rule out another city with a major subway system as the target."

"Four days after I start, you'll have the details," Andrew assured them. "Where's the subject being rendered?"

"Uzbekistan."

Andrew's beefy neck crinkled when he nodded. "They know how to be discreet."

"They ought to, given how much we pay them."

"But I don't want any foreign interrogator involved," Andrew emphasized. "Thugs have unreliable methods. A subject will confess to anything if tortured sufficiently. You want reliable information, not a hysterical confession that turns out to be baseless."

"Exactly. You're completely in charge."

"In fact, there's no reason why this needs to be an extraordinary rendition." Andrew's use of "rendition" referred to the practice of moving a prisoner from one jurisdiction to another, a common occurrence in the legal system. But when the rendition was "extraordinary," the prisoner was taken out of the legal system and placed where the normal rules no longer applied and accountability was no longer a factor. "The interview could just as easily take place in the United States."

"Unfortunately, not everyone in the United States appreciates the difference between torture and your methods, Andrew. A jet's waiting to fly you to Uzbekistan."

● ● ●

ANDREW'S FATHER had been heavyset. Andrew was more so. A big man with a large chest, he resembled a heavyweight boxer, an impression that frequently made a detainee's eyes widen at first sight of him. With his deep raspy voice, he exuded a sense of menace and power, causing his subjects to feel increasing dread, unaware that Andrew's true power came from numerous psychology courses taken at George Washington University, where he earned a Master's degree under a created identity.

A burly American civilian guard greeted him at a remote Uzbekistan airstrip next to a concrete-block building that was the rendering facility, the only structure in the boulder-dotted, mountain-rimmed valley.

Andrew introduced himself as Mr. Baker.

The guard said he was Mr. Able. "I have the subject's documents ready for you. We know his name and those of his relatives, where they live and work, in case you want to make him talk by threatening to kill people he loves."

"That won't be necessary. I'll hardly ever speak to him." A cold wind tugged at Andrew's dark suit. When working, he always dressed formally, another way of expressing authority.

Escorted by the guard, he passed through the security checkpoint, then entered the facility, which had harsh overhead lights and a row of doors with barred windows. The walls were made from unpainted cinder blocks. Everything felt damp.

"Your room's to the right," the guard told him.

Andrew's travel bag contained four days of clothes, the maximum he would need. He set it on the concrete floor next to a cot. He barely looked at the stainless-steel sink and toilet. Instead he focused on a metal table upon which sat a laptop computer. "The other equipment should have arrived."

"It's been installed. But I don't know why we needed to bother. While we waited for you, my men and I could have put the fear of God into him."

"I can't imagine how that's possible when he's convinced God's on his side. Is the interpreter ready?"

"Yes."

"Reliable?"

"Very."

"Then let's get started."

• • •

ANDREW WATCHED the guard unlock a metal door. Holding a .45-caliber Glock pistol, the guard and two others armed with identical pistols entered the cell and aimed at the prisoner. Andrew and the interpreter stood in the open doorway. The compartment was windowless, except for the barred opening in the door. It felt damper than the corridor. The echo was sharp.

A short, gaunt Iraqi man was slumped on the concrete floor, his back against the wall, his wrists shackled to chains above his head. In his mid-thirties, he had a thin, dark face and short, black hair. His lips were scabbed. His cheeks were bruised. Dried blood grimed his black shirt and pants.

As if dazed, the subject stared straight ahead, not reacting to Andrew's entrance.

Andrew turned toward the senior guard, his stark expression making clear that he'd sent explicit instructions not to abuse the prisoner.

"That happened when the team grabbed him in Paris," the guard explained. "He's lucky he didn't get killed in the gun battle."

"*He* doesn't think so. He wants to die for his cause."

"Yeah, well, if he doesn't talk, we can arrange for him to get his wish," the guard said. "The thing is, as much as he'd like to be a martyr, I'm sure he didn't intend for any suffering to be involved." The guard faced the prisoner. "Isn't that right, chum? You figured you'd jump over the agony and get straight to the virgins in paradise. Well, you were wrong."

The prisoner showed no reaction, continuing to look straight ahead. As an experiment, Andrew raised his arm above his head and pointed toward the ceiling, but the prisoner's eyes didn't follow his broad gesture. They remained so resolutely fixed on the opposite wall that Andrew became convinced the subject wasn't as dazed as he appeared.

"Translate for me," Andrew told the interpreter, then concentrated on the prisoner. "You have information about a soon-to-occur attack on a subway system. This attack will involve smallpox. You will tell me exactly when and where this attack will take place. You'll tell me how the smallpox was obtained. You'll tell me how the attack will be carried out. The next time you see me, you'll tell me all of these things and anything else I wish to know."

The prisoner kept staring straight ahead.

When the interpreter finished, Andrew pointed toward a narrow cot bolted to the floor along one wall. He told the senior guard, "Remove it. Leave a thin blanket. Unshackle him. Lock the room. Cover the window in the door."

"Look, is all this really necessary?" the guard complained. "Just give me two hours with him and—"

Andrew left the cell.

• • •

THE WAY *he avoids eye contact*, Andrew thought. *He's been warned about some types of interrogation.*

Like most intelligence operatives, Andrew had received training in the ways humans processed information. According to one theory known as neuro-linguistic programming, most people were either sight-oriented, sound-oriented, or touch-oriented. A sight-oriented person tended to favor language that involved metaphors of sight, such as "I see what you mean." From an observer's point of view, that type of person tended to look up toward the left when creating a thought and to look up to the right when remembering something. In contrast, a sound-oriented person tended to use metaphors such as "I hear what you're getting at." When creating a thought, that type of person looked directly to the observer's left and, when remembering something, looked directly to the observer's right. Finally, a touch-oriented person favored metaphors such as "I feel comfortable with what you're saying." When that type of person looked down to the left or the right, those movements, too, were revealing.

People were seldom exclusively one type, but through careful observation, a trained interrogator could determine the sense orientation an individual favored. The interrogator might ask, "What city will be attacked?" If a sound-oriented prisoner glanced directly to the left and said, "Washington," that statement was a created thought—an invention. However, if the prisoner glanced to the right and said the same thing, that statement was based on a memory. Of course, the prisoner might be remembering a lie he was instructed to tell. Nonetheless, through careful observation of eye movements, a skilled interrogator could reach reasonably certain conclusions about whether a prisoner was lying or telling the truth.

The trouble was, this particular prisoner obstinately refused to look Andrew in the eyes.

Hell, he knows about neuro-linguistic programming, Andrew thought. *He's been warned that his eye movements might tell me something about his mission.*

The sophistication made Andrew uneasy. To consider these fanatics as ignorant was a lethal mistake. They learned exponentially and seemed dangerously more complex every day.

He couldn't help thinking of the simplicity of an interrogation technique favored during his father's youth in the 1950s. Back then, a prisoner was injected with sodium pentothal or one of the other so-called truth serums. This relaxed a detainee to such a degree that his mental discipline was compromised, in theory making him vulnerable to questioning. But the process was often like trying to get information from a drunk. Fantasy, exaggeration, and fact became indistinguishable. Needing clarity and reliability, interrogators developed other methods.

● ● ●

IN HIS room, Andrew sat at his desk, activated the laptop computer, and watched an image appear. Transmitted from a hidden camera, it showed the prisoner in his cell. In keeping with Andrew's instructions, the cot had been removed. The barred opening in the door was covered. A thin blanket lay on the concrete floor. The subject's arms had been unshackled. He rubbed his chafed wrists. Now that he was alone, he confirmed Andrew's suspicions by looking around warily, no longer fixing his gaze toward a spot on a wall.

Andrew pressed a button on the laptop's keyboard and subtly increased the glare of the overhead lights in the cell. The change was so imperceptible that the subject couldn't notice. During the next four days, the intensity would continue to increase until the glare was blinding, but no moment in the gradually agonizing change would be perceptible.

Andrew pressed another button and reduced the cell's temperature a quarter of a degree. Again, the change was too small for the prisoner to notice, but during the next four days, the damp chill in the compartment would become extreme.

The subject sat in a corner with his back against the wall. In a moment, his eyes closed, perhaps in meditation.

Can't allow that, Andrew thought. He pressed a third button, which activated a siren in the prisoner's cell. On the screen, the prisoner jerked his eyes open. Startled, he looked up at the ceiling, where the siren was located. For now, the siren was at its lowest setting. It lasted only three seconds. But over the next four days, at unpredictable intervals, it would be repeated, each time louder and longer.

The prisoner would be given small amounts of bread and water to keep his strength at a sufficient level to prevent him from passing out. But the toilet in his cell would stop functioning, his wastes accumulating, their stench adding to his other sensory ordeals. Meanwhile the cell was on rollers and would subtly shift, not enough to be consciously noticed but sufficient for the subject's balance to be affected.

Andrew was reminded of the story his father had told him long ago on the sailboat. In his father's case, there had been various increasing challenges to his perceptions. In the prisoner's case, there were increasing *assaults* to his perceptions. He would soon lose his sense of time. Minutes would feel like hours, and hours would feel like days. The intensifying barrage of painful stimuli would tear away his psychological defenses, leaving him so overwhelmed, disoriented, and worn down that he'd reveal any secret if only he could sleep and feel steady.

• • •

THE PRISONER lasted three and a half days. The sporadic faint siren eventually became a prolonged wail that forced him to put his hands over his ears and scream. Of course, his scream could not be heard amid the siren. Only the O of his mouth communicated the anguish escaping from him. The eventual searing glare of the lights changed to a pulsing light-dark, light-dark strobe effect that made the prisoner scrunch his eyes shut, straining to protect them. The thin blanket he'd been allowed was merely an attempt to give him false hope, for as the cold intensified, seeping up from the concrete floor and into his bones, the blanket gave him no protection. He huddled uselessly under it, unable to stop shivering.

• • •

AGAIN, THE guard and two others entered the cell. Again, Andrew and the interpreter stood in the open doorway.

The prisoner twitched, this time definitely affected by Andrew's size.

"When and where will the attack occur?" Andrew asked. "Does the attack involve smallpox? If so, how did your group obtain it? How will the attack be carried out? Tell me, and I'll dim the lights. I'll also shut off the siren. I'll make the room's temperature comfortable. I'll allow you to sleep. Wouldn't it be wonderful to sleep? Sleep is the greatest pleasure. Sleep will refresh you."

Hugging himself to keep from shaking, the prisoner confessed. Because he hadn't slept for almost four days, the information wasn't always clear. Andrew needed to rephrase questions and prompt him numerous times, on occasion reactivating the siren and the throbbing lights to jolt his nerves. In the end, Andrew learned all that he wanted, and the prisoner no longer avoided looking at him. With a besieging gaze, the desperate man told him what he needed, and the movement of his red, swollen, sleep-deprived eyes told Andrew that he wasn't lying.

The target was New York City. The attack did involve smallpox. In four days, at five p.m. on numerous subway platforms, aerosol canisters that looked like hair-spray dispensers would be taken from backpacks. Their tops would be twisted, then returned to the backpacks. Their pressurized air would be vented through a tube in the knapsack, dispersing the virus among the crowd. The victims wouldn't know about the attack until days later when symptoms of the disease began to appear, but by then, the victims would have spread the virus much farther.

As Andrew hurried toward a scrambler-equipped satellite radio to report what he'd learned, he heard muffled screams coming from another cell. Water splashed. Disturbed by the significance of the sounds, Andrew ran to an open doorway through which he saw a man strapped to a board. The board was tilted so that the man's head was lower than his feet. His head was in a brace so that he couldn't turn it from side to side. He was naked, except for his underwear. His features were covered by a cloth, but the brown color of his skin matched that of the prisoner Andrew had interrogated, making Andrew conclude that this man, too, was an Iraqi.

Mr. Able stood over this new prisoner, pouring water onto his covered face. The prisoner made a gagging sound. He squirmed desperately, barely able to move.

"Our team in Paris caught the guy who escaped," the guard told Andrew, then poured more water over the prisoner's face. "He arrived while you were questioning the other prisoner."

"Stop," Andrew said.

"You took almost four days. At the start, I told you I could get someone to confess in two hours. But the truth is, all I really need is ten minutes."

What Andrew watched helplessly was called waterboarding. The immobilized prisoner was subjected to a heavy stream of water over his face. The soggy cloth on his nose and mouth added to the weight of the water and made breathing even more difficult. The cloth covered his eyes and increased his terror because he couldn't see to anticipate when more water would strike him. The incline guaranteed that the water would rush into his nostrils.

Unable to expel the water, the prisoner kept gagging, relentlessly subjected to the sensation of drowning. Andrew knew of cases in which prisoners did in fact drown. Other times, panic broke their sanity. Intelligence operatives who allowed themselves to be waterboarded in an effort to understand the experience were seldom able to bear even a minute of it. Those prisoners who were eventually set free reported that the panic they endured created life-long traumas that made it impossible for them to look at a rain shower or even at water flowing from a tap.

In this case, the prisoner thrashed with such force that Andrew was convinced he would dislocate his limbs.

"Okay, asshole," the guard said through a translator. He yanked the drenched cloth from the victim's face.

Andrew was appalled to see tape stretched over the prisoner's mouth. The only way the man could breathe was through his nose, from which water and snot erupted as he fought to clear his nostrils.

"Here's your chance not to drown." The guard yanked the tape from the prisoner's mouth. "Which subway system's going to be attacked?"

The prisoner spat water. He gasped for air, his chest heaving.

"Speak up, jerk-off. I haven't got all day."

The prisoner made a sound as if he might vomit.

"Fine." The guard stretched the tape across the prisoner's mouth. He threw the dripping cloth over his face, picked up another container of water, and poured.

With his feet tilted above him, the prisoner squirmed and gagged insanely as water cascaded onto the smothering cloth and into his nostrils.

"One last time, pal." Again, the guard yanked the cloth and the tape from the prisoner's face. "Answer my question, or you'll drown. What subway system's going to be attacked?"

"Paris," the prisoner managed to say.

"You won't like it if I find out you're lying."

"*Paris.*"

"Wait right there, chum. Don't go away." The guard left the prisoner strapped to the board and proceeded along the corridor to the man in the other cell.

"No," Andrew said. He hurried after the guard, and what he saw when he reached the cell filled him with dismay. Guards had stripped the first prisoner and strapped him to a board, tilting his head down. A cloth covered his face.

"Stop," Andrew said.

When he tried to intervene, two other guards grabbed him, dragging him back. Frantic, Andrew strained to pull free, but suddenly the barrel of a pistol was rammed painfully into his back, and he stopped resisting.

"I keep getting radio calls from nervous, important people," the burly guard said. "They keep asking what the hell's taking so long. A lot of people will die soon if we don't get the right information. I tell those nervous, important people that you've got your special way of doing things, that you don't think *my* way's reliable, that you think a prisoner'll tell me anything just to make me stop."

"It's true," Andrew said. "Panic makes him so desperate he'll say anything he thinks you want to hear. The information isn't dependable. But *my* way strips away his defenses. He doesn't have any resistance by the time I finish with him. He doesn't have the strength to lie."

"Well, Mr. Baker, waterboarding makes them too terrified to lie."

The guard began pouring water over the prisoner's face. It took less time than with the other man because this prisoner was already exhausted from the sensory assaults that Andrew had subjected him to. He struggled. He gagged. As water poured over his downward-tilted face, rushing into his nostrils, he made choking sounds beneath the smothering cloth.

"What subway system's going to be attacked?" the guard demanded.

"He already told me!" Andrew shouted.

"Well, let's hear what he answers *this* time." The guard pulled the cloth from his face and ripped tape from his mouth.

"Paris," the prisoner moaned.

Andrew gaped. "No. That's not the answer he gave me. He told me New York City."

"But now he says Paris, and so does the other guy. Paris is where they got captured. Why else would they be there if they weren't going to attack it? Enough time's been wasted. Our bosses are waiting for my report. We don't need you here. I'm the interrogator they should have hired."

"You're making a mistake."

"No, *you* made the mistake when you took so damned long. We can't waste any more time."

Andrew struggled to pull away from the guards who held his arms so tightly they made his hands numb by restricting the flow of blood. "Those people you want to impress—tell them the target's either New York *or* Paris. Tell them to increase surveillance at *all* the major subway systems but to emphasize New York and Paris. Four days from now. Thursday. Five p.m. local time. The attackers will wear backpacks. They'll have hair-spray canisters inside the backpacks. The canisters hold the smallpox."

"I haven't started questioning these maggots about the other details," the guard said. "Right now, I just want to let everybody know the target area."

"When they confessed to you, they never looked at you!" Andrew shouted.

"How the hell could they look at me when their heads were braced?" the guard demanded. "I was standing to the side."

"Their eyes. They should have angled their eyes toward you. They should have used their eyes to beg you to believe them. Instead they kept staring at the ceiling, the same way the first prisoner stared at the wall when I got here."

"You expect me to believe that NLP shit? If they look to my left, they're making things up. If they look to my right, they're remembering something. So, they look at the ceiling to keep me from knowing if they're lying or not."

"That's the theory."

"Well, suppose what they're remembering is a lie they rehearsed? Left. Right. None of it means anything."

"The point is *they* think it means something. That's why they won't look at you. After three and a half days, when the man I interrogated was ready for questioning, he couldn't stop looking at me. His eyes wouldn't stop pleading for me to let him sleep. And he always looked to the right. Maybe he remembered a lie, but at least, his eyes didn't tell me he was inventing

173

something. The men you waterboarded, though, when they confessed, they didn't give you a chance to learn *anything* from their eyes."

"But..." A sudden doubt made the guard frown. "If you're right, the only way that would work..."

"...is if they were waterboarded other times. As part of their training," Andrew said. "Once they adjusted to it, their trainer could condition them to control their eyes."

"But the panic's overwhelming. No one would agree to be waterboarded repeatedly," the burly guard insisted.

"Unless they welcome death."

The stark words made the guard cock his head, threatened by Andrew's logic.

Apparently the other guards reacted the same way. Confused, they released him. Feeling blood flow into his arms, Andrew stepped forward. "All these prisoners want is to die for their cause and go to paradise. They're not afraid of death. They welcome it. How can waterboarding make them panic?"

A long moment passed. The guard lowered his gaze toward the water and scum on the floor. "Report whatever the hell you want."

"I will in a moment." Andrew turned toward the other guards. "Who stuck the pistol into my back?"

The man on the right said, "I did. No hard feelings."

"Wrong." Andrew rammed the palm of his hand against the man's face and shattered his nose.

• • •

FOUR DAYS later, shortly after five P.M. Eastern Standard Time, Andrew received a radio message that five men with backpacks containing smallpox-dispersal cans had been arrested as they attempted to enter various sections of the New York City subway system. A weight seemed to fall from his chest. For the first time in three days, he breathed freely. After the confidence with which he'd confronted the guard, he'd begun to be troubled by doubts. So many lives depended on his skills. Given the sophistication of the prisoners, he'd been worried that, for once, he might have been fooled.

He was in Afghanistan now, conducting another sensory-assault interrogation. As before, the person usually in charge resented his intrusion and complained that he could get results much faster than Andrew did.

Andrew ignored him.

But on the eve of the third day of the interrogation, when Andrew was sure that his prisoner would soon lose all his psychological defenses and reveal what Andrew needed to know, he was again reminded of his father. He sat before the computer on his desk, watching the image of the prisoner, and he recalled that his father had sometimes been asked to go to the Agency's training facility at Camp Peary, Virginia, where he taught operatives to extend the limits of their perceptions.

"It's like most things. It involves practice," his father had explained to Andrew. "For old times' sake, I made my students read *The Ambassadors*. I tried to distract them with blaring music. I inserted conversations behind the music. A layer at a time. After a while, the students learned to be more aware, to perceive many things at once."

As Andrew studied the computer screen and pushed buttons that flashed the blinding lights in the prisoner's cell while at the same time causing a siren to wail, he thought about the lesson that his father had said he took from that Henry James novel.

"Lambert Strether becomes increasingly aware as the novel progresses," Andrew's father had told him. "Eventually, Strether notices all sorts of things that he normally would have missed. Undertones in conversations. Overtones in the way someone looks at someone else. All the details in the way people dress and what those details say about them. He becomes a master of consciousness. The sentences dramatize that point. They get longer and more complicated as the novel progresses, as if matching Strether's growing mind. I get the sense that James hoped those complicated sentences would make the reader's mind develop as Strether's does. But this is the novel's point, Andrew. Never forget this, especially if you enter the intelligence profession, as I hope you will. For all his awareness, Strether loses. In the end, he's outwitted. His confidence in his awareness destroys him. The day you become most sure of something, that's the day you need to start doubting it. The essence of the intelligence profession is that you can never be aware enough, never be conscious enough, because your opponent is determined to be even more aware."

Andrew kept watching the computer screen and the agony of his prisoner as lights flashed and sirens wailed. Abruptly, he pressed buttons that turned off the lights and the siren. He wanted to create ten minutes of peace, ten minutes in which the prisoner would be unable to relax, dreading the further assault on his senses. It was a hell that the prisoner would soon do anything to end.

Except, Andrew thought.

The day you become most sure of something, that's the day you need to start doubting it. His father's words echoed in Andrew's memory as he thought about his conviction that the only sure method of interrogation was his own. But was it possible that...

A threatening idea wormed into Andrew's imagination. An operative could be trained to add one perception onto another and then another until he or she could monitor multiple conversations while reading a book and listening to brassy music.

Then why couldn't an operative of a different sort be trained to endure deepening cold, throbbing lights and wailing sirens for three and a half days without sleep? The first time would be agony, but the agony of the second time would perhaps be less because it was familiar. The third time would be a learning experience, testing methods of self-hypnotism to make the onslaught less painful.

Watching the prisoner's supposed anguish, Andrew felt empty. Could an enemy become that sophisticated? If they learned NLP in order to defeat it, if they practiced being waterboarded in order to control their reactions to it, why couldn't they educate themselves in other methods of interrogation in order to defeat *those?* Any group whose members blew themselves up to destroy their enemies and thus attain paradise was capable of anything.

Andrew pressed buttons on his computer keyboard and caused the strobe lights and siren to resume in the prisoner's cold cell. Imagining the blare, he watched the sleepless prisoner scream.

Or was the prisoner only pretending to have reached the limit of his endurance? Andrew had the troubling sense that the man on the screen was reacting predictably, almost on schedule, as if the prisoner had been trained to know what to anticipate and was behaving the way an interrogator would expect.

But how can I be sure? Andrew wondered. *How much farther do I need to push him in order to be confident he isn't faking? Four and a half days? Five? Longer? Can anyone survive that and remain sane?*

Andrew recalled his father telling him about one of the most dramatic interrogations in American espionage. During the 1960s, a Soviet defector came to Washington and told the CIA that he knew about numerous Soviet moles in the U.S. intelligence system. His accusations resulted in investigations that came close to immobilizing the Agency.

Soon afterward, a second Soviet defector came to Washington and accused the first defector of being a double agent sent by the Soviets to paralyze the Agency by making false accusations about moles within it. In turn, the first defector claimed that the second defector was the true double agent and had been sent to discredit him.

These conflicting accusations finally brought American intelligence operations to a standstill. To break the stasis, the second defector, who'd been promised money, a new identity and a consulting position with the Agency, was taken to a secret confinement facility where he was interrogated periodically for the next five years. Most of that time was spent in solitary confinement in a small cell with a narrow cot and a single light bulb in the ceiling. He was given nothing to read. He couldn't speak to anyone. He was allowed to bathe only once a week. Except for the passage of the seasons, he had no idea what day or week, month or year it was. He tried making a calendar, using threads from a blanket, but each time he completed one, his guards destroyed it. His boarded window prevented him from ever breathing fresh air. In summer, his room felt like a sweat box. For five hundred and sixty-two days of those five years, he was questioned intensely, sometimes around the clock. But despite his prolonged ordeal, he never recanted his accusation, nor did the first defector, even though their stories were mutually contradictory and one of them must have been lying. Nobody ever learned the truth.

Five years, Andrew thought. *Maybe I'm being too easy. Maybe I need more time.*

Suddenly wishing for the innocent era of sodium pentothal, he pressed another button and watched the prisoner scream.

It seemed the man would never stop.

THE GRANITE KITCHEN

My wife enjoys watching kitchen shows on television. One day, I was struck by the direct relationship between the chef and the viewer. It gave me an idea for a story about someone in a kitchen (not a chef) speaking directly to the reader, who's part of the story. My wife contributed the title, "The Granite Kitchen." Earlier I mentioned that in 1971 I sold my first story to Ellery Queen's Mystery Magazine. *In 2016, that magazine asked me to contribute this story to help celebrate its 75th anniversary. I felt honored to be invited to return to where I began.*

YOU LIKE THE GRANITE COUNTERTOP? THANK you. When people arrive for the open house, make sure you tell them how difficult it was to choose the right color. My husband Arthur, God rest his soul, told me, "Edith, if that's what you want, go to the design store and pick something." But I told him this was too big a decision to make on my own and in six months I didn't want him telling me he wished I'd chosen another color, so he went with me to the stores, more than once to a few of them, and we finally decided on something. But as I predicted, there were second thoughts—from me, I admit, not from him—the granite wasn't the right shade of grey—so I had it torn out and replaced with this.

The kitchen's the most important room in a house, don't you agree? That's the first thing people coming here today will want to see. It's what the new owners will face every morning when they wake up—yes, the bathroom certainly, if you don't mind me being indelicate—but the kitchen is what people really pay attention to in the morning, and if it isn't cheery and perfect, the rest of the day is downhill from there. Shiny and new and clean and promising.

Do you ever watch those home-remodeling shows on television? Yes, of course, you do. As a Realtor, you need to keep up with the market. What's your favorite part of those remodel shows? Exactly. The part where the designers and the new owners look at a kitchen and say, "What a dump! Look at those tired-looking appliances, and the colors are old-fashioned, and the island's in the wrong place. We need to tear it all out and start over." Isn't it wonderful when they pound a sledgehammer against an old countertop and tear down old cabinets and rip out an old stove, and what do they always find? Horrors like pipes that've rusted through and slimy water's dripping into spaces between the walls, or mice have chewed through insulation on electrical wires and if the old cabinets hadn't been torn out, the house might've caught on fire the next time somebody turned on a light switch.

But it's more than just finding the mold and the mouse droppings. It's about starting over. People want to feel like they're buying a *new* house even if it might be twenty years old. They want to believe they're making a brand-new fresh start. Who wants to put food into a refrigerator that somebody—maybe they had a terrible disease—kept their five-day-old milk in? Who wants to cook in an oven that, if you lean in and breathe deeply enough, still has the odor of a turkey that somebody cooked in there last month, even if the oven's been cleaned a half-dozen times since then?

My sister, God rest her soul, never understood. Ethel. That was her name. Edith and Ethel. My father thought it was cute. My mother's name was Edwina, and his name was Edward, and he loved it when he introduced us to strangers. "Hi, my name's Edward. This is my wife Edwina, and these are my daughters Edith and Ethel." My father always had a big grin to show how pleased he was with his cleverness. I used to cringe.

My father owned two dry-cleaning shops, the ones on Maple Lane and Crestview. When he came home from work, he always had that chemical smell that's in dry-cleaning shops. Not just on his clothes. I swear it was in his skin. When he hugged me, I always felt uncomfortable. A girl I used to play with came over to the house once and told me even the furniture had that chemical smell. Later she told me that she was sorry, that she just made that up to tease me. But the damage was done and I never played with her again, although even if I'd wanted to, there wasn't much chance because she fell from a slide at school and hit her head and had to be put in the facility over on Chestnut Lane.

But I was telling you about my sister. Ethel was always happy with what she had and if something broke, she'd just have it fixed, or if it wasn't broken, she'd find a way to update it. She had a doll my parents gave her, and at Christmas or her birthday, all she wanted was new clothes for it or a toy high chair for it or a tiny bed for it. Same old doll, just new things around it. The toy *I* liked, though, was a doll house that my parents gave me. It had an open back, and I could move furniture around inside it and rearrange the rooms on the two levels. Even then, the kitchen was what most interested me. As soon as I had it exactly the way I wanted, I asked for a newer, bigger doll house.

What? Yes, I suppose I'm still doing the same thing. It's sort of a hobby you could say, except that I get to live in the houses instead of peering into the back of them and reaching in to move furniture around. I'd use a kitchen knife, the kind with a serrated edge like a saw, to take down walls, and then I'd arrange them in a different pattern and glue them into place. Sometimes I'd add a new addition until eventually my parents had to give me a newer, bigger doll house. In a way, there's not much difference, except that it's a lot more expensive to tear out cabinets and rearrange appliances and pull down walls in a real house.

My husband used to complain that every time I had a house completely remodeled until it was exactly the way I wanted, I'd start looking at the real-estate listings in the Sunday newspaper. Of course, we couldn't afford a brand-new house, so I'd find a gem of a fixer-upper, and by the time I was finished, it'd be as good as new, and then I'd need to start another project. Arthur used to complain because the granite and the oak cabinets and the latest appliances and the marble floor cost too much for us to make a profit and if we averaged everything out, it would've made better financial sense to buy a brand-new house, even if the mortgage was bigger. Then we'd be done with all the improving, he told me. He didn't understand that improving is exactly the point. Starting over. Making everything better.

The previous house we owned, over on Beacon Drive, was Arthur's favorite. Did I mention he was an insurance salesman? Of course, he always insisted on being called a broker. Life insurance, house insurance, car insurance, boat insurance, health insurance, personal liability insurance—whatever kind of insurance you wanted, Arthur had a policy for it. You can't imagine how hard he worked to find clients. Friends and relatives, of course, my parents and my sister and anybody he went to school with, and he joined all kinds of fraternal organizations to look for clients, and the two golf clubs in town even though Arthur didn't know a nine iron from a putter. I'm learning about it, though. After he died, I finally decided that I had to do something besides sit around and feel gloomy. I needed to get out and meet people, try to see a bright side.

Thank you. Yes, it's been difficult. Arthur and I were married twenty years. We shared so many things. That's why I'm selling the house—too many memories. What happened to him? A terrible accident. I thought I heard water running in the basement. He went down to see if a pipe had burst. He tripped and broke his neck. I still have nightmares about finding him down there.

Children? No, Arthur and I were never blessed with children. Sometimes I think it was the stress he felt from working all the time. Who can understand these things? My sister had two children, a boy and a girl. Of course, those children only brought my sister pain. How? Well, they died in a car accident. Ethel's husband—he managed the supermarket over on the highway—was driving the family to a birthday party I was having, and a tire blew. Flipped the car three times before it landed upside down in a ditch. Ethel's husband and their two children died instantly, the medical examiner said. Ethel survived, but she always had a limp after that. When she recovered—a surgeon had to put a pin in her leg—she went back to teaching at the grade school on the east side, so in a way she still had children, but of course, it wasn't the same.

Enough gloom. Let's talk about the dishwasher. That model—top-of-the-line German manufacturer, as you can see—has been on the market for only three months. As people start to arrive, turn it on. After a while, as more people arrive and everyone's talking, let them know that the dishwasher's been working all the time and nobody could hear it. Tell them to lean down and put an ear against it. Even then, people will barely hear it. The same with the cooktop ventilation hood. Turn it on. Can you hear it? Of course not. It's so super-baffled, each minute it can suck twelve hundred cubic feet of food odor out of this kitchen and the only thing you notice is a pleasant breeze drifting toward the hood.

Look at how that granite countertop shines. I polish it every morning and every two weeks I put on a sealer that keeps bacteria from seeping in. The manufacturer says once a month is enough, but I don't think it's possible to be too careful. My parents died from food poisoning, you know. Worst case of salmonella the health department ever saw. From that new Chinese restaurant over on Fifth Street. Well, I guess it isn't new any longer. They had to go out of business after I sued them. My parents absolutely adored Chinese food. Spring rolls and won-ton soup and chicken fried rice and all that other stuff I can't stand. Maybe it's the soy sauce I don't like. It gives me a headache and makes my face red.

Anyway, my parents had invited me to dinner. My father sold the dry-cleaning places a couple of years ago, but I swear I could still smell the chemicals in the furniture. As soon as I saw that they'd brought in Chinese food, I told them I wasn't feeling hungry. I was surprised that they didn't remember how I felt about Chinese food, but I thought why ruin the evening, so I lied and told them I still felt full from a big lunch I'd had. I drank a cup of coffee and ate a piece of cherry pie when they had dessert. You can imagine how shocked I was when I phoned my mother the next morning and couldn't get an answer, and I couldn't get an answer that evening either, so I drove over and found them dead. I guess they were too weak to even pick up a phone and call for help. Terrible. I don't even want to think about how close I came to being polite and having some of those spring rolls.

The refrigerator used to be over there, and the oven was here. The layout is more convenient this way, don't you think?

You wouldn't believe how small this kitchen was. I had to move that wall to make the room large enough to accommodate everything, and then I had to move another wall so the pantry would be big enough. One thing always leads to another.

My sister lived in the same house that she lived in when she was first married. For Ethel, it was a big deal if her microwave broke down and she needed to buy another one, and it was always the cheapest model she could find. She could have afforded better after our parents died, although my father hadn't made as much on the dry-cleaning places as I thought and my husband turned out not to have been as good an insurance salesman as he led me to believe. It was an old policy and Arthur hadn't gotten around to persuading them to update it. A hundred thousand dollars doesn't go far, especially when it's split between Ethel and me, and to tell the truth, Arthur's own life insurance policy turned out to need upgrading. So did my sister's. I never thought of him as a lazy man, but I guess eventually you learn all sorts of things about people.

We had a lot of debts that Arthur didn't tell me about, and of course the mortgage. Over the years, Ethel—living in the same house—paid off her mortgage, and she didn't have anyone to spend her money on, so I asked if she'd loan me enough money for me to move from here and the gloomy memories of Arthur, but she told me she needed to be careful with her money because her limp was getting worse from arthritis and with the pain she might have to retire from teaching. She said she had to plan for old age and taking care of herself. I told her she could always count on me. She thanked me and said, "Something might happen to you, though, and then where would I be? Completely alone." "Don't worry. Nothing's going to happen to *me*," I told her. Every day's bright and new. It's important to have a positive attitude.

When people arrive, make sure you show them how that television set folds down from under that cabinet, and there's a fold-down computer dock from under this other cabinet. That coffee maker is better than the kind you see in those expensive coffee shops. I swear, if you put a bed in here, you wouldn't need to leave the kitchen, except for the bathroom of course, if you don't mind me being indelicate again.

Do you know what carbon monoxide is? Colorless and odorless? Yes. You don't realize you're breathing it, and all the while, it's stealing the oxygen out of your blood. The police finally decided it came from Ethel's furnace. She was so careful with a dollar. She should have bought a new furnace the way *I* did, or at least she could have paid the furnace company to come to the house and make sure it was safe before she turned it on for the cold weather, but that wasn't her way. She and I were so close, I don't know what I'll do without her.

A positive attitude. It's so important to be positive. Every day's a new start. Otherwise, how would we ever manage? Goodness, look at the time. The doorbell's ringing. I'll get out of your way. To stop from being nervous, I'm going to an open house over on Summit Ridge. I'll be back in two hours, and you can tell me how things went. But if people complain about the price I'm asking, just tell them to take a good look at this kitchen. Tell them about that tri-sensor, climate-controlled refrigerator and that under-counter microwave with a convection feature and that stovetop with a power burner under a glass ceramic surface and that double oven with a dual-flow fan system, a built-in temperature probe, halogen lighting, satin-glide racks, and a green porcelain enamel interior. Tell them how much effort it took to choose the color of that marble floor and that perfectly gorgeous granite counter top. Tell them that they won't find a kitchen this perfect anywhere else, that they're getting a bargain, that it all cost more than they can imagine.

THE SPIRITUALIST

After the imaginary version of J. D. Salinger in "The Architecture of Snow," here's a story about another famous author: Sir Arthur Conan Doyle. It's an offshoot of the research I did for my Victorian mysteries, Murder As a Fine Art, Inspector of the Dead, and Ruler of the Night, which feature Thomas De Quincey, one of the most fascinating and brilliant literary figures of the 1800s. De Quincey's "Postscript to 'On Murder Considered As One of the Fine Arts'" helped establish the popularity of sensation literature (what we call thrillers). He influenced Edgar Allan Poe, who in turn inspired Conan Doyle to create Sherlock Holmes, so it was natural for my fascination with De Quincey to transfer to Conan Doyle, giving me the chance to write more historical fiction. As with my De Quincey novels, most of "The Spiritualist" is true. In this detective story, Sherlock Holmes solves the mystery of Sir Arthur Conan Doyle.

A GAIN, THE NIGHTMARE WOKE HIM. AGAIN, he couldn't go back to sleep.

As the bells of nearby Westminster Abbey sounded two o'clock, Conan Doyle rose from his bed. Always determined not to waste time, he considered going to the desk in his sitting room to write a few more thousand words, but instead his troubled mood prompted him to dress and go down the stairs. Careful not to wake his housekeeper, he unlocked the door and stepped outside.

A cold mist enveloped shadowy Victoria Street in the heart of metropolitan London. During the day, the rumble and rattle of motor vehicles reverberated off the area's three-story buildings, but at this solitary hour, the only sound was the echo of Conan Doyle's shoes as he reached the pavement and turned to the left, proceeding past dark shops.

Even in the night and the mist, the back of Westminster Abbey dominated, its hulking presence rising over him. He recalled his sense of irony a year earlier when he'd finally found a suitable location for the most important enterprise of his life, noting that it was only a stone's throw from one of England's most revered religious sites. He hadn't spoken with His Grace about their competing views, but he suspected that the archbishop wasn't amused.

A hazy streetlamp revealed the sign above the door: PSYCHIC BOOK SHOP, LIBRARY & MUSEUM. Because a sense of urgency always propelled him, Conan Doyle stretched his long legs to walk the short distance, but of late, those legs—once so strong in rugby, soccer, and cricket—had betrayed him, as had his once-powerful chest, making him pause to catch his breath before he unlocked the door and entered.

A bell rang. During the day, its jangle was welcome, announcing that a rare visitor had arrived, but at night, the bell violated the stillness. Gas lamps would have provided an appropriate moody atmosphere. This was 1926, however. Instead of striking a match and opening a valve, Conan Doyle reached to his left and turned an electrical switch. Two bulbs on each wall provided instant illumination, as did dangling globes in the ceiling.

The yellow lights revealed numerous rows of bookshelves, the smell of old and new pages pleasantly filling his nostrils.

He knew their titles without needing to see them: among them, *Letters on Animal Magnetism*, *Footfalls on the Boundary of Another World*, *The Spirit Manifestations*, *Experiments in Thought Transference*, *Phantasms of the Living*, *Minutes of the Society for Psychical Research*, *Survival of Bodily Death*, and—

Brittle rapping startled him. Turning sharply, he saw a constable frowning through a window.

Conan Doyle opened the door.

"Unusual to see you at this late an hour, Sir Arthur." The constable peered into the shop, straining to see its back corners. "Is everything all right?"

"Perfectly. I couldn't sleep, so I decided to come here and catch up on some work." It had been more than four decades since Conan Doyle left Edinburgh, and yet his Scottish burr remained thick.

"You're certain nothing's wrong?" the constable persisted.

"Absolutely. Thank you for your concern."

The constable gave him a troubled nod, seeming baffled about why one of the most revered authors in Great Britain was wasting his time in this strange shop and why he now lived in a small flat just down the street rather than at one of his large country houses.

Only when Conan Doyle closed and locked the door did the constable continue along the misty street, his footsteps receding.

Stillness again enveloped the shop.

Of course, everything was definitely *not* all right, but what troubled Conan Doyle wasn't anything that a constable could correct.

He faced the first display that patrons saw when they entered—not that the shop enjoyed many patrons. Conan Doyle's name was featured prominently above titles that he'd spent much of the past ten years writing but that hardly anyone wanted to read: *The Wanderings of a Spiritualist, The Coming of the Faeries, The Case for Spirit Photography, The New Revelation, The Vital Message,* and *The History of Spiritualism.*

No preposterous fictions here. No supercilious Sherlock Holmes, who solved improbable mysteries about homicidal hounds and trained serpents. No fawning Watson, who was so befuddled that he should never have been allowed to acquire a medical degree. To the contrary, these particular books contained the truth, and yet the world didn't care. Visitors didn't even need to *buy* these books. They could borrow them. It didn't help. Nor did Conan Doyle's exhausting lecture tour throughout the United Kingdom and around the world—to the United States, Canada, France, Germany, South Africa, Australia, and New Zealand. People came to hear him only because they wanted to know why a man whose name was associated with Sherlock Holmes couldn't stop talking about ghosts and faeries.

The floor creaked as Conan Doyle walked toward the rear of the shop. His shoulders were so broad that he needed to shift sideways between rows of bookshelves. He came to murky stairs, their wood protesting as he descended toward the dark basement.

At the bottom, a damp chill greeted him. Emerging from an archway, he turned an electrical switch on a wall. Overhead lights chased the long room's shadows, their glow reflecting off glass cases and framed photographs, creating an otherworldly effect. Some visitors, no matter how skeptical, might have felt uneasy and even fearful about coming down here in the middle of the night, but Conan Doyle felt comforted by the truth before him.

After all, here were photographs of actual ghosts and faeries. Here were the wax gloves of a spirit's hands. Here were a Syrian vase, a Babylonian clay tablet, and a pile of Turkish pennies that had materialized on a séance table. Here were intricate drawings of flowers that someone under the influence of a spirit had impossibly created within seventeen seconds. Here was a brilliant seascape that a woman without any artistic training had painted while under a spirit's influence. Here were pages of automatic writing that mediums had scribbled, responding to questions that loved ones asked and that only the departed could answer correctly.

How can anyone see these proofs, and not be convinced that the dead are capable of communicating with us? Conan Doyle wondered in despair. *I need to try harder, to write more books about the afterlife, to travel to more cities and countries and give more lectures.*

Seeking reassurance, he turned toward a photograph of three faeries next to a waterfall. He was reminded of a painting that his father had—

A creak of footsteps on the stairs surprised him. Had the constable returned to make certain that nothing was amiss? But how would that be possible? The front door was locked. Had someone broken into the shop? To what purpose? If hardly anyone bought or even borrowed the shop's books, why would somebody go to the effort of stealing them as opposed to burglarizing the valuable contents of the garment shop next door?

"Who's there?" he called.

The creak on the wooden stairs became louder as the footsteps neared the bottom.

"Mary, is that you?"

Conan Doyle's daughter—from his first marriage—managed the shop. Perhaps she'd come here in the middle of the night to attend to a pressing detail she'd suddenly remembered.

But in that case, wouldn't she have called out as he himself had, demanding to know who was in the shop?

Conan Doyle stepped backward when a shadow appeared at the bottom of the stairs. The shadow didn't belong to Mary but instead to a tall, thin man emerging from the murky archway.

The man wore an Inverness cape, the gray color of which matched the figure's intense eyes. He was perhaps thirty-five, with an ascetic face, a narrow chin, a slender nose, high cheekbones, and an intelligent forehead that was partially covered by a deerstalker hat.

The basement became damper and colder.

"My dear fellow, you're as pale as if you've seen a ghost," Sherlock Holmes said.

Conan Doyle felt a tight pain in his chest. "If you were indeed a ghost, I'd rejoice."

Holmes surveyed the photographs of faeries, the wax gloves of a spirit, and the pages of automatic writing. "Then look joyous. You murdered me, and yet here I am: proof of what you're looking for."

"Proof?"

"Of life after death."

"I'm still asleep. I never woke from my nightmare. Those fools who send me letters asking for your autograph might think you're real, but—"

"Then how can I be standing here, talking to you? Why are you responding to me?"

"I didn't murder you."

"Perhaps you prefer a more delicate word such as 'killed'."

"You never died. When you and Moriarty grappled on the ledge, it was only he who plummeted into the Reichenbach Falls."

"But you didn't believe that at the time," Holmes corrected him. "When you wrote 'The Final Problem,' you truly intended to get rid of me. You even bragged to your mother that you'd seen the last of me, even though your mother begged you not to do it."

"You'd become a burden," Conan Doyle protested. "Readers wouldn't let me write about anyone else."

"Ha. You earned a fortune from writing stories about me, and that's a burden? Tell that to my Baker Street Irregulars when those little beggars are desperate for their next meal. Then eight years later, when you needed more money, you suddenly decided I wasn't a burden after all. So you wrote another novel about me, but even then I remained dead, because you had my hound adventure occur years before you killed me. Then a magazine offered you even *more* money to write a story that showed I hadn't actually died at the Reichenbach Falls, so you invented that nonsense about Moriarty falling alone while I escaped to Tibet. Tibet? Is that the best you could think of? Obviously you lacked conviction. You can't fool readers, though. They sensed that something was amiss, that it wasn't really I in those later stories, only someone to whom you gave my name. Certainly I'm not an aged beekeeper. As you can see, I'm still in my thirties. Ghosts don't age."

"Take off that blasted deerstalker hat."

"Readers prefer it."

"I didn't include it in any of my stories about you."

"But Sidney Paget had the inspiration to put it in one of his illustrations of me. Now readers imagine it when they read about me. It's as real as if you'd written it. But if it troubles you..."

Holmes removed the deerstalker hat. Now that his forehead was fully exposed, it seemed even more intelligent, his receding hairline emphasizing the height of his brow.

He set the hat on a counter next to a photograph of wispy light in a dark room.

"Ectoplasm?" Holmes asked, referring to a placard in front of the photograph.

"The strongest evidence so far."

"There are various types of evidence. I see that you walked in Hyde Park today, that you're unusually troubled, and that you have limited domestic help," Holmes said.

"Yes, yes. I'm not impressed by your parlor tricks. Remember, I invented them. There are spots of mud on my shoes and my trouser cuffs. The mud has a reddish color that's typical of sections of Hyde Park. The mud would have been removed if I had sufficient domestic help, but at the moment, I have only the assistance of a single housekeeper: Mrs. Hudson."

"Mrs. Hudson is *my* housekeeper," Holmes reminded him.

"A slip of the tongue. Mrs. *Murray*. My housekeeper is named Mrs. Murray."

"Of course. Soon you'll have as addled a memory as you gave to dear old Watson. He can't keep dates or names consistent from one story to the next. He can't even keep straight how many wives he had. Two? Five? I confess that even with my superior powers of deduction, I'm unable to determine the exact number, although it's probably two because you yourself had two. And with regard to my 'parlor tricks,' as you call them, *you* didn't invent them. You learned them from Dr. Bell at the University of Edinburgh medical school. By the way, you didn't ask me how I knew that you were unusually troubled."

"Obviously because I'm here in the middle of the night."

"I'd have known you were troubled even if we were speaking on Victoria Street at noon. You have a mark on your lower lip, where you've been chewing it."

Conan Doyle raised a hand to his lip, suddenly aware of how tender it felt. "Please leave me alone. Go away and solve a mystery."

"Solving a mystery is precisely what I'm doing."

"I don't understand."

"You, my dear fellow," Holmes said. "*You're* the mystery. This business about ghosts and faeries. People worry that you're delusional."

Conan Doyle stepped forward, clenching his fists. "Never say that to me."

"My apologies. Kindly relax your hands. Although you were once a pugilist, that was many years ago, and if you couldn't walk the short distance to this shop without feeling out of breath, I doubt that an altercation between us would have a successful conclusion for you, especially because I'm an expert in boxing, Baritsu, and singlestick fighting. To change the subject, do you recall that Watson climbed the steps at 221 B Baker Street many times before I asked him how many steps there were? He couldn't answer the question. Together, he and I climbed the steps while we counted to seventeen. I told Watson, 'You see, but you do not observe.' That's an interesting comment, given that your specialty as a physician involves diseases of the eyes."

"I fail to see the relevance."

Holmes pointed toward the photograph of the faeries at the waterfall. "That photograph was produced by combining two images in what is called a double exposure."

"Prove it," Conan Doyle demanded.

"I cannot unless I have the original two images so that I can demonstrate how the illusion was created."

"Then you don't know for certain. The photograph of ectoplasm that you ridiculed—"

"I did no such thing. I merely implied doubt. Were you at the séance where the ectoplasm appeared?"

"I was."

"Did you see the ectoplasm?"

"I did not. But the medium did and told my photographer to press the shutter on his camera."

"After the plate was removed from the camera and developed, this image appeared?" Holmes asked, pointing.

"Yes."

"Your friend Houdini would perhaps—"

"Mr. Houdini is no longer a friend. He insulted my wife."

"—would perhaps suggest that the medium had prepared a photographic plate beforehand and substituted it for the plate that was in the camera."

"But *our* plate was marked," Conan Doyle emphasized.

"Perhaps an assistant to the medium had the opportunity to examine the photographic plate prior to the séance and apply an identical mark on the plate that was eventually substituted."

"'Perhaps' is not proof."

"Indeed." Holmes reached into a pocket and removed a large, curved pipe.

"I didn't give you a calabash pipe, either," Conan Doyle said disapprovingly.

"But the great actor, William Gillette, used it as a prop when he portrayed me on stage. It looks more dramatic than an ordinary straight pipe. Illustrators took to including it in their depictions of me. Now people imagine it whenever they think of me. It's as real as the deerstalker hat."

Holmes tamped shag tobacco into the bowl of the calabash.

"Do you absolutely need to? There's no ventilation down here," Conan Doyle objected.

"The smoke will cover the odor of the mildew." Holmes prepared to strike a match.

"Stop. These exhibits are delicate. The smoke will damage them."

Holmes sighed. "Very well. But I suspect that the spirits wouldn't mind the aroma. They're probably desperate for a puff now and then."

"That isn't humorous."

"No humor intended. Convince me, my dear fellow. Why did you suddenly believe that there are spirits in an afterlife— spirits who can communicate with us?"

"I don't expect that a man who's obsessed with the surface of things will understand, but my belief wasn't sudden at all. When I set up my medical practice in Southsea, near Portsmouth—"

"Southsea. Aptly named. Almost as far from Edinburgh as it's possible to go and still remain in Great Britain," Holmes noted.

"And your point is?"

"Just an observation. Please continue." Holmes gestured with the unlit pipe. "When you set up your medical practice in Southsea…"

"I had a friend there: Henry Ball. Southsea was a Bohemian community that enjoyed discussing new ideas. Mediums and séances were a popular topic. Henry and I participated in several attempts to contact the other world—table rapping, automatic writing, and so forth. We decided that since thought transference was essential to communicating with the dead, we'd conduct an experiment. He and I sat back-to-back, with pencils and notepads in our hands. He'd draw something on his pad and concentrate on it. Then I'd try to imagine what he was thinking and draw it. Neither of us had any artist's skill. What we drew were stick figures and geometric shapes. Amazingly I often reproduced what was on Henry's pad, and Henry did the same with regard to shapes that *I* had drawn."

"Fascinating," Holmes said. "In what year did you conduct these experiments?"

"Eighteen eighty-six."

"When you started to write your first novel about me: *A Study in Scarlet*."

"As a matter of fact, now that I think of it, yes."

"A creative period for you. And what was your marital status at the time?"

"I married my first wife the year before, in eighteen eighty-five." Memories of Louise, of that long-ago innocent time—his fond nickname for her had been Touie—made him pause. He shook his head. "Where are you going with this?"

"I'm merely looking for context." Holmes shrugged and sat in a chair next to a photograph of a ghost's head floating above a man in a doorway. "Kindly continue."

"Because of the successful experiments that Henry and I conducted, we were motivated to go to more séances. What made the difference for me was an evening when a medium spoke in several voices and then wrote frantically on a notepad, referring to me as a healer. But I hadn't been introduced as a physician, so the medium couldn't have known that. Then the medium astonished me by writing a note in which the spirit told me not to read Leigh Hunt's book."

"Why was that astonishing?" Holmes eased back in the chair, crossing his long legs.

"I had a book by Leigh Hunt next to my bed! I was just about to start reading it. How could the medium have possibly known this?"

"Perhaps..."

"Perhaps what? Say what you're thinking."

"When you arrived for the séance, did the medium's assistant ask you and your friend to wait in an anteroom?"

"That's the customary procedure."

"Perhaps the medium stood on the other side of a wall and listened to your conversation, learning personal details, repeating them later, claiming to receive this information from a spirit. Did you have any religious convictions that prepared you for your belief in a spirit world?"

"Not at all. I was raised as a Roman Catholic. When I was nine, I was sent to a Jesuit preparatory school and then a Jesuit college. All told, I spent eight years in those schools, but the only afterlife I hoped for was one in which the priests would stop beating me. No, nothing prepared me for my interest in the spirits."

"Nine is an early age for your parents to have sent you away."

"My family life was..."

"Yes?"

"It isn't relevant," Conan Doyle said. "My belief in the attempts of spirits to reach us was reinforced in eighteen ninety. I remember vividly that the month was November. I read an item in the *British Medical Journal* about a conference that was about to convene in Berlin. The subject of the conference was new ways to treat tuberculosis."

Holmes gestured, encouraging him to proceed.

"I can't explain the urgency that suddenly compelled me," Conan Doyle said. "All at once, I knew that it was essential for me to go to that conference. I packed a bag and immediately departed for Germany."

"Leaving your wife and your almost two-year-old daughter," Holmes noted.

"That's why my urgency is so difficult to explain," Conan Doyle emphasized. "I had every reason to remain with my family. Earlier that year, I'd studied ophthalmology in Vienna. Then I'd moved my family to London, and suddenly I felt a desperate need to travel yet again, to go to Germany to attend a conference about a disease that wasn't even related to my specialty. My abrupt journey didn't make sense. But I soon understand why I'd felt the urgency."

"Now I'm the one who fails to see the relevance," Holmes said.

"Tuberculosis. Three years later, my first wife was diagnosed with the disease. Isn't it obvious? The spirits compelled me to learn what I could about the latest in treatments. They knew I would soon need that vital information when my wife displayed her terrible symptoms."

"But there might be another explanation," Holmes suggested.

"And what would *that* be?" Conan Doyle asked impatiently.

"You're a physician. Perhaps you subconsciously sensed the early indications of your wife's disease."

"There *weren't* any early indications—none whatsoever! My wife thought nothing of joining me on thirty-mile daily bicycle rides. Her lungs were strong. But then, three years later, in eighteen ninety-three, she became ill."

"Eighteen ninety-three, "Holmes said. "Didn't your father die that year?"

"It was a difficult time."

"He was in a mental institution near Edinburgh, I believe."

"I prefer not to discuss my father's illness."

"Alcohol addiction," Holmes said. "I gather that on one occasion, when he couldn't obtain gin or wine or beer, he drank furniture varnish. He sold his clothing in order to buy alcohol. The bed linen. His sketches. Children's toys. Anything. Please, remind me of what your father sketched."

Conan Doyle stood straighter. "I told you I prefer not to discuss my father's illness."

"Were you able to journey to Edinburgh and attend his funeral?"

"Unfortunately, my wife's tuberculosis prevented me."

"And while all this was happening in eighteen ninety-three," Holmes said, "you killed me."

"I didn't kill you! Only Moriarty plunged into the falls! How many times must I explain it?"

"As far as you were concerned, I was dead. Whoever that imposter is in the later stories, it isn't me. But let's move on. It wasn't until fifteen years later, in nineteen eighteen, that you published *The New Revelation* and your readers finally learned about your belief in spiritualism. They were surprised that you'd shifted from an interest in science to mysticism."

"There's nothing mystical about it," Conan Doyle protested. "Twenty years ago, people would have mocked me if I'd said that voices could travel great distances through the air, and yet Marconi's radio accomplished what until recently would have been thought a supernatural occurrence. Science will eventually prove that an afterworld exists just as certainly as *this* world exists."

"Your first spiritualist book coincided with the end of the war."

"Yes, the blasted war." Conan Doyle looked down at the stone floor. "I imagined that the conflict would be noble, that a cleaner, better, stronger nation would come out of it. How wrong I was." His voice faltered. "How far the war was from anything that was noble. So many died, and so brutally. I wasn't prepared."

"One of the dead was your son, Kingsley. Please accept my sympathy," Holmes said.

"He was the second child that Touie and I had," Conan Doyle managed to say. "By then, my relationship with Kingsley wasn't the best. He went to war to defend our nation, of course, but I suspect that he also took risks to prove himself to me. He was wounded at the battle of the Somme. He seemed to be recovering, but then the Spanish Influenza took him down. And my brother, Innis, died in the war. And my brother-in-law, Malcolm. And another brother-in-law..." He didn't have the strength to say the name. "And two nephews. And... So many of them gone. Surely it couldn't be forever. Surely their souls hadn't merely ceased to exist. At séances, my son contacted me, assuring me that he was contented and that he'd met my brother over there and..."

Again, Conan Doyle's voice dropped.

"Perhaps that's when your true conversion to spiritualism occurred, not many years earlier," Holmes suggested. "Could your intense grief have made you want to believe desperately that your son and your brother and all the others weren't truly dead?"

"It was more than my emotions playing tricks on me." Conan Doyle pointed angrily. "Do you see those wax gloves of a spirit's hands?"

"Indeed."

"Prior to a séance, an associate and I prepared a container of heated wax. A dim red light allowed us to see the medium lapse into a trance. Suddenly a spirit's hands plunged into the heated wax. As suddenly, when the hands emerged, they disappeared, leaving these wax gloves on the table. Look at the cuffs on the gloves. They're the size of a man's wrists. If the hands were those of an ordinary person, the gloves couldn't have been removed without being damaged. The only way these gloves could have survived in the perfect way that you see them is if the hands became disembodied."

"Master illusionist that he is, Houdini would perhaps—"

"Don't mention his name."

"—suggest the following. The hands that plunged into the heated wax were those of the medium's assistant. The assistant withdrew his wax-covered hands into the darkness beyond the pale red light, leaving wax gloves that had been prepared in advance."

"You sound exactly like Houdini. But I anticipated his usual smug objection. The gloves couldn't have been prepared in advance. I put an identifying chemical into the wax, and the wax of these gloves contains the same chemical."

"When did you obtain the chemical?"

"The day before the séance."

"If *I* had been the medium's assistant, I'd have observed your activities for a few days before the séance. When you went to the shop to buy the chemical, I'd have followed. When you left the shop, I'd have entered the shop and found a pretense to persuade the shopkeeper to tell me what you'd purchased."

Conan Doyle stared at him. "But you don't know for certain that such a thing happened."

"That is correct."

"Then you haven't disproved the validity of these wax gloves, any more than you disproved the validity of these photographs."

"Granted. Earlier, you said that Houdini insulted your wife."

"My second wife, Jean, is herself a medium. She receives messages from an Oriental spirit named Pheneas. These visitations began five years ago. With her deep honesty, Jean at first resisted the impulses, wondering if perhaps she subconsciously self-willed them. But eventually, through her inspired automatic writing and through a process in which she lapsed into a trance, Jean and I became convinced that the visitations were authentic. Through Pheneas, we received messages from my mother and my brother and our son and all our other dear departed loved ones."

"I gather that Houdini is skeptical about your wife's ability," Holmes said.

"If the wretch had expressed his doubts to me personally, I would have perhaps made allowances! But instead he did it publicly, telling American newspapers—the newspapers, mind you—that my wife's...that she's...a *fake!* Equally unforgiveable, he accused *me* of thinking I was a Messiah come to save mankind through the mysteries of spiritualism. He claimed that I misled the public with teachings that are, to use his words, 'a menace to sanity and health.' I never spoke to him again."

"Understandably," Holmes said.

"Pheneas has been immensely helpful. He warned me that if Jean and I went on a proposed trip to Scandinavia last year, the consequences would have been dire, perhaps a horrible accident. But through Jean, Pheneas approved of a resort in Switzerland for the same vacation. Pheneas also approved of the new country house that I bought for Jean to stay in while I'm here in London, doing what I can to attract people to this shop."

"You mentioned that your mother, brother, son and other dear departed loved ones visited you through Pheneas. Did that include your first wife?"

"No."

"Doesn't that seem strange?"

"Touie didn't approve of my interest in spiritualism."

"But now your first wife would know that you're right. She ought to be happy to tell you so. What about your father? Was *he* one of the loved ones who visited you from the afterlife?"

"No."

"Doesn't *that* strike you as odd? At one time, didn't your father say that he received messages from the unseen world?"

Conan Doyle didn't reply.

"The sketches that your father drew. What was their subject?" Holmes asked.

"What are you up to?"

"I'm merely attempting to solve a mystery. What was the subject of your father's sketches?"

They regarded each other, neither of them speaking for at least a minute.

"Faeries," Conan Doyle finally said.

"Faeries and phantoms. One of your father's drawings is a self-portrait in which demons swirl around him."

"Alcohol made my father insane. He sketched what his poisoned mind caused him to see."

"Or perhaps..."

"Every time you say 'perhaps'..."

"Perhaps your father actually did see faeries, demons, and phantoms, so horrifying that he used alcohol to try to stop the visions. Perhaps alcohol didn't cause the visions. It might have been the other way around. Could your father's visions have caused his need for alcohol?"

"But that would mean..." Abrupt understanding made Conan Doyle stop.

"I'm only considering every possibility," Holmes explained.

"I want you to leave."

"We haven't finished our conversation."

"Leave. Now. If you don't respect my wishes, we might indeed have the physical altercation that almost happened earlier."

Holmes considered him and nodded. "Very well. The mystery might be better solved by you instead of me. But the clues are all before you."

Holmes stood, put on the deerstalker cap, and walked toward the archway.

"Good night, Sir Arthur."

He climbed the stairs, his tall thin figure disappearing, the creak of his footsteps becoming fainter.

Silence settled over the museum.

Conan Doyle stared toward the shadowy stairs for a long time. At last he turned toward the photograph of the three faeries next to a waterfall. When he'd last looked at it, he'd been reminded of a sketch that his father had drawn in which faeries lay among blades of grass in a field.

Somehow that recollection had made him imagine that Sherlock Holmes had visited him. The intense chill Conan Doyle felt told him that he was in fact here in this basement and not in his bed still enduring a nightmare.

The power of imagination never failed to astonish him: wide-awake trances possessing him, prompting him to envision a lost world of dinosaurs, the White Company of the Hundred-Years War, and...

Sherlock Holmes.

"The clues are all before you," Holmes had told him.

Or rather, something in my mind made me imagine that he told me, Conan Doyle thought.

Although he would never have admitted it, his characters often spoke to him. It didn't seem strange to him, but he knew what others would think if he admitted he heard voices. His father had heard voices. "Voices from the unseen world," his father had told people.

And look where his father had ended.

"Perhaps your father actually did see faeries and demons," Holmes had suggested. "Could your father's visions have caused his need for alcohol?"

"But that would mean..." Conan Doyle hadn't dared to finish his thought.

What would *it mean?* he asked himself. *That my father was insane? Did my father consume massive quantities of alcohol to drown the faeries and demons he saw?*

Conan Doyle leaned close to the photograph of the faeries. Holmes had said that the photograph consisted of two images combined in a double exposure. It wasn't the first time Conan Doyle had heard that criticism. Skeptics were quick to offer objections that they couldn't prove.

"You see, but you do not observe," Holmes had said.

Conan Doyle peered even closer toward the photograph. Was there possibly a blur around the fairies? Did they resemble children made to look extremely small?

But if that photograph was fraudulent, then he would need to consider that the photograph of the ghost hovering above the man in the doorway was fraudulent also, and then he would need to consider that the Syrian vase, the Babylonian clay tablet, and the pile of Turkish pennies that had dropped onto a séance table were fraudulent—and the pages of automatic writing, and the ornate drawing of flowers that a medium had somehow completed in seventeen seconds. Certainly Holmes had implied that the wax gloves of a spirit and the photograph of ectoplasm weren't authentic.

But Holmes hadn't been here to imply anything, Conan Doyle forcefully reminded himself. No one had actually been in this basement, sitting in that chair. To believe differently would truly be a sign of madness.

And yet...

Why did Holmes emphasize that Southsea, near Portsmouth, is almost as far from Edinburgh as it's possible to go and still remain in Great Britain? Was he suggesting that I felt compelled to put as much distance between my father and myself as I could?

Why did Holmes seem to think it significant that I didn't go to my father's funeral? My father died the same year I killed Holmes. Was he implying that by killing Holmes I was somehow finally ridding myself of my father and my fear that I shared his...?

Stop thinking this way, Conan Doyle warned himself.

But he couldn't stop the voice inside his head.

Did Holmes nod with suspicion when I described all the traveling I did after I was married the first time? Did he seem to think that I suddenly traveled to Germany not because of the tuberculosis conference but because I wanted to get away from my wife and two-year-old child?

Did he seem to nod with greater suspicion when I described how my second wife was a medium who received messages from the spirit Pheneas about where we should take vacations and whether I should buy another country house for her?

Conan Doyle picked up the framed photograph of the faeries by the waterfall. He made his way to the chair that Holmes had occupied. It troubled him that the cushion felt warm, as though someone had sat in it recently.

He studied the faeries, so innocent, so free of cares.

Did Holmes intend him to conclude that Jean wasn't a medium at all and that she'd taken advantage of his beliefs in order to guide his actions?

Madness, Conan Doyle told himself. *Stop thinking this way. If I believed that Jean was fraudulent, then I'd need to believe that everything in this room was fraudulent, that my* life *was fraudulent.*

He clutched the photograph of the faeries and stared as hard at it as he'd ever stared at anything. He desperately tried to will himself to enter the photograph, to stand with the faeries next to the waterfall whose chill resembled that of this basement. He had a sudden vision that the basement was a crypt and that Holmes was in it, tearing coffins apart, hurling bones into a corner. Bones. Perhaps that's all his dead son and his first wife and his brother and his brother-in-law and his nephews and his mother...and his father...had become and nothing else. No. He couldn't believe it.

That would be the true madness.

VASTATION

Let's remain in a literary mood and consider a story about Henry James, one of my favorite authors. His work taught me more about writing fiction than that of any other author, except Ernest Hemingway, James M. Cain, and Geoffrey Household. James pioneered the third-person-limited viewpoint in The Ambassadors *(1903). Long before Gillian Flynn's* Gone Girl *(2012) established a trend, James's classic ghost novel,* The Turn of the Screw *(1898, 1908) gave us the unreliable first-person narrator.*

James sometimes acted like a character in one of his horror stories. For example, he had a pet praying mantis that he walked on a leash made of string; when he accidentally stepped on the insect, squashing it, he vomited on his lawn. His eerie stories can be contagious, prompting some of his fans to step into surreal James-land. What are we to make of the biographer who absorbed himself so deeply in James's life that he acquired James's furniture and wore James's clothes, not to mention his watch chain and ornate ring? That biographer's numerous volumes about James's life, to which the scholar devoted most of his own life, became stalled when he discovered letters that suggested James was a homosexual. But the biographer had dismissed that possibility throughout his many years of research. To consider this new view of James would have meant that he needed to revise everything he'd written. The biographer developed a serious case of writer's block and finally went to a psychiatrist, who cured his block by convincing him to doubt the validity of the new evidence. The analyst was female. Possibly suspecting that this wouldn't be the last of his writing crises, the biographer married her.

O F LATE HE'D FELT—HE PAUSED TO select the proper words—not quite himself. He felt indifferent, not to the letters and notebooks, stories and novels: they were his life, after all, his Master's voice. But everything else, the mundane chores of life, depressed him. Classes he had to prepare and teach, exams to grade, meetings to attend, people to converse with—he felt no identity with them, as if his alterego wandered through the fog of ordinary existence while his true self read before a fireplace, absorbed in the house of James's fiction.

His own house had been chosen because it closely resembled Lamb House, James's country home at Rye in Sussex, redbricked with a high old Georgian doorway, a tall brick garden wall, and an ancient cobblestoned lane in front. He'd remodeled its interior to match the photographs of James's drawing room and study. He'd lined the walls with photographs of James, with sketches and paintings of him, especially those by John Singer Sargent, and even the cruel caricature that showed James chained to his desk, writing furiously. He'd purchased James's tea set, his watch chain, and his dinner jacket. His finest acquisition was the diamond ring that James had worn for Sargent's famous portrait of him. Such devotion drained his bank account, but since, like James, he'd never married, there was no one who could object. He didn't miss companionship. He had the Master's work to occupy him, shelves and shelves of it, the best, the most refined of thought and taste. As well he had his own work, his vast monument to James, begun when, as a long-ago student at Oxford, he'd enjoyed his initial exposure to James's work: *The Portrait of a Lady*. Fondly, he remembered his first of countless readings of it. And "The Aspern Papers" and *The Spoils of Poynton*. With each book he closed, he'd quickly opened another. He had never questioned who would be the subject of his graduation thesis. But its fifty pages hadn't seemed sufficient. He'd felt the need to learn more, so much more, to read and reread, then to publish his discoveries so that the world could share his wonder.

But three hundred pages hadn't been sufficient either. His first volume stretched to two. His subsequent discoveries soon produced a *third* volume, a fourth. The Master's genius seemed bottomless, his insights and his awareness. Now five volumes prompted him to write a sixth. At fifty-two, he hoped for many fruitful years to come when, sitting at James's writing desk, he would eventually complete the longest, most definitive biography of any writer, so infused with facts, so documented it would stand forever as a testament to James's brilliance.

He'd immersed himself. Although most of James's friends were dead, a few acquaintances in youth had seen the Master in old age. He'd sought them out and stimulated their remembrance. He'd tracked down the children of the now-dead friends who'd known James throughout his life. A hint from one, a clue from another. He connected this new information with fresh revelations from unpublished diaries and letters entrusted to him by—and sometimes bullied from—his interview subjects.

Like James, he'd accumulated weight from years of sitting. He'd grown a beard to complete the resemblance. Wearing James's clothes, his watch chain, and his ring, surrounded by his trove of objects that James had touched, he felt totally content. He almost felt the Master's spirit.

What happened next seemed inevitable. James's father had recorded the experience; so had James's brother, William. *A vastation.* James's father had sat alone in a kitchen, digesting before the pale coals of a fire, when he'd sensed an invisible presence in the shadowy corner of the room. The experience had filled him with dread, just as James's brother had been horror-stricken when he encountered a similar presence in the murky confines of a dressing room. When James's father had turned to the philosophy of Emmanuel Swedenborg for an explanation, he had learned that this distressing mystical phenomenon was called a *vastation,* an awareness of the spirits hovering unseen around us.

Given his ever-deepening research, he wasn't surprised, then, when he had his own *vastation.* A week ago, near midnight, with the drapes closed and the only light provided by a desk lamp barely dissipating the shadows, he'd sensed a presence, had felt it thickening behind him. Alarmed, he'd swung around in time to see its afterimage, the vague form of a figure vanishing like a black hole squeezing inward. He'd gaped. Instead of trembling, he'd become rigid, dizzy until he realized he wasn't breathing. Gulping air in a panic, sweating coldly, he'd stared at the gloomy corner between dark curtains and a bookshelf. Was he mistaken, or had the curtains moved as if touched? Standing weakly, he'd gone to the corner. He'd shivered and blamed his imagination. There'd been nothing. But unsettled, he hadn't been able to continue writing.

The next night, the same thing had happened. He feared for his sanity, yet swore that he saw the figure: indistinct, insubstantial, but unmistakably there. It vanished as soon as he became aware of it and turned. Desperate for an explanation, at last he'd remembered the *vastation* that James's father and brother had experienced. It's only the power of suggestion, he'd told himself. You've been writing about James's relatives. Now you imagine you've seen what *they* saw. You've been working too hard.

But the next night was the same, and every night thereafter, the presence hovering in the corner. He'd grown accustomed to it. Indeed he'd now decided it wasn't the power of suggestion but an actual *vastation*. As he wrote about James, he felt more in tune with him, privileged, on a higher level of awareness as if visited by James himself. His fear became contentment.

But tonight contentment turned to dread. As he worked at James's desk, he felt the figure loom behind him, stronger, darker. He refused to look, determined not to break the spell. He stared at a newly discovered letter he'd been analyzing— from James to one of his male friends. It offered rare, unambiguous evidence of James's homosexuality. *That I might kiss your...*

At once he felt the shadow move from its corner, drifting toward him, inching closer. As he tensed, he felt it rise behind him, leaning nearer, stooping over him to read the letter...*to hold your body, to smother it with...* Suddenly he flinched. He felt the shadow's brooding rage, its frantic anger. Was it possible that what he thought was encouragement had been disapproval? Years ago, at the start of his lifelong tribute to the Master, he'd been aware of James's hatred toward biographers. Before he died, James had burned his private papers. In "The Real Right Thing," a writer's ghost had scared away a biographer. But nothing in the Master's life could possibly need to be excised. James represented the ultimate in sensitivity and taste.

...to press my love...

He felt the shadow's wrath. "You're wrong!" he told the shadow, struggling not to turn. "These days, it doesn't matter! No one cares! I'm gay also! It doesn't make a difference any longer!"

Desperate to defend his monument to James, he swung to face...

• • •

HE BURNED the letter, dropping the ashes in the fireplace. Rifling through the other letters, he discovered one addressed to him from William. It began "Dear Harry." That annoyed him. He had never addressed William as "Bill," so why should William feel at liberty to call him "Harry"? Henry was his name. He burned that letter as well, then picked up his pen and opened his notebook.

Possible story, he wrote. *Slim. To the point. A variation on "The Real Right Thing." Somewhat ghostly. Ironic revenge. A biographer becomes so obsessed with his subject (buys the man's clothes, his furniture, his jewelry, etc.) that he becomes the subject about which he's writing. "Of late he'd felt—"*

He paused to select the proper words.

"—not quite himself."

BLUE MURDER

In my introduction to "The Interrogator," I mentioned the G. Gordon Liddy Academy of Corporate Security and Private Investigation, where I learned some of the espionage tradecraft that I used in my spy novels. One of the Academy's instructors was a retired U.S. marshal, which brings me to the background of the following three stories.

The U.S. Marshals Service is one of the three groups in the U.S. government that specialize in protecting people. The other two are the Secret Service and the Diplomatic Security Service. The famous Witness Relocation Program, sometimes erroneously called the Witness Protection Program, is the responsibility of the Marshals Service. The man who taught the protective-agent classes at the Liddy Academy had been part of the security detail that guarded John Hinckley, Jr., after he shot President Reagan in 1981. For several days, I listened in awe as he explained the ethics of being a protector, the unusual mindset that motivates someone to step in the way of a bullet or a knife or any other kind of threat intended for a stranger, a criminal, a politician whose views a protector might not agree with, and sometimes even an enemy. Through selflessness, a protector has the power of life and death over someone whom the protector might barely know and might not even like. This unique relationship fascinated me.

The Liddy Academy was the first of many opportunities I found to broaden my understanding of protective agents and their unusual code. Over the years, I received training from several of them, including members of an Ohio sheriff's department that contributed to the high-level security for the 1995 Dayton (Bosnian) Peace Accords. Eventually I wrote three novels about the subject: The Fifth Profession, The Protector, and The Naked Edge. The latter two books feature a man named Cavanaugh (no first name and "Cavanaugh" isn't his actual last name). He's a protector. If you refer to him as a bodyguard, which he regards as a synonym for a thug, you won't like his reaction. His hatred of bullies compelled him to enlist in Special Forces. Now as a civilian, he runs Global Protective Services, the world's finest security company. Along with his wife, Jamie, he defends the helpless and keeps predators from their prey. "Most people muddle through their lives," he tells a client. "I hope that if I keep them from dying a while longer, maybe they'll find a way to justify remaining alive."

I grew so fond of writing about protectors that, over the years, when an editor asked me to contribute a short story to a magazine or an anthology, I looked for a way to do so. Cavanaugh's wife, Jamie, doesn't appear in "Blue Murder," the initial Protector story you're about to read. Hence she's all the more welcome in "The Controller" and "The Attitude Adjuster." Apart from their devotion to the safety of others, I enjoy writing about these characters because there aren't a lot of married couples in thrillers, and these two obviously enjoy each other's company.

As a bonus, in "Blue Murder," you'll meet another imaginary author.

"**D**O YOU CARRY A GUN?" THE woman asked.

"That's a very personal question," Cavanaugh replied. "*I* carry one."

"Yes, you mentioned that on *Good Morning, America*. Now just you and I and several million viewers share your secret."

"I have a good reason."

"For carrying a gun or for telling everyone about it on national television?"

They were in the rear of a black Cadillac, whose driver was following a carefully chosen indirect route to their Los Angeles destination. Tinted windows muted the glare of passing headlights. The glass was bullet resistant.

"You saw the notes this creep sent me," the woman continued. "You heard the phone messages. The bastard even snuck onto my property in Connecticut and shot my dog. Don't worry. I know how to use a firearm. Even before the threats started, I carried one. It's good publicity. A female thriller writer who's as tough as the bad guys she writes about."

She pulled a nine-millimeter Beretta from beneath her jacket, cradling it in her lap.

Cavanaugh became very still.

"I'm serious," she said. "If I pay someone to protect me, I want to make sure I get my money's worth. I showed you mine. Now you show me yours."

"We barely know each other." Cavanaugh noted that the pistol's safety was on. Nonetheless, he continued to be still. "And if I were you, Ms. Ryder, I'd get a different handgun."

"You've got to be kidding. This has a fifteen-round magazine, plus one in the chamber. I could take down a small army with this."

"Except that your bullets hit to the left of where you're aiming."

"Have you been spying on me? Just how the hell do you know *that?*"

"A magazine that big makes the pistol too large for the size of your hand. You need to stretch your finger to reach the trigger. That nudges the barrel to the left."

Amanda Ryder took a harder look at him. Cavanaugh was six feet tall. In one of her thrillers, she might have described him as "ruggedly good-looking," although he wasn't so handsome that he attracted attention. He was in his mid-thirties and had average-length brown hair. His sport coat, turtleneck, and slacks were anonymously casual. The only two things that might have seemed noteworthy to a discerning eye were that his shoes had sturdy soles and that his shoulders looked strong.

"I'm told you used to be in Delta Force. Jonathan's right. I need somebody like you to protect me," Amanda said. The reference was to Jonathan Kramer, one of the last remaining independent publishers now that international conglomerates dominated the business. Jonathan's company, Kramer House, released Amada Ryder's two bestsellers each year.

"But I'm not sure I want the assignment," Cavanaugh said.

"Not sure? Of all the... Then why in God's name are you here?"

"Because Mr. Kramer asked me to meet with you." Six months earlier, Cavanaugh had protected Amanda's publisher when Arab terrorists got the impression that a novel Kramer House was about to release contained anti-Islamic passages. The crisis had passed when the novel turned out to have a small section depicting an American diplomat learning the positive aspects of Islam prior to being sent to the Middle East. That serious novel about international relations had sold a meager five thousand copies, which was why the bestselling thrillers of Amanda Ryder were important enough for her publisher to pay Cavanaugh to assess her situation.

"Anyway," Cavanaugh continued, "as it is, you've got plenty of security." He pointed ahead toward a black Cadillac, a match to the vehicle they were being chauffeured in. A third black Cadillac followed.

"Can't be too careful," Amanda said.

"On *that* subject, you and I agree."

"Almost there," she ordered the driver. "Make the switch."

The heavyset man behind the steering wheel spoke into a walkie-talkie, then slowed, allowing the Cadillac that followed to pass them and shift into the middle slot.

"So what do you think?" Amanda asked Cavanaugh.

"The old shell game. Which car are you in? The one in the middle seems the probable choice," Cavanaugh agreed.

"But you don't look impressed."

"I don't like conspicuous vehicles. At Global Protective Services, we use cars so popular they're anonymous. Tauruses. The ones the Ford racing team uses. High-performance engines with suspensions to match. Armored, with bullet-resistant windows."

"I wouldn't be caught dead in a Taurus."

"I've had numerous clients who've experienced the reverse effect."

The convoy turned a corner onto brightly lit Hollywood Boulevard. After years of neglect, an ambitious urban-renewal program had returned many of the boulevard's theaters, night spots, and restaurants to their former glory. Ahead was a soft blue, art-deco façade and a nineteen-thirties-style neon sign that announced THE BLUE MURDER BOOK STORE AND CAFÉ.

A group of women hurried inside as the convoy reached a poster announcing that America's favorite thriller novelist, Amanda Ryder, creator of the globe-trotting investigative journalist Abigail Adams, would be reading from her work and signing her new novel at seven this evening.

Avoiding the numerous tourists on the street, the convoy steered toward a parking lot in back, where another neon sign indicated Blue Murder's back door.

As the vehicles stopped, Amanda's cell phone rang. Scowling at the name on the phone's screen, she jabbed a button and told whoever was calling, "That publicity release you wrote was crap. Your mother's in the hospital? Well, you were hired to raise my numbers, and you didn't. Now you'll have plenty of time to visit your mother. You're fired."

Amanda broke the connection and holstered her handgun beneath her jacket. "What are they waiting for?" she demanded to the driver.

The driver picked up his walkie-talkie and ordered someone, "Get started."

Doors on the middle Cadillac opened. Its driver stepped out to assist the back seat's occupant. Cavanaugh had met Amanda in her bungalow at the Beverly Hills Hotel after she'd finished a day of interviews. Most of her entourage had already been waiting in the Cadillacs. Thus, he wasn't prepared for what he now saw.

A woman who could have been Amanda Ryder's twin got tensely out of the middle car. Like Amanda, she was in her thirties and exceptionally attractive. Like Amanda, she had long straight blond hair that fell back behind her shoulders, evoking Veronica Lake's *femme fatale* look in *noir* movies of the nineteen forties. Her gray linen suit and gleaming white blouse, accentuated by pearls, were identical to what Amanda wore.

"Let's see if my number one fan's hanging around," Amanda murmured.

The driver and the decoy nervously entered the building. Twenty seconds later, the driver came out and gave the all-clear sign to the third car.

"You don't look impressed by that, either," Amanda told Cavanaugh.

"Actually, I'm amazed. This woman—"

"My assistant."

"—was chosen for the job because she resembles you?"

"Well, she certainly wasn't chosen for her brains. Even with the resemblance, it took a lot of effort and money to make the match as close as it is."

"What amazes me even more is, since you're setting her up to take a bullet in your place, why don't you provide her with more protection?" Cavanaugh asked.

"*I'm* not paying for this. *Jonathan* is."

The driver of the first car joined the driver of the second car and walked to the third car, where they formed a corridor while the third driver opened the door for her.

"Wait," Cavanaugh said. "I might as well be useful."

"I thought you didn't want to work for me," Amanda said.

"Call this a favor to Mr. Kramer." Cavanaugh got out of the Cadillac, scanned the shadowy parking lot, assessed the low rooftops, studied the numerous cars, and hated the entire set up. "We should have gotten out in front of the store. The street is well lit. There are fewer places to hide. Anybody standing still would look conspicuous."

Cavanaugh joined the corridor that the drivers had formed, noting with approval that they kept their backs to Amanda, watching for a potential attack as they hurried with her into the store's back office.

"Someone like me should have been here ahead of time to study the people coming in and check for warning signs," Cavanaugh told Amanda.

A gray-haired, fiftyish woman, presumably the store's manager, fluttered. "Welcome to Blue Murder, Ms. Ryder. We're all terribly excited to—"

"Count the draw," Amanda told her look-alike assistant.

When the uneasy decoy opened the door to the main part of Blue Murder, excited conversations came to a halt. The sudden silence was interrupted by intense applause as the fans out there thought they were seeing the real Amanda Ryder.

Five seconds later, the assistant shut the door. "Looks to be about two hundred."

"*Two hundred?*" Shocked, Amanda spun toward the manager. "Weren't you told I don't make an appearance for less than *four* hundred people?"

"We did everything we could. We put up signs, sent out notices, paid for ads in the newspapers, and promoted it in our online newsletter. But with competition from cheaper-priced stores on the Internet, people don't want to pay full price for hardbacks and—"

"I risked my life to come here for a lousy two hundred people?"

"They're eager to hear you speak."

"My royalties would only be a thousand dollars. No way." Amanda motioned fiercely for everybody to leave.

The apprehensive look-alike opened the door to see if the parking lot remained safe. Her solitary guard followed.

"No," Cavanaugh told the others. "We all go out first to provide cover."

"Quit wasting my time," Amanda told him. "We already know the creep isn't there."

With a caustic look, Cavanaugh led the other men outside, where they formed a corridor, permitting the look-alike to get safely into the middle Cadillac.

"See." Amanda stepped into view and pushed past them, heading toward the rear car. "He's nowhere around."

As Cavanaugh hurried to catch up to her, a bullet whacked the brick wall above Amanda's head. Hearing a shot echo across the parking lot, Cavanaugh dropped her to the pavement a moment before a second bullet struck the wall. Ears ringing, he dragged her into the rear Cadillac. A third bullet slammed the wall, chunks flying. Only then did the drivers overcome their shock, two of them ducking back into the store while the third man ran to get behind the steering wheel of Amanda's car.

"I'm driving," Cavanaugh told him. Outside the Cadillac, he took the keys and shoved the man into the passenger seat. He hurried into the front seat, rammed the gearshift into reverse, sped backward, hit the brakes, and twisted the steering wheel, spinning the car 180 degrees in the so-called bootlegger's turn. Now facing the exit, he shoved the gearshift into drive and raced from the parking lot. If a hostile car had been blocking his way, he knew how to crash through by hitting the side of the rear fender and pivoting the car away from him. But the exit was clear, except for traffic on the side street, which parted as Cavanaugh blared the Cadillac's horn. He slid smoothly into the sudden gap between vehicles and sped along the side street, away from Hollywood Boulevard.

"Take me back to the hotel!" Amanda shouted.

"That's the first place somebody would look.

"Then where the hell are we going?"

"The Van Nuys airport."

"Why are we going *there?*"

"I'm curious about something."

After LAX and Burbank, the next two important airports in the Los Angeles area were located in Van Nuys and Santa Monica. These were known as "reliever" airstrips because they channeled corporate, chartered, and private aircraft away from commercial traffic at the larger airports, helping to relieve congestion. Because Cavanaugh's clients often had their own jets, he made a point of knowing the most efficient routes to various reliever airstrips near major cities and now used the Hollywood and Ventura Freeways to get to Van Nuys within twenty-five minutes. Its proximity to Blue Murder was the reason he chose it. He assumed that the same ease would attract his target. Taking care that he and the guard flanked Amanda, they hurried into one of the airport's small terminals that catered to private aircraft.

Behind a counter, a woman looked up.

"We're late," Cavanaugh lied to her. "I hope they didn't take off without us. We're supposed to be on a Gulfstream." He told her the tail number of a jet.

"You're not late at all," the woman assured him. "It's still outside."

Security in the non-commercial area of reliever airstrips tended to be minimal. The logic was that passengers of private planes trusted each other, so there was no need to scan for weapons or explosives. Cavanaugh thus had no trouble reaching a window, through which he noticed the sleek Gulfstream among other aircraft on the harshly lit tarmac. Its hatch was open. Its steps had been lowered. A pilot stood next to it, as if waiting for someone.

"Good. We got here ahead of him."

"Ahead of...? Who are you talking about?" Amanda insisted. "And how did you know the number on the jet?"

"I was on it six months ago. I flew here on it."

"What?"

"Be quiet so he doesn't hear your voice."

Cavanaugh guided Amanda toward an out-of-the-way spot, from where he could discreetly watch the doors that led to the tarmac.

Three minutes later, a harried man rushed into the compact terminal, carrying a metal suitcase. He was in his forties, tall, overweight, with thinning, brown hair. His face was flushed and sweaty.

"Mr. Kramer." Cavanaugh stepped forward.

The man spun in shock.

"Jonathan? My God, what are *you* doing here?" Amanda asked.

"I had an emergency business meeting."

"Sure you did." Cavanaugh turned toward Amanda. "He's the one who shot at you tonight."

"*What?*"

"I shot at Amanda? Don't be absurd," Kramer said.

"It's easy enough to prove. We'll test your hands for gunpowder residue."

Despite the sweat on his face, Kramer's gaze remained confident.

"Okay, I understand," Cavanaugh said. "You used latex gloves and threw them away."

He studied Kramer's dress slacks and designer shirt. "I'm betting you wore coveralls and threw those away, too. No residue on your clothes. But there'd be residue on your face and hair because you needed to rest your cheek against the rifle to aim it."

"*Jonathan, what's he talking about?*"

Cavanaugh answered for him. "Poor sales for books that he really cares about. Kramer House is one of the last independent publishing firms, and if I'm right, it's close to bankruptcy."

"I haven't the faintest idea what you—"

Cavanaugh cut him off. "Whoever fired those shots tonight aimed too high to be serious. The first bullet hit way above us. The next two should have been lower, but they didn't even hit the car, so either the shooter was too incompetent to adjust his aim, or else he didn't want to. Under the circumstances, the second possibility makes more sense. You're not trying to hurt anybody. You're just trying to get enough publicity to boost sales for the new book. You paid me to come here so I'd be an expert witness to the shooting and make the threat credible to the media."

"This is the craziest—"

"Then you won't mind opening that suitcase," Cavanaugh told him. "I'm betting it contains a disassembled rifle. That's the one thing you couldn't risk abandoning because it might have been traced back to you. You can carry a firearm aboard a private plane without going through a security check. So you figured why not take it back to New York and get rid of it there. Tomorrow morning, the plan was you'd be back in your office. No one would suspect you'd come to Los Angeles. But when I realized what was happening, I remembered that we used your Gulfstream to fly here for a meeting when I protected you six months ago."

"This is absolute nonsense."

"Then open the suitcase. Prove I'm wrong."

Kramer stared at him.

The moment lengthened. As Cavanaugh reached for the suitcase, Kramer stepped back.

"Amanda..." Kramer sighed. "An independent publisher can't compete with the international conglomerates. I desperately need this new book of yours to be a mega-hit. It's not as if you were ever in danger. No one got hurt."

"My dog, you creep. You snuck onto my property and shot my dog."

"I didn't have a choice. I needed to make it look as if you were actually being threatened. Otherwise, you wouldn't have been convincing. Honestly, it had to be done."

"You bastard."

"For the good of the book, Amanda. Believe me, if this had worked out, with all the publicity about the threats against you, we could have made a fortune."

"Thank you, Jonathan."

"For what? Are you telling me that you see my point?"

"Yes, not that you'll profit from it. You're going to prison, Jonathan. I won't publish any more books with your company, and I intend to sue you for all you're worth. But I do thank you for the idea."

Two weeks later, Amanda Ryder's new globe-trotting thriller reached number one on the *New York Times* bestseller list. Cavanaugh happened to be watching the *Today Show* the morning she was interviewed.

"Yes," she said, "this book's outselling all my others. I think it's because my readers understand how much I'm devoted to them. When I was being shot at, when I risked my life again and again on my publicity tour, the fans knew I was doing it for them. The fans mean everything to me. Even at the risk of my life, nothing can stop me from getting to my fans and showing my appreciation."

Cavanaugh shut off the television.

THE CONTROLLER

In this second Protector story, you have the honor of meeting Jamie.

"**Y**OU DON'T HAVE A FIRST NAME?" the man asked.

"I have one. I just don't use it. The less people know about me, the better."

"Sure. The bodyguard with only one name. Cavanaugh. Like a trademark. Creates a mystique. Clever."

"Actually, Cavanaugh isn't my real last name."

"I don't understand."

"I try to be invisible, starting with my identity. What you called me just now—a bodyguard—that's not what I am."

"But I was assured you could help me."

"A bodyguard's what a mobster uses," Cavanaugh said. "His skills are limited to his size and his ability to inflict pain. I'm a protective agent."

"Okay. All right. Fine. A protective agent."

"If I take this assignment—"

"If?"

"I need to be assured of something. A man with your power and wealth. You didn't get where you are by being passive. It's your nature to take charge and assume control."

"I have three former wives who'll testify to that."

"Well, I won't risk my life for someone who'll put us both in danger by not doing what I tell him," Cavanaugh said. "The paradox of hiring a protective agent is that while you're the employer, I'm the one who gives the orders. Can you accept that? Can you follow my directions without question and allow yourself to be controlled?"

• • •

F. SCOTT Fitzgerald once wrote, "The very rich are different from you and me." To which, Hemingway replied, "Yes, they have more money." In Cavanaugh's experience, however, the true difference was that the extremely rich were able to shield themselves so thoroughly from the basic messes of life that after a while they forgot that messes existed. Problems with vehicles, plumbing, appliances, hot water heaters, furnaces, roofs, on and on, the sort of breakdown that a person of ordinary income might lose sleep over or feel was a sign of impending doom were unknown to the very rich. Fixing messes—that's what servants were for. That's what personal assistants were for. That's what money was for. Fires, floods, earthquakes. Inconvenient, certainly, but while others took care of the mess, a Gulfstream V soared toward Rio or Monte Carlo or Dubai or one of many other resort locations. Of course, even the rich had dental problems, eye problems, bladder problems, but the best medical specialists in the world could correct those things if you threw enough money at them. Meanwhile, it was best to pretend that dental problems, eye problems, and bladder problems didn't exist.

But inevitably, even the rich encountered a problem so severe that it couldn't be ignored or fixed by wealth—a mortal illness, for example—and it always came as a shock that they weren't as entitled as they assumed. Something similar had happened to

Martin Dant. At the age of twenty, he'd inherited his father's oil-refinery business. Because of not-in-my-backyard issues, it was almost impossible to expand that business and build new refineries, so Dant invested in the broadcasting industry. Photogenic, he appeared frequently on news programs he owned, and after expensive instruction by advisors to former presidents, he became—at the age of twenty-eight—a wunderkind public-affairs moderator to whom politicians learned to pay court. At the age of thirty-five, he almost entered the governor's race in Georgia, but by then, his numerous romantic affairs had jeopardized his first marriage (to a television producer), and he decided that the freedom to have a private life was more appealing than the nuisance of hiding scandals. Besides, he could gain far more power by using his wealth to influence politicians than he could ever gain by being a politician himself.

When Dant was forty-two, his second marriage (to a Washington political commentator) went the way of the first. By then, his empire included a motion-picture company, which resulted in his third marriage—to a *Vogue* model, who aspired to be a movie star. She shared his interest in environmental issues, particularly wetland preservation, and in the pursuit of that goal, Dant acquired huge tracts on the U.S. eastern seaboard and in South America. His marriage to the fashion model lasted even fewer years than did his previous marriages, however, and at that point, Dant decided that connubial bliss was probably not something he was destined to achieve. Acquiring possessions and power was far more rewarding and long lasting.

Cavanaugh knew these details—and considerably more—because of a thick profile that his security company, Global Protective Services, had compiled. The extent of Dant's financial tentacles was even greater than Cavanaugh expected, but the strength of the man's ambition, determination, and sense of destiny didn't surprise him at all. Cavanaugh had provided security for tycoons on numerous occasions, and they all exhibited the same confidence, bordering on ruthlessness, when it came to generating wealth and obtaining what they wanted. Some had a degree of charm comparable to Fitzgerald's Great Gatsby. Others made no effort to ingratiate themselves. If you didn't like the crude, cruel, or imperious way they treated you, well, tough shit. There were plenty of others who'd be more than happy to take your place.

Cavanaugh reserved his opinions about this. People who didn't have money could be crude, cruel, or imperious, also. His business was saving lives, not making judgments. He protected the defenseless against predators, and sometimes even the very rich could be defenseless.

That was the case with Martin Dant. No one amassed an empire without making enemies. Over the years—Dant was now sixty-four—his enemies had accumulated until it was impossible to keep track of them. One particular enemy had decided to seek revenge. A month earlier, a sniper fired at Dant as he stepped from his limousine and approached his private jet at Teterboro airport outside New York City. Dant heard the snap of the bullet passing his head and then its impact against the limousine. Two weeks afterward, as Dant and a female companion approached a boathouse at his Cape Cod estate, the building exploded, knocking them to the sand. Two days ago, a bullet shattered the window of a Grand Cayman office where Dant was negotiating to buy a struggling airline. Glass sprayed over him, cutting his face.

• • •

"WE NEED to give his attacker credit for being persistent," Cavanaugh said as the elevator closed.

"And for frequency," his companion noted as the elevator rose. Her name was Jamie Travers. She was his wife.

"But whoever it is, isn't very good at it."

"Unless the idea is to scare Dant for a long time before killing him," Jamie observed.

"If so, the tactic's working," Cavanaugh said. "Whoever's doing this has definitely got Dant's attention. He's not twitching or sweating or pissing his pants, but I can see in his eyes how much strength he needs to appear calm."

"Right," Jamie agreed. "For most of his life, he controlled everything around him, and now someone's showing him what it feels like to *be* controlled."

They got off the private elevator and reached the entrance to the penthouse of Dant's Fifth Avenue office building in Manhattan. In the marble lobby, a guard had phoned to announce that Cavanaugh and Jamie were on their way up. The elevator had a security camera. So did the vestibule to the penthouse.

Two solid-looking men emerged from alcoves on either side of the elevator doors. They wore loosely fitted suits that Cavanaugh had no doubt concealed firearms. Their shoes were sturdy, presumably with steel caps. Their belt buckles had a design that Cavanaugh recognized, hiding knives.

"I.D.," the man on the right said, curtly adding, "please."

While the man on the left stood a careful distance back, Cavanaugh and Jamie complied.

"Are you armed?" the man on the right asked.

"Of course," Jamie answered. "But you already knew that. The elevator has a scanner, doesn't it?"

The sentries looked uncertainly at one another.

"You'll have to surrender it," the man on the right said.

"I don't think so," Jamie told him.

"No one gets in there with a weapon."

"I guess word didn't reach you. We're on the security team."

"Mr. Novak says there's been a change of plan."

"Mr. Novak?" Cavanaugh frowned. "Who's *he*? We're here to see Mr. Dant."

"Let them in," a voice announced from a speaker next to the camera above the door.

"Yes, Mr. Novak."

The sentry on the left pressed buttons on a keypad. Electronically released, a lock on the door made a metallic sound. Cavanaugh opened the door, revealing a spacious room with a magnificent view of the city.

A tall, well-dressed man was silhouetted against the bright skyline. Cavanaugh took for granted that the wall-to-wall windows were bullet resistant and that the man had chosen his position for dramatic effect. Crossing the room, he noted metal-and-glass furniture whose rigid lines matched those in several modernistic paintings. A rough guess put the value of the room's artwork at ten million dollars.

The man at the window made his own assessment, shifting his attention between Jamie and Cavanaugh, although it was Jamie he mostly looked at: an attractive, athletic-looking woman wearing slacks, a blazer, and a white blouse. He lingered over her auburn hair and green eyes.

"I'm Ben Novak, Mr. Dant's security chief." In his forties, Novak had a thin, stern face and short, military-style hair. "I watched a monitor when you met with Mr. Dant yesterday, so I know who *you* are," he told Cavanaugh. "But I don't know who your associate is."

"Jamie Travers."

"Pleased to meet you." Novak offered his hand.

When they shook, Novak held Jamie's hand a moment longer than necessary. "You have calluses on your thumb and your index finger."

"That's awfully personal."

"There's only one way to get calluses like that," Novak said.

"Definitely personal."

"How many rounds do you shoot a day?"

"Two hundred," Jamie replied.

Novak referred to the calluses that a habitual shooter developed from repeatedly thumbing ammunition into a magazine and pulling a trigger.

He raised his eyebrows, reluctantly impressed.

"Good. Now that we've gotten to know one another, here's our threat assessment." Cavanaugh put a thick folder on a glass desk. "We have an appointment to discuss it with Mr. Dant."

"Yes, well, there's been a development," Novak said. "Mr. Dant decided you won't be needed."

"Oh?"

"He asked me to give you this check for your trouble." Novak indicated an envelope on the desk. "I think you'll find the amount satisfactory."

"It's hardly satisfactory if he gets himself killed." Cavanaugh turned quickly, addressing a security camera in the upper left corner. "Mr. Dant, you're making a mistake."

"I'll escort you to the—"

"Mr. Dant," Cavanaugh said louder toward the camera. "When we spoke, I told you a man doesn't acquire your power and wealth by being passive. I guess I was partly wrong. I didn't realize your management technique was *passive aggressive*. Is this how you do business? You don't have the balls to deal face-to-face with an awkward situation, so you arrange for an employee to take care of it?"

A door opened. Martin Dant stepped from a room filled with computers, monitors, printers, and a variety of other electronic equipment. Men were occupied in front of screens that provided financial statements and stock-market information. One of several security-camera displays showed Cavanaugh, Jamie, and Novak.

Dant wore designer loafers, khaki pants, a blue linen shirt with its sleeves rolled twice, a gold bracelet on one wrist and a Patek Philippe watch on the other. He wasn't tall, but he exuded a power that gave him presence. His silver hair, healthily thick, contrasted with the golden tan that enhanced his television good looks. He had a square face, distinctive features, and penetrating eyes. Even the half-dozen scabs from the flying glass that had cut his face reinforced the masculinity he projected.

His gaze rested on Jamie, then focused on Cavanaugh.

"If this is a question of ego," Dant told Cavanaugh, "remember you haven't actually been fired. After all, you never really had the opportunity to start the job. Nothing personal. I merely changed my mind."

"But we *did* start the job," Cavanaugh responded, "and you might as well receive some value for that check you want to give us. We found some interesting items."

"We? If you mean Ms. Travers, I wish you'd brought her to yesterday's meeting."

"I was preparing your threat assessment," Jamie told him.

"The thing is, I already know there's a threat," Dant emphasized. "I confess I was nervous, but then I reminded myself that risk is a fact of life. It's just a question of keeping it away from me. So the answer is to increase my protection. Isn't that right, Mr. Novak?"

"Well, yes, sir, I think there's—"

"It's the control issue," Cavanaugh interrupted.

"Excuse me?" Dant asked.

"Yesterday, I wondered if you were willing to take orders from someone who worked for you. Now I have your answer."

"None of this concerns you any longer."

"Please look at the threat assessment," Jamie requested. "If it doesn't convince you, we'll gladly leave. After we tear up the check."

Dant paused. He glanced at the folder. He looked at Jamie. He considered Cavanaugh.

Absently, he scratched one of the scabs on his face. When he lowered his hand from his cheek, blood was on his finger.

"Maybe I was wrong. Maybe we should begin again."

• • •

CAVANAUGH TOOK a page from the folder and showed it to Dant. "In the past five years, you had a seventy percent turnover on your protective detail. Mr. Novak is your fifth security chief in that same period."

Dant looked surprised.

"Surely you knew this," Cavanaugh said.

"Of course. But that information is confidential."

"Apparently not, or else we wouldn't be discussing it with you."

"How did you learn this?"

"I hacked into your computer system," Jamie answered matter-of-factly.

Dant looked more surprised. "My system is state of the art."

"So is ours," Jamie assured him.

"The district attorney will want to know all about them."

Cavanaugh pointed at the file. "Here's the agreement you signed, authorizing us to use any means necessary to prepare a threat assessment."

"It's better this way," Jamie continued. "I'll plug the holes. Then I'll hire a friend who's smarter than me to try to hack in. Meanwhile, the flaws in your computer security might have been how the person who's trying to kill you learned your schedule. Teterboro airport. Cape Cod. The Grand Caymans. You can't be followed easily, so that means somebody's ahead of you."

"Another thing that stands out," Cavanaugh said, pointing at the file, "is the absence of any female personnel on your security team. There hasn't been any in the past three years."

"I don't know why you think that's significant." Dant sounded annoyed. "Men are obviously more suited for dangerous work. Besides, it's difficult to find properly trained female bodyguards, given that almost everyone in that business is a former member of a special-operations military unit. Isn't that right, Mr. Novak?"

"Not exactly, Mr. Dant. There's a female special-ops unit that—"

Dant cut him off, asking Cavanaugh, "Why do you think women should be on my security team?"

"The men in the lobby and outside your door showed more interest in Jamie than they did in me. So did Mr. Novak. So did *you*. In your case, that's a function of your fondness for female companionship."

"Which is none of your business."

"It is if your protectors need to accommodate that fondness. The team might be more objective if some of them are female. It's not that Mr. Novak or the men outside stopped being professional. On the contrary, I got the impression they worried that a woman could be a greater threat than a man and that they weren't sure how to deal with that. A female protector would know how to handle the situation."

"I won't give up my social life."

"No one's asking for that," Jamie emphasized. "But you can have patience enough to wait until background checks are made. Three years ago, you had female protectors. What happened? The unusually high turnover in your security staff. What do you suppose is the problem?"

Dant shrugged. "Maybe they find better money somewhere else. How would *I* know?"

"You pay higher than the standard rate. No, the problem is you treat them like bodyguards instead of protectors."

"Back to that again. Whatever you want to call them, I won't allow anyone to tell me how to run my life."

"Even if that's what's necessary to save it?" Jamie pointed at his face. "By the way, one of your scabs is bleeding again."

This time, Dant didn't touch it. "Whoever's trying to kill me won't have the satisfaction of making me cower. To prove it, tonight I'm going to Lincoln Center."

"What?"

"A charity benefit."

"*Tonight?* But that doesn't give us enough time to plan the security arrangements," Cavanaugh objected.

"It's not a problem. Mr. Novak has already taken care of everything."

• • •

AT NIGHT, Lincoln Center was one of Cavanaugh's favorite places in Manhattan. Its brilliantly lit buildings, spacious plaza, and spectacular fountain represented what the city could be at its best, never failing to impress him.

Except when Cavanaugh was working. Then all he saw were unlimited vantage points and uncontrollable crowds.

Dant's limousine arrived by an indirect route that might have fooled someone into thinking he'd changed his mind about going to the benefit. It was one of four that had left the basement parking area of Dant's Fifth Avenue building, their tinted windows making it impossible for an observer to see inside and detect which limousine Dant had chosen to use. Near Lincoln Center, the vehicles had separated and approached all four entrances: Columbus Avenue, West Sixty-Fifth Street, West Sixty-Second Street, and Amsterdam.

Dant rode in the second limousine, sipping Armand de Brignac champagne. Cavanaugh sat in back with him while Novak sat in the front, using a scrambler-equipped two-way radio to communicate with the rest of the security team and coordinate Dant's arrival. Jamie had gone ahead.

The black of Dant's Brioni tuxedo made his thick silver hair seem more lustrous and emphasized his photogenic features. Expertly applied makeup disguised the scabs on his face.

"Have you ever been shot at when you protected someone?" he asked Cavanaugh.

"A couple of times."

"Were you hit?"

"Once."

"Let me ask you something. It's obvious you don't like me, and yet you're willing to risk your life for me. Is the money that important to you?"

"I barely know you, so how can I have an opinion about whether you're likeable or not? If it matters, I admire how hard you worked to build your empire. Not many people have your determination."

"I got that from my father." Dant didn't say it happily. He glanced toward the glow of traffic. "Would you risk your life for someone you detested?"

"Drug dealers have tried to hire me. Mob bosses. Corporate CEOs who aren't any better than con men, looting pension accounts. Financial advisors cheating the investors who trusted them. Sometimes evil is obvious. Otherwise, it's not my place to judge. Most people muddle through their lives. All I can do is hope that if I keep them from dying a while longer, maybe they'll find a way to justify remaining alive. The truth is, I'm less interested in the people I protect than the bullies I protect them from."

"Bullies? Do I detect anger?"

"My father beat my mother."

"Ah, yes, fathers." Dant pointed through the window toward Lincoln Center. "Did you ever see the movie, *The Producers?*"

"Sure."

"You remember the plot? Zero Mostel and Gene Wilder embezzle money from widows by getting them to invest in a

Broadway play that they do everything to make sure is a flop. The widows invest more than the play cost to produce, so Mostel and Wilder are guaranteed a profit."

"Yes, Wilder's an accountant, as I recall."

"They dream up that plan at Lincoln Center. At night at the fountain. When the idea comes to them, the fountain gushes. I couldn't stop laughing when I was a kid and I saw that fountain gush. The first time I came to Manhattan, the only place I wanted to see was Lincoln Center and that fountain." Dant looked amused. "I donated five million dollars for tonight's fundraiser. It underwrites cultural events at the Center."

"Nice to have culture."

"I don't mind having that publicized. It isn't self-serving. What I *don't* publicize are the considerably greater amounts I donate to after-school programs, homeless shelters, food banks, day-care centers, inner-city health clinics, and so on."

"You just gave me a lot of reasons to risk my life for you."

• • •

THEY USED the garage entrance on West Sixty-Second Street, proceeding past harsh underground lights to a guarded area that provided access to an elevator reserved for VIP donors. Cavanaugh and Novak got out first, joining six protective agents, three on each side, who shielded Dant as he moved from the vehicle to the elevator.

The lobby doors opened, revealing tuxedos and evening gowns, the drone of hundreds of conversations, lights glinting off champagne and cocktail glasses—and diamonds, an abundance of diamonds. Uniformed servers moved through the crowd, offering canapés from polished trays. A string quartet played in the background.

For most attendees, the occasion seemed festive. For Cavanaugh, it was a nightmare. At the other entrances, security personnel presumably made sure that everyone who came through the various doors had an invitation, just as a guard now took Dant's invitations and the ones he'd arranged for Cavanaugh and Novak. But invitations were easy to counterfeit. Plus, there weren't any metal detectors. If Cavanaugh and Novak could enter with concealed firearms, so could someone with violent intentions. To add to the problems, while Cavanaugh wore a tuxedo, Novak did not. Nor did any of his security team. The rule was, Always match what your employer wore. Not only did you blend with the environment, disguising your function, but also you might confuse a gunman's aim, making it hard for him to distinguish his target from similarly dressed people around him.

Dant merged with the crowd. Following, Cavanaugh watched him approach a woman whose blond hair was combed above her head, emphasizing her statuesque figure. As she turned toward Dant and smiled, her movement had a dancer's grace. He kissed her on the cheek, so low that his lips almost reached her neck.

Cavanaugh stopped a discreet distance away.

"Champagne?" a server asked.

"No, thank you."

"Looking for a good time, lover?" a woman asked.

It was Jamie, who shifted in front of him so that he seemed to be focusing on her while he actually concentrated on the people around Dant a dozen feet away. She wore an evening dress with a loose hem, allowing her to move quickly if she needed to.

"As long as you're with me, it's always a good time," he said, the murmur of nearby conversations floating over them.

"Well, I'll tell you one thing that's not good," Jamie said quietly.

"You mean, apart from the fact that Dant's security team is wearing suits instead of tuxedos, so they can't move into the crowd without attracting attention? Hell, even if they did, their military haircuts would give them away."

Looking past Jamie's shoulder, Cavanaugh watched Dant whisper into the woman's ear. She nodded, as if experiencing pleasure.

"He certainly has a way with the ladies."

"With her, he's had practice," Jamie said.

"What do you mean?"

"She was his second wife."

"What?" Cavanaugh concealed his surprise. "But she doesn't look like her photographs. She's too young. She ought to be in her late fifties by now."

"The kind of alimony she gets from Dant, she can afford the Elixir of Youth. That's the name of the office of her cosmetic surgeon. By the way, I got a look at the seating chart. Dant has a balcony seat. First row."

"Novak should have caught that. What else hasn't he checked? We need to—"

"I should have said Dant *had* a balcony seat. I arranged for him to sit behind you."

Cavanaugh's feeling of relief lasted all too briefly. "Wait a minute, what's he doing?"

Dant and the woman left the crowd, moving toward an exit.

Cavanaugh spoke into a microphone on his lapel, warning the team that Dant was headed outside. He and Jamie followed, trying to disguise their urgency.

"Mr. Dant," Jamie called. "Can we speak with you, Mr. Dant?"

Dant turned, annoyed.

"Sorry to interrupt," Cavanaugh said, "but an old friend asked me to give you a message."

"Not now."

"He said the message was very important."

"It's too loud in here," Dant complained. "This lady and I want some fresh air. It's been a while since we had a chance to talk."

Impatience with Cavanaugh's interruption made the ex-wife's features harden.

"You know it *is* loud in here," Jamie said. "I'd like some fresh air, too."

She and Cavanaugh followed Dant and his ex-wife into the nightglow of the plaza outside Lincoln Center. The blare of traffic replaced that of conversations and the string quartet.

Cavanaugh saw Novak and the rest of the security team coming outside. If they'd worn tuxedos, Dant might have been indistinguishable from his protectors.

Dant headed toward the fountain.

Cavanaugh hurried in front of him. "All you needed to do was tell us in advance what your plan is."

"Sometimes I don't have one."

"Look, just give us a half hour, and we'll make sure the area's clear."

"The opera's scheduled to start by then."

"Please."

"What good does all the money in the world matter if..." Dant shook his head. "I knew this wouldn't work."

Cavanaugh looked ahead toward the huge, circular fountain. Lights shimmered under the water. A tarpaulin covered part of the fountain's curve. Cones stood in front of a sign: UNDER REPAIR.

"At least, let me check the tarpaulin."

"Get out of our way."

The explosion had the force of hands shoving at Cavanaugh's chest. His ears felt slapped. Stumbling back, he closed his eyes from the glare of the blast. He winced as Dant and his ex-wife walloped against Jamie and him, all four of them crashing onto the plaza. Sickening smoke swirled around him. Bystanders screamed.

• • •

"HOW MANY fingers do you see?" the doctor asked.

Cavanaugh told him.

"What year is it?"

Cavanaugh told him.

"What's your social security number?"

"You're kidding, right? You expect me to give you my social security number?"

"Just wanted to see if you're alert. Are you sick to your stomach?"

"No."

"Are your ears still ringing?"

"Not as much."

"I wouldn't try to handle any heavy machinery." The doctor looked at Jamie, whom he'd already checked. "Otherwise, I think it's okay for the two of you to leave the hospital."

"What about Mr. Dant? Is he okay?" Jamie asked.

"The same condition as you. I released him twenty minutes ago."

"Released him? No. We need to talk to him."

"The police wanted to talk to him downtown. But even if they hadn't, it would have been impossible to keep him here. He definitely knows what he wants. Speaking of the police, there's a detective waiting to ask you more questions."

• • •

TWO HOURS later, Cavanaugh and Jamie were escorted by Global Protective Services agents to a car outside the hospital. They were driven to the security firm's headquarters on the fortieth floor of a building in midtown Manhattan, where they met with the hastily summoned heads of GPS's various divisions.

"Dant's been treating his protective team so badly, no one with any talent wants to work with him," Cavanaugh said, his ears continuing to ring from the explosion.

"You should buy a lottery ticket," the director of the Far East division said. "That close to the blast, somehow you didn't get hit with shrapnel. All things considered, this was your lucky night."

"What about the other people in the area?"

"No serious injuries," the head of electronic-security devices replied.

"None? That doesn't seem possible. Unless there wasn't *any* shrapnel."

"Maybe the idea wasn't to kill Dant as much as to keep attacking him," Jamie wondered. "To prolong the revenge."

Cavanaugh thought about it and nodded. The motion aggravated his headache. "The same as the other times, whoever's after Dant had information that allowed him or her to know in advance where the target would be."

The director of corporate security shrugged. "It's a big leap from knowing that Dant would be at Lincoln Center and predicting that he'd go out to the fountain. It would have taken a lot of trouble to hide the bomb there. Nobody would have risked doing it without being sure that Dant would go out there."

"The fountain." Cavanaugh remembered something. "Dant has a thing about it. From a movie he saw. The first time he visited New York, that's immediately where he went."

"So whoever's doing this has personal information about him," Jamie said, "more than just the sort of details available by hacking his computer system and learning his schedule. Really personal information. The sort of thing only someone close to him would know."

• • •

"I'M SORRY," the receptionist's voice said. "Mr. Dant isn't available."

"Then put me through to Mr. Novak," Cavanaugh said into the phone.

"He's not available, either. Would you like to leave a message?"

"Yes." Cavanaugh gave his name and phone number. "Do you know when they'll be free?"

"Not for quite a while. Both of them are in Europe."

Neither Dant nor Novak returned his calls.

• • •

A CLIENT had a television tuned to a business channel. He kept it on during a meeting with Cavanaugh and Jamie, wanting to track a story about hedge funds. As he glanced toward the television, Jamie did the same and suddenly pointed.

"My God."

Above the stock-market quotes streaming along the bottom of the screen, a photograph of Dant appeared next to a caption that said BREAKING NEWS.

"...near this peaceful Greek island," an announcer somberly reported.

The television showed wreckage floating on water.

"According to Martin Dant's security officer," the announcer continued, "he went for a moonlight sail. Despite recent attempts to kill him, Dant was known for being determined not to let threats control his life. He was alone when the bomb went off on his boat. Windows were shattered within three blocks of the harbor. Local authorities are still searching for the body."

• • •

"FIVE ATTEMPTS on his life," Jamie said. "Two with a rifle, three with explosives. Ever hear of an assassin who didn't specialize in a single method?"

"And that explosion at the Lincoln Center fountain," Cavanaugh said. "All flash-bang but no shrapnel. What the hell's going on?"

• • •

SAUDI ARABIA.

Gunshots echoed across the desert. With Jamie beside him, Cavanaugh drove a Range Rover to a checkpoint. They showed their identification to a Saudi guard, who studied a list, nodded, and motioned for Cavanaugh and Jamie to get out of the vehicle. In the stark heat, other guards approached them.

The gunshots persisted.

Jamie wore the black cloak that all women in Saudi Arabia were required to wear. The head cover wasn't as strictly enforced for Western women. Even so, Jamie made sure that she had a black scarf in a pocket in case she was ordered to wear it. Meanwhile, a floppy brimmed Helios sun hat covered her head while dark sunglasses concealed her eyes.

The vehicle was checked for weapons and explosives.

So were Cavanaugh and Jamie.

The guard motioned for them to get back in the Range Rover and proceed, but not before one of the guards slid into the rear of the vehicle, staying with them.

Although unpaved, the desert road was remarkably smooth, not surprising given that the area was owned by a member of the Saudi royal family. The gunshots became louder.

Buildings appeared ahead. Some were functional, containing what Cavanaugh assumed were offices, a lecture hall, a cafeteria, a dormitory, and bathrooms. Other buildings— mere shells—formed mock urban streets, along one of which a three-car motorcade was attacked by men with submachine guns and a rocket launcher. The motorcade slammed into reverse gear, pivoted one hundred and eighty degrees, surged into forward gear, and raced away, only to be confronted by more fire from submachine guns and a rocket launcher.

However realistic, it was a practice exercise using non-lethal ammunition.

The people engaged in the exercise were Saudis. The men supervising it were American, German, and Australian, all of them former members of special-operations units. Cavanaugh knew their backgrounds because he recognized all the instructors, having worked with them from time to time.

After a siren blared and the gunfire ended, a burly sunburned man in desert camouflage fatigues came over.

"It's been a long time, Cavanaugh." The man's accent was Australian.

"Good to see you, Randall, especially alive." They shook hands. "Anytime you want a job at Global Protective Services…"

"I like it better on my own."

Cavanaugh nodded. "Training a protective detail for the royal family?"

"A favored cousin. The man you asked me about on the radio—he's over there."

"Thanks for the favor."

Cavanaugh and Jamie approached the street on which the mock ambush had occurred. The man they wanted to talk to was explaining something to one of the drivers.

Sensing, he looked toward Cavanaugh and Jamie, narrowed his eyes, finished his explanation to the driver, and reluctantly walked over.

"Hi, Novak," Jamie said.

Hardly pleased, Novak asked, "What brings you two here?"

"Old times," Cavanaugh said.

"Our feelings are hurt," Jamie added. "After everything we've been through, you don't return our phone calls or answer our emails. It's enough to make us feel rejected."

"Look, you know what Dant was like. He did what he wanted. Half the time, it was impossible to get ahead of him and clear the way. What happened to him wasn't my fault. He insisted on taking that sailboat out, and short of restraining him, I couldn't have stopped him."

"We want to talk to you about your girlfriend," Jamie said.

The smell of burned gunpowder hung in the air.

"Girlfriend?" Novak asked.

"You've been in Saudi Arabia only two weeks, and already you forgot the woman you've been living with for the past year?"

"Sure. Right. My girlfriend."

"Dant was smart enough to have a woman on his security team until three years ago," Jamie pressed on. "Laura Evans. Used to be in the Army. In a special-ops unit for women who accompany members of Delta Force on some of their missions—the kind of missions that involve infiltrating a foreign country by posing as tourists. A young married couple on a holiday blends easier than a man traveling alone."

Novak nodded. "I know about that female unit."

"Yes, as I recall, you tried to tell Dant about it, but he interrupted you. We haven't had the pleasure of meeting Laura yet. She dropped out of sight. But Dant's computer records indicate that she was the last woman hired to protect him. Why do you suppose she was the last?"

"I have no idea, but I bet you're going to tell me."

"We contacted agents who worked with your girlfriend on that assignment," Jamie said. "Seems that Dant treated her as a bodyguard instead of a protector, or maybe it's more accurate to say he treated her as a body. Kept trying to strike up a relationship with her. Wanted to take her to dinner. To have a drink with her. To be alone with her. Wouldn't let her do her job. Pissed her off so much that she quit before the way he distracted her might get both of them killed."

"Okay," Novak said, "I see where this is going."

"You and Laura crossed paths on an assignment a year and a half ago. You started dating and eventually moved in together."

"I don't deny it. Not that we see each other a lot. When I'm working, she isn't—and the other way around."

"We know Laura *wasn't* working when a sniper fired at Dant at Teterboro Airport," Cavanaugh said.

"Hey, that's an awfully big accusation you're—"

"You complained to her about the way Dant wouldn't follow directions to keep him safe," Cavanaugh continued. "In turn, Laura complained about how he treated her when she worked for him. She said, 'If anybody ever tries to kill the son of a bitch, if he gets the hell scared out of him, he'll appreciate what his security people do for him.'"

"You're dreaming," Novak said. "There's no way to prove a conversation like that ever happened. If you went to the police, they'd laugh at you."

"We're not the police."

Novak pointed toward drivers getting into the motorcade vehicles. "Look, we're about to start another exercise. I don't have time for this."

"You told her when Dant would be at Teterboro," Jamie said. "It's a small airport, mostly for business jets. Not hard for a professional to infiltrate. Laura shot at him, deliberately missing. Later, the two of you enjoyed the practical joke. Hell, there was even the possibility that he might pay you extra to increase his security."

"Bullshit."

"You enjoyed it so much that you couldn't stop," Jamie insisted. "The bomb in the Cape Cod boathouse. The sniper attack in the Grand Caymans. The two of you were determined to see Dant sweat. But I'll give him credit. He didn't."

"I've heard all I'm going to—"

"We have hotel receipts and witnesses that prove Laura was at the Grand Caymans when the sniper shot at him there. We figured she wouldn't risk bringing a rifle into the country, so we asked around and found the drug dealer she bought it from."

"The police won't believe a goddamn drug dealer."

"But I told you we're not the police," Cavanaugh emphasized.

The fierce sun had terrible force.

Novak studied them. "Dant's death wasn't our fault. We had nothing to do with it."

"Sure sounds like a practical joke that went bad."

"The first three attempts..." Novak sighed. "Okay, that was Laura and me. Wanting to get him to come to his senses and realize how important his security was."

"What about the bomb at the Lincoln Center fountain?" Jamie asked.

"As big a surprise to us as it was to you," Novak replied. "After that, I was scared. Believe me, I tried everything I could to keep Dant off that fucking boat. I have nightmares about it. In a way, I did kill him. Because somebody got the idea from Laura and me. The difference is they wanted to do it for real. God knows he had a lot of enemies. Look at how his empire collapsed after he was killed. The bastard couldn't stop doing whatever he wanted, taking chances regardless of the risk. He borrowed against one corporation to prop up another, then borrowed against *that* one to save yet another. He even raided pension funds to meet his payroll, but nobody realized it because he had a genius for cooking the books. He ruined a lot of people. Maybe one of them realized what was going on and decided to get even. Or maybe..."

"Maybe what?"

"Maybe Dant couldn't bear the idea of going to prison. Laura and I wondered if maybe he killed himself, going out as dramatically as he did everything else."

A siren blared.

"I need to get back to work," Novak said.

"Don't bother," Jamie told him. "You and your girlfriend aren't protective agents anymore."

"What? But this is the only thing I know how to—"

"You swore to risk your life for Dant. You accepted money from him. Then you attacked him. You make me sick," Cavanaugh said. "We don't have enough proof to go to the police. But we've got plenty enough proof to convince the agents who depend on you to watch their backs. If we ever hear that you're on another protective detail, we'll spread the word about what you did. You won't like what happens to you."

The siren blared.

• • •

"I BELIEVE him," Cavanaugh said, driving away.

"So do I," Jamie told him. "But we're not any closer to find-ing who killed Dant. He had so many enemies, it could take years to investigate them all."

"Maybe it isn't a question of who hated him most. How about, who benefited most?"

• • •

THE PACIFIC island was so out of the way that it didn't have regular aircraft or boat service. In Hawaii, Cavanaugh—who had a pilot's license with multiple ratings—chartered a two-engine seaplane with extra fuel tanks that gave it an extreme range. He and Jamie, accompanied by two protective agents and a special passenger, took four hours to reach the island, whose palm trees, white beach, and gentle surf seemed like a vacation poster when seen from above.

After touching down in a sheltered cove, Cavanaugh guided the seaplane toward a dock. Beyond it, a village nestled among palm trees.

Puzzled natives waited for them.

"Does anybody speak English?" Cavanaugh asked as he and Jamie and the agents tied the aircraft to the dock. "*Français? Español?*"

No one responded.

One agent guarded the plane while the other agent and the special passenger followed Cavanaugh and Jamie past the villagers toward the end of the dock. Beyond the soft beach, they reached the grass huts of the village.

The sound of engines guided them to electrical generators and numerous barrels of fuel. The primitive façades of some huts contrasted with their sophisticated interiors, which included air conditioning, a stove, a refrigerator, a freezer, satellite television, computers, even a wine cooler.

"Where *is* he?" Cavanaugh demanded of the natives.

They looked baffled by his question. Or maybe they just pretended to be baffled.

"Fine. We'll get him. It'll just take a little longer."

The island was eight miles long and four miles wide, with a ridge along the middle. Plenty of spots in which to hide.

Not that it mattered. The special passenger was a bloodhound.

Cavanaugh let the bloodhound sniff the interior of the master hut. When the dog found a scent, it barked repeatedly, ran outside, and led them toward the interior of the island.

The trees became thicker, the undergrowth denser. They made their way to a stream and took fifteen minutes to find where the scent emerged a hundred yards to the left on the other side of the water. They squirmed over fallen trees and reached a steep rocky slope, the start of the ridge that formed the island's spine. Sniffing along the bottom of the slope, the dog stopped in confusion, circled, came back to the same spot, and again was confused.

"Dant couldn't just vanish," Jamie said. "How did he hide his scent?"

She and Cavanaugh looked above them, noticing a tree branch.

"He jumped up, grabbed the branch, squirmed toward the slope, and touched down several feet above where the dog could smell him," Cavanaugh realized.

They lifted the dog onto the slope. Instantly it retrieved the scent and scrambled upward, with Cavanaugh, Jamie, and the handler working to follow. They reached a bluff and hurried along it. Sweat stuck their clothes to their skin. Along another slope, the dog again lost the scent.

But this time, there wasn't a tree branch above them to explain how Dant could have lifted himself and fooled the dog.

"Well, if he didn't go up and he didn't go forward...," Cavanaugh said.

"He backtracked and jumped off the trail," Jamie concluded.

They ran back the way they'd come and almost passed the cave before they realized it was there, camouflaged by bushes. The bloodhound barked frantically, wanting to charge in.

The handler restrained it.

Cavanaugh wiped sweat from his face and unclipped a canteen from his belt.

"Dant, are you thirsty?" he yelled toward the cave. "You covered a lot of distance in a hurry. I've got water." He shook the canteen so that Dant could hear the water sloshing.

The shadowy cave was silent.

"Or maybe you planned for an emergency," Jamie said, "and stocked the cave with food and water."

Cavanaugh raised the canteen to his mouth, taking several swallows. Although the water was unpleasantly warm, his parched tongue absorbed it.

"Fine. We'll set fire to the bushes and smoke your miserable ass out of there."

He and Jamie gathered dead leaves and branches, stacking them in front of the bushes that obscured the cave.

He struck a match.

"Okay," a voice said from the enclosure.

The bushes rustled. Gradually a figure emerged.

But he didn't look anything like Dant. He was bald and bearded. His nose had a bony ridge. A scar disfigured his neck.

"Never heard of anyone getting cosmetic surgery to look ugly," Jamie said. "Since you went to all this trouble, why didn't you try to pretend to be someone else when we arrived?"

"I was prepared to until I saw who was getting off the plane." Dant's expression was sour. "I figured I could fool most people, but not anybody who spent up-close time with me and specializes in paying attention."

"Yeah, those camera-friendly blue eyes of yours are hard to disguise," Jamie said. "Tinted lenses might have done the job, but I suspect you forget to put them on day after day when only the natives are around to see you. Even with tinted lenses, you wouldn't have fooled us, though. Your cosmetic surgeon told us what you look like now."

"But..."

"Yes, I know—you thought you'd guaranteed his silence by promising him a quarter-million dollars a year," Jamie said. "The trouble is, the second check you sent him bounced. Worse, he believed what you told him about how well your companies were doing. To impress his clients, he said he had a stock tip that couldn't go wrong. They invested heavily. When your house of cards collapsed, the clients blamed him for their losses. His practice is ruined."

"There are plenty like him," Cavanaugh added. "Thousands of people lost their jobs because of you. Their pensions are worthless. They can't pay their mortgages or feed their families. Their lives are destroyed. All because you did whatever you wanted whenever you felt like it."

"Big gains require big risks."

"Keep telling yourself that in prison. Did you figure the first three attempts to kill you were only the beginning? Novak was behind them, incidentally. He couldn't stand you any more than anybody else does. Did the explosion at your Cape Cod property give you the idea to arrange for the last two explosions on your own, so when your boat blew apart, people would decide you were blown apart also and finally give up searching for you?"

"Something like that." Dant glared. "How the hell did you find me?"

"Once we figured out what you were doing, it became a matter of asking the right questions," Jamie answered. "Naturally you'd want to change your appearance. After that, you'd want to hole up someplace remote for a couple of years until you felt it was safe to return with a new identity. What property did your companies own that would be useful to you, particularly in terms of your appetite for female companionship? We spent months going through your records. One of your shadow companies bought this island just before your empire started to teeter. That seemed a good clue. So did the half-dressed native women."

"Damn it, why couldn't you leave me alone? I gave you a generous check."

"Which bounced. But that's not what pissed me off," Cavanaugh said. "I told you protecting people is a very personal thing for me, but you treated it like a joke."

"I needed to. It was part of the act. I had to show I was so determined to do what I wanted, that I was so controlling, even the best bodyguards couldn't have kept me from getting on that boat."

"Protectors, not bodyguards."

"Whatever."

"Now *you're* the one who'll be controlled."

THE ATTITUDE ADJUSTER

In a final Protector story, here again are Cavanaugh and Jamie.

A ROAD-RENOVATION CREW. TRUCKS, GRINDERS, ROLLERS. Only one lane of traffic is open. As you drive toward the dust and noise, a man holds a pole with a sign at the top. The pole's bottom rests on the dirt, so all he needs to do is turn the shaft to show you one side of the sign or the other. SLOW, you are directed, or else STOP.

The man is tall and scarecrow lanky, exuding the impression of sinewy strength. He wears battered work boots, faded jeans, and an old blue work shirt with the sleeves rolled up, revealing a rose tattoo above the hand with which he holds the pole. His shirt has sweat blotches. His face is narrow, sun-browned, and weather-creased. He wears a yellow vest and hardhat.

According to the radio's weather forecaster, the temperature on this Illinois August day is ninety degrees Fahrenheit, with eighty-seven percent humidity. But the sun radiates off the road, increasing the temperature to one hundred and five. Because the project is behind schedule, the man is required to work overtime. He holds that sign twelve hours a day—for the past three months. You've seen countless versions of him. Passing him, you might wonder what he thinks.

Stupid son of a bitch. Sits in his damned air-conditioned SUV, stares at my sign, speeds past, almost hits me, throws dust in my face. Can't you read, you moron? The sign says SLOW! One of these days, I'll whack this pole against a fender, hell, through a window. Teach these bastards to show respect. Everybody's got a snotty attitude. Here comes another guy barreling toward me. King of the road. Hey, see this sign I'm pointing at, dummy! SLOW! It says SLOW!

The man's name is Barry Pollard. He is thirty-nine, but years of working outdoors have made him look much older. His previous jobs involved strenuous physical labor, lifting, carrying, digging, hammering, which he never minded because he felt content when he had something to fill the time, to weary him and shut off his thoughts. But months of nothing to do except stand in the middle of the road, hold the sign, and watch motorists ignore it have given him plenty of opportunity to draw conclusions about the passing world.

Dodo, how'd you ever get a driver's license if you can't read? The sign says SLOW. For God's sake, you came so close, you almost knocked it out of my hand. You think you can do whatever you want. That's what's wrong these days. Nobody pays attention to the rules. When I was a kid, if I even thought about doing something my old man didn't like, he set down his beer can and punched me to the floor. Certainly taught me right from wrong. "You've got a bad attitude," he used to tell me. "We gotta correct it." From what I've seen the past three months, there's a lot of bad attitudes that need correcting.

A voice squawked from a walkie-talkie hooked to Barry's belt. "Okay, that's enough cars going north for a while. Stop 'em at your end while the cars on *my* side get a chance to go through."

"Roger," Barry said into the walkie-talkie, feeling a little like he was in the military. He swung his sign so the message now read STOP.

A guy in a van tried to go past.

"Hey!" Barry shouted and jerked his sign down in front of the windshield.

The guy barely stopped before the pole would have cracked the glass.

"Back up and get off the road!" Barry shouted. "There's a bunch of cars coming this way!"

Red-faced, the guy charged from the van. "You almost broke my windshield!"

"I could have, but I didn't!" Barry said. "Maybe next time!"

"You jerk, I ought to—"

Barry pointed the pole at the guy. "Oughta what? I told you to back up your van and get off the road. You're interfering with the project."

"You could've waited to stop traffic until I went past!"

"When the boss tells me to stop vehicles, I do it. You think you're more important than the guy in the car behind you? I should stop *him* but not *you?*"

"I've got a job I need to get to!"

"And *he* doesn't have some place to go? You think you're a big shot? A VIP? That stands for Very Important Prick. An attitude like yours, it's no wonder the country's going to hell. Here comes the other traffic, bozo! *Move your vehicle.*"

The guy spit on Barry's work boots, then stormed back to his van.

Barry stared down at the spit.

A sign on the van read MIDWEST CABLE AND HIGH-SPEED INTERNET INSTALLATION. A phone number was under it. As the guy got into the truck and backed from approaching traffic, Barry took his cell phone from his belt and pressed numbers.

"Midwest Cable," a female voice said.

"One of your installers was at my place today. He did such a good job, I thought I'd phone and tell you how impressed I am."

"What's his name?"

"Just a second. I've got his... Of all the... Dumb me, I lost the card he gave me. He's about forty-five. Kind of on the heavy side. Real short red hair."

"Yeah, that's Fred Harriman."

"He did a great job."

At seven, after the job shut down for the day, Barry drove home, looked up Fred Harriman's address on the Internet's White Pages and made a note of it. He waited a month, wanting to be certain that no one at the cable company would remember his phone call. At last, he drove to Fred's neighborhood, passed a blue ranch house with two big flowerbeds, saw a pickup truck in the driveway, and stopped at a park down the street. With lots of other cars near him, no one paid attention as Barry watched the truck. Soon, the sun went down, and the people in the park went home, but Barry continued watching. Lights glowed through the front windows.

At nine thirty, as Barry began to worry that a police car would cruise the area and wonder why he was sitting alone in a car in the dark, the front door opened. Fred came out, got in the truck, and drove away.

Barry followed him to a bar called the Seventh Inning Stretch, where Fred joined a couple of buddies at a table, drank a pitcher of beer, and watched the end of a baseball game. They cursed when the Cubs didn't win. Fred was such a putz, he didn't notice Barry watching among drinkers in the background. But Barry was gone when they paid for their beers.

In the shadowy parking lot, they made a couple of jokes. One of them burped. The others laughed. They went to their separate vehicles. Fred got to his about the same time the others got to theirs. He climbed into the truck, started to drive away, then felt that the truck handled wrong, and got out. The shadows were so dense that he needed to crouch to see the flat tire on the front passenger side. He cursed more seriously than when the Cubs lost. His pals were gone. As he straightened and turned toward the locked tool kit in back of his truck, he groaned from a two-by-four to the side of his jaw, although he never knew what hit him or saw who did it. Barry felt the satisfying crunch of flesh and crack of bone. To make it look like a mugging, Barry took all the cash from Fred's wallet.

Two weeks later, the roadwork was finished. With time on his hands, Barry unhappily discovered that everywhere he went, people had attitude problems. A guy in a sports car cut him off at an intersection and gave him the finger when Barry blared his horn. A woman pushed in front of him at Starbuck's. A clerk at a convenience store made him wait while the clerk used the store's phone to gab with his girlfriend. A waiter at a diner brought him a bacon and tomato sandwich that had mayonnaise, even though Barry had distinctly told him he didn't want any mayo. When Barry complained, the waiter took the sandwich away and brought a replacement, but when Barry opened it, he saw traces of white. All the waiter had done was scrape some off.

In movie theaters, people wouldn't stop talking.

"That cop better stay out of that warehouse," a woman said, pointing at the screen.

"Yeah, he should radio for backup," the man next to her said.

"He didn't radio for backup when he searched the abandoned house, either," the woman said.

"Well, if he did, the stupid writers wouldn't have a plot."

"Please, be quiet," Barry said behind them.

"And look at this. The lights don't work, and he doesn't have a flashlight, but he's going inside anyhow."

"Please, don't talk during the movie," Barry said.

"Yep, here's the vampire sneaking up on—"

"SHUT THE HELL UP!"

The man turned and glared. "Have you got a problem, buddy?"

"This isn't your living room! I'm trying to—"

"You want me to shut up?"

"That's what I've been telling you."

"Make me."

Barry left the theater, waited outside, followed the couple home, put a ski mask over his head, and taught them to shut up by knocking their teeth out. Then he smashed all their TV sets and set fire to their car. He took money from the guy's wallet and the woman's purse. Another job well done.

●●●

"THERE, YOUR computer system's updated," the technician said.

"High-speed Internet." Barry marveled. "I figured it was time I joined the twenty-first century."

He found an online company that specialized in surveillance equipment.

FOLLOW ANYBODY ANYWHERE, an ad announced. JUST HIDE THIS TINY RADIO TRANSMITTER ON THEIR CLOTHES OR IN THEIR BRIEFCASE OR THEIR PURSE. IT GIVES OFF A SILENT BEEP THAT ONLY YOU CAN HEAR THROUGH YOUR MATCHING RADIO RECEIVER.

But when Barry got the transmitter, it was the size of a walkie-talkie and the even-larger radio receiver needed to be less than thirty feet from the transmitter or else Barry couldn't hear the beep.

He sent an email, asking for his money back, but never received an answer. He repeatedly phoned the number on the company's website, but all he ever heard was a recorded message, telling him that "every available technician is talking with another customer."

Barry drove four hours to St. Louis, where the company had its post-office box. From his car in the parking lot outside the post office, he stared through windows toward the company's PO box. After a rumpled guy took envelopes from the box, Barry followed him to an office above an escort service. When Barry finished teaching the guy the error of his ways, he had his money back, plus the guy's driver's license and his FOLLOW ANYBODY ANYWHERE business card, which allowed Barry to cash all the checks in the envelopes.

Compensation for my time, Barry thought. *It's only fair.*

Back home after the long drive, he counted his money yet again, almost eight hundred dollars, and opened yet another beer. *Sure beats standing on the road, holding that damned sign.* He chased a shot of bourbon with a gulp of beer and told himself that he was actually performing a public service. *Protecting people from jerks. You bet. Teaching bozos to mend their ways.*

He slumped on his sofa, chuckling at the thought that some guys with attitude problems might even be thankful if Barry set them straight. *For all I know, they're ashamed of being dorks. Like my father said, everybody knows they need direction.*

Amused, Barry staggered to his computer. Alcohol made his fingers clumsy. He thanked God for the computer's spell-check program. After all, he needed to make the proper impression.

EBOD
THE ADULT ALTERNATIVE TO EBAY
LOWER COMMISSION—LESS MONITORING—
MORE FUN
SELLERS ASSUME ALL RESPONSIBILITIES FOR
LISTING ITEMS

I WILL ADJUST YOUR WAYS
ITEM 44735ABQE

High bidder receives an attitude adjustment.

I am strong and tough from years of outdoor work. If you win this auction, I will teach you to walk the straight and narrow. I promise not to cripple or kill you. No weapons, just my boots and fists. Maybe a club, depending on how much your attitude needs adjusting.

Barry chuckled.

I will perform this service only if you promise not to resist and not to have me arrested afterward.

Clever point, Barry thought.

You will provide travel expenses and directions to your home and work. You will also provide motel expenses, but these should be low because I plan to do the job swiftly so that I can proceed to giving adjustments to other people. I will pick a time that you least expect. Perhaps while you're asleep or in the bathroom or going to work. During your adjustment, I may be forced to break windows or furniture. The costs for these are your responsibility. If you have a family or whatever, warn them to stay out of my way unless you want their attitudes adjusted also.

Ha! Barry thought.

No checks or PAYPAL. I accept only money orders made out to CASH. Good luck.

• • •

THE NEXT morning, Barry foggily remembered what he had done and cursed himself for wasting time when he could have continued drinking. EBod was part of a porn site, for God's sake. The only reason he'd used it was that eBay wouldn't have allowed him to post his auction. For all he knew, nobody visited that portion of the site.

Anyway, who's going to bid on getting beat up? he asked himself.

To prove his point, all week he didn't get a response.

Then, on Sunday, with a half hour left in the auction, he received the following:

QUESTION TO SELLER

I thought about your auction quite a while: all week, every day and night. I have done something bad that makes me feel awful. I can't stop thinking about it. I need to be punished. How could I have done such a terrible thing? Are you serious that you won't kill me? I'm a devout Roman Catholic, and if you kill me, God might see it as a kind of suicide. Then I'd go to Hell. I need to know that you won't endanger my soul, which is in danger enough already.

• • •

DAN YATES stuck the OPEN HOUSE sign into the lush lawn and walked past rose bushes toward the two-story Spanish Colonial Revival. Another sign was prominently displayed, YATES REALTY, under which was a phone number and a website address. Dan wore a navy sport coat, white shirt, and conservative striped tie. He paused on the porch and surveyed the handsome yard and pleasant neighborhood, nodding with confidence that someone would make an offer by the end of the afternoon.

Dan left the front door open and proceeded to the kitchen, where he brewed coffee and arranged cookies next to bowls of peanuts and potato chips. He set out bottled water and canned soft drinks. He stacked brochures with eye-catching photographs of the house and information about it. The asking price was $899,000. Two months ago, it had been $939,000. With low mortgage rates and the housing market starting to return, he felt sure that the house would sell for $889,000, close to what the sellers wanted.

His preparations completed, Dan gave his best smile to his first visitors, a man and a woman, who were obviously impressed by the marble-topped kitchen counter but tried not to show it. Thirty seconds later, another couple arrived, then another soon after, and the show was on.

"The house is three years old. This subdivision used to be the Huntington Beach airport. As you can see, there's no house behind you, only this low attractive wall, beyond which is a Mormon church. Very quiet. Plenty of sky. You attend that church? The Latter-Day Saints? My, this house would certainly be convenient for you. On Sundays, you could practically crawl over the wall and go to services. The subdivision has its own swimming pool and park. There's a golf course down the street as well as a shopping center three blocks away and a school three blocks in the other direction. You've heard the old saying about what makes property valuable? Location, location, location. Ten minutes to the beach. Honestly, this has it all."

And so it went, forty visitors, three promises to make offers and one firm offer for cash. *Not a bad afternoon's work*, Dan thought.

"The owners are visiting family in Seattle," he told the prospective buyers. "I'll fax the material to them. They have until noon tomorrow to respond. I'll let you know what they say as soon as possible."

Dan escorted the couple to the door, checked his watch, saw that the hours for the open house were over, and allowed himself to relax. When the last visitors drove away, he went to the street and put the OPEN HOUSE sign in his SUV. He returned to the kitchen, where he cleaned the coffee maker and cups. He put all the empty cans and bottles into a garbage bag along with the coffee grounds and the remnants of the cookies, the peanuts, and the potato chips.

The Baxters are coming for dinner, he thought. *Laura's expecting me to bring home the steaks. I'd better hurry.*

Giving the kitchen a final inspection, Dan saw movement to the right and turned toward a lanky man standing in the doorway to the living room. The guy had a creased, rugged face. He wore sneakers, jeans, and a pullover. His hair was scraggly.

"I'm sorry," Dan said. "The open house is over. I was just about to leave and lock up."

"I warned you I'd show up when you least expected," the man said.

"Excuse me?" Dan asked.

"You've been bad."

"What the hell are you talking about?"

"Your attitude adjustment."

"Adjustment?"

"The one you paid for. You're Dan Yates, correct?"

"That's my name, but—"

"Two-One-Five Sunnyvale Lane?"

"How do you know my—"

"No sense in putting it off." The guy rolled up his long sleeves, as if preparing for physical labor. He had a rose tattoo on his right forearm.

"Look, I don't get the joke," Dan said. "Now if you'll come with me, we'll just step outside and—"

"No joke. You bid on the attitude adjustment. You won the auction. Now you get what you paid for. I don't know what you did that was so terrible, but I swear I'll ease your conscience. You'll be sore, but you'll feel a whole lot better after I finish with you."

Dan reached for his cell phone. The man threw it against the wall, punched him in the stomach, kneed him in the face, whacked his cheek, struck his nose, then started beating him in earnest.

At five, when Dan didn't return home with the steaks for the dinner with the Baxters, his wife called his cell phone. An electronic voice announced, "That number is out of service." Out of service? What was going on? Laura called several more times, with the same response. The Baxters arrived at six. At seven, when Dan still hadn't arrived, Laura phoned the police, but no one named Dan Yates had been reported in a traffic accident. The Baxters agreed to watch the Yates's ten-year-old daughter while Laura went to where Dan had the open house. The front door was unlocked. She found him unconscious on the kitchen's marble floor, lying in a pool of blood.

"Fractured arm, ribs, and clavicle," an emergency-ward doctor told her after an ambulance hurried Dan to the nearest hospital.

"Auction. Rose tattoo," Dan murmured as he drifted in and out of consciousness.

"Must be the pain killers. The poor guy's delirious," a police detective said.

• • •

BARRY, WHO had never been to California, used the generous travel fee he'd demanded to stay a few extra days. He watched the surfers near Huntington Beach's famous pier. He planned to drive north to Los Angeles and cruise Hollywood Boulevard, then head up to Malibu. With luck, he'd cross paths with movie stars.

Those plans ended when he read the next morning's edition of the *Orange County Register*. With increasing anger, he learned that Dan Yates had attempted to identify him.

Auction. Rose tattoo. That wasn't the damned deal! Barry thought as joggers passed him at the beach. *You weren't supposed to resist, and you weren't supposed to try to have me arrested afterward! Doesn't anybody keep his word? Didn't I adjust your attitude hard enough?*

In the hospital's lobby, he requested the number for Dan Yates's room.

"Are you a member of his family?" the receptionist asked.

"His brother. When I heard Dan was in the hospital—I still can't believe it—I drove all the way from Phoenix."

"Room eight forty-two."

One of many things Barry had learned while holding the sign for the road crew was that people got so absorbed in their affairs, they didn't pay attention to what was around them. They'd drive over you before they noticed you. Walking along the hospital corridor, a newspaper in one hand, a bunch of flowers in the other, just one of many visitors, Barry might as well have been invisible. The door to room eight forty-two was open. He passed it, glancing in at banged-up Dan lying in a bed, the only patient in the room. Dan's face looked like an uncooked beefsteak. Various monitors were attached to him. An IV tube led into his arm.

I'd almost feel sorry for you if you hadn't broken our deal, Barry thought.

A not-bad-looking woman sat next to Dan. Roughly Dan's age, she was pale with worry. *The wife*, Barry decided.

That was all he saw as he continued down the corridor. He went into a men's room, lingered, then came out, and returned along the corridor. Visiting hours were almost over. People emerged from various rooms and headed toward the elevators. The woman left Dan's room and did the same.

Barry went into Dan's room and used a knee to close the door so he wouldn't leave fingerprints. He set down the flowers and pulled his shirtsleeve over his hand, again so he wouldn't leave fingerprints. He turned off the monitors, grabbed a hospital gown from a table, shielded himself, pulled a section of garden hose from the newspaper he'd brought, and whacked Dan several times across the face. Blood flew. He set the crimson-soaked section of hose on Dan's chest, dropped the spattered gown on the floor, opened the door, and went down the corridor with the other departing visitors.

Twenty seconds, Barry thought. *Damned good.*

• • •

A NURSE went into Dan's room. She was used to seeing blood in a hospital, but not this much. Screaming, she rang for an emergency team, then hurried to turn on the monitors, which immediately began wailing, the waves and numbers showing that at least Dan was still alive.

• • •

From: Laura Yates <earthlink.net>
To: <jamietravers@gps.com>

Subject: trouble, postpone visit

Jamie, I hate to do this at the last minute, but I've been so worried and tired that I haven't had the time or energy to send an email. I've got so much trouble. I need to withdraw my invitation for you and your husband to stay with us for a few days while you're in LA on business. Dan was nearly beaten to death on Sunday afternoon at an open house he was giving. Then he was beaten again in his hospital room. We have no idea who on Earth did it or why. I spend so much time with him at the hospital that I won't be able to see you. Plus, I'm so sick with worry that I won't be very good company. Sorry. I was looking forward to meeting your husband and reminiscing about our sorority days. Life can sure change quickly. Laura.

• • •

From: Jamie Travers <gps.com>
To: <laurayates@earthlink.net>
Subject: coming regardless

Laura, Since we're in the area, we've decided to visit you anyhow. But you won't need to babysit us. This won't exactly be a social occasion. My husband's in a line of work that might be helpful to you. I'm pretty good at it myself. Apologies for sounding mysterious. It's too complicated to explain in an email. Kind of a secret life I have. All will be revealed tomorrow. What's the name and address of the hospital? Can we meet you there at noon? We'll see if we can sort this out. Don't despair. Love, Jamie.

• • •

ALTHOUGH LAURA hadn't seen Jamie in five years, her former college roommate looked as radiant as ever. Five feet ten, with a jogger's slim build. A model's narrow chin and high cheek bones. Long brunette hair. Bright green eyes. She wore brown linen slacks, and a loose-fitting jacket over a beige blouse. But Laura processed these details only later, so distracted by her emotions that all she wanted to do was hug Jamie as she came into the room.

Laura wept again. She'd been doing a lot of it. "I'm so glad to see you."

"You couldn't have kept me away," Jamie assured her.

Laura's tear-blurred gaze drifted toward the man next to her.

"This is my husband," Jamie said proudly. "His name's Cavanaugh. And this is my good friend Laura," she told her husband. "She and I raised a lot of hell at Wellesley."

"Pleased to meet you," the man said.

Again, Laura paid attention to his appearance only later. He was around six feet tall, not muscular but somehow solid looking. Handsome, with a strong chin that somehow didn't intimidate. Hair that wasn't quite brown and not quite sandy, not long but not short. Alert eyes that were hazel and yet seemed to reflect the blue of his loose sports coat. He had an odd-looking black metal clip on the outside of a pants pocket. But all that mattered was his handshake, which was firm yet gentle and seemed to communicate a reassurance that as long as you were with him, you were secure.

"Cavanaugh?" she asked. "What's your first name?"

"Actually"—he grinned—"I've gotten in the habit of just being called 'Cavanaugh'."

Laura looked at Jamie. "You call him by his last name?"

"It's sort of complicated," Jamie said.

"But it sounds kind of cold."

"Well, when I want to be friendly, I call him something else."

"What's that?"

"'Lover.'"

"Perhaps I should leave the room," Cavanaugh said.

"No, stick around," Jamie said. "We're finished talking about you. You're not the center of attention anymore."

Cavanaugh nodded. "Exactly. *He* is."

They turned toward Dan, who lay unconscious in a hospital bed, all sorts of equipment and tubes linked to him. His face was purple with bruises.

"Laura, the initials GPS on my website address stand for Global Protective Services," Jamie said. "My husband watches over people in trouble. He takes care of them. He's a protector."

Laura frowned, puzzled.

"Sometimes I help," Jamie said. "That's why we're here. To find out what happened."

"And make sure it doesn't happen again," Cavanaugh said.

"But I *don't know* what happened, only that Dan was attacked. *Twice*." Laura's voice shook.

"Tell us what you can," Jamie said. "Tell us about Sunday."

Ten minutes later, wiping more tears from her cheeks, Laura finished explaining.

"I don't understand *any* of it." Laura raised her hands in a gesture of helplessness.

"Has Dan been able to say anything?" Jamie asked.

"Nothing that makes sense."

Unconscious, Dan fidgeted and groaned.

Cavanaugh studied the room and frowned. "Why isn't someone watching the door?"

"The police said they don't have the budget to keep an officer here."

"Jamie said you had a daughter."

"Yes. Bethany. She's ten years old."

"And where is she now?"

"At school. I need to pick her up at three. She's worried sick about her father."

Cavanaugh pulled out his cell phone and pressed numbers.

"Vince," he said when someone answered, "can you bear it if you don't do any sightseeing in LA? I need you to come down to Huntington Beach." Cavanaugh mentioned the name of the hospital. "A patient needs watching. Dan Yates. Jamie went to college with his wife. That's right—this one's for friendship. I'll fill you in when you get here. If Gwen's available, bring her with you. A little girl needs watching also. Great. Thanks, my friend."

Cavanaugh put away his phone and told Laura, "They're a brother and sister team. We brought them with us on the Gulfstream for a job that starts two days from now."

"Gulfstream?" Laura looked more bewildered.

"Global Protective Services has a lot of resources," Jamie said. "That's why I married him."

It was a joke. Jamie, who sold a promising dot-com company during the Internet stock frenzy of the 1990s, owned plenty of resources of her own.

"Laura, we need to ask the obvious question," Jamie continued. "Does Dan have any enemies?"

"Enemies?" Laura made the word sound meaningless.

"Surely, the police asked you the same question."

"Yes, but... Enemies? Dan's the nicest man in the world. Everybody likes him."

"From everything Jamie told me, he's kind and decent," Cavanaugh agreed.

"That's right."

"A loving husband. An attentive father."

Laura wiped her eyes. "Absolutely."

"Good-natured. Generous."

Laura frowned. "Where are you going with this?"

"In my experience, a certain type of person hates those virtues," Cavanaugh said. "Despises anyone who exhibits them.

Takes for granted that someone who's kind and good-natured is weak. Assumes he or she is a mark to be exploited."

Laura looked at Jamie in confusion and then again at Cavanaugh. "That's awfully cynical, don't you think?"

"I work in a cynical profession," Cavanaugh said. "You'd be surprised how many kind, good-natured, generous people have enemies."

Laura, who'd been thinking a lot about the times she and Jamie shared at Wellesley, recalled an American fiction course they'd taken. "*Billy Budd?*" She referred to a work by Herman Melville, in which a ship's officer hates a kind-hearted sailor simply because he's kind hearted.

"Something like that," Cavanaugh said. "Some people— sociopaths—get their kicks taking advantage of what they consider weakness."

"Then *anybody* could be Dan's enemy."

"It's just something to think about," Jamie said. "The point is, often the enemy isn't obvious."

"Often, it's someone who appears to be a close friend," Cavanaugh said. "You mentioned *Billy Budd*. Think about Iago in *Othello*."

Again Laura looked at Jamie. She might have been trying to change the subject. "I doubt many bodyguards know Shakespeare."

"Not a bodyguard," Jamie said. "A protector. As you'll see, there's a difference. We need to consider something else, Laura. Please, don't take this wrong. Don't be offended. Are you absolutely certain Dan's faithful to you?"

"*What?*" Laura's cheeks reddened.

"Stalkers tend to be motivated by sexual anger," Cavanaugh said. "If Dan were having an affair, if the woman were married, the husband might have been furious enough to attack Dan. Or if Dan tried to call off the affair, the woman might have hired someone to put him in the hospital. 'Keep our agreement, jerk, or you'll get an even worse adjustment.' The note can be interpreted to fit that scenario."

"I don't want to talk about this anymore."

"I understand," Cavanaugh said. "I'm a stranger, and suddenly I'm asking rude questions. I apologize. But I did need to ask, and now it's important for you to look at your world in a way you never imagined. Suppose someone thought Dan was making sexual overtures even when he was perfectly innocent. Did you ever have a fleeting suspicion that someone was needlessly jealous? If we're going to find who did this to your husband and stop it from happening again, we might need to suspect what seemingly couldn't be suspected."

Laura eased into a chair. "I don't feel well."

"I'm surprised you're holding up as strongly as you are," Cavanaugh said. "Why don't you let Jamie take you home? There's nothing you can do for Dan at the moment. Get some rest."

Laura looked at Dan, where he lay unconscious in the bed. "But..."

"I'll stay with him. Nothing's going to happen to him while I'm here. I promise."

Laura studied Cavanaugh for several long seconds. "Yes," she finally said. "I could use some rest."

Jamie helped her to stand. As they walked toward the door, Laura turned and studied Cavanaugh again. "What's that metal clip on the outside of your pants pocket?"

"This?" Cavanaugh pulled on the clip and withdrew a black folding knife from the pocket. With a flick of his thumb, he opened the blade. He touched his loose-fitting jacket. "I also carry a firearm that I have a permit for."

"So do I," Jamie said.

Bewildered but more certain of the reassurance they communicated, Laura let Jamie guide her from the room.

• • •

CAVANAUGH IDENTIFIED himself to a nurse and doctor who came in. Although they frowned, they seemed relieved by his presence. Sitting next to the door, out of sight from the hallway, he performed the hardest, tensest activity in his profession: waiting. Bodyguards might pass the time by reading, but protectors didn't distract themselves—they kept their hands free and watched.

In a while, he sensed a change in Dan and glanced toward the bed, keeping most of his attention on the doorway.

Dan's bloodshot eyes were open, squinting. "Who..."

"I'm a friend."

Dan's eyes closed.

In a further while, a man walked into the room. Like Cavanaugh, he had strong-looking shoulders and wore a loose sport coat. He looked immediately toward Cavanaugh's sheltered position next to the door, as if that were the proper place for Cavanaugh to be.

"Vince, thanks for coming," Cavanaugh said.

"Well, you said the magic word 'friendship.'"

"Where's Gwen?" Cavanaugh asked.

"Jamie phoned and gave us directions to the house. Gwen's helping to pick up the little girl from school."

"That finally covers the bases," Cavanaugh said.

Again, Dan's eyes struggled open. "Who..." He squinted at Vince.

"Another friend," Cavanaugh said. "Isn't it nice to be popular?"

Dan's eyes drooped.

"Somebody sure worked him over," Vince said.

• • •

"HAD A tattoo," Dan said a day later. His words were hard to understand because he spoke through mangled lips. "A rose. Here." Dan pointed toward his right forearm.

"Yes, you told that to your wife and me when you were unconscious," a police detective said. "Ever see him before?"

"No." Dan breathed and rested. "But he knew my address."

Cavanaugh leaned close.

"He claimed I paid him. For what he called an attitude adjustment," Dan murmured.

"What does *that* mean?" the detective asked.

"He said I won an auction."

"Yeah, you mentioned that, too. He must have been crazy. A crack head who wandered into the house you were showing," the detective concluded.

"But then why would he go to the hospital and attack Dan a second time?" Jamie asked.

"That's the thing about crack heads. They don't make sense," the detective told her.

"He said I'd done something terrible." Dan forced out the words. "...said he was easing my conscience."

"By beating you? Crazy for sure," the detective decided. "We'll check our files for crack heads who are religious fanatics."

A physician entered the room, examined Dan, and announced that there wasn't any reason for him to remain in the hospital any longer. "I'll prescribe some pain medication. You'll probably get a quieter rest at home."

• • •

HELPING TO get Dan settled in the master bedroom, Cavanaugh asked, "Do you feel alert enough to answer more questions?"

"Anything to catch him." Dan took a painful breath. "To stop him."

"Do you have any enemies?"

Dan looked puzzled.

"Sweetheart, he asked me the same thing," Laura said. "I told him I couldn't imagine anybody hating you."

"How big is your real-estate firm?" Jamie asked.

"Twenty brokers."

"One big happy family?"

"They're all a great team."

"No exceptions?" Cavanaugh asked.

"No." Dan's pain-ridden eyes clouded. "Except..."

"There's always an 'except'," Jamie said.

"Now that I think about it..."

"Exactly. Now that you think about it... It's a great team because the ones that didn't fit got sent away."

"Six months ago. I had to tell a broker to leave the firm," Dan remembered.

"Why?"

"Sexual harassment. Sam Logan. He kept bothering a secretary."

"I remember now," Laura said. "But that's so long ago..."

"But wouldn't he have tried to get even with me earlier?"

"Not if he made himself wait until he hoped you'd forgotten him," Jamie said.

"But Sam wasn't the guy who attacked me."

"So he hired somebody," Jamie suggested.

"Auctioned somebody," Cavanaugh added, referring to the word the detective had mentioned.

"But *what* auction?" Dan winced from the pain of talking.

"Set that aside for the moment. Tell us more about your business. Is anything unusual or dramatic happening?"

"Just that this year was fabulous for us. Enough that Ed Malone made an offer."

"Ed Malone? Offer?"

"He's the best broker I have. He wants to buy a share of the firm and open a branch office close to the beach."

"You seriously considered his proposal?" Jamie asked.

"Not much. I told him I liked things the way they are."

"Do you suppose he wanted a share strongly enough that he decided to put you on your back for a while?" Cavanaugh wondered. "If business suffered, maybe he could buy a share of the firm for a lower amount."

"Ed?" Dan looked astonished. "Never in a million years. We get along perfectly."

"Tell us about the Baxters. Laura told Jamie you were supposed to have dinner with them the day you were beaten."

"Yes," Laura said. "They watched our daughter while I went to look for Dan. They're close friends. They'd never do anything to hurt us."

"Because of the dinner invitation, they'd be the last people you'd suspect," Cavanaugh noted.

"You know," Dan said painfully, "I don't like the way you think."

"I don't blame you," Cavanaugh told him. "You're tired and sore, and we're badgering you with questions. We'll talk about this later. Meanwhile, arrangements need to be made. Jamie and I have an assignment in Los Angeles tomorrow. Vince and Gwen go with us. But you need at least two protectors. Also, you need to tell your daughter's school to take precautions while she's there."

"Two protectors?" Laura asked.

"Three would be better," Jamie answered.

"We'd hire them?"

"Jamie and I were happy to do this for friendship," Cavanaugh said. "Vince and Gwen did it as a favor to us. But protectors who don't know you would certainly expect to be paid."

"How much?" Laura frowned.

"A reasonable rate would be three hundred dollars a day."

"Times *three?* Per *day?*" Laura looked shocked.

"Good God, for how long?" Dan wanted to know.

"Until you're recovered. Meanwhile, they'd teach you how to secure the house and to change your patterns and behavior when you're outside. We call it Condition Orange, a basic alertness that helps you anticipate trouble. You should read Gavin de Becker's *The Gift of Fear*. It teaches you to pay attention to your instincts when they warn you something's wrong."

"*The Gift of Fear?*" Dan asked. "Condition Orange? This is insane. You make it sound like we're living in a war zone."

"Not far from the truth. The world's a dangerous neighborhood," Jamie said.

Laura studied her. "You've certainly changed."

"Things happened that forced me to change," Jamie said. "I wouldn't be alive today if I hadn't started thinking this way. I'll explain it to you later."

"Meanwhile, think about this while you rest," Cavanaugh told Dan.

"I don't have time to rest." Dan shifted in the bed, wincing. "Not when I'm losing business. Laura, get me my laptop. I need to see the new listings and—"

"Do you really think working as soon as you get home from the hospital is a good idea?" Laura asked.

"The alternative is to let Ed try to replace me. That's how your friends have got me thinking."

"Sorry," Cavanaugh said, and started backing from the room.

Laura brought Dan his laptop and helped him sit up. Groaning, he opened it and used the hand on his unbroken arm to turn on the computer.

"We'll let you do your work." Jamie left the room with Laura.

"Please, close the door," Dan said.

Halfway down the stairs, Laura halted. She thought about something, then glanced up toward the bedroom.

"Excuse me for a minute," she told Jamie and Cavanaugh.

Laura climbed the stairs and opened the door. After a motionless moment, she stepped inside and closed the door. The back of her neck was red.

● ● ●

AT THE bottom of the stairs, Cavanaugh and Jamie looked at each other.

"Something's not what it seems," Cavanaugh said. "Laura was more upset about the expense of hiring protectors than Dan was. Do they have money problems?"

"Not if somebody's trying to buy into Dan's business and he keeps refusing."

"I'm bothered by something else," Cavanaugh added. "The police detective said Dan talked about an auction and a rose tattoo when he was unconscious, but Laura never mentioned a word about the auction and the tattoo when we met her. Why would she leave those details out of her explanation?"

"Auction. What does that mean to you?" Jamie asked.

"Christie's. Sotheby's. Paintings. Statues."

"Sure. But... Maybe it's because I used to be in the dot-com sector. Christie's and Sotheby's aren't what I immediately think of."

"I don't understand."

"I'll give you a hint. The auction's on the Internet."

"eBay?"

Jamie went into a study next to the living room and approached its desk-top computer. "Just out of the hospital, Dan was far too impatient to get on the Internet." She turned on the computer, tapped a few keys, and pointed toward a list that appeared on the screen. "These are the ten sites that this computer accesses the most."

"No eBay," Cavanaugh said. "That hunch didn't work out."

"But what's this bod.com and eBod?" Jamie wondered. "Let's see if this computer and the one upstairs are networked. Yep." Jamie tapped more keys. "Dan already signed off. Strange. He couldn't wait to get on, and now he couldn't wait to get off as soon as Jamie went back to the bedroom."

Jamie typed www.bod.com. A prompt asked for a password.

"Looks like this has a parental control," Jamie said. "Let's check out the site on my iPhone."

The image that popped up on her iPhone made her say, "Gosh." She tilted her head, trying to look at the screen upside down.

"Double gosh," Cavanaugh said, peering over her shoulder.

"I didn't know that position was physically possible," Jamie decided.

"Just goes to show, we never stop learning. But I suspect they needed a chiropractor after doing it that way."

"A porn site," Jamie said.

"Chiropractor or not, would you mind if *we* tried that position?" Cavanaugh asked.

"I have no idea where we'd find the harness."

"Can't wait to see what *eBod* is." Cavanaugh pointed toward a directory, where eBod was an option.

After Jamie pressed that portion of the screen, the new page made them motionless.

"An auction site," Cavanaugh finally said.

"Well, now we know where to get the harness. Also weird-shaped dildos, erotic creams, exotic vibrators, and inflatable dolls."

"Anatomically correct," Cavanaugh said. "Hey, the bid for that one is only up to twenty dollars. At that price, it's a steal. Let's try for it."

A directory at the top of the screen included the word "services."

"I wonder where *that* leads," Jamie said.

When she clicked on it and they read about the things that people were willing to be paid to do to one another, Cavanaugh said, "The road of lost souls."

"Seen enough?"

"To last a lifetime."

As they returned to the living room, Laura descended the stairs.

"Hey, Laura," Cavanaugh said. "Remember, at the hospital, I told you we might need to suspect what seemingly couldn't be suspected?"

Laura frowned. "What's wrong?"

"How long has Dan been addicted to computer porn?"

"What kind of question..."

"Is that what he was looking at when you went back to the bedroom just now?" Cavanaugh asked. "Were you checking up on him? Even fresh out of the hospital after taking a beating, he couldn't resist taking a peek. Is he that far gone?"

"I have no idea what you're talking about."

"Bod-dot-com and eBod."

Laura's cheeks paled.

"We all agreed Dan was kind and decent. A loving husband. An attentive father. Good-natured. Generous," Cavanaugh said. "None of that's incompatible with a porn addiction. He's not hurting anybody, right? If he enjoys watching, what's the big deal?"

The room became silent.

"Unless he gets more turned on by fantasy than reality," Jamie said. "Then the expression 'loving husband' has a limited application."

"Jamie, you're supposed to be my friend."

"I couldn't understand why were you so concerned about the cost of the protectors. If you were worried about Dan, the price would have been cheap," Jamie said. "Unless you knew who'd attacked him and why. Unless you were fairly confident the guy who did it wouldn't return after the second attack."

"You hired the attacker," Cavanaugh added. "You used the auction directory of the porn site that Dan's most addicted to. Poetic justice."

"Did he stop having sex with you?" Jamie asked. "Did he get all his satisfaction from the porn site?"

"Jamie, really, I'm begging you as a friend. Leave this alone."

"Did you resent the way he ignored you? Did you plead with him to stop going to the site? Did you promise he could indulge all his fantasies on you, but even *that* didn't tempt him to pay attention to you?"

Trembling, Laura hugged herself.

"I'm sorry," Jamie said.

"Damn him, he wouldn't stop. I wanted to punish him. I wanted to put him in a position where he needed me, where he'd appreciate that I took care of him."

"The second attack?" Cavanaugh asked.

"A mistake," Laura answered. "I contacted the man and made sure he knows not to come back."

"That's why the cost of the protectors bothered you. Because you knew they wouldn't be needed."

Laura's knees bent. She eased onto a chair. "I don't think I can bear going to jail. Being away from Bethany will kill me."

"We're the only ones who know," Cavanaugh said.

Jamie looked at him in surprise.

"Except for Dan," Cavanaugh added. "*Dan* has to know."

"You mean you're not going to tell the police about this?"

"It seems to me there's been enough suffering," Cavanaugh said.

Laura looked hopeless. "But you insist I tell Dan?"

"Otherwise we won't stay quiet."

"When he finds out, he'll leave me."

"Possibly. But the way things were going, one of you would have left soon anyhow. So you're not exactly losing anything. Do you still love him?"

"Yes, Lord help me."

"And maybe, despite everything, he still loves you."

"Do you seriously expect me to believe Dan will forgive me? That's not going to happen."

"Perhaps if you can forgive *him*. There's no denying this is a mess," Jamie said. "But you won't know if this marriage can be saved until the two of you face the truth."

"I feel nauseous."

"I know." Jamie went over, crouched next to her, and held her hands.

No one moved for several minutes. Finally, Laura took a deep breath, freed her hands, and stood. "There's no sense waiting to tell him. It only hurts worse."

Gripping the banister, Laura slowly climbed the stairs.

"The attacker," Cavanaugh said.

"He called himself an 'attitude adjuster'."

"What's the email address you used to get in touch with him?"

Laura paused at the top of the stairs. Her face was even paler.

"Don't worry. We won't tell the police," Cavanaugh said. "If we did, he'd implicate you. Then he wouldn't be the only one going to prison."

"But he needs to feel responsible for his actions," Jamie said. "*He* should do some soul searching the same as you and Dan are."

• • •

EBOD
I WILL ADJUST YOUR WAYS

High bidder receives an attitude adjustment. I am strong and tough from years of outdoor work. If you win this auction...

QUESTION TO SELLER

I have been bad. Frightfully horribly bad. I have never felt so ashamed. I can't eat or sleep because I feel so god-awful guilty. I need to be punished as soon as possible. Please. I'm begging you to adjust my...

• • •

BARRY PUT on his leather gloves. A refinement he was proud of, they protected his knuckles. At the same time, they guaranteed he wouldn't leave fingerprints. *I don't know why I didn't get the idea earlier*, he told himself. The gloves were shiny black. Their thin leather fit snugly on his hands. He loved their smell.

Time to earn my pay, he thought.

He was in San Francisco, another interesting city he had not visited until his auctions led him in new directions. Cable cars. Fisherman's Wharf. The Golden Gate Bridge. The cemetery where James Stewart followed Kim Novak in that spooky Hitchcock movie. There was certainly plenty to see, and the food was wonderful, especially at that fancy Italian restaurant *Fior d'Italia*, where the waiters wore tuxedos and the wood-paneled walls were dark with age. A little pricey, but adjusting attitudes was bringing in cash, especially when he robbed people after beating them senseless, making it look like a mugging. The world was purer by the day.

Almost midnight. A thick fog came in off the bay. A ship's horn blared. Barry was outside a warehouse. At a corner of the building, a light glowed faintly in an office. He peered past moisture on the window. A man sat at a desk. His head down, he sorted through documents. Crutches leaned against the wall behind him.

Barry nodded. The man had sent him an email about a car accident in which his drunken driving had caused his Mercedes to veer toward a van full of high-school kids on their way to a party after their prom. Swerving to avoid him, the kids hit a concrete wall, the impact killing all of them. The man who caused it managed to drive home. Nobody witnessed the incident. Thus he avoided punishment, except that when he got out of his Mercedes at home, he was so drunk that he fell and broke his leg. *That's not enough punishment. I don't want to go to prison, but I can't bear feeling this guilty,* his email said.

You've come to the right person, Barry had replied. *I will make you feel better.*

Now Barry tried the door. As promised, it wasn't locked. He pushed it open, stepped into a dark hallway, and walked toward light seeping under a farther door. As promised, *it* wasn't locked, either. Barry swung it open, revealing the grief-stricken man hunched over his desk.

"You've been bad," Barry said.

"You have no idea," the man murmured, his face down.

"I'm here to adjust your attitude. You'll be sore afterward, but I swear I'll ease your conscience."

"Actually," the man said, "I planned on doing some adjustments of my own."

"What?"

The man looked up. His intense hazel eyes reflected some of the brown from the desk. His strong chin and forehead radiated the wrath of hell.

"I think I'm in the wrong place." Turning, Barry faltered at the sight of a gorgeous woman with searing green eyes and a pit bull on a leash.

"No, you're definitely in the right place," the woman said.

A noise made Barry pivot toward the man. The noise came from the chair scraping as the man stood and grabbed one of the crutches from the wall.

"Wait," Barry said.

"Why?" The man held the crutch as if it were a baseball bat.

"There's a mistake," Barry said.

"You think so? Roll up your right sleeve."

"My...?"

"Right sleeve. Don't make me tell you twice."

Barry rolled up the sleeve, revealing a rose tattoo.

"Call me the auctioneer," the man said.

"Uh," Barry murmured.

The man swung the crutch with all his might. It slammed across the desk. With an ear-torturing crack, it split apart, one end flying across the roof, crashing against a cabinet.

"Uh," Barry said. Feeling something wet on his legs, he realized that his bladder had let go.

Growling, the dog bared its teeth as the woman urged it forward. Barry stumbled back and tripped over a chair, crashing into a corner. The man whacked the broken crutch against the wall above Barry's head. The impact sent plaster flying. It was so loud it made Barry's ears ring. The dog growled nearer. The man picked up the other crutch, towered over Barry, and swung it toward—

• • •

A ROAD-REPAIR crew. A man holds a pole with a sign at the top. SLOW, it says on one side. STOP, it says on the other. The man holds it listlessly. Tall and scarecrow lanky, he looks even more weary than his dawn-to-dusk workday would explain. His cheeks are sunken. His shoulders sag. A chill November wind blows dust across his face. His coat and yellow vest hang on him. Cars speed past, ignoring the SLOW sign, almost hitting him.

You've seen countless versions of him without ever paying attention. As snow starts to fall, he looks so pathetic that you actually give him a sorrowful look. What kind of dismal life does he have? What on Earth is he thinking?

Is that them in that van? The light was so dim, I never got a good look at their faces. The bit bull. Jesus. Snapping at me. Foam spraying over my face.

No matter how much Barry had begged, the guy wouldn't stop hitting him with the crutch. "We'll keep track of you, Barry," the guy had said after taking all of Barry's money and the airline ticket folded in his pocket so that Barry didn't even have a way to get back to Illinois after he got out of the hospital. "We'll make sure you learned the error of your ways. If we find out you've been doing more adjusting, we'll put the fear of God into you, Barry."

The fear of God? They're the ones I'm afraid of. I was never so shit-scared in my life. That van's gotta be doing sixty. Slow down! You almost hit me! But I don't dare shout. If that's them and I shake my sign at them, they'll wait for me after work. They'll—

"Barry! What the hell's wrong with you?" a voice shouted.

"Huh?" As the snowflakes got larger, Barry turned toward his big-chested foreman stomping toward him. The man had angry red cheeks.

"Don't you listen to your walkie-talkie!" the foreman yelled. "I've been giving you orders for the last five minutes!"

"Orders?"

"To stop traffic from coming through! Turn the frigging sign! Make everybody stop!" As passing traffic almost hit them, the foreman raised his beefy hands. "This has been going on too damned long. How many times do I have to tell you to do your job?"

"I'm sorry I…"

"Look, I hate to do this. You're just not fit for the job anymore. Don't show up tomorrow."

"But—"

"Can't risk it, Barry. Somebody'll get hurt. Get your head straight, man. You need to adjust your attitude."

THE ABELARD SANCTION

Earlier I mentioned my espionage novel, The Brotherhood
of the Rose, *which is about two young men, Chris and Saul,
raised in an orphanage and recruited into the CIA by a man
who treats them as his foster children. (I spent time in an
orphanage when I was three and identified with the main characters.) When I finished that novel, I so missed its world that
I wrote a similarly titled novel,* The Fraternity of the Stone, *in
which I introduced a comparable character, Drew MacLane.
Still hooked on the theme of orphans and foster fathers, I then
wrote* The League of Night and Fog, *in which Saul from the
first book meets Drew from the second. I intended to write a
further novel in the series and left a deliberately dangling plot
thread that would have led into the fourth book. But then my
fifteen-year-old son, Matthew, died from a rare bone cancer.
Suddenly, the theme of orphans searching for foster fathers no
longer spoke to me. I was now a father trying to fill the void
left by my dead son, a theme I explored in several non-Broth-
erhood novels, especially* Desperate Measures *and* Long Lost,
and a memoir, Fireflies: A Father's Tale of Love and Loss.

*For many years, readers curious about the unresolved plot
element asked me to write the fourth novel. Finally Saul and
his wife, Erika, returned to me in this story. "The Abelard
Sanction" explains why Saul's village in Israel was attacked*

at the start of The League of Night and Fog. *Fans of Drew and his friend, Arlene, might sense them in the background— unnamed "friends"—at the story's conclusion.*

AT THE START, ABELARD SAFE HOUSES existed in only a half dozen cities: Potsdam, Oslo, Lisbon, Buenos Aires, Alexandria, and Montreal. That was in 1938, when representatives of the world's major intelligence communities met in Berlin and agreed to strive for a modicum of order in the inevitable upcoming war by establishing the principle of the Abelard Sanction. The reference was to Peter Abelard, the poet and theologian of the Dark Ages, who seduced his beautiful student Heloise and was subsequently castrated by her male relatives. Afraid for his life, Abelard took refuge in a church near Paris and eventually established a sanctuary called "The Paraclete" in reference to the Holy Spirit's role as advocate and intercessor. Anyone who went there for help was guaranteed protection.

The modern framers of the Abelard Sanction reasoned that the chaos of another world war would place unusual stress on the intelligence operatives within their agencies. While each agency had conventional safe houses, those sanctuaries designated "Abelard" would embody a major extension of the safe-house concept. There, in extreme situations, any member of any agency would be guaranteed immunity from harm. These protected areas would have the added benefit of functioning as neutral meeting grounds in which alliances between agencies could be safely negotiated and intrigues formulated. The sanctuaries would provide a chance for any operative, no matter his or her allegiance, to rest, to heal, and to consider the wisdom of tactics and choices. Anyone speaking frankly in one of these refuges need not fear that his or her words would be used as weapons outside the protected walls.

The penalty for violating the Abelard Sanction was ultimate. If any operative harmed any other operative in an Abelard safe house, the violator was immediately declared a rogue. All members of all agencies would hunt the outcast and kill him or her at the first opportunity, regardless if the transgressor belonged to one's own organization. Because Abelard's original sanctuary was in a church, the framers of the Abelard Sanction decided to continue that tradition. They felt that, in a time of weakening moral values, the religious connection would reinforce the gravity of the compact. Of course, the representative from the NKVD was skeptical in this regard, religion having been outlawed in the USSR, but he saw no harm in allowing the English and the Americans to believe in the opiate of the masses.

During the Second World War and the escalating tensions of the subsequent Cold War, Abelard sanctuaries proved so useful that new ones were established in Bangkok, Singapore, Florence, Melbourne, and Santa Fe, New Mexico. The latter was of special note because the United States representative to the 1938 Abelard meeting doubted that the Sanction could be maintained. As a consequence, he insisted that none of these politically sensitive, potentially violent sites would be on American soil. But he turned out to be wrong. In an ever more dangerous world, the need for more Abelard safe houses became so great that one was eventually established in the United States. In a cynical profession, the honor and strength of the Sanction remained inviolate.

• • •

SANTA FE is Spanish for "Holy Faith." *Peter Abelard would approve*, Saul Grisman thought as he guided a nondescript rented car along a dusk-shadowed road made darker by a sudden rainstorm. Although outsiders imagined that Santa Fe was a sun-blistered, lowland, desert city similar to Phoenix, the truth was that it had four seasons and was situated at an altitude of seven thousand feet in the foothills of a mountain range known as Sangre de Cristo (so-called because Spanish explorers had compared the glow of sunset on them to what they imagined was the blood of Christ). Saul's destination was toward a ridge northeast of this artistic community of fifty thousand people. Occasional lightning flashes silhouetted the mountains. Directions and a map lay next to him, but he had studied them thoroughly during his urgent flight to New Mexico and needed to stop only once to refresh his memory of landmarks that he'd encountered on a mission in Santa Fe years earlier. His headlights revealed a sign shrouded by rain: CAMINO DE LA CRUZ, the street of the cross. Fingers tense, he steered to the right along the isolated road.

There were many reasons for an Abelard safe house to have been established near Santa Fe. Los Alamos, where the atomic bomb was invented, was perched on a mountain across the valley to the west. Sandia National Laboratories, a similar research facility important to U.S. security, occupied the core of a mountain an hour's drive south near Albuquerque. Double-agent Edward Lee Howard eluded FBI agents at a sharp curve on Corrales Street here and escaped to the Soviet Union. Espionage was as much a part of the territory as the countless art galleries on Canyon Road. Many of the intelligence operatives stationed in the area fell in love with the Land of Enchantment, as the locals called it, and remained in Santa Fe after they retired.

The shadows of piñon trees and junipers lined the pot-holed road. After a quarter mile, Saul reached a dead end of hills. Through flapping windshield wipers, he squinted from the glare of lightning that illuminated a church steeple. Thunder shook the car as he studied the long low building next to the church. Like most structures in Santa Fe, its roof was flat. Its corners were rounded, its thick, earth-colored walls made from stuccoed adobe. A sign said MONASTERY OF THE SUN AND THE MOON. Saul, who was Jewish, gathered that the name had relevance to the nearby mountains called Sun and Moon. He also assumed that in keeping with Santa Fe's reputation as a New Age, crystal-and-feng shui community, the name indicated this was not a traditional Catholic institution.

Only one car, as dark and nondescript as Saul's, was in the parking lot. He stopped next to it, shut off his engine and headlights, and took a deep breath, holding it for a count of three, exhaling for a count of three. Then he grabbed his over-the-shoulder travel bag, got out, locked the car, and hurried through the cold downpour toward the monastery's entrance.

Sheltered beneath an overhang, he tried both heavy-looking wooden doors, but neither budged. He pressed a button and looked up at a security camera. A buzzer freed the lock. When he opened the door on the right, he faced a well-lit lobby with a brick floor. As he shut the door, a strong breeze shoved past him, rousing flames in a fireplace to the left. The hearth was a foot above the floor, its opening oval in a style known as kiva, the crackling wood leaning upright against the back of the firebox. The aromatic scent of piñon wood reminded Saul of incense.

He turned toward a counter on the right, behind which a young man in a priest's robe studied him.

The man had ascetic, sunken features. His scalp was shaved bare. "How may I help you?"

"I need a place to stay." Saul felt water trickle from his wet hair onto his neck.

"Perhaps you were misinformed. This isn't a hotel."

"I was told to ask for Mr. Abelard."

The priest's eyes changed focus slightly, becoming more intense. "I'll summon the housekeeper." His accent sounded European but was otherwise hard to identify. He pressed a button. "Are you armed?"

"Yes."

The priest frowned toward monitors that showed various green-tinted night-vision images of the rain-swept area outside the building: the two cars in the parking lot, the lonely road, the juniper-studded hills in back. "Are you here because you're threatened?"

"No one's pursuing me," Saul answered.

"You've stayed with us before?"

"In Melbourne."

"Then you know the rules. I must see your pistol."

Saul reached under his leather jacket and carefully withdrew a Heckler & Koch 9 mm handgun. He set it on the counter, the barrel toward a wall, and waited while the priest made a note of the pistol's model number (P2000) and serial number.

The priest considered the ambidextrous magazine and slide release mechanisms, then set the gun in a metal box. "Any other weapons?"

"A HideAway knife." Modeled after a Bengal tiger's claw, the HideAway was shorter than a standard playing card. Saul raised the left side of his jacket. The blade's small black grip was almost invisible in a black sheath parallel to his black belt. He set it on the counter.

The priest made another note and set the knife in the box. "Anything else?"

"No." Saul knew that an x-ray scanner built into the counter would tell the priest if he was lying.

"My name is Father Chen," a voice said from across the lobby.

As thunder rumbled, Saul turned toward another man in a priest's robe. But this man was in his forties, Chinese, with an ample stomach, a round face, and a shaved scalp that made him resemble Buddha. His accent, though, seemed to have been nurtured at a New England Ivy-League university.

"I'm the Abelard housekeeper here." The priest motioned for Saul to accompany him. "Your name?"

"Saul Grisman."

"I meant your code name."

"Romulus."

Father Chen considered him a moment. In the corridor, they entered an office on the right, where the priest sat behind a desk and typed on a computer keyboard. He read the screen for a minute, then again looked at Saul, appearing to see him differently. "Romulus was one of the twins who founded Rome. Do *you* have a twin?"

Saul knew he was being tested. "Had. Not a twin. A brother of sorts. His name was..." Emotion made Saul hesitate. "Chris."

"Christopher Kilmoonie. Irish." Father Chen gestured toward the computer screen. "Code name: Remus. Both of you were raised in an orphanage in Philadelphia. The Benjamin Franklin School for Boys. A military school."

Saul knew he was expected to elaborate. "We wore uniforms. We marched with toy rifles. All our classes—history, trigonometry, literature, et cetera—were related to the military. All the movies we saw and the games we played were about war."

"Philadelphia: the city of brotherly love. What is the motto of that school?"

"'Teach them politics and war so their sons may study medicine and mathematics in order to give their children a right to study painting, poetry, music, and architecture.'"

"But that quotation is not from Benjamin Franklin."

"No. It's from John Adams."

"You were trained by Edward Franciscus Eliot," Father Chen said.

Again, Saul concealed his emotions. Eliot had been the CIA's director for counter-espionage, but Saul hadn't known that until years later. "When we were five, he came to the school and befriended us. Over the years, he became…I guess you'd call him our foster father, just as Chris and I were foster brothers. Eliot got permission to take us from the school on weekends—to baseball games, to barbecues at his house in Falls Church, Virginia, to dojos where we learned martial arts. Basically, he recruited us to be his personal operatives. We wanted to serve our father."

"And you killed him."

Saul didn't answer for a moment. "That's right. It turned out the son of a bitch had other orphans who were his personal operatives, who loved him like a father and would do anything for him. But in the end he used all of us, and Chris died because of him, and I got an Uzi and emptied a magazine into the bastard's black heart."

Father Chen's eyes narrowed. Saul knew where this was going. "In the process, you violated the Abelard Sanction."

"Not true. Eliot was off the grounds. I didn't kill him in a sanctuary."

Father Chen continued staring.

"It's all in my file," Saul explained. "Yes, I raised hell in a refuge. Eventually Eliot and I were ordered to leave. They let him have a twenty-four-hour head start. But I caught up to him."

Father Chen tapped thick fingers on his desk. "The arbiters of the Sanction decided that the rules had been bent but not broken. In exchange for information about how Eliot was himself a mole, you were given unofficial immunity as long as you went into exile. You've been helping to build a settlement in Israel. Why didn't you stay there? For God's sake, given your destructive history, how can you expect me to welcome you to an Abelard safe house?"

"I'm looking for a woman."

Father Chen's cheeks flared with indignation. "Now you take for granted I'll supply you with a prostitute?"

"You don't understand. The woman I'm searching for is my wife."

Father Chen scowled toward an item on the computer screen. "Erika Bernstein. A former operative for Mossad."

"The car in the parking lot. Is it hers?"

"No. You said you're *searching* for her?"

"I haven't seen her in three weeks. Does the car belong to Yusuf Habib?"

As thunder again rumbled, Father Chen nodded.

"Then I expect Erika to arrive very soon, and I'm not here to cause trouble. I'm trying to stop it."

A buzzer sounded. Frowning, Father Chen pressed a button. The image on the monitor changed to a view of the lobby. Saul felt blood rush to his heart as a camera showed Erika stepping from the rain into the lobby. Even in black-and-white, she was gorgeous, her long dark hair tied back in a pony tail, her cheek bones strong but elegant. Like him, she wore running shoes and jeans, but in place of his leather coat, she had a rain slicker, water dripping from it.

Saul was out of the office before Father Chen could rise from his chair. In the brightly lit lobby, Erika heard Saul's urgently approaching footsteps on the brick floor and swung protectively, hardly relaxing when she saw who it was.

She pointed angrily. "I told you not to come after me."

"I didn't."

"Then what the hell are you doing here?"

"I didn't follow you. I followed *Habib*." Saul turned toward Father Chen. "My wife and I need a place where we can talk."

"The refectory is empty." The priest indicated the corridor behind them and a door on the left, opposite his office.

Saul and Erika stared at one another. Impatient, she marched past him and through the doorway.

Following, Saul turned on the overhead fluorescent lights. The fixtures hummed. The refectory had four long tables arranged in rows of two. It felt cold. The fish smell of the evening meal lingered. At the back was a counter behind which stood a restaurant-sized refrigerator and stainless-steel stove. Next to containers of knives, forks, and spoons, there were cups and a half pot of coffee on a warmer. As rain lashed at the dark windows, Saul went over and poured two cups, adding non-dairy creamer and the sugarless sweetener Erika used.

He sat at the table nearest her. Reluctant, she joined him.

"Are you all right?" he asked.

"Of course, I'm *not* all right. How can you ask that?"

"I meant, are you injured?"

"Oh." Erika looked away. "Fine. I'm fine."

"Except that you're not."

She didn't reply.

"It's not just *your* son who's dead." Saul peered down at his untasted coffee. "He was *my* son, too."

Again, no reply.

"I hate Habib as much as you do," Saul said. "I want to squeeze my hands around his throat and—"

"Bullshit. Otherwise, *you'd* do what *I'm* doing."

"We lost our boy. I'll go crazy if I lose you also. You know you're as good as dead if you kill Habib here. For breaking the Sanction, you won't live another day."

"If I don't kill Habib, I don't *want* to live another day. Is he here?"

Saul hesitated. "So I'm told."

"Then I'll never get a better chance."

"We can go to neutral ground and wait for him to leave. I'll help you," Saul said. "The hills around here make perfect vantage points. Will a shot from a sniper's rifle give you the same satisfaction as seeing Habib die face-to-face?"

"As long as he's dead. As long as he stops insulting me by breathing the same air I breathe."

"Then let's do it."

Erika shook her head from side to side. "In Cairo, I nearly got him. He has a bullet hole in his arm to remind him. For two weeks, he ran from refuge to refuge as cleverly as he could. Then six days ago, his tactic changed. His trail became easier to follow. I told myself that he was getting tired, that I was wearing him down. But when he shifted through Mexico into the southwestern United States, I realized what he was doing. In the Mideast, he could blend. In Santa Fe, for God's sake, Mideasterners are rarely seen. Why would he leave his natural cover? He lured me. He *wants* me to find him here. I'm sure his men are waiting for me outside right now, closing the trap. Habib can't imagine that I'd readily break the Sanction, that I'd gladly be killed just so I could take him with me. He expects me to do the logical thing and hide among the trees outside, ready to make a move when he leaves. If I do, his men will attack. *I'll* be the target. Damn it, why didn't you listen to me and stay out of this? Now *you* can't get out of here alive any more than I can."

"I love you," Saul said.

Erika stared down at her clenched hands. Her angry features softened somewhat. "The only person I love more than you is...was...our son."

A voice said, "Both of you must leave."

Saul and Erika turned toward the now-open doorway, where Father Chen stood with his hands behind his robe. Saul had no doubt that the priest concealed a weapon.

A door farther along the refectory wall opened. The ascetic-looking priest from the reception counter stepped into the doorway. He, too, had his hands behind his robe.

Saul took for granted that the refectory had hidden micro-phones. "You heard Erika. Habib has a trap arranged out there."

"A theory," Father Chen replied. "Not proven. Perhaps she invented the theory to try to force me to let the two of you stay."

"Habib's an organizer for Hamas," Erika said.

"Who or what he works for isn't my concern. Everyone is guaranteed safety here."

"The bastard's a psychologist who recruits suicide bomb-ers." Erika glared. "He runs the damned training centers. He convinces the bombers they'll go to paradise and fuck an end-less supply of virgins if they blow themselves up along with any Jews they get near."

"I'm aware of how suicide bombers are programmed," Father Chen said. "But the sanctity of this Abelard safe house is all that matters to me."

"Sanctity?" Saul's voice rose. "What about the sanctity of our *home?* Four weeks ago, one of Habib's maniacs snuck into our settlement and blew himself up in a market. Our home's near the market. Our son..." Saul couldn't make himself continue.

"Our son," Erika said in a fury, "was killed by a piece of shrapnel that almost cut off his head."

"You have my sincerest and deepest sympathy," Father Chen said. "But I cannot allow you to violate the Sanction because of your grief. Take your anger outside."

"I will if Habib calls off his men," Erika said. "I don't care what happens to me, but I need to make sure nothing happens to Saul."

Thunder rumbled.

"I'll convey your request," Father Chen said.

"No need." The words came from a shadow in the corridor.

Saul felt his muscles tighten as a sallow face appeared behind Father Chen. Habib was heavy-set, with thick dark hair, in his forties, with somber eyebrows and intelligent features. He wore dark slacks and a thick sweater. His left arm was in a sling.

Keeping the priest in front of him, Habib said, "I, too, am sorry about your son. I think of victims as statistics. Anonymous casualties. How else can war be waged? To personalize the enemy is to invite defeat. But it always troubles me when I read about individuals, children, who die in the bombings. *They* didn't take away our land. *They* didn't institute laws that treat us as inferiors."

"Your sympathy almost sounds convincing," Erika said.

"When I was a child, my parents lived in Jerusalem's old city. Israeli soldiers patrolled the top of the wall that enclosed the area. Every day, they pissed down onto our vegetable garden. Your politicians have continued to piss on us ever since."

"Not me," Erika said. "I didn't piss on anybody."

"Change conditions, give us back our land, and the bombing will stop," Habib said. "That way, the lives of other children will be saved."

"I don't care about those other children." Erika stepped toward him.

"Careful." Father Chen stiffened, about to pull his hands from behind his robe.

Erika stopped. "All I care about is my son. *He* didn't piss on your vegetables, but you killed him anyhow. Just as surely as if you'd set off the bomb yourself."

Habib studied her as a psychologist might assess a disturbed patient. "And now you're ready to sacrifice the lives of both you and your husband in order to get revenge?"

"No." Erika swelled with anger. "Not Saul. He wasn't supposed to be part of this. Contact your men. Disarm the trap."

"But if you leave here safely, you'll take their place," Habib said. "You'll wait for me to come outside. You'll attack me."

"I'll give you the same terms my husband gave his foster father. I'll give you a twenty-four-hour head start."

"Listen to yourself. You're on the losing side, but somehow you expect me to surrender my position of strength."

"Strength?" Erika pulled down the zipper on her rain slicker. "How's this for strength?"

Habib gasped. Father Chen's eyes widened. Saul took a step forward, getting close enough to see the sticks of dynamite wrapped around Erika's waist. His pulse rushed when he saw her right thumb reach for a button attached to a detonator. She held it down.

"If anybody shoots me, my thumb goes off the button, and all of us go to heaven, except I don't want any virgin women," Erika said.

"Your husband will die."

"He'll die anyhow as long as your men are outside. But this way, you'll die also. How does it feel to be on the receiving end of a suicide bomb? I don't know how long my thumb can keep pressing this button. When will my hand start to cramp?"

"You're insane."

"As insane as you and your killers. The only good thing about what you do is you make sure those nut cases don't breed. For Saul, I'll give you a chance. Get the hell out of here. Take your men with you. Disarm the trap. You have my word. You've got twenty-four hours."

Habib stared, analyzing her rage. He spoke to Father Chen. "If she leaves before the twenty-four hours have elapsed…"

"She won't." Father Chen pulled a pistol from behind his robe.

"To help me, you'd risk being blown up?" Habib asked the priest.

"Not for you. For this safe house. I pledged my soul."

"My thumb's beginning to stiffen," Erika warned.

Habib nodded. Erika and Saul followed him along the corridor to his room. Guarded by the priests, they waited while he packed his suitcase. He carried it to the reception area, moving awkwardly because of his wounded shoulder. There, he used a phone on the counter, pressing the speaker button, touching numbers with the index finger of his uninjured right arm.

Saul listened as a male voice answered with a neutral, "Hello." Rain made a staticky sound in the background.

"I'm leaving the building now. The operation has been postponed."

"I need the confirmation code."

"'Santa Fe is the City Different.'"

"Confirmed. Postponed."

"Stay close to me. I'll require you again in twenty-four hours."

Habib pressed the disconnect button and scowled at Erika. "The next time, I won't allow you to come close to me."

Erika's thumb trembled on the button connected to the detonator on the dynamite. She nodded toward a clock on the wall behind the reception desk. "It's five minutes after ten. As far as I'm concerned, the countdown just started. Move."

Habib used his uninjured right arm to open the door. Rain gusted in. "I am indeed sorry," he told Erika. "It's terrible that children must suffer to make politicians correct wrongs."

He used his car's remote control to unlock the doors from a distance. Another button on the remote control started the engine. He picked up his suitcase and stepped into the rain.

Saul watched him hurry off-balance through shadowy gusts toward the car. Lightning flashed. Reflexively, Saul stepped back from the open door in case one of Habib's men ignored the instructions and was foolish enough to shoot at an Abelard safe house.

Buffeted by the wind, Habib set down his suitcase, opened the driver's door, shoved his suitcase across to the passenger seat, then hurried behind the steering wheel.

Father Chen closed the sanctuary's entrance, shutting out the rain, blocking the view of Habib. The cold air lingered.

"Is that parking lot past the boundaries of the Sanction?" Erika asked.

"That isn't important!" Father Chen glared. "The dynamite. That's what matters. For God's sake, how do we neutralize it?"

"Simple." Erika released her thumb from the button.

Father Chen shouted and stumbled away.

But the blast didn't come from Erika's waist. Instead, the roar came from outside, making Saul tighten his lips in furious satisfaction as he imagined his car and Erika's blowing apart. The vehicles were parked on each side of Habib's. The plastic explosives in each trunk blasted a shockwave against the safe house's doors. Shrapnel walloped the building. A window shattered.

Father Chen yanked the entrance open. Slanting rain carried with it the stench of smoke, scorched metal, and charred flesh. Despite the storm, the flames of the gutted vehicles illuminated the night. In the middle, Habib's vehicle was blasted inward on each side, the windows gaping, flames escaping. Behind the steering wheel, his body was ablaze.

The rumble of thunder mimicked the explosion.

"What have you done?" Father Chen shouted.

"We sent the bastard to hell where he belongs," Erika said.

In the nearby hills, shots cracked, barely audible in the downpour.

"Friends of ours," Saul explained. "Habib's team won't set any more traps."

"And don't worry about the authorities coming to the monastery because of the explosion," Erika said.

A second explosion rumbled from a distance. "When our friends heard the explosion, they faked a car accident at the entrance to this road. The vehicle's on fire. It has tanks of propane for an outdoor barbecue. Those tanks blew apart just now, which'll explain the blasts to the authorities. Neither the police nor the fire department will have a reason to be suspicious about anything a half mile farther along this deserted road."

By now, the flames in the cars in the parking lot were almost extinguished as the rain fell harder.

"We had no idea there'd be a storm," Saul said. "We didn't need it, but it makes things easier. It saves us from hurrying to put out the flames in the parking lot so the authorities don't see a reflection."

Another shot cracked on a nearby hill.

"We'll help clean the site, of course," Erika said. "The Monastery of the Sun and the Moon will look as if nothing had ever happened."

"You violated the Sanction." Father Chen raised his pistol.

"No. You told us the parking lot wasn't part of the safe house," Saul insisted.

"I said nothing of the sort!"

"Erika asked you! I heard her! This other priest heard your answer! You said the parking lot wasn't important!"

"You threatened an operative within a sanctuary!"

"With what? That isn't dynamite around Erika's waist. Those tubes are painted cardboard. We don't have any weapons. Maybe we bent the rules, but we definitely didn't break them."

The priest glowered. "Just like when you killed your foster father."

Erika nodded. "And now another black-hearted bastard's been wiped from the face of the earth." Tears trickled down her cheeks. "But my son is still dead. Nothing's changed. I still hurt. God, how I hurt."

Saul held her.

"I want my son back," Erika whimpered.

"I know," Saul told her. "I know."

"I'll pray for him," Father Chen said.

"Pray for us all."

THE OPIUM-EATER

In 2009 one of my granddaughters, Natalie, died from the same rare bone cancer (Ewing's sarcoma) that killed my son, Matthew. Only around 200 people contract the disease each year in the United States. Ewing's is not believed to be inherited. The odds against it striking twice in the same family are almost incalculable. Grieving for my lost granddaughter and suffering renewed grief for my son, I tried to escape reality by retreating into the past (becoming like my characters in Creepers *and* Scavenger*). The past I retreated to was 1854 London, where my curiosity about a notorious literary figure of the time, Thomas De Quincey, prompted me to engage in several years of research. Literally, with my 1850s London map and my shelves of Victorian volumes, I thought I was there.*

De Quincey was the first author in English literature to write about drug addiction, inventing the modern memoir in his famous Confessions of an English Opium-Eater *(1821-22). I don't know why he referred to himself as an opium-eater when he was actually drinking the stuff via a combination of alcohol and powdered opium known as laudanum (legal, cheap, and available everywhere, the only effective pain reliever at the time). Many people took the hint of the skull and crossbones on the label and used it sparingly, but contemporary drawings and photographs of Victorian drawing rooms with the draperies*

313

closed and every surface covered with thick, muffling fabric that had intricate patterns make me suspect those drawing rooms were respectable versions of opium dens. In any case, De Quincey acquired his life-long nickname of the Opium-Eater because he admitted publicly to a habit (the Victorians didn't have the concept of addiction) that others kept hidden.

His opium nightmares made him wonder where those nightmares came from and led him to conclude that the human mind is filled with "chasms and sunless abysses, depths below depths," in which there are secret chambers where alien natures can hide undetected. With this and other theories, such as "there is no such thing as forgetting" (memories are like the stars—they disappear during the day but come back at night), he anticipated Freud's psychoanalytic theories by more than half a century. In his 1854 blood-soaked postscript to "On Murder Considered as One of the Fine Arts," he described England's first publicized mass murders, the Ratcliffe Highway killings, with such vivid detail that he invented the modern true-crime genre. He influenced Edgar Allen Poe, who in turn inspired Sir Arthur Conan Doyle to create Sherlock Holmes. In "On the Knocking at the Gate in Macbeth," he also invented what he called psychological literary criticism.

As I tumbled down this Victorian rabbit hole, I couldn't resist making De Quincey and his amazing daughter, Emily, the main characters in three Victorian mystery/thrillers, Murder As a Fine Art, Inspector of the Dead, *and* Ruler of the Night. *The story you're about to read is a cousin to those novels, the heartbreaking true tale of two deaths during a harrowing blizzard in England's Lake District and how a further death, that of a three-year-old child (one of Wordsworth's children), caused De Quincey to become the Opium-Eater.*

London, 1855

THE STRANGER STEPPED FROM THE STORM-RAVAGED street, dripping rain onto the sand-covered floor.

"I'm told that the Opium-Eater is here." Thunder rumbled as he pushed the door shut against a strong wind.

"Aye. A lot of other people heard the same," the tavern's owner replied, wiping a cloth across a counter. "He's in the back. Thanks to him, even with the foul weather, business is good tonight."

The stranger approached a crowd at the rear of the tavern. Everyone was strangely silent. Dressed in cheap, loose-fitting garments that identified them as laborers, men held glasses of ale and cocked their heads, listening to faint words through an open doorway.

"Murder as a fine art? Not *this* time," a voice said, its tone suggesting a man of advanced years. "There aren't any killings in *this* story."

From the back room, murmurs of disappointment drifted out toward the crowd.

"But there are several deaths," the voice continued.

Now the murmurs indicated anticipation.

"Father, you don't need to do this," a young woman's voice objected.

"This man asked me a question."

"Which you aren't obliged to answer."

"But on this particular night, I do feel obliged," the voice insisted. "There's no such thing as forgetting, but perhaps I can force wretched memories into submission if I confront them."

Recognizing the voices, the stranger touched two men at the edge of the crowd. "Pardon me. I need to move past you."

"Hey, the rest of us want to go in there too. Who appointed *you* lord and master?"

"I'm a Scotland Yard detective inspector."

"Ha. That's a good one. Tell me another."

"Better do it," a man cautioned. "His name's Ryan, and he is in fact a detective inspector. I saw him at the Old Bailey last week, testifying against my brother."

Grudgingly, the crowd parted.

Detective Inspector Ryan squeezed his way into a congested room that was thick with the odor of pipe smoke and ale. People sat at tables or else stood along the age-darkened walls, their attention focused on an elderly man seated in front of an iron-lined fireplace.

The man was Thomas De Quincey. More than forty years earlier, in 1821, he'd become notorious for writing the first book about drug addiction, *Confessions of an English Opium-Eater.* The nickname had followed him ever since. De Quincey's troubled opium nightmares, in which all of history marched before him and the ghosts of loved ones haunted him, made him conclude that the mind was filled with chasms and sunless abysses, layer upon layer. Writing about this unsuspected subconscious world, the Opium-Eater had established a reputation as one of the most controversial and brilliant literary personalities of the era.

Because of De Quincey's notoriety, people often expected to see someone larger than life. To the contrary, he was slight, so short that his boots didn't reach the bottom of his chair. From a distance, he might have been mistaken for a youth, but when seen this close, his wrinkled face conveyed a lifetime of sadness. His melancholy blue eyes had a dry glitter, as if years of sorrow and regret had exhausted his capacity for tears.

Next to him stood an attractive young woman whose blue eyes resembled his. Her name was Emily, and Ryan's gaze shifted toward her as quickly as it had toward De Quincey— perhaps even quicker, because in the months that Ryan had known her, his impatience about the way she spoke her mind and exerted her independence had turned to respect and indeed much more than that.

Emily's clothing was an example of that independence. If she'd been wearing a fashionable hooped skirt, the immense space it consumed would have prevented her from fitting into the packed room. Instead, her skirt hung freely, with a hint of female trousers beneath them, a style that the newspapers sneeringly called "bloomers," an insult to which Emily paid no attention.

Worry strained her features as she tugged at her father's frayed coat, urging him to leave.

Beside her, a tall, burly man wore shapeless street clothes similar to Ryan's. His name was Becker. In his mid-twenties, he had a scar on his chin suggesting that he was the kind of man whom Ryan customarily arrested, although in fact he, too, was a police detective.

Both he and Emily looked relieved when they saw Ryan enter the room.

"I began searching as soon as I learned that he'd gone missing," Ryan told them. "Finally a constable mentioned a little man walking along this street muttering to himself, and a woman and a detective sergeant asking about him."

"It took us hours to find him," Emily said, sounding exhausted. "For the past week, Father wouldn't stop brooding about this date. When he disappeared, I was afraid that he might have done something to hurt himself."

"The nineteenth of March?" a man in the crowd asked, puzzled. "What's so special about tonight?"

Ryan ignored the question. "I'll find a cab," he told Emily. "We'll take him back to Lord Palmerston's house."

The reference to the most powerful politician in the land made the crowd lean forward with even greater interest.

"Please come with us, Father," Emily implored. She increased her effort to raise him from the chair.

"But I haven't answered this man's question—about how I became an opium-eater."

"It's none of his business," Ryan said.

"All I wanted to know was whether his obsession with murders gave him nightmares that led to *this*," a man protested, pointing at a glass of ruby-colored liquid on the table in front of De Quincey.

The liquid appeared to be wine, but Ryan had no doubt that it was laudanum. The skull-and-crossbones warning on bottles of the opium/alcohol mixture—legally, cheaply, and easily purchased from chemists and even grocers—was normally sufficient to discourage people from swallowing more than a teaspoon of the pain reliever, lest it kill them. In contrast, De Quincey's tolerance was such that he sometimes drank sixteen ounces of laudanum per day.

"After I read his essay about the Ratcliffe Highway murders, all I dreamed about were bodies and blood," the man in the crowd continued. "He was starting to tell us if *he* suffered the same nightmares from writing about so much killing, but then these two"—he indicated Emily and Becker—"and *you*"—he indicated Ryan—"barged in and interrupted him."

"Bodies, yes," De Quincey agreed, staring at the glass of laudanum. "Terrible deaths. But if they were murders, God is the one who committed them."

"Father!" Emily said in shock.

"Perhaps the happiest day of my life was when I met William Wordsworth," De Quincey said.

"What does Wordsworth have to do with this?" someone complained. "The opium makes his mind jump around."

"Not at all," Emily corrected the man, giving him an annoyed look. "It's just that other minds aren't quick enough to follow my father's."

"Wordsworth? Who's *he*?" a shabbily dressed customer wanted to know.

"Didn't you learn to read?" a better-dressed man asked. "William Wordsworth was one of our great poets."

"Who cares about a poet? I thought this was a story about a murderer."

"That's not what he said."

"I loaned Coleridge three hundred pounds," De Quincey said.

"Another great poet," the better-dressed man explained, but he looked worried that De Quincey's mind was indeed jumping around.

"Neither man was considered great at the time." De Quincey kept staring at the ruby-colored liquid before him. "I was twenty-two. In those long-ago years, hardly anyone knew about Wordsworth, but I admired his verses to the point of obsession. I loaned his friend Coleridge three hundred pounds from an inheritance I received, hoping to gain his favor so that he'd introduce me to Wordsworth. Mind you, it wasn't my first attempt to meet Wordsworth. Twice before, I'd made my way to Grasmere."

"You talk too fast about too many things. Grasmere? Where's *that*?"

"The Lake District," De Quincey replied. "It's a village that Wordsworth called 'the loveliest spot that man hath ever found.' Twice before, I'd traveled there to pay my respects to him, but each time, I'd felt so nervous that I stayed in a village in a neighboring valley. Twice, with a volume of Wordsworth's poetry in my coat, I climbed to the ridge that looked down on Grasmere's lake and a particular white cottage gleaming among trees. Twice, my courage failed me, and I retreated.

"But this time, I wasn't an intruder, for Coleridge had asked me to escort his wife and children to his home near Grasmere. This time, my nerves didn't falter as our carriage stopped before that white cottage. I hurried through a little gate. I heard a step, a voice, and like a flash of lightning, a tall man emerged. He held out his hand and greeted me with the warmest welcome that it's possible to imagine. The week in which I enjoyed Wordsworth's hospitality was the happiest time of my life. But such is the wheel of fortune that only a few months later, a catastrophe plunged me into the *worst* time of my life."

"Is this where the murders come in?" someone asked.

"Pay attention. He said *terrible deaths*, not *murders*," the better-dressed man objected.

De Quincey gripped the glass of ruby liquid, raised it to his lips, and took several swallows. The crowd gasped. For an average person, that quantity of laudanum would have been lethal.

Ryan gave Emily a troubled look.

"Today, Wordsworth's fame brings many visitors to the Lake District," De Quincey explained. "But a half century ago, the Grasmere valley was as unknown as his poetry. Fewer than three hundred people lived in the area. Above the lake, only five or six cottages were scattered among the woods and meadows on the rugged mountains."

The rain lashed harder against the room's window.

"The solitude was so extreme that the few families who found shelter on those mountains waited eagerly for the rare social events that occurred in Grasmere and the scarce other villages. These events were usually auctions of cattle, sheep, wood, and such. To attract buyers, the auctioneers provided refreshments—biscuits, tea, and even brandy—to make the atmosphere resemble a party. It was during one of those occasions, on March the nineteenth, forty-seven years ago tonight, that George and Sarah Green descended from their cottage in a remote upper valley."

De Quincey shuddered.

He pointed as though the mountains loomed before him. "Looking up from Grasmere, you can't see any indication of that valley. Hovering mists conceal it. A rough path was the only approach. After ascending through dense woods and difficult ridges, the path crossed a wooden bridge with a gap in the middle. Great care was required to avoid falling through the hole and into the force."

"The force?" someone asked. "The force of what?"

"The Lake District has a private language. A raging stream is called a force. From that seclusion, George and Sarah Green set out for an auction that was eight miles away in a village called Langdale. In that direction, there wasn't even a path."

"Father, I beg you not to upset yourself. Please, let's go," Emily urged.

But De Quincey persisted. "The auction involved furniture. Two elderly parents were disposing of their household goods, preparing to spend their remaining years with a married son and his family. But it wouldn't have mattered to Sarah Green *what* type of auction it was. She and her husband were too poor to buy even the smallest object. As the auctioneer made jokes and attempted to raise the bids on the various items of furniture, Sarah's fervent purpose was to obtain a future for her eldest daughter. In her youth, Sarah had fallen prey to a man whose intentions were base. Her first daughter had been the result, burdened with the stigma of being illegitimate. Sarah's unfortunate history was familiar to everyone in the area. That George Green, whom she'd met later, had offered to marry her made people think of him as compassionate. Perhaps her past was the reason that she and her husband lived in that remote valley. Perhaps it pained Sarah to mingle among townspeople and know that they still whispered about her.

"But on this day, Sarah didn't care what people whispered. Her out-of-wedlock daughter was grown, and Sarah had come to Langdale to beg various people of means to provide a position for her. Perhaps the girl could work in a shop, or she could learn to be a cook in a great house, or she could feed and dress children at a manor. Sarah's hope was that her daughter would meet families who offered opportunities, and perhaps one day the daughter would find a suitor who didn't care about her origins. The alternative was that the daughter, who now worked in a tavern, might succumb to the peril of that environment and suffer the same misfortune that Sarah had."

Everyone looked at Emily to see how she responded to this immodest topic. But if they'd expected her cheeks to redden with embarrassment, they were disappointed. She displayed no reaction, accustomed to hearing her father speak of matters that were far more indelicate than illegitimacy.

"Try as Sarah might, rushing from group to group with increasing urgency, she couldn't persuade anyone to consider her petition," De Quincey said. "People later remembered the earnestness with which she approached them and the regret with which they declined her pleas. Then, all they cared about was the auction. They had a vague recollection that she and her husband departed just before sunset. Voices were heard hours afterward, from high in the mountains—perhaps shouts of alarm, but more likely the echoes of jovial partyers going home. No one paid attention."

De Quincey stared at the glass of ruby liquid before him.

"As the sun descended, snow fell in the mountains. From the front door of a distant stone cottage, an eleven-year-old girl, Agnes, watched the flakes accumulate. In the gathering silence, she strained to hear sounds that might indicate the approach of her parents. She closed the door and looked at her five younger brothers and sisters.

"Little Agnes studied an old clock on the mantel, one of the few items of worth that the Green family owned. Her parents had told her that they would try to return by seven, but that hour was long past. The children had already eaten the simple meal that their mother had laid out before departing. Agnes assured the children that their parents would arrive soon, that there wasn't anything to worry about. When the clock's hands showed eleven, she finally made the children wash their faces and get into their sleeping clothes, all the while promising that their mother and father would be in the kitchen to greet them when they wakened in the morning. Agnes led the children in their evening prayers and put them to bed. She sang a lullaby to the very youngest. Then she looked out the window in the direction from which her mother and father would approach, but the blowing snow prevented her from seeing anything.

"George and Sarah Green were not in the cottage when the children wakened. Agnes told her brothers and sisters that their parents, seeing the foul weather, had decided to remain in Langdale and would set out in the morning. 'They'll be here before noon,' the little girl predicted, looking at the hands on the clock, which were now only three hours away from the promised time. Feeling a jolt, she remembered that the clock needed to be wound.

"The fire was fueled with peat. During the night, Agnes's uneasy mind had wakened her several times, prompting her to put more peat on the flames. The family's tinderbox was broken, and if the fire went out, there wouldn't be any way to restart it—she and the other children would freeze to death. To give her younger brothers something to occupy them, she put on their coats and made them follow her outside to a shed where the peat was stored.

"As the snow fell harder, they went back and forth, piling a large stack of peat in a corner of the kitchen, lest the snow become so deep that reaching the shed would be difficult. 'Perhaps Mama and Papa won't come back to us today,' Agnes told her brothers and sisters. 'Because of the snow, they might not be able to set out from Langdale until tomorrow. We'll show them how grown up we are.'

"Agnes examined the almost empty cupboard and made porridge, conserving what she had, giving small portions to every child, with a little extra for the two youngest. 'Until Mama and Papa bring the oatmeal that they planned to buy in Langdale,' she said. Then the cries of the cow in the barn warned her about other duties. Again, Agnes went outside, the snow even deeper. Holding her often-mended coat tightly around her, she reached the barn and climbed to the loft, where she pushed hay down to the animal. The bundle was almost too heavy for so tiny a girl. Then she milked the cow, but the animal was so aged that it provided less than a pint.

"There was other milk in the house, a small quantity of skimmed milk, of little value, purchased cheaply the last time her father had journeyed down to Grasmere. Agnes worried that it might spoil, even though it was kept near a cold wall. She remembered her mother telling her that a way to stop milk from turning sour was to scald it, so Agnes put the old milk in a pan and boiled it. When the skin on it cooled and thickened, she divided the milk among the children, providing their midday meal.

"She kept peering out the window but still detected no sign of her parents. When the wind slanted the falling snow toward the cottage, she assigned the children the task of stuffing rags beneath the windows and the door to keep drifts from blowing under. She went to a corner of the kitchen where potatoes were stored in a bin, but as it was near the end of winter, few remained. She chose the two that were least spoiled, cut off the bad parts, and boiled them, providing supper. She dressed the children for bed. She led them in their prayers. She drowsed near the fire, taking care to add more peat whenever she snapped awake."

"I feel cold," someone murmured.

Others in the tavern hugged their arms and nodded their agreement.

"On the second morning, the snowfall continued. Normally, the children might have been able to walk the several miles to Grasmere, with Agnes carrying the youngest, but the weather made that impossible. The force was too wide for them to leap over, and the narrow wooden bridge could not be crossed, as the deep snow concealed where the treacherous hole in its timbers was located. A false step would drop them into the raging, ice-cold water.

"Agnes assured her brothers and sisters, 'As soon as the snow stops, Mama and Papa will come back to take care of us.' She wound the clock. She put more peat on the fire. She boiled the last of the oatmeal, of which there was so little that when she discovered a small quantity of flour, she added water and baked tiny cakes on the hearth. She persuaded the smallest children, who didn't realize the danger, that they were having a party. Agnes even made tea, although the family was so poor and the leaves had been boiled so often that there was almost no taste."

"You're making me hungry," someone in the tavern told De Quincey.

"After milking the cow, which gave even less than on the previous day, eleven-year-old Agnes discovered that the water in the cow's trough was frozen. In the house, she boiled snow and carried a pail of the steaming water to the barn. She did this several times until the gathering darkness felt so rife with threats that she ran through the drifts back to the cottage, afraid that she would lose her way. She prepared the last two potatoes for supper. She put the children in their nightclothes. She led them in prayers. She went to sleep."

"Pray God that she didn't let the fire go out," someone said.

"Indeed she did not," De Quincey assured the crowd. "Not Agnes. She slept upright in a chair. Whenever her head jerked, she opened her weary eyes and made sure that the fire had more fuel."

"I knew it!" the man exclaimed.

"The third day brought a gleam of hope," De Quincey told them.

Everyone straightened with excitement—except Ryan, Emily, and Becker, who knew the harrowing direction that the story was about to take.

"The wind changed, shifting the drifts so that portions of the ground were exposed," De Quincey resumed. "Agnes put on her coat and hurried to the bridge, but it remained blocked, the hole in it still hidden. Farther along the force, a wall had been exposed. Agnes rushed to the house and brought her younger brothers. The wall was made from rocks that weighed upon one another without the need for cement. In the chilling wind, Agnes and her brothers pushed the rocks away until the wall was low enough for them to climb over. They picked up the rocks and threw them into the water, ignoring how difficult the labor was, until they had created a small island. Agnes's brothers watched in dread as she leaped onto it and then to the opposite bank, the cascading water splashing on her. She waved good-bye, then raced from one bare patch of ground to the next, disappearing into the snowfall. The brothers hurried back to the cottage and prayed for her.

"The difficult route to Grasmere took Agnes over ridges and through dense trees. Sometimes she had to wade through hip-deep snow. But other times, she reached wind-cleared ground and rushed onward in her desperate mission. Cold gusts numbed her cheeks. Her hands and feet lost sensation. Exhaustion made her plod. At last, the odor of smoke pinched her nostrils and directed her toward a screen of trees, where she found a house.

"With senseless hands, she pounded on the door. The woman who opened it looked surprised that anyone would come visiting on so hostile a day, especially a little girl. The woman smiled in welcome, then opened her mouth in horror as Agnes screamed, 'Help us!'

"'Is that Agnes Green?' the woman asked. 'Good heavens, child, come in where it's warm! What happened?'

"'Mama and Papa didn't come home!' Agnes cried.

"'From the auction at Langdale? But that was three days ago!'

"As the woman warmed Agnes by the fire, her husband quickly dressed and braved the storm. When he finally reached Grasmere, he banged on the rectory at St. Oswald's Church. He and the minister took turns ringing the church's bell, sounding the alarm.

"Perhaps only sixty families lived in the village. Meeting at the church, the men of those families made their plans. One group would climb to the Greens' farmhouse and rescue the children. The rest would proceed over the ridges toward Langdale. There was still a possibility that the Greens had stayed with a family in that village, and there was also a chance that they'd found shelter in a shed along the way, although without a hearth and a fire, a shed would offer little protection from the cold."

The crowd squirmed nervously.

"Each group of searchers carried a bell so that they could signal to the others if they found something or if they themselves were suddenly in need of rescue," De Quincey told them. "Indeed, the dangers of the expedition were considerable, and the women of Grasmere didn't relax until night brought their men back unharmed.

"George and Sarah Green hadn't been found, but at least their children were now safe. As various families sheltered them, the village learned what Agnes and her brothers and sisters had endured, how brave the children had been, and how heroically Agnes had acted. The village also learned how truly impoverished the Greens were. Whenever they'd come to town, they'd worn their least-mended clothes, never letting anyone see the tattered garments that they were reduced to in their cottage. Only the most meager of furniture remained, everything else having been sold to buy food, of which there was now virtually none.

"The next day and the day after that, the search teams pursued their desperate mission, never giving a thought to the risk. Every half hour of daylight was made use of. No man came back to eat and rest until long after dark.

"On the fourth night, Wordsworth's sister, Dorothy, asked a neighbor—a young shoemaker—what he intended to do the next morning.

"'I'll go up again, of course,' the young man replied.

"'But what if tomorrow should turn out like all the rest of the days?' Miss Wordsworth asked.

"The young man told her, 'Then I'll go up with greater determination on the *next* day.'

"It became evident that George and Sarah Green must have veered off the direct route from Langdale, if *direct route* can be used to describe the uneven landscape that they needed to climb and descend to reach their cottage. Falling snow can cause a person to wander off course without knowing it, possibly moving in a circle, becoming hopelessly lost.

"Finally, dogs were added to the search, in the hope that the animals might hear faint cries for help that the searchers couldn't. Few men said out loud what everyone was thinking— that the dogs might also detect the odor of corpses, even if the cold kept the bodies from deteriorating.

"Around noon on the fifth day of the search, the clanging of a bell echoed throughout the mountains. A shout from a misty ridge produced other shouts that spread with what we would now call telegraphic speed from group to group. The Greens had been found."

"*Alive?*" a man asked breathlessly.

"George Green lay at the bottom of a precipice," De Quincey answered.

"No," someone murmured.

"The severe damage to his body indicated that he had fallen. The precipice was in the opposite direction from the Greens' house, which showed how severely he'd become disoriented in the blowing snow.

"Sarah Green's body was at the top of the cliff. Trying to establish what had happened, the searchers concluded that husband and wife had stopped in confusion. Sarah wore her husband's greatcoat. Perhaps George Green had gone forward, hoping to catch a glimpse of a ridge or a peat field that he might recognize. The precipice from which he had fallen was only a few yards from where Sarah's body was found.

"It was later decided that the mountain voices heard in Langdale on the night of the auction were in fact only one voice, Sarah Green's, first calling to her husband and then, when she didn't receive an answer to her repeated calls, shrieking. Perhaps she had stepped forward to do her best to help her husband, but when she realized how close she was to falling, she lurched back. One of her shoes was found at the edge of the precipice, as if she had recoiled so violently that the motion caused her to lose the shoe.

"Her body was on an outcrop of the precipice, with steep drops on three sides. Wanting to find a way to reach her husband, but with danger seemingly at every turn, she must have remained in place in the darkness, hugging his greatcoat around herself as numbness crept up through her shoeless foot and invaded her body. She was found covered with snow in a seated position, as if she had succumbed to exhaustion or as if she had never stopped waiting, convinced that her husband would somehow return. She probably died dreaming of the warm fire in her house and of the darling faces of her little children whom she would never see again.

"The funeral took place eight days later in the graveyard at Grasmere's church. The weather provided a perfect contrast to the conditions that had killed George and Sarah Green. Although snow remained here and there on the ground, the azure sky was unstained by a cloud, and golden sunlight warmed the hills over which they had struggled. What had been a howling wilderness was now a green lawn in the lower regions and a glittering expanse of easily crossed snow on the higher bluffs. Wordsworth himself read a memorial poem, referring to the 'sacred marriage-bed of death / That keeps them side by side / In bond of peace, in bond of love / That may not be untied.'"

"What happened to the children?" someone quickly asked.

"In a letter, Wordsworth's sister told me that the grief of Sarah Green's illegitimate daughter was the most overwhelming she had ever witnessed. Throughout the valley, people volunteered to take the children. Even the poorest families put in a claim. But it was decided that none of the children should be entrusted to those who, because of slender means or old age, might need to surrender the obligation they had asked to assume. Two of the orphans were twins and stayed together with a childless couple who took them in. The others were dispersed, but into such kindhearted, attentive families that there were constant opportunities for the children to meet one another on errands, or at church, or—ironically—at auctions.

"Thus, in the brief period of a fortnight, a family, which by the humility of poverty and the simplicity of their lives seemed sheltered from all attacks, came to be utterly broken up. George and Sarah Green slept in a single grave in Grasmere's churchyard, never to want for anything again. Their children were scattered among guardians who offered opportunities that never would have been available to them otherwise.

"Meanwhile, the Wordsworths applied themselves to raising funds for the children's education. Wordsworth's sister circulated an account of the terrible deaths, prompting people to offer what they could, sometimes only sixpence and sometimes several pounds. I was a student at Oxford during that fateful March, and if Wordsworth's reputation had been what it is now, I would have had no difficulty collecting a large sum from my classmates. But given the low esteem with which his poetry was then regarded, no Oxford contributions were forthcoming. When the royal family heard about the children's plight, however, they sent a generous donation. In the end, more than one thousand pounds were collected, enough to ensure the children's welfare."

"What happened to Sarah Green's illegitimate daughter?" a man asked.

"She was rescued from working at the tavern where Sarah Green had feared that the girl's reputation would be destroyed. A better position was found for her. As for Agnes, the brave little girl grew up to have a happy marriage with a loving husband and many sons and daughters."

"So the story had a satisfactory end. Although the parents died, the children triumphed," the better-dressed man decided.

"But that wasn't the end."

"Father, please don't take your mind in this direction. I beg you to go away with us," Emily said.

But De Quincey seemed not to have heard. "Consider the perfect symmetry of these events. A desperate woman leaves her six children at home while she and her husband journey down to an auction so that the woman can attempt to protect another of her children, one who seems destined to repeat her mother's misfortune. Sarah Green fails in her frantic appeals. Despondent, she and her husband return to the mountains and die miserably in their effort to reach their farmhouse, where their other children wait for them. But the deaths of Sarah and George Green result in every success that Sarah Green wished for her children. Without knowing it, by dying she achieved her desperate goal. I could never hope to invent a story that contains such geometric proportions. Even the family's last name, Green, is perfectly apt, suggestive of springtime, new life, and new hope. If I put that name in a story, readers would accuse me of being too obvious. But in life, we say 'How appropriate that the family was named Green.'"

De Quincey picked up the glass of ruby-colored liquid.

"Only God can create a story like that," he said, his voice edged with anger.

He swallowed the rest of the laudanum.

The crowd gasped as they had earlier, only this time louder. The shocked expressions on their faces made clear that they didn't understand why so much opium didn't put De Quincey to sleep or into a coma. For him, the drug wasn't a sedative but a stimulant. As he had told the story, his voice had become faster, energized by anguish.

"Father, it's time to leave," Emily insisted.

"Indeed," Ryan said, he and Becker stepping forward. Ryan knew where the story was going, and he feared that De Quincey's attempt to confront the harrowing memory wouldn't restrain it but would only make it worse.

De Quincey resisted. "We say that what happened to George and Sarah Green was a terrible accident," he said. "But if we look closely, we realize that it wasn't an accident at all. It was the unavoidable result of a series of events that began years earlier when a young man convinced Sarah to succumb to his faithless charms. Everything followed from that. If not for the illegitimate daughter, Sarah Green would never have gone to that auction. She and her husband would never have died. The children would never have enjoyed a future free of poverty. The faithless suitor began the decades-long sequence that led Sarah Green to be accepted into the Wordsworth household."

"Your mind's jumping around again!" someone objected. "You said that Sarah Green died in a mountain storm."

"But one of the rescued children, nine years of age, was also named Sarah—after her mother," De Quincey said, "and *that* Sarah Green..."

"Please," Ryan urged, trying to raise him from the chair. "Don't take this any farther. We should have left a long time ago."

Despite being a little man, De Quincey squirmed from Ryan's hands, telling the crowd, "In October of 1809, eighteen months after George and Sarah Green died in that winter storm whose anniversary is tonight, I moved to Grasmere. I established residence in Dove Cottage, the humble white dwelling where Wordsworth had lived until his growing family required him to move to larger accommodations. Wordsworth's new residence wasn't far from Dove Cottage. I often walked there to visit him, hardly able to believe that only two years earlier I had finally met my idol and that I now lived in the cottage where we had first shaken hands.

"Wordsworth's younger daughter, Catherine, was then an infant. A more adorable child was never seen. I made faces to her or ducked below her cradle and popped up waving, making her giggle. She enjoyed my company more than that of any other person except her mother. In April of 1810, more than two years after the Greens died, the Wordsworths assigned young Sarah, now eleven, to watch over her, but this Sarah Green was listless and inattentive, as far removed from the energy and duty of her mother and of heroic Agnes as it's possible to imagine.

"Coleridge told me of the morning when, as Wordsworth's guest, he came down to the kitchen and found young Sarah Green feeding uncooked carrots to infant Catherine. Coleridge warned Sarah that raw carrots were an indigestible substance for an infant and might cause her to choke. But this warning went unheeded, and a short time later, Catherine was seized with strong vomiting. I was shocked to find her convulsing when I arrived that afternoon. By sunset, the convulsions finally stopped, but the fit affected Catherine's brain, and from that time onward, her left arm and left leg drooped, capable of only limited motion. Perhaps because of little Catherine's pathetic affliction—or perhaps because of my dead sisters—I became more devoted to her."

"Your dead sisters?" a man asked.

De Quincey drew a long breath.

"Please don't, Father," Emily said.

"My younger sister Jane died when I was four and she was three. When a strange fever struck her, she was taken to a sickroom from which she never emerged alive. A servant—annoyed by the constant vomit that needed to be cleaned—struck her in exasperation. That was my first experience with evil.

"My sister Elizabeth was the next to die. I was six, and she was nine, my constant playmate, the joy of my life. She, too, experienced a strange fever. After she died, I snuck into her room and stared at her corpse. She had an unusually large head. A physician theorized that perhaps water on her brain had caused Elizabeth's death. I found out later that before she was buried, a surgeon sawed into her skull and declared that her brain was the finest he had ever examined.

"Catherine Wordsworth's head was large also. Perhaps that's why I was reminded of Elizabeth and why the affection for my sisters was transferred to Catherine. As one year and another passed, I often visited Wordsworth's house to see Catherine. Frequently she came to Dove Cottage and spent the day with me. When she napped, I sat next to her, gazing at her innocent face. She had a spirit of joyousness that made me feel as if my sisters had been reincarnated.

"In June of 1812, I was in London. I received a letter from Wordsworth's sister. It had a seal of black wax, and I can never forget the words. 'My dear friend, I am grieved to the heart when I write to you—but you must hear the sad tidings. Our sweet little Catherine was seized with convulsions last night. The fits continued until after five in the morning when she breathed her last. She never forgot you, De Quincey.'"

He paused, trying to steady his voice. "Catherine had difficulty saying 'De Quincey' and called me 'Kinsey.' The Wordsworths told me that when I was traveling, she used to search their house to try to find me. She was only three years old, the same age as my sister Jane when *she* died. But never, not even when Jane and Elizabeth died, did I feel so fierce a grief as that which struck me when I learned of dear little Catherine's passing.

"I hurried back to Grasmere as swiftly as I could. I went to Catherine's grave in the churchyard at St. Oswald's, and I found the thought of being away from her so unbearable that every night for the next two months, I stretched upon that tiny resting place and clawed at the earth. People later told me that in the darkness they heard me moaning there. When I wasn't in the graveyard, I took long agonizing walks through the valley. On the opposite side of every field, Catherine and my sisters materialized. They each carried a wicker basket filled with flowers. They walked toward me, their short legs moving in the long grass, but they never gained any distance."

De Quincey picked up his glass and studied the ruby-colored remnant.

"I first became acquainted with opium when I was nineteen. A toothache led me to a chemist's shop where, for only pennies, I made my first purchase of laudanum. In an hour, oh, heavens, what a lifting of my inner spirit. That my pain vanished was a trifle compared to the immensity of pleasure that opened before me. This was an abyss of divine enjoyment, a panacea for all human woes. Paradise! Or so I mistakenly believed. For the next eight years, I indulged in opium on an occasional basis, foolishly convinced that I was stronger than it until, by the time I was twenty-seven, it got the better of me, torturing me when I tried to stop, forcing me to ingest ever greater quantities merely to feel reprieved from hell.

"Catherine Wordsworth's death tipped the balance. Throughout the last of June and then all of July and August, my frenzy of grief persisted until, at the end of that summer, having relied on opium in a desperate attempt to relieve my sorrow, I was doomed."

De Quincey looked at the man who had asked the question that began it all.

"When I first came in here, you saw me pour laudanum into this glass and wanted to know why I became an opium-eater—or, in this case, an opium-*drinker*. Was Catherine Wordsworth's death to blame? Was Sarah Green's daughter to blame for feeding Catherine uncooked carrots and causing the convulsions that crippled the darling little girl and permanently damaged her health? Were the deaths of George and Sarah Green to blame, flooding the Grasmere valley with tears, prompting villagers, including the Wordsworths, to take the children into their households? Was the long-ago faithless suitor to blame for tricking Sarah into surrendering her virtue and conceiving an illegitimate daughter, the fate of which so worried Sarah that she and her husband descended into Langdale forty-seven years ago today and then returned without hope, dying in the mountains?

"The string of causes and effects is overwhelming. Suppose my sisters hadn't died as they did. Suppose a sudden storm hadn't trapped George and Sarah Green. Suppose they were able to arrive home when they'd promised they would. Suppose another of the Green children, and not young Sarah, had joined Wordsworth's household. Suppose I hadn't idolized Wordsworth and lent Coleridge three hundred pounds so that Coleridge would favor me enough to arrange for me to meet my idol. Remove any one of these elements, and the chain is broken. I wouldn't be sitting here tonight holding this empty glass."

De Quincey peered up at Emily, tears trickling down his face, tears that Ryan would have thought impossible an hour earlier when he'd noted that De Quincey's melancholy eyes had a dry glitter, as if years of sorrow and regret had exhausted his capacity for tears.

"I weep for George and Sarah Green. I weep for Catherine Wordsworth. I weep for my weakness," De Quincey told his daughter.

Emily hugged him tightly. "And I weep for you, Father. Please, will you go with us now?"

This time, Ryan and Becker didn't need to try to raise him. He set down the glass and slowly stood. Emily led the way, the crowd silently parting for them.

THEY

Here's one last story—and another about an author. When my daughter, Sarie, was ten, she became fascinated with a popular 1970s television series, Little House on the Prairie. *Cultural memories tend to be short, so it might not hurt to explain that the series dramatized the experiences of an American pioneer family in the late 1800s. The characters were Pa and Ma Ingalls and their four daughters, one of whom, Laura, was Sarie's favorite, to the point that Sarie often wore imitations of the pioneer dresses that Laura wore.*

The series was based on several memoirs that the actual Laura Ingalls Wilder wrote about growing up on the American prairie. She lived to see the modern era and was buried in 1957 at the farm where she and her husband eventually settled near Mansfield, Missouri. Sarie discovered Wilder's memoirs during one of our family visits to the library in Iowa City. She read those books repeatedly and finally asked for copies of her own.

Her enthusiasm was contagious. Curious, I read Wilder's books and was amazed by their vividness. They made me feel transported to the prairie-settlement era. One volume, The Long Winter, *especially impressed me with its depiction of what it had been like to endure a Minnesota winter in a remote cabin, carefully rationing food and fuel. In another memoir,* On the Banks of Plum Creek, *Wilder described prairie grass as tall as an adult and how she went exploring in it, only to lose her bearings. When she tried to retrace her path, she discovered that the grass had popped back up, so high that she couldn't see the sun and use it as a way of determining the direction she needed to take in order to escape from the grass. Only the alarmed shouts of her parents guided her to safety.*

Of course, an adult sees things differently than a child does. For me, these incidents didn't have the sentimentality that my daughter imposed on them. As I imagined the life-and-death reality of the homesteading period, Wilder's books were often terrifying. What's more, Pa Ingalls didn't strike me as being the good-natured, optimistic, grinning, easy-to-get-along-with guy whom Michael Landon portrayed in the television series. Producer, writer, and director as well as actor, Landon favored emotional stories that brought his viewers to tears and then made them conclude that, after all, the world remained a wonderful place because of Landon's beaming smile in the final image.

To the contrary, my interpretation of the Little House *books led me to suspect that Pa Ingalls was emotionally disturbed. In book after book, Wilder described how her father forced the family to build a cabin and plow fields and tend crops in what supposedly was a perfect location, only to have him decide that, once everything was the way he wanted, another remote place would be better. First, they lived in Kansas. Then they moved to Minnesota, then Iowa, then back to Minnesota, then South Dakota, this at a time when roads were few and belongings were transported by horse and wagon.*

All this painful uprooting made me wonder if Pa Ingalls made enemies in various places or if he was manic-depressive. I began to imagine an alternate Little House on the Prairie *that emphasized the hell of being a settler and enduring the close proximity of family members who thought that living under inhuman conditions was normal. In one of her books, Wilder describes rattlesnakes falling through a frozen sod roof when the spring sun thaws it. She seems to think that this incident is quaint. I decided that one day I would write a story that began with those snakes, but they wouldn't be quaint at all.*

These thoughts occurred to me in the 1970s, but it wasn't until the early 2000s, after I moved to Santa Fe, New Mexico, that something happened to make me want to write the story. Santa Fe is in the foothills of the Rocky Mountains, dependent on snow for much of its water supply. One December evening, I stood at a window as a snow storm swept into the area. Soon a road fifty feet from my house was obscured. As daylight failed and the wind howled, I saw a shadow rush past. Its shape was that of an animal the size of a large dog, although something about its silhouette and rhythm made me believe that it wasn't a dog. Then I saw another animal rush past. Not dogs. I became more certain of that. Coyotes perhaps. But maybe not coyotes either. Then what else could they be?

At once the shapes were gone. Perhaps they'd been a trick of the snow and the fading daylight. Perhaps I'd only imagined them. Nonetheless, for a moment, I was taken back to Laura Ingalls Wilder and her father and what truly might have happened during the terror of that long winter.

PAPA WAS CLEVER. IN THE SPRING, when the sod roof thawed and the snakes fell through, he hooked blankets to the ceiling and caught them. Usually they were bull snakes, but sometimes they were rattlers. Those sounded like somebody shaking a bundle of seeds. Papa said the snakes were still sleepy from hibernating, which was why he wasn't worried about going near them. He tied each blanket and carried the squirming weight to the far edge of the pasture, where he dumped them into our creek. The snowmelt from the mountains made the water high and swift and rushed the snakes away. Just to be safe, Papa warned us never to go downstream past where he dumped them. Mama wanted to kill them, but Papa said they were too sleepy to mean us harm and we shouldn't kill what we didn't need to.

The snakes dropped from the ceiling because Papa dug the back of the cabin into a slope. He piled dirt over the sod on the roof beams. That kept us cool in the summer and warm in the winter, and shielded us from the wind that shrieked through the valley in bad weather. Grass grew on the roof. Snakes burrowed into the dirt. We always heard them shifting before they fell, so we had warning, and it wasn't many, and it was only for a few weeks in the spring.

Papa was so clever. He made the best soap in the valley. Everybody knew how to make the soft kind. Pour water over wood ashes. Add the ash water to boiling animal fat. Let the two of them cool and use the scummy stuff at the top. That was the soap. But we had an outcrop of salt on our property, and Papa experimented by adding salt to the boiling water and fat. When the mixture cooled, it got hard. Papa also put sand in his soap, and everybody thought that was his secret, but they could never get their soap hard because his real secret was the salt, and he made us promise not to tell.

We had ten chickens, a horse, a cow, a sheep, a dog, and a cat. The dog was a collie. It and the cat showed up a day apart. We never knew where they came from. We planted lettuce, peas, carrots, beans, potatoes, tomatoes, corn, and squash. We had to build a solid fence around the garden to keep rabbits away. But birds kept trying to eat the seed, so Papa traded his hard soap for sheets and tented the sheets over the vegetables.

The birds got discouraged. The rabbits that kept trying, Papa shot them. He said they needed to be killed to save the garden and besides they made a good stew.

We were never hungry. Papa dug a root cellar under the cabin. It kept the carrots, potatoes, and squash through the winter. Mama made preserves of the peas and beans, using wax to seal the lids the way Papa showed her. We even had an old apple tree that was there when we came, and Mama made the best pies, and we stored the apples, too. All of us worked hard after Papa showed us what we needed to do.

Hot summer nights, while Papa and Mama taught us how to read from the Bible, we sometimes heard the coyotes howling in the hills. *Yip, yip, yip, yip.* Baying at the moon.

"God's dogs," Papa said. "That's what the Indians call them."

"Why?" my little sister, Judith, asked.

"Because they stay away from people," Papa answered. "They're practically invisible. Only God can see them."

"What do they look like?" Daniel asked.

"Silly," I told him. I was only twelve, but I felt smarter than my older brother. "If only God can see them, how can anybody know what they look like?"

"They're brown," Papa said. "They've got pointy ears and black tips on their tails."

"How big are they?" Judith asked, snuggling in his arms.

"A little bigger than Chester," Papa said. Chester was our dog. "They weigh about thirty pounds. They look something like a dog, but you can tell them from a dog because they run with their tails down while a dog runs with its tail *up.*"

"Sure sounds like *somebody* got a good look at one," I said.

Papa nodded. "I saw one a long time ago. Before I met your mother. I was alone at a campfire. It came out of the darkness and stared from the edge of the light. It must have smelled the rabbit I was cooking. After a while, it turned away. Just before it disappeared into the darkness, it looked over its shoulder, as if it blamed me for something."

"Were you scared?" Daniel asked.

"Time for you to go to sleep," Mama said. She gave Papa a look.

"No," Papa said. "I wasn't scared."

The harvest moon was full. The coyotes howled in the hills for several hours.

The next year, the rains held off. The other farmers lost their wells and had to move on. But the drainage from the snow in the mountains kept water in our creek, enough for the garden. The aspens on the slopes had it hard, though. They got so dry, lightning sparked fires. At night, the hills shimmered with flames. Smoke drifted into the valley. Judith had trouble breathing.

At last, we had a storm.

"God's mercy," Mama said, watching the rain chase the smoke and put out the flames in the hills.

The morning after the first hard freeze, Daniel ran into the cabin. His face was white.

"Papa, come quick!"

Our sheep lay in the middle of the pasture. Its neck was torn. Its stomach was chewed. Blood and chunks of wool lay everywhere. The other animals shivered with fright, keeping a distance.

I saw the veins in Papa's neck pulse as he stared toward the hills.

"At night, we'll fence the cow and the horse next to the shed," he decided. "There's meat on the carcass. Ruth," he told me, "get the ax and the knife. Daniel and I need to butcher the sheep. Get the shears," he told Mama. "We'll take the wool that's left."

The morning after that, Papa made us stay inside while he went out to check the rest of the animals. He was gone quite a while. Mama kept walking to our only window. I heard Papa digging.

When he came back, his face looked tight. "The chickens," he told us. "They're all killed." He turned toward Mama. "Heads and feathers. Nothing else left. Not enough meat for you even to make soup from. I buried it all."

"What about eggs?" Mama asked, hoping.

"No."

That night, Papa loaded his rifle, put on his coat, and went out to the shed beside where the horse and cow were fenced.

Yip, yip, yip, yip.

I stared at the ceiling and listened to them howl. But they were far away, their echo shifting from one part of the valley to another. When Papa came inside the next morning, the breeze was cold. Snow dusted the ground. His eyes looked strained, but he sounded relieved.

"Seems they moved on." He put his rifle in a corner.

"We'll trade soap for more chickens," Mama said.

By noon, it was colder. Clouds capped the mountains.

"Looks like an early winter," Papa said.

"Thank God," Mama told him. "As dry as it's been, the mountains need moisture. Our creek needs snowmelt."

At supper, we heard wood snapping outside, the horse whinnying. Papa dropped his fork and grabbed his rifle. Mama handed him a lantern. From the window, we watched his light jerk this way and that as he rushed toward the corral next to the shed.

He kept running. He passed the fence. The light from the lantern got smaller until I couldn't see it in the darkness.

I listened to the wind. I flinched when I heard a shot. Then all I heard was the wind again.

Snow was in the air. Mama whispered something as she stared through the window toward the night. I think she said, "Please God."

We waited.

"Ruth, get Daniel his coat and a lantern," Mama told me. "He needs to go out and see if Papa wants help."

"No, wait, look." Standing on tiptoes, Judith pointed.

Through the window, we saw a speck of light. It got bigger, moving with the wind and Papa's arm.

Cold filled the room as he came in. Judith coughed. Papa locked the door and set down the lantern.

"Something scared the horse so bad it broke through the fence and tried to run off," Papa said.

"Tried?" Daniel asked.

Papa looked toward the window. "Whatever scared the horse took it down. When I shot, they ran into the dark."

"They?" I asked.

"No need to alarm the children," Mama told him.

"But everybody has to know so you can all be careful," Papa insisted.

"We're already careful."

"You need to be even more careful."

"*They*, Papa?" I asked.

"I saw five."

Judith coughed.

"Five of *what?*" Daniel asked. "God's dogs? Did they run with their tails down?"

"Now they're the *devil's* dogs. I think I hit one. I found a trail of blood, but maybe it was the horse's blood dripping from their mouths."

Nobody moved.

"Ruth, get the ax and the knife," Papa told me. "Daniel and I need to butcher the horse before they come back."

"Butcher?" Judith asked. "We're going to eat *horse* meat?"

"It's meat, no matter what. When winter comes this early, we need all the food we can find."

With the dark around us, Mama and I shivered and held lanterns that swung in the wind while Papa and Daniel cut up the horse. Papa told us to keep staring toward the night, to watch in case *they* came back. He kept his rifle protected in a blanket beside him. Only Judith didn't work. She staying inside, shivering too much to hold a lantern.

"Look at the paw prints in the snow." Daniel pointed.

"I know," Papa said. "They don't look natural."

I took my gaze away from the darkness and frowned at the prints. I'd never seen anything like them. They were like huge blobs of melted wax, none of them the same size, all big and grotesque and misshapen.

"Ruth, keep watching the night," Papa warned me.

We put big chunks of horse meat in burlap bags and carried them to the storage pit Papa had dug next to the cabin. That's where the meat from the sheep was. Papa set planks over the hole and put rocks on them.

"The cold will freeze the meat all winter," he said. "At least, we won't starve."

"But what about the cow?" Mama asked.

"We'll put her in the shed at night," Papa answered.

In the cabin, we found Judith coughing in a chair by the fire. Even though the logs roared, she couldn't get warm. Her face was red.

"Has anybody seen Chester?" she managed to ask.

I thought a moment. I hadn't seen the dog since the morning.

"And where's the cat?" Judith asked, coughing.

I looked at the others, who frowned.

"Did the dog and cat smell what was out there and run off?" Mama wondered.

"They'd need to be awfully scared to do that," Daniel said.

Maybe they didn't run off, I thought.

Yip, yip, yip, yip. We turned toward snow blowing at the window and listened to the howls. They were close.

"I'll put more wood on the fire," Mama said.

Yip, yip, yip. The howls sounded even closer.

Papa stopped unbuttoning his coat. "I'd better stay with the cow in the shed."

Dawn was only a few hours away. The morning light was gray from the clouds and the blowing snow. As Judith coughed, I peered through the frost-edged window and saw Papa step from the shed, which was large enough to hold him, the cow, and bales of alfalfa stacked at one end. He looked pale and stiff. His shoulders were hunched. It was the first time I thought of him as old. He peered around, ready with his rifle. Then he motioned for me to come out and start my chores and milk the cow.

The day was busy as we raced against the night. Daniel went with Papa to the woods at the edge of the valley, rigged ropes to logs, and dragged them back for more firewood. They had the rifle. I washed clothes and helped make mutton stew while Mama used snow water for a sponge bath to try to lower Judith's fever.

"The only smoke in the valley is from our chimney," Papa said when he and Daniel came back.

Through the window, I saw it starting to snow again, flakes hitting the pane.

Mama turned from wiping Judith's brow. "I guess more people moved on than we thought."

Papa nodded. "Maybe that's why those things are coming here. After the drought and the fires, there's no game in the mountains. Maybe all the other farms are deserted, and there's no other livestock in the valley."

After supper, Daniel put on his coat. He took the rifle from the corner. "You spent the last two nights in the shed, Papa. Tonight, it's my turn."

Yip, yip, yip, yip.

In the dark, I listened to them. Judith kept coughing. Mama came in with tea from bark that Papa said would lower her fever.

"Maybe we should have moved on with the others," Mama said so low I almost didn't hear her.

Just before dawn, a shot made me jerk awake.

"I'm okay!" Daniel yelled from the shed. "The moon came out! I saw them coming! Five like you said! One was limping! Probably the one you shot, Papa! I put a bullet into it! The others ran off!"

In the morning, we all dressed warm, except for Judith, and went out to see what Daniel had shot. The sky was cold blue. The sun glinted off the snow, making me squint. A breeze numbed my cheeks. We took the cow into the pen next to the shed and fed her some of the alfalfa. Then we walked for a while, following bloody, strange-looking paw prints.

We came to something in the snow.

"Fine shot," Papa said. "At night, with no sleep, at this distance."

Daniel looked pleased. "I had the moon to help me, but thank you, Papa."

The snow was red. The thing was brown with pointy ears and a black tip on its tail, just like Papa described. Its sharp teeth were bared, as if it had died snarling. The cold wind blew snow across the ground.

"Hard to tell," Daniel said, "but that looks like a bullet wound in its right front leg."

"Probably *my* shot," Papa said. "And that's *your* shot through its chest. That's what brought it down."

The reason it was hard to tell is that the animal had been chewed on. Its stomach was gnawed open. Its left flank was raw.

"Damned things ate one of their own." Papa scowled. "That's how hungry they are. I didn't know they got this big. Must have bred with something else. Maybe wolves."

"But the mutilation isn't just from being eaten," Daniel said. "What happened to its paws, its ears, and its snout?"

"Burn scars. From the fires in the mountains," Papa answered.

I couldn't make myself look at it any longer. Its paws made me think of the melted wax I mentioned earlier. Its skin was bare in spots. Its ears were gone. Its snout was deformed.

"Yeah, this one got trapped up there in the flames," Papa told us.

Yip, yip, yip.

We turned toward the nearby hills.

"In daylight?" Papa frowned. "They're howling in daylight?"

Yip, yip, yip.

"They're watching us," Daniel said.

"Yes," Papa said. "Ruth, get the knife so we can skin what's left of it. Even if it's scarred, we can use the pelt. There's no point in wasting anything, including this. Plus, I want them to see what we do to them. I want to put the fear of God into them."

"You talk as if they're smart and can think," Mama said.

"Oh, they're smart, all right. A trapper once told me, these things hunt in packs better than wolves."

That night, as Judith coughed, I used the knife to scrape the last of the meat from the pelt. Then I stretched it on a frame, the way Papa taught me, and put it just close enough to the fire so it would dry without shrinking. Mama gave Judith more of the bark tea. Daniel sharpened the knife and the ax. As their metal scraped on the stone, I went to the window and looked toward the lamplight in the shed, where Papa guarded the cow.

Judith died in the night. She kept coughing, and her chest heaved, and she couldn't catch her breath. Her cheeks were scarlet. She kept fighting to breathe. Then her lips got blue, and so did her face, and after two hours, she died. Mama held her and sobbed. Daniel kept looking at the floor. I stood at the window and stared at the shed.

A shadow ran between the cabin and the shed. Then I saw another shadow, dark against the snow on the ground. The howls were very close. I heard a shot, but Mama didn't react. She just kept sobbing.

"I'm okay!" Papa yelled from the shed. "They're running away! But just in case, don't open the door!"

Then the night was silent, except for a rising wind and Mama's sobbing.

"We need to tell Papa," I said.

"When it's light," Daniel answered. "It won't help Judith if we bring him in now."

Mama started murmuring, "In the valley of the shadow."

I went over and took her hand. "I'm sorry, Mama."

Her eyes were red. "Fear no evil." She kept holding Judith.

When Papa came in at dawn, he stopped in the doorway and knew right away what had happened. His face looked heavy. He closed the door and crossed the room. He knelt in front of Mama, who was still holding Judith.

"Lord, give us strength," he said.

Through the window, I saw more tracks in the snow.

Papa sobbed. I wanted him to know I was brave. "I'll do my chores," I said. "I'll take care of the cow."

My coat barely kept me warm as I milked the cow, then fed her in the pen. I took a pitchfork to the manure in the shed, throwing it in a pile at the side of the pen.

Four brown specks watched from the rim of a hill.

Mama dressed Judith in her best clothes, her "church clothes," Mama called them, although we hadn't seen a church in two years. Papa set Judith on the kitchen table. We took turns reading from the Bible. About Job and Lazarus and Jesus on Easter morning. All of us, except Mama. She sobbed and couldn't bring herself to read.

Papa and Daniel put on their coats and went to the shed, where they got the shovel and the pickax. They spent the rest of the day digging. I was reminded of when they buried my other brother and sister when we lived in another valley far away. This grave was in a nice spot near the apple tree. Judith would like that. Judith loved apples. The ground was frozen hard, and Daniel and Papa were soaked with sweat when they came back to the cabin.

Daniel spent the night in the shed with the cow. Papa and I stayed up with Mama as she held Judith's hand. We prayed more.

"Eternal life," Papa said.

I expected to hear them howling, but there wasn't any sound, not even a wind. Daniel came in at dawn. I've never seen him look so exhausted. I went out and took care of the cow.

Then we said our last prayers. Judith's face was gray now. She seemed a little swollen. Papa carried her outside into the cold. The rest of us followed. Mama sobbed as Daniel and I guided her.

When Papa set Judith into the ground, Mama murmured, "Not even a coffin."

"Don't have the wood," Papa said.

"She'll be so cold," Mama whispered.

Papa and Daniel took turns shoveling dirt onto Judith. Mama couldn't bear to look. I guided her back to the cabin. Papa carried stones from a fence he was making and put them on the grave. Daniel went to the shed. I heard hammering, and Daniel came out with two branches nailed to form a cross. Papa pounded it into the ground that had been dug.

Papa stayed in the shed that night. At dawn, we heard him wailing. Daniel and I ran to the window.

"No!" Papa screamed.

He charged toward the apple tree.

"No!" he kept screaming.

Daniel and I raced out to see what was wrong. Dirt was scattered over the snow. Rocks were shoved aside. Judith's grave was empty.

Papa's voice broke. "Fell asleep! No! Didn't mean to fall asleep!"

"Eternal life," Mama said.

I didn't hear her come up behind us. She wasn't wearing boots or a coat.

"Judith has risen," Mama said.

A swath in the snow went across a field and into the woods. Grotesque paw prints were on each side.

"The sons of bitches dragged her that way," Papa said. I'd never heard him speak like that before.

Daniel hurried to the cabin to put on his coat. He and Papa followed the tracks.

"Risen," Mama said.

I helped her back to the cabin. From the window, I saw Papa and Daniel disappear into the woods.

It snowed again. I stood at the window, straining to see. I leaned against the wall and must have dozed. A gust woke me. The door was open. Snow blew in.

"Papa!" I cried. "Daniel! Thank God, you're back! You had me so worried!"

But no one came in. The wind blew more snow.

"Mama?" I swung toward the chair by the fire. It was empty. "Mama!"

I rushed to the open door and saw footprints going away. I grabbed my coat and hurried outside. The snow filled the footprints. I tugged the door shut. The quickly vanishing footprints led me toward the apple tree. The prints went past the tree. Then I couldn't see them any longer in the gusting snow.

"Mama!" The wind shoved the word back into my mouth.

The snow swirled thicker. The air got darker. I stumbled forward but didn't know which direction to take. Then I realized that I didn't know how to go back even if I found her. I couldn't see the cabin. My tracks were almost full. I followed them as best I could. The wind wanted to push me to the ground. I thought I saw a low moving shadow. I struggled to my feet and ran, only to bang into the fence near the shed. But now I knew where I was and stumbled forward. Whispering "Thank God," I bumped into the cabin and sank to the ground before the fire.

In the dark, I woke and heard them howling. Next, I heard the cow panicking. Then the only sound was the wind. In the morning, there was two feet of snow. It took me a long time to stamp through it to get to the shed. Somehow they had pried the latch open. The cow was all over the inside. Mostly blood, hide, and bones. Hooves. The head. Its eyes were wide with shock. I saw where the tracks went off in the snow in single file. The first animal made it easier for the second, and the second made it easier for the third and fourth.

"Oh, they're smart, all right," Papa had said.

They'll eat Mama next, I thought. *They've probably already eaten Papa and Daniel. When there's nothing else left in the valley, they'll come for me.*

For a moment, I couldn't move, unable to decide what to do. *Think like Papa,* I decided.

I could stack wood in the cabin. I could bring meat from the storage pit. I had carrots, squash, potatoes, and apples in the root cellar. I could stay inside all winter. I'd need water, but if I was careful and I opened the door real quick and scooped up a pail of snow, I could close the door before they got me.

I dug my way down through the snow to the boards across the storage pit. Unlike the rocks on Judith's grave, the ones on the boards were still there. I didn't understand. Why had the animals taken Judith's body before trying to get at the meat in the pit? Had they wanted to get even because Papa and Daniel had killed one of them?

I managed to pry two chunks of horse meat from the frozen pile. The rest was frozen so solid, I couldn't break anything else off. The things hunting me wouldn't be able to gnaw it off, either.

I set the chunks in a corner of the cabin, planning to stuff myself on the meat before it rotted. I carried tools from the shed: the shovel, the pickax, the hammer, and the pitchfork. I spent the day bringing in wood. I kept looking over my shoulder as I split logs. My arms ached.

Too soon, it was dark. I went in, cut away a slice of thawing meat, and cooked it over the fire. It was tough and bitter, but I didn't care. I ate it in a frenzy and fell asleep.

In the night, when I needed to relieve myself, I used a pail in a corner. In the morning, the smell was so bad that I wanted to carry the pail outside and dump it. But there were tracks in the snow. Across from the window, something watched past the shed's open door. When I used the pail again, the stench got worse, and I knew I couldn't bear it for a whole winter.

What would Papa do?

I got the pickax, went to a corner, and chopped the dirt floor. I got the shovel and scooped out the dirt. I kept chopping and scooping. My arms ached worse. But eventually I had a hole deep enough. I dumped the pail of waste into it, covered the waste with dirt, and still had plenty of space to dump more.

I heard scratching against the wall. They must have heard me digging and burrowed down through the snow to the bottom of the wall. I put my ear against the logs. I heard them out there trying to dig under. But Papa had built the wall with two logs below ground to guard against flooding. I listened to them working to claw through, but the ground was frozen too hard. They clawed and clawed, and at last I no longer heard them.

Again it snowed. In the morning, I opened the shutter. A drift sloped up to the window. Seeing me at the glass, one of the things came out of the shed.

Be as clever as Papa.

I went to the shelf where he kept the box of poison he used on prairie dogs to keep our cow and horse and sheep from breaking a leg in one of their holes. I cut off some of the horse meat, sliced it open, filled the cavity with poison, and squeezed the meat together. As I went toward the door, I heard wood creaking above me. The roof beams were bending from the weight of the snow and dirt.

I said a prayer, jerked the door open, hurled the meat over a drift, and slammed the door shut. Or tried to. Some of the snow fell, blocking the door. Panicking, I scooped frantically at the snow. I heard something straining to run through the drifts toward the open door. My heart beat so fast, I thought I'd be sick as I scooped the rest of the snow away and slammed the door. The animal banged against it and growled.

Trembling, I looked out the window. Sunlight reflecting off snow almost blinded me as I saw three of them fighting over the meat. They had terrible burn scars. One didn't have a tail. The fourth, the biggest, was the most deformed. Its lips had been burned off.

It glared from the door to the shed. When it snarled, the others stopped fighting and looked at it. With another snarl, it moved forward, its mashed paws rising and falling in the snow.

It sniffed the meat and growled for the others to leave the meat alone. Two stepped back.

But the one without a tail took its chance, bit into the slab, and ran off. At a distance, it gobbled the meat and sat contentedly.

In a while, it squirmed. A while longer, it started writhing.

It vomited and vomited. Finally it died.

Darkness gathered. As snowy wind howled past the cabin, I cooked horse meat, but not before I used Papa's soap to wash my hands. "Make yourself clean," I remembered him saying. "It's the difference between us and animals."

I pushed the blanket from the wall at the back of the cabin and went down the sloped floor to the root cellar, from where I brought a potato. I set it on a clean spot next to the fire. I listened to the shriek of the wind and the creak of the roof beams.

The storm was too fierce for the things to be prowling out there in the dark. They'd have taken shelter in the shed. I filled a lantern with coal oil and lit it. I put on my coat and went to the door.

But what if I'm wrong? I thought.

I'm not. Papa would be proud of me for being clever.

Breathing quickly, I opened the door and scurried to the top of the drift. The wind was so cold, it made my face feel burned. I squirmed through the gusts. When I saw the dark outline of the shed, I hurled the lantern through the front door and raced toward the cabin. Glass broke. Behind me, flames whooshed as I slid down the drift and tumbled inside. Kicking fallen snow away, I slammed the door.

Outside, something wailed. So numb I didn't feel the cabin's warmth, I ran to the window and saw fire consuming the shed. A thing raced from the door, its fur ablaze. Yelping in agony, it fled into the darkness, the flames on it getting smaller in the distance. The alfalfa in the shed ignited. The fire grew larger, the shed's roof collapsing, sparks erupting.

Soon, the wind and the snow killed the blaze. I closed the shutter and went to the fireplace, where I discovered that the potato was cooking and hissing near the fire. The horse meat tasted better. I dozed on a blanket near the hearth. Sometimes, the creak of the roof beams wakened me.

In the morning, cracks of sunlight peeked through the boards of the shutter. It was the first windless morning in several days. I went to the pit in the corner, relieved myself, shoveled dirt down, and washed my hands with Papa's soap. I nibbled on a piece of leftover potato, the skin crusty.

The silence encouraged me that the fire had killed the remaining three. I went to the shutter, swung it open, and one of them crashed through the window. Screaming, I stumbled back and struck the table.

The thing was two-thirds through. Spit flying, it dangled, thrusting with its paws to get all the way in. Its snout was bloody, covered with fresh blisters and burns. Hate gave it strength.

I grabbed the pitchfork. As the thing landed on the floor, I charged. A tine caught its throat. But the animal was as big as I was. Wrenching free, it snarled and lunged. I stabbed but only nicked skin. Twisting away, leaving a trail of blood, it braced itself, leapt, and caught the pitchfork straight in its chest. The force against the pitchfork's handle knocked me down. The handle yanked this way and that as the thing snarled and writhed and bled.

I hurried to the shutter and locked it. The thing on the floor struggled to stand despite the pitchfork in it. Its eyes were red, dimming, going blank.

For a time, I didn't move. Then I went to the water pail, where I rinsed my mouth, spat into the pit in the floor, and drank. The water soothed my throat, which was raw and swollen from screaming.

Four dead, I thought. *Only one more.*

But I knew that the last one was the smartest, and I knew something else. It didn't want me only for food now.

It hated me.

Without shelter, it'll freeze out there, I hoped. But I seemed to hear Papa say, "No. It'll dig a cave in the snow."

"That doesn't matter," I told him. "If I don't go out again, it'll need to move somewhere else to find food."

Papa answered, "The stench of the decaying carcass will poison you. You'll need to open the door to shove the carcass out or else open the shutter to breathe. The thing'll charge in."

"No, Papa. I can bear anything. The door and the shutter stay closed."

I cooked more horse meat. It tasted delicious. As shadows gathered beyond the cracks in the shutter, I lit the lantern on the table, edged toward the carcass on the floor, and tugged the pitchfork from its chest.

The roof creaked.

It creaked again.

Louder.

"Be clever," Papa said.

Hurrying, I pushed away the rug on the wall and took the ax and the knife down the ramp to the root cellar. I carried down a pail of water. I rushed back to get the lamp, but I never got that far. With a massive *crack*, the roof collapsed. The crush of dirt and snow sent me rolling down the ramp. My head struck something hard.

For a moment, colors swirled inside my mind. Then my vision cleared, and I saw that the top of the ramp was almost entirely blocked by wood, dirt, and snow. Dust made me cough, but as it settled, I saw a gap behind which flames rose. The collapsed roof had knocked the lamp over. The table was on fire.

The flames will suck the air from the cellar, I thought. I climbed to the top. Because the shovel was still in the cabin, I needed to use my hands to push dirt into the gap. As the space got small, I saw the flames grow brighter. Smoke filled the opening. Frantic, I pushed dirt until the space was closed and the smoke stopping coming in. Surrounded by darkness, I retreated to the bottom, sat, and tried to calm myself. My breathing echoed. I shivered.

Hunger woke me. I had no way of telling how long I'd slept. I was slumped against potatoes. My back ached. The cellar, which was about five feet wide and high, had wood across the top to keep earth from falling. It smelled damp, like rotted leaves. Darkness continued to surround me.

My hunger insisted. Papa used to say that raw carrots were bad for digestion. But it was either them or raw potatoes or squash, so after waiting as long as I could, I felt for a carrot and bit into it. Its cold hardness made my teeth hurt. I didn't choose the apples because they felt soft and wormy. Continuing to shiver, I chewed until the piece of carrot was mush in my mouth. Only then did I swallow. I did that for a long time, hoping I wouldn't get sick.

I tried to count the passing seconds, but my mind drifted in the stale air. For all I knew, it was now day outside. I needed to relieve myself but forced myself to wait. Finally I crawled up the ramp. About to dig through the blockade of dirt and snow, I heard noises beyond it. Where the gap had been, dirt began to shift. I backed away.

At once, a speck of light appeared. A snout poked through, clustered with outcrops of scars and blisters. The thing growled. As the light widened and the head thrust into view, its ears merely nubs, I grabbed a potato and hurled it as hard as I could. It thudded off the creature's grotesque snout. I threw a second potato and heard a snarl. The creature clawed to widen the hole, shoving its neck through as I grabbed the pail of water and threw its contents. Water splashed over the raging head but made no difference. I banged the empty pail against the head, but the creature was halfway through. The handle on the pail broke. The creature's hind legs were almost free. I raised the ax but didn't have room to swing, so I jabbed, but the thing kept coming, and abruptly it wailed.

It snapped its head to the side, staring wildly behind it. Its wail became a savage yelp as it whirled and bit at something. The fierce motion widened the hole, allowing it to turn and bite harder. Daylight blazed in. I heard a noise like someone shaking a package of seeds. As the creature spun, the snake came into view, flopping like a whip, rattling, its fangs buried in the creature's haunch. The snake must have fallen when the roof collapsed. The heat of the fire wakened it. It kept its fangs sunk in as the creature whirled and yelped. The poison made the creature falter. Breathing heavily, the thing steadied itself, as if it knew it was dying and had to concentrate on unfinished business. It took a step toward me. It opened its mouth to bite. I shoved the ax handle between its jaws and leaned forward, thrusting the handle down its throat.

Choking, the creature thrashed. I struggled with the ax, pressing harder, feeling vibrations through the handle. Gagging, the thing frothed, wavered, slumped, trembled, and after a while lay still. Only then did the snake stop rattling. It released its fangs and dropped to the ground.

Papa said, "Its poison sacs are empty. For a while, it can't hurt you."

But I didn't believe Papa. As the snake slithered down the ramp toward me, I pressed against the wall, trying to keep a distance. The snake crawled over the pile of squash and disappeared behind it.

I edged around the carcass, fearing that any moment it would spring to life. The cold air smelled sweet. Wary of other snakes, I emerged from the dirt and snow and surveyed the wreckage. Clouds hovered. Knowing I needed shelter before the next storm, I saw that beams had fallen on an angle in front of the fireplace, forming a kind of lean-to. I found the pelt that Papa had cut from the creature he and Daniel had shot. I secured it over a hole between beams. I tugged down the scorched blanket from the entrance to the root cellar and hooked it over another hole between beams. I found other scorched blankets and did more of the same.

But there were still holes, and the blankets wouldn't keep moisture out, so I clenched my teeth, went into the root cellar, found the knife, and skinned the creature. "Damn you," I said all the time I cut away its pelt. I stuck it over other holes between beams. Then I skinned the carcass of the thing that had come through the window, and I crammed that pelt between beams. In time, I would look for the one I had poisoned and use *its* pelt, but snow was falling, and I had to complete my shelter. A few embers glowed under charred wood in the fireplace. I layered kindling and blew on the embers. I was almost out of breath before the sticks sparked and the wood began to burn.

As the snow thickened, I went down to the root cellar and carried as many potatoes and carrots as I could, all the time keeping a wary eye on the pile of squash. While a potato cooked next to the fire, I bit a chunk from a carrot. Papa was wrong that uncooked carrots would make me sick. Maybe Papa was wrong about a lot of things.

Darkness settled, but despite the falling snow, my shelter felt secure. Tomorrow, I planned to make it stronger. I chewed another carrot and watched the potato sizzle. I thought about Papa, about the many valleys in which we had built cabins and how he was never satisfied and we always had to move past every town.

I thought of the brother and sister who were buried in one of those valleys. I thought about the bark tea Papa gave Judith for her fever. Papa always told us how clever he was, but maybe he didn't know as much as he thought about bark and it made Judith sicker. Maybe Papa wasn't so clever when he and Daniel chased after the things that took Judith's body. Maybe he should have kept control and stayed home and Mama wouldn't be dead and he and Daniel wouldn't be dead.

I think about that a lot. I sit in this tiny room and listen to motorcars rattling by outside. Seventy-eight years is a long time to remember back. You ask me what it was like living in the valley when I was twelve. The old days as you call them. For me, the young days, although I was never really young. Streets and houses and schools and churches are now where our farm was, where everyone died, where I spent the winter eating carrots, potatoes, and horse meat. But never the squash. I never went near the squash.

Damned stupid Papa.

ABOUT THE AUTHOR

David Morrell was born in Kitchener, Ontario, Canada. As a teenager, he became a fan of the classic television series, *Route 66,* about two young men in a Corvette convertible driving across the United States in search of themselves. The scripts by Stirling Silliphant so impressed Morrell that he decided to become a writer.

The work of another writer (Hemingway scholar Philip Young) prompted Morrell to move to the United States, where he studied with Young at the Pennsylvania State University and received his M.A. and Ph.D. There, he also met the esteemed science-fiction author William Tenn (real name Philip Klass), who taught Morrell the basics of fiction writing. The result was *First Blood*, the novel that introduced the character of Rambo, a returned Vietnam veteran suffering from post-traumatic stress disorder who comes into conflict with a small-town police chief and fights his own version of the Vietnam War.

That "father" of modern action novels was published in 1972 while Morrell was a professor in the English depart ment at the University of Iowa. He taught there from 1970 to 1986, simultaneously writing other novels, many of them *New York Times* bestsellers, including the classic spy trilogy *The Brotherhood of the Rose* (the basis for the only television mini-series to be broadcast after a Super Bowl), *The Fraternity of the Stone*, and *The League of Night and Fog.*

Eventually wearying of two professions, Morrell gave up his academic tenure in order to write full time. Shortly after-ward, his fifteen-year-old son Matthew was diagnosed with a rare form of bone cancer and died in 1987, a loss that haunts not only Morrell's life but his work, as in his memoir about Matthew, *Fireflies*, and his novel *Desperate Measures*, whose main character lost a son.

"The mild-mannered professor with the bloody-minded visions," as one reviewer called him, Morrell is the author of more than thirty books, including *Murder as a Fine Art*, *Creepers*, and *Extreme Denial* (set in Santa Fe, New Mexico, where he lives). An Edgar, Anthony, Thriller, and Arthur Ellis finalist, Morrell has Nero, Anthony, Inkpot, and Macavity awards and is a three-time recipient of the distinguished Bram Stoker Award from the Horror Writers Association. The International Thriller Writers organization gave him its prestigious Thriller Master Award. Bouchercon, the world's largest crime-fiction convention, gave him its Lifetime Achievement Award.

With eighteen million copies of his work in print, Morrell's work has been translated into thirty languages. His writing book, *The Successful Novelist*, analyzes what he learned during his more than four decades as an author. Please visit www.davidmorrell.net, where you can contact him, learn more about him, and sign up for his newsletters.

COPYRIGHT PAGE